The
Price *of a*
Contract

Ellen Kingman Fisher

CLIO MUSE PRESS

The Price of a Contract, by Ellen Kingman Fisher
Copyright © 2022 Ellen Kingman Fisher
All rights reserved

Published by Clio Muse Press
Denver, Colorado

ISBN: 978-0-9994950-2-5
LCCN: 2021923371

Cover image © Everett Collection/Shutterstock
Cover and interior design by Pratt Brothers Composition
Maps by Jay P.K. Kenney
Editing by Eva Fox Mate

This book is printed in the United States of America

Quantity Purchases: Schools, companies, professional groups, clubs, and
other organizations may qualify for special terms when ordering quantities
of this title. For information, email: ClioMusePress@gmail.com

Cover and page design by Pratt Brothers Composition

For Dayton, Hadley, James, and Will
and their bright futures

Our lives are defined by our choices. It's nothing more than that but so much more.

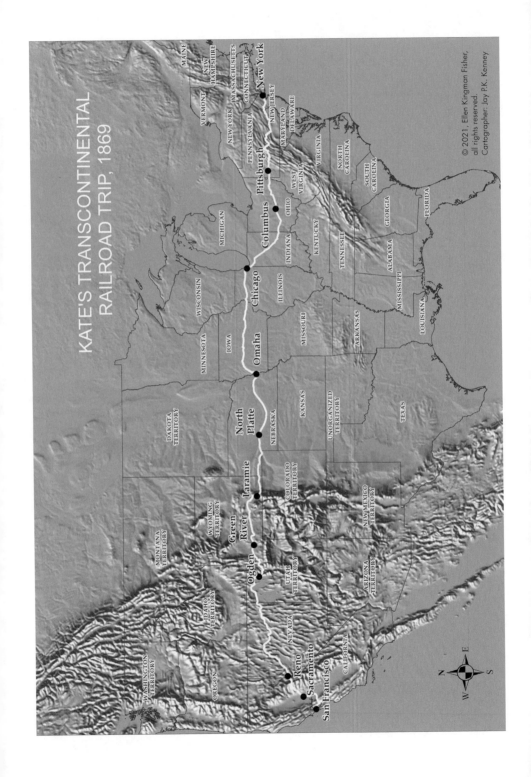

KATE'S TRANSCONTINENTAL RAILROAD TRIP, 1869

The Price of a Contract

The memory of that day had been like a hidden secret no one wanted to discover. Kate had been swimming in the pond at the edge of the green open meadow. Wanting to prove herself to her two older brothers, she began to climb the boulders towering above the pond's east edge. Placing her toes into the cracks between the rounded sandstone, she reached the top, ready to send a high splash on top of them. Steadying herself to gain her balance, she sprang up full force, folded her knees, knobby as a young fawn's, and wrapped her arms around them as she hurtled down. Eyes closed, she anticipated the cold water. Instead, she felt hot, breath-sucking pain. Her ankle seared, almost making her faint. A pointed branch, protruding above the surface, had ripped her skin. Struggling to keep afloat, she looked over at Bill and Jim. Their usual horseplay had taken them to the west end, and they had not noticed her effort to impress them.

Pulling herself onto the bank, she snatched her towel from where she had laid it on the grass, and dabbed at the blood flowing from the jagged tear. She stood up, and before her brothers noticed, ran up the long path to the house. Kate soundlessly crossed the threshold into the foyer on her bare feet. She was startled by the sounds of her parents' sharp voices. Frozen, she did not move. In the next room, her mother said her name, followed by an angry retort from her father. "Disown . . . don't you dare . . . you too . . ." The words came in snippets rather than full meaning, but she could tell they were arguing about her and what she should be allowed to do. It was not the first time. Somehow her father always made her feel like an unwanted little girl. She bent down, again pressing the soft towel against her wound so she would not drip blood on the carpet as she fled up the stairs.

After wrapping a bandage tight around her ankle in the bathroom, she flopped down on her bed, lying against the familiar green and pink patterned quilt as she tried to devise a plan. Nothing came except the determination to make up for being an unlovable child by being smart and accomplished. With an overwhelming desire never to depend on anyone other than herself, she would go face forward to control her own future.

Over time, self-reliance became her mantra, one she could and would overdo. With that determination, some decisions would resemble wild animals fleeing from danger—thinking not of direction, but of escape. Her choices would be a dilemma of conflicting options—none entirely ideal.

ONE

A shrieking whistle sounded through the heavy air. Cool mist surrounded San Francisco Bay—not uncommon, Kate knew, but weather in September was supposed to be clearer. When they left Sacramento, the noon sun had been bright, but that had been five hours ago. With a shiver, she pulled her wool coat from the seat. Dust puffed up from the thick fabric. Brushing was futile; railroad dust clung to every surface. She pushed her slender arms through the coat sleeves. A smile replaced her brief frown. Nothing, not even dirt and weather, could dispel the elation of finally arriving at her long-sought destination.

Even though fog shrouded the San Francisco cityscape across the bay, Kate could picture the details. During months of planning, she had studied maps until she could have drawn the route from Providence to California, and even the streets of San Francisco, from memory. She had scoured every available account of cross-country travel. Her favorites were personal journals. Some writing was so eloquent, she imagined she was traveling with the little-known chroniclers, absorbing their aspirations as well as the scenery they described.

As the final station neared, passengers became too eager for arrival to remain seated. They began standing in the aisle like tipsy revelers, trying to keep their balance. Lively conversations surrounded her. The celebratory mood was a mixture of regret about leaving their traveling hotel and expectation of what lay ahead.

"Kate, where did you decide to stay in San Francisco?" The crush of people with their hand luggage, angling for position by the door, crowded Doris next to Kate as they stood in the aisle. She had found Doris a cheerful soul who sought company while her husband, Ralph, was preoccupied talking business with other men. Doris was usually on her own.

"The Occidental," Kate said, although she was still ambivalent about choosing it over the Lick House. Both were a splurge on her limited budget. "The Occidental, because so many famous people stay there . . . Mark Twain, Robert Louis Stevenson, Ralph Waldo Emerson . . ." she mused as much to herself as Doris, her voice muffled by the hubbub of passengers waiting to exit the train.

"Oh," Doris exclaimed, clapping her plump hands. "We're staying there too. It's one of the most luxurious hotels on this side of the country—even better than the Pullman train." Then doubt clouded her eyes. "It's such a bother to have to take the ferry to San Francisco."

"It's the only way to get there," Kate said, but she too felt the incongruity of having to take a steamboat for the last part of the trip to get across the bay from Alameda to San Francisco.

Tired of the blurred landscape, she turned to make a final survey of the railroad car where she had spent the last three days; before that, an additional five days on the previous train from New York, and the first from Providence to New York. This luxurious journey was far different from what she knew travel had been only five years ago. In 1864, her close friend Alice Hill had shared her husband's letters, written while he went west to Colorado Territory. Sitting side by side in Providence, Alice and

Kate savored every description, often of hardship and danger. They were relieved after each reading that, at least as of the date at the top of the thin stationery, Nathaniel was still alive.

In the five intervening years, trains had spanned the continent. Kate had read every printed account she could find of the achievements and pitfalls of the Overland Route's construction from 1863 to 1869. Union Pacific had built west from a network of eastern railroads, and the Central Pacific east from Sacramento. They eventually connected at Promontory Point in Utah Territory the past spring. The last link, from Sacramento to San Francisco, was not quite finished.

Kate had enthusiastically bought a ticket to take one of the first through-trains since the transcontinental connection in Utah. Rails across the continent had revolutionized travel from horseback or stage to the comfort of the railroad, especially for those who paid for first class. Her train had three luxury Pullman Palace passenger cars, as well as dining cars, and at the end, two baggage cars. All pulled by a steam locomotive.

Kate had expected some of the two-thousand-mile journey to have long, boring stretches. Instead, time had vanished as she looked out at the ever-changing scenery, wrote in her journal, read, or talked to other passengers. One station after another came and went at a surprisingly rapid pace.

When Kate's grandmother died three years ago, she bequeathed her estate to her nine grandchildren. The will stipulated that a trustee at the Old Stone Bank in Providence manage and invest it. The heir or heiress got a monthly allotment until forty years of age, when each would receive a lump sum portion of the remaining funds. The restraint had prickled her. Kate knew her grandmother had good reason to worry about several of her grandchildren, who might squander their inheritance—the money she had so carefully saved. Kate had caused no such concern. Economical by nature, she was determined to make the gift last because, if used judiciously, she would be free from teaching and able to travel and explore. Occasionally, she might have to supplement her money, perhaps by tutoring students, but even that would give her flexibility for traveling.

"We had to pay a dollar each to have our trunks moved from the railroad to the ferry and then to the hotel," Doris interrupted Kate's thoughts.

"It does seem like a lot." Kate barely noticed Doris' prattle, but she, too, was frustrated. "I wish we could *see* something. At least I decided to stay for a week...."

"I know the weather will change during our stay," Doris said. "We have no definite return date." She had a top knot of strawberry blonde hair; beneath it, her brown eyes gleamed with enthusiasm.

The engine jolted to an abrupt, chuffing stop, sending passengers flailing to clutch something for balance. Kate grabbed a seatback, barely staying upright. Passengers bumped one another as they pushed toward the doors the conductor had opened. Their excited laughter mixed with mechanical sounds of steamboats and wagons outside. Kate picked up her tan leather satchel and followed the conductor to the wharf and the Alameda ferryboat. She could hardly wait to cross the bay to San Francisco.

TWO

"May I join you?"

Kate looked up with a start, feeling her face color in surprise.

"Frank Ellsworth," he said, tipping his felt bowler, hesitating without taking a seat. "I regret we were never seated together at a meal on the train."

Flustered, she gestured an invitation to sit across the table from her on the ferryboat.

They had never met, but his eyes were nevertheless familiar. She remembered him as the man who had occupied a seat at the back of her railroad car, and like all passengers, he had to walk down the aisle to get to the washroom at the front of the car. At night, the aisles were made even narrower after a steward had taken each pair of facing seats, folded them over, and put a mattress across to provide a lower berth. The upper berth came down from the luggage compartment high on the wall. Kate's upper berth was empty because she was alone in her compartment. More comfortable than sitting in earlier trains with their hard, wood-slatted chairs, constantly in the view of other passengers, the so-called palace cars still had their failings. Curtains provided some privacy—curtains, she discovered, cut with negligible yards of fabric that parted most inconveniently. The confining sleeping arrangements were comfortable only if you planned precisely what you needed and stored the rest underneath. No matter how carefully Kate planned, she always forgot to set aside some essential item from her satchel. Retrieving anything from under the berth required the most annoying amount of squirming that knocked the shortchanged curtains askew, revealing her embarrassing position to anyone who happened to be walking down the hallway—and her curtains seemed destined to be ajar just as this man, in particular, did his walking.

"Frank Ellsworth," he repeated, placing his hat on the adjacent chair. "I started in Chicago."

She realized he was waiting for her name. "Kate Sinclair. I started in New York, then made the switch in Omaha; my home is Providence." During the long journey across the country, she had become accustomed to telling others details of her travels.

"From one ocean to the other," he said, eyes twinkling good-naturedly. "Why did you come?"

Kate smiled back, although inwardly she sighed: *It's because I'm a woman traveling alone that makes people so curious. They judge my life by their own inhibitions.* Then enthusiasm erased her impatience. "Ever since California's gold rush and then Pike's Peak, reporters have been filling newspapers with stories about the West. Who wouldn't be interested? And artists like Moran, Bierstadt, and Catlin have painted landscapes that make you die to see it for yourself."

Kate could tell he was amused by her passion, but as she studied him, she read appreciation too. She found him handsome, with full muscular features and ruddy cheeks that made his face alert and vigorous. Not overly tall, he was square-set, with strong shoulders and broad hands. Looking more closely, she realized his eyes were not quite brown but a blend of gold, green, and brown—a sort of hazel, and very beguiling.

The waiter interrupted by putting down a hand-printed menu, and then asking, "What can I get you to drink?"

"Tea," she responded.

"Coffee for me."

They perused the menus in silence until the waiter returned, carrying a tray clinking with cups and two china pots of steaming liquid. After giving their food orders, Kate took a sip of her tea before starting her story. "You asked me why I came. Actually, it's not my first journey. I made half this trip in 1868—only a year ago, though it seems much longer."

"I'm surprised to meet someone who's already traveled so much." Frank said. "This new transcontinental travel is changing everything, don't you think?"

"Yes, and it seems like overnight, but of course it wasn't."

"Tell me about your first trip."

Kate ran her story through her mind, trying to figure out how much she could shorten it and still make sense. Making sense might not be possible, though, given any amount of time. The first trip had transformed her from someone who merely dreamed into someone willing to act.

"A year ago, we traveled on a series of trains, a steamship, and finally a stagecoach. Worry was constant—"

"We?"

She nodded and explained that her closest friend had moved to a mining town in Colorado Territory. Stories about attacks during cross-country travel filled newspapers and conversations. They made the Hills too fearful to expose their young children to the potential danger. Crawford was six and Isabel four. Instead, they left them with Alice's parents, but without them, Alice told Kate her life in Black Hawk was meaningless.

"She wrote me frequently about the beauty of her new world, but mostly about missing her children. So, I offered to bring them."

"You just decided to go?" Frank chuckled.

"The trip was a chance to help my friends, and by happenstance, see more of the country." Kate did not know why he drew her in, making her an open book.

She pulled her coat collar up around her neck. The memory chilled her. "I worried constantly about something happening to Crawford and Isabel—they were so young—one not even in school. Trepidation about a mishap prayed on my mind every minute. How could I have looked Alice and Nathaniel in the eyes if I had allowed harm to come to their children? That would have haunted me for the rest of my life." She squirmed in her seat. "In the end, determination to prevent any injury reduced my fear—I was more afraid of failing than I was of being attacked."

"And you made it. What an accomplishment. It's not what I expected when we started talking about travel." Frank folded his napkin by his empty plate.

"Danger was real. The people who lived at the places where we resupplied faced it every day. Some of the water stations had streams running through surrounding green fields, and you could understand being there, but others were wind-blown and barren—harsh propositions. Mostly lonely. I suppose there are occasional conversations with travelers, but what about friends? People you can count on if there's trouble? Lonely!" she repeated.

"Some people call it self-reliance," Frank said. "It's the definition of the West—finding the wherewithal to go it on your own, not depending on anyone else."

His wide shoulders and calm bearing evoked confidence, with a mixture of seriousness and amiability that appealed to her. Kate would not have been surprised if self-reliance defined him as well.

THREE

Glimpsed through a veil of condensation, San Francisco seemed to Kate little different from New York City— horse carts, wagons, and pedestrians crowding everywhere. With other disembarking passengers, Kate and Frank followed the crew of the Alameda ferryboat to the dock's reception hall, where they could sit in relative comfort until their luggage arrived. Ornately paneled high walls held gilt-framed paintings depicting scenes of the Pacific Coast, from Washington to California. Two rows of scroll-topped wooden benches occupied much of the waiting room. Some of the ferry's passengers searched for empty seats. Others remained standing, engaged in conversation. Frank disregarded the noisy hubbub and took Kate's arm, guiding her through the throng until he found empty places on a bench. They sat side by side, waiting for instructions.

She wedged her satchel safely beside her before turning to Frank. "What brought you to California . . . was taking the train your objective?"

He shook his head. "Not really, but the timing happened to be favorable." He surveyed the crowd momentarily. "I bargained for one adventure and got two by chance. I hope the second turns out as well as the first." The trimmed beard framing his square jaw had a hint of red not evident in the dark brown of his hair. He radiated an infectious enjoyment of life. Kate estimated by his looks that they were roughly the same age—just about to slip out of their twenties—or perhaps he was a couple of years older. She was relieved that if he had any inquisitiveness about her single status, he kept it to himself.

"I'd like to hear about why you came to California."

"I came for a job, he said, "the telegraph—Western Union—has hired me. They're stringing telegraph lines across the country, mostly alongside train tracks because the railroad often pays to put up the poles. It's a great opportunity for me to see how the telegraph is changing things. The company footed my transportation. That was another bit of good fortune."

The reference gave Kate's heart a lurch. Finding the Western Union office was one of the first things she had to do in San Francisco. A telegram was supposed to arrive directing her to a bank where she could pick up the small monthly distribution from her grandmother's trust. She had planned her trip west carefully, looking for ways to save money because transportation and lodging were expensive. When she had asked Mr. Finney, the bank's trustee—an old fuddy-duddy as far as she was concerned—for an early allocation, he refused, infuriating her. It was the first time she had ever requested one, and she suspected if she'd been one of the male heirs, he would have made an exception. Because she was a woman, taking what he called "a trip of self-indulgence," Mr. Finney exerted his control, as if it were his money instead of hers.

"Did I say something wrong?" Frank asked with a frown.

"Oh, no," Kate said, shaking herself back into the present. She had accidentally quashed his enthusiasm about his trip and new job. "I'm sorry, Frank; your mention of Western Union made my mind slip to something I have to take care of before I do any sightseeing . . . or anything else."

"Is there something I can do to help?"

"No, but thank you; it's just a business matter," she said, stuffing her gloves deeper in her coat pocket so they would not get lost. His thoughtfulness increased her regret about not listening. "Tell me what you'll be doing for your new job," she said, but the moment was lost. A wharf employee rang a hand-held bell, alerting them that the crew had delivered all the luggage from the ferry.

"Line up for transport to hotels," the worker shouted several times to be heard. Other transit staff held up lettered signs indicating various hotels. The clamor of voices intensified as people sought their proper lines, laughing, pointing, and saying goodbye to people whom they most likely would never see again. Identification tags hung from handles of trunks and other traveling accoutrements lined up against the wall.

Frank almost shouted to be heard. "I have to get settled in my job in the next few days, but then I should have some free time. May I send you a note to have dinner with me? I'm at the Lick House."

Kate hesitated, and then said, "I'm staying at the Occidental, but I'm going to leave for Yosemite next week." She looked up at his engaging eyes. She liked this man. "Yes, if our schedules match, I'd enjoy that."

"I'll look forward to it." He nodded with a smile before joining the line for the Lick House.

FOUR

Pullman berths were luxurious compared to her first cross-country trip, but her room at the Occidental rewarded her with the pleasure of space and privacy after so many days of travel. The four-story, Italianate edifice at Bush and Montgomery Streets was even more beautiful than a photograph she had seen before leaving Providence. Fatigue infused her in her peaceful surroundings. All she managed to do was don her nightdress, pull back the covers, and sink into bed. Her shoulders relaxed as she scanned her surroundings: floral wallpaper, a mahogany chifforobe, and narrow writing table. An image of handsome Frank Ellsworth flitted through her mind as sleep overtook her.

In the morning, desultory fog had turned to light rain. The patter of drops mixed with the sounds of clopping horses pulling carriages laden with early morning deliveries. Kate reached over to wind her watch and then leisurely pulled the feather comforter closer, loath to give up her cozy solitude, although her mind churned with what she had to do, wet weather or not. Finally, the sight of her travel trunk across the room beckoned her. Upright and open, it had a row of six drawers on the right side and a horizontal rod with a dozen hangers on the left. She had carefully selected and meticulously organized every item she brought. Opening a middle drawer, she picked out a suit that did not have too much train dust and would stand up to the rain. She had wedged her tall black umbrella next to her hanging clothing.

She washed her face, smoothing her light-brown arched brows. Her unrestrained, honey-colored hair fell on her shoulders. After a hundred vigorous brush strokes, she wound her hair in its usual tight chignon above the nape of her neck. Whisking off her lacy white nightdress, she caught a glimpse of her trim figure in the full-length looking-glass. Kate sensed people found her attractive, especially when a smile dimpled her cheeks, but she resisted that image, knowing that admiration for beauty often discounted intellect. She put on her tan suit. It revealed the curves of her body without being tight. Its matching plaid skirt reached just midway over her brown leather boots. *All dirt colored*, Kate chuckled.

Before going down for breakfast, she wanted to catch up on her daily journal and correspondence—she had been too tired to write before she went to bed. As a young girl, she had developed the habit of writing a paragraph—or more, if enthusiastic—about the day. She always ended with one sentence summarizing what she had learned, forcing herself to think and remember. Journal writing was a discipline she had stuck to even if she occasionally had to catch up after missed days.

Letter-writing was next. Time disappeared as Kate filled sheets of stationery with flowing script, describing to Alice her arrival in San Francisco, concern that she did not have all the necessary cash in hand, and even the conversation with Frank, holding back little. She wrote shorter notes to other friends and to her brothers, Bill and Jim, describing highlights and relaying her safe arrival. They had both moved to Missouri and had married. She rarely heard from them or saw them, but on the few occasions when she did, they always thanked her for her letters and apologized for the lack of their own.

Writing to her parents was a different matter. They thought it was nonsense for a woman to travel to rough territories. Focus at her age should be on finding a mate, and time was slipping away—time she was wasting on extravagance. It was ironic, knowing what she did about their marriage. Kate vacillated about what to say, so she returned her pen to its holder. She would wait to write them until after she had seen some of the sites in San Francisco, and then more after Yosemite. Descriptions of places interested them, even if they did not share her enthusiasm about travel.

Over several years, Kate had closely followed newspaper reports of a battle to save Yosemite after the California gold rush. Mining had attracted tens of thousands of non-residents to California. The state's beauty and mild climate persuaded many to stay whether they had made their fortune or not, spreading civilization far beyond the mining districts. When the increasing populace began encroaching into the Yosemite Valley, alarmed conservationists pleaded with Congress to protect the beloved granite peaks that towered over everything, waterfalls that thundered down from vast heights in the springtime, and groves of Sequoias so large they defied the imagination. Fortunately, President Lincoln had realized the value of preserving land for public enjoyment, and in 1864, he declared Yosemite Valley a public trust of California.

The stories of saving Yosemite inspired people to visit the public land. She had been tempted to continue west after she brought the Hills' children to them in Colorado Territory. Kate remembered a conversation she'd had with Alice a year before as clearly as if it had happened yesterday. Light from the sunny fall day streamed in the double-hung window in the Hills' home in Black Hawk, warming the kitchen where they sat drinking tea in familiar companionship. Crawford and Isabel played a few feet away by the warm hearth. Nathaniel had already left for work.

"The view from here is beautiful," Kate had said. "Some of the mountains already have a dusting of snow, like confectioner's sugar, on top."

Alice's gaze joined Kate's. "Every changing light gives them a different appearance, and I agree, they're beautiful."

"They make me want to see Yosemite. Maybe I should go on to California instead of turning around and going home."

"You mean now?"

"It's a thought," Kate said, watching the reaction on Alice's smooth face, plump with her pregnancy. "Then I wouldn't have to cross from coast to coast."

"Kate, that doesn't make sense." Lines creased Alice's brow. "Winter comes early here. How would you get to California?"

"I just survived getting across half the continent with, may I remind you, two merry children," Kate laughed playfully. "The other half should be easy."

"Going across alone would be foolish," Alice repeated more firmly.

"It would be formidable, no doubt, but, honestly Alice, others have done it . . . even women." Kate kept her tone light. It was their forever difference of sensible versus daring—each admiring the characteristic in the other and at the same time resisting those opposite traits.

"Did the other women travel alone?" Alice's eyes squinted skeptically.

After a moment, Kate sighed, "No, you're right, and it is already late in the season. A better thought is to wait for trains to go all the way through. It's bound to happen next year."

As planned, Kate returned to Providence in late fall of 1868. The scope of sweeping scenery on her trip to Colorado had accelerated her desire to see more of the country. Consequently, she had spent the past year determined to resume her travels as soon as the transcontinental railway was completed. She'd searched for accounts of those who had already made the trip to Yosemite. Kate had read and re-read their detailed advice about how to manage the rigorous trip, egged on by their final words: "The pleasures of travel survive its pains." Kate had no delusions. After a long railroad trip to reach California, she would be squeezed in a confining stagecoach with unknown passengers to get to Yosemite. Outside, exposure to rain, wind, and sun would create more challenges.

Yet, like the diarists, she considered the discomforts a small price to pay for experiencing unfamiliar places.

During the summer, she had spent time corresponding back and forth from Providence to California, investigating leads for excursions to Yosemite and Lake Tahoe to the north. Previous travelers recommended spending ten to fifteen days to get a taste of the area. She discovered many available types of transportation. A private carriage was the most flexible way to go, where she could designate destinations and lodging, but the carriage alone cost three dollars a day with many other costs in addition. Regular stagecoaches provided another option, but they had set schedules and did not always stop at desirable lodging. Hiring a guide was possible for a dollar a day, plus money for meals, horse rental, and lodging. She had to mind the costs.

Least expensive was to travel alone on horseback and camp out each night. Intrepid as she considered herself, Kate knew it was unrealistic for her to travel alone to a place she had never been. Making a solitary trip did not even sound like fun. Rather than fending for herself, she had decided to sign up for a tour. It would reduce her costs, and sharing the experience might be a bonus.

Of all the tour companies, Ahwahnee Adventures had come out on top. The tour lasted fourteen days and went to both Yosemite and the south end of Lake Tahoe. It would be a whirlwind, but she thought worth it. Ahwahnee planned a meeting the second full day of Kate's time in San Francisco, where she could learn final details of the itinerary and meet the guide face-to-face. She had decided to take a chance that a place would still be available.

FIVE

At breakfast, lively conversation encircled her in the Occidental Hotel's main dining room. Chandeliers lit the room since the cloudy day provided little light through the narrow two-story windows. Kate was overjoyed to finally be in California. She flipped through her journal as she waited for her breakfast, remembering all the planning that went into getting her this far. She leisurely read the newspaper as she ate two soft-boiled eggs on toast and sipped musky oolong Chinese tea. After finishing, she walked down the carpeted hallway to the front desk to ask the clerk for directions to the telegraph office. The mahogany front desk extended across the center of the formally appointed lobby. At the far end stood a tall glass vase with aromatic pale-yellow jasmine flowers. Open square compartments for room keys and mail stretched across the back of the desk. She found the elegant surroundings appealing, but had second thoughts about being so extravagant.

"Western Union is several blocks away, Miss Sinclair. Have you noticed the weather? It's really wet out there. I'd be glad to call you a carriage." Peter, the young clerk, was solicitous.

Kate contemplated for a moment, but wanted to experience the city as closely as possible. The ambiance would not be the same through the misty windows of a cab. "Thank you, I appreciate your offer," she told him. "Fortunately, I've come prepared for any weather." It was true. The travel accounts of those who had already been to Yosemite had included lists of everything to take along from clothing to equipment and even medicinals. Kate had brought boots—well-worn, as instructed—a slicker, and a broad-brimmed, waterproof hat. A smile flashed. If she was ready for Yosemite, she must be ready for the streets of San Francisco. "No, she replied, "I think I'll walk."

The desk clerk frowned, still unconvinced. "If you change your mind, you can always hail a cab and put the charge on your hotel bill," he said, attentively.

"Thank you again. I'll keep that in mind." She turned from the sweet jasmine-scented desk to go up and arm herself against the weather.

— · — · — — · ·

Western Union Telegraph occupied a small storefront in a block-long gray brick building. Kate had wondered if she might bump into Frank, but when she saw the office, she knew better; Frank must be involved in something more important than sending and receiving telegrams. Entering, she found a thin man with angular cheekbones sitting behind the counter. The nameplate said Mr. Twindle. Telegraph machines clattered on each side of him. At the back, another man, this one squat with a protruding belly, sat at a table under a bank of cubbyholes, pasting lettered strips on yellow telegraph paper.

The skinny clerk rolled back his chair and stood up to greet her. "Good day, ma'am. Do you wish to send a telegram?" He clasped his narrow fingers. His thinning gray hair stuck tight to his head.

"Not send one," Kate drew in her umbrella, not sure what to do about the accumulating drops puddling on the tile floor. "I'm expecting one . . . from the Old Stone Bank in Providence . . . Rhode Island. I'm hop-

22

ing it's arrived. I gave the bank this office address because it was close to my hotel."

"Your name?"

"Kate. Katherine Sinclair."

With his lanky arms, Mr. Twindle reached to pull papers from a cubbyhole. He riffled through them, then took out another stack from a neighboring compartment. "Nothing here." He turned toward her, his eyes flat and all business. "I checked under your name as well as the bank's. Do you know when it was sent?"

Kate shifted her feet in annoyance, suspecting sabotage on the part of the bank's trustee. "It should have been sent the early part of the month and this is already the middle. Would you have returned it because it wasn't picked up?"

"Oh no, regulations say to keep anything for a month."

She drew in a breath of frustration, trying to contain her temper and contemplate any recourse.

"Could it have gone to your hotel?" The clerk asked.

She recalled Peter, the young desk clerk, doing everything he could to be helpful. "No, I'm staying at the Occidental, and I'm sure someone would have given me a telegram if one had arrived." She regretted blurting out the name of her hotel. She need not divulge details to every stranger she met.

"What about a bank? Would your bank have sent it to another bank?" His skimpy eyebrows met across his brow as he thought.

"I don't know," she admitted, trying to remember if Mr. Finney had mentioned a particular San Francisco bank. She sighed, "I guess I'll have to send a telegram. I'm trying to be careful with my money." *I've done it again. Don't broadcast everything.* "I'd like to send one to Edwin Finney." She waited for Mr. Twindle to fold himself into the chair and begin to tap on the telegraph key. EIGHT-SIX SOUTH MAIN STREET PROVIDENCE RI. Tap. Tap. Tap. NO FUND TRANSFER PLEASE WIRE KATE. Then corrected herself. WIRE AT ONCE. No need to be polite, although she knew it would gratify the pompous banker to realize he had nettled her.

The telegraph clerk counted the letters and wrote the price on a small square of paper and slid it across the counter.

She reached under her slicker for her purse and carefully counted out nine dollars and ten cents, stifling a groan. Mr. Finney knew she had to count every penny, and the delay and extra cost might be intentional.

After a perfunctory thanks, she opened the door and unfurled her umbrella. Her spirits were as damp as the weather. For three hours she explored the soggy streets, recognizing some of the buildings from her reading. She did not want to ruin her map by examining it in the rain. Occasionally, a shop, such as Watkins Photography on Market Street, looked interesting enough to enter. Finally, she returned to the Occidental to dry off and have her noon meal. Foreboding gripped her. There was little time before the tour of Yosemite departed. If she did not have the cash to pay for it, she would miss the primary reason for taking the long cross-county trip.

SIX

Over lunch, Kate brooded about what to do. She could think of little else than her lack of cash. The absence of information from her bank was unraveling all her careful planning. She had over two hundred sixty dollars divided between her purse and a hidden compartment of her steamer trunk, but it was all reserved for San Francisco expenses and travel back to Providence. Even if the inheritance payment arrived in the next few days, it might be too late for her to get a spot on the tour.

From the tall dining room window, a sliver of sunshine unexpectedly shone in her eyes, making her blink. Her spirits rose with the sight of the sun. If it stayed out, she could explore the city in the afternoon without an umbrella.

On the lunch table, her travel log lay open. In it was a list of sights Kate wanted to visit. She had seen a photograph taken from Telegraph Hill by Carleton Watkins showing the deep channel carved in California's coastal mountains by the Sacramento and San Joaquin Rivers on their way to the Pacific Ocean. After the gold rush, people began calling the break in the mountains the Golden Gate. She wanted to take a tour boat there, and if the weather held, she would hike up Telegraph Hill. Her tour book said the name came from a type of windmill, or semaphore, built in 1849, to inform the city about the ships entering the Golden Gate. Two arms on a pole were raised in different configurations to signal what type of boat was entering the harbor. With the arrival of the electric telegraph in 1862, the semaphore was no longer needed, but the hill kept its name.

There was more on the list, but Kate thought boating to Golden Gate and climbing Telegraph Hill were more than enough to fill the afternoon. She paused, reflecting on the telegraph. One way or another, it was interjecting itself into her life: Frank's job, her need for a telegram from her bank, and now the symbolic hill. She put her leather-bound book aside and finished her lunch.

— ·— ·— — ·

The air was cool when Kate boarded the small tour boat to see Golden Gate. She buttoned her coat tightly and tucked a wool scarf around her neck to protect against the harbor breeze. Thin clouds occasionally skipped across the sun, but the view of Angel Island and Mount Tamalpais was inspiringly clear. San Francisco harbor was much less built out than Providence's Narragansett Bay. The boat pilot, doubling as tour guide, told his half-dozen sightseers that a project had begun two years ago to build a seawall to eliminate the clutter of private wharves and jagged lines. Dredging the mudflats to construct a sixty-foot-wide channel, workers had pumped out and filled the area inside the wall using rock, rubble, and even trash. Eventually, they would construct a clean, wide surface ending at an embarcadero.

Progress was evident, but there was no sign of ongoing work as their boat traveled out toward the ocean and "gate." The gnarled boat pilot, with a dark wool hat rimming his weathered face, explained that the opening of the transcontinental railroad had halted construction on the seawall. Only half the tonnage of vessels arrived now as had in the past, but he assured his visitors, even if only to lessen his own worry, that the State Harbor Commission was working determinedly to restart the complicated project.

Kate's mind brimmed with information when she disembarked from her tour. She had found the boat pilot completely satisfactory. When she asked him for directions to Telegraph Hill, he puffed up with pride. "Only one of forty-four hills in San Francisco," he said, and explained the way.

The air had dried, and the temperature warmed to pleasantly mild. The steep grade and the weight of her raincoat made her brow bead with perspiration. When she paused to remove it, she breathed in the aroma of the abundant and unfamiliar foliage. Coat slung over her arm, she trudged up to the top and was buoyed by a glorious panoramic view. It was a different perspective of the natural formation of the Golden Gate than from the boat. Kate stood immobile, exhilarated by the aerial view of the bay. Experiencing the sight in person fulfilled something in her that the books she had read could not. It verified remaining unattached and unfettered in order to travel, even though she paid a price to do so.

By the time she got to the bottom of Telegraph Hill, it was late afternoon. She considered every step of what she thought must have been ten miles worthwhile, but was worn out and ready to return to the Occidental.

After dinner, she retreated to her room, got ready for bed, and wrote in her journal. The process of documenting what she had seen cemented the details in her mind. She included facts, not only about what she had seen, but also history taken from a guidebook or newspaper article. Her writing was as much essay as travelogue. She considered her attempt at illustrations frustratingly crude, but she did a small sketch of what she remembered of the architecture and plants. Only at the end did she include a sentence about money worries. Then she stretched, put away her pen, and fell into bed in an exhausted sleep, too tired to agonize over the upcoming meeting about the Yosemite trip.

SEVEN

Once again, Kate had found her breakfast table beautifully set, with a glass bud vase of jasmine next to the steaming pot of tea. The poached eggs were cooked just the way she liked them: when pierced, the yellow yoke spread luxuriously onto the toasted bread. After a few bites of egg and crisp bacon, she turned her attention to the rest of the dining room, wondering who of the other hotel guests would be at the Yosemite meeting. Most, she suspected, planned to stay put in San Francisco, but a few, like her, would be eager to tackle an arduous excursion. And she assumed that, unlike her, all of them would have ready cash to book the tour. Her shoulders slumped. There was no help for that right now; she might as well work on her breakfast until it was time for the meeting.

Ahwahnee Adventures had arranged for a meeting room to solicit business for its excursion. Kate arrived early and took a far seat where she could scrutinize the others filing in the door. Most of the prospective customers were men, intermingled with only a few couples but no other unaccompanied women. At the front, beside an unfurled map tacked to the wall, was a muscular man wearing dark, shapeless trousers and a well-worn buckskin jacket. He was bareheaded, but a stained, wide-brimmed hat rested on the table in front of him. His hair was dark brown and, with his long sideburns and full beard, he reminded her of something straight out of nature—maybe a bear.

He's sizing us up, Kate surmised, guessing who might ante up, who might be good company, and who might be more trouble than compensated for. She determined not to be one of the latter . . . if she managed to go.

After a few minutes the guide checked his pocket watch and stepped forward to greet the gathering. "Let's get started, folks."

His hair flowed behind his ears just to his collarless shirt. Kate guessed him to be around forty, with the tanned skin of outdoor exposure and wrinkles that fanned at the corner of his eyes from squinting at the sun. She found him ruggedly handsome.

"My name is Ned Jones, and I've been guiding for Ahwahnee Adventures for five years." He picked up a narrow pointer from the table. "By the way, the name comes from what the local Indians originally called the Yosemite Valley. I'm going to start by showing you the route we'll take."

Using the pointer, he traced the route on the map, pausing to indicate where they would stay overnight. Kate's heart pumped with enthusiasm. He described the scenery they would encounter with detail that dazzled her. Jones' deep affection for the outdoors was contagious. The trip would take fourteen days and cost over two hundred and fifty dollars, a little less than she had calculated.

With burly confidence, Ned stepped forward to invite questions.

A hand shot up. "Any chance we will get snow? It will be the end of September."

"It's happened this time of year, but unlikely. It won't turn us back." Ned said assuredly before turning to the next questioner.

"What about grizzlies? I've heard even a gun won't deter them."

"More likely than snow," Ned replied with a tight smile. "We'll keep our eyes open, but generally they shy away from groups of people."

After answering a handful of additional questions, Ned said, "Come on up and take a closer look at the map. I have contracts for those of you who haven't already signed up." He swept his hand toward the paper-filled table. "We have space for twelve and leave the twenty-fourth. Payment is your reservation."

Kate's heart jumped to her throat, knowing it was just what she wanted, and worried that it would fill before she received her monthly inheritance. Instead of walking to the front, she hung halfway back and stood inconspicuously. From her position next to a wall, she observed at least four couples glide toward the exit instead of to the table and map. The trip was not for them, apparently, and they would not compete for a spot. Nevertheless, two dozen people approached the front to ask Ned more questions and examine the map. As the crowd thinned, she edged toward the front, step by step, straining to see the details of the map, until she was standing next to the table . . . and face-to-face with Ned Jones.

Her hand shot forward to shake the large man's hand, while she examined him close-up. His outdoor ruggedness was palpable. She could easily envision him in the woods at night, fearlessly sleeping on a pile of gathered leaves, protected by nothing more than tree branches overhead.

"I'm Kate Sinclair. I wrote in early summer from Rhode Island, inquiring about a trip." She rushed on. "To be honest, San Francisco was my destination, but Yosemite is my true goal. I've read so much about it and Lake Tahoe." Her words bunched together with enthusiasm. "Now that I'm here in the West and heard your talk, I'm even more eager to go."

His full brows arched above deep brown eyes, flickering in reaction. Kate was not sure it was interest at her genuine eagerness or doubt about her gushing.

"Reading about the outdoors and traveling to the mountains are as different as dinner at the Occidental and slogging on mules in the rain," Jones said. He remained unhurried and firmly planted. "Once we start, there's no turning back, and you'll have no one to take care of you."

With a deep inhale, Kate took time to study his expression. His weathered face seemed etched with genuine concern, not an assumption that single women needed to be taken care of more than others. Her shoulders relaxed. As a guide he would be responsible for a dozen people, who may have more bravado than realistic expectations about backwoods travel. No doubt after five years' experience he had had to reckon with temperamental travelers getting more than they bargained for and putting everyone at risk.

"No," Kate faced him, now calm, "you described what we should expect in travel and lodging quite explicitly. The trip you described is what I hoped for."

"Well then, little lady, I'd be happy to have you come along. Have a seat." Jones stepped sideways to pull back the chair from the table. "The agreement states what you just heard, but give it a once-over before you sign. I'll write up a receipt for your payment, official-like."

Two stacks of papers were on the table, most likely those that had been signed and those waiting, Kate guessed. She put her hand on the back of the chair to steady herself, and remained standing. "Mr. Jones, after months of planning, I managed to come all the way by train from Rhode Island. My most fervent desire is to see Yosemite Valley and Lake Tahoe." Kate tightened her grip on the chair to control her voice, determined to sound confident instead of pleading. He had to know how determined she was to go. "What you described is exactly why I made my long journey."

A look of curiosity washed over his face as he turned his attention from the paper-filled table to observe her, his own hand not far from hers on the chair, ready to push it forward when she sat down.

Her cheeks flushed warm. "I did a great deal of study about cost and options. Your fee matches what I estimated." She lifted her eyes to look directly at him.

With her free hand, she motioned toward the stacks of paper. "I have enough money back in Providence to pay for your Yosemite tour and, of course, for additional expenses to stay in San Francisco for a few days afterward, and then the return trip home to Providence." She swallowed her pride at the crassness of discussing money with a stranger and one with whom she might be traveling. "My money was to be transferred from my Rhode Island bank to San Francisco, but I've checked with the Western Union office and no word has arrived yet." Doubt creased the space between her eyes. "I'm not sure why there's a delay. The Western Union clerk knows my hotel and will send me a message right away. Hopefully, soon . . ." she hesitated, dropping both arms to her side. "I wonder if I could sign an agreement for a spot and pay you as soon as a wire about my money arrives."

"Hmm," he concealed any emotion that might give her hope or not. "Here," his chapped hand patted the chair, "take a seat and let's have a word about it." He took a long step to reach for a second chair while she scooted hers toward the table.

"Well, well, well now, little lady, it seems your problem puts a hitch in both our plans." He hunched his broad shoulders. "My dilemmy is that my income is cheek-to-jowl with my expenses—there's not a lot of play in them. I need to hire helpers and transportation. When it comes to lodging, the owners need their pay when we walk in the door." He shifted positions, making his chair wobble with his weight. "We're all living hand to mouth."

"I'm very sorry, Mr. Jones. It was not my intention to be difficult." Her lips compressed in fury at her impossible banker. "I have only one opportunity; with the travel season ending, I'm running out of time. There won't be many more tour groups going, and yours is ideally suited."

Ned paused, probably considering what she said before answering. "I stand on my reputation, but it don't pay the bills. I need eight people minimum to break even and ten to make any profit—with winter coming that's a necessity. Twelve is what I'll try for, frankly. Lodging won't hold no more so I can't add on. If I save one for you, and turn people away, and then find your money is still back East, there goes my profit." Ned reached down to a hip pocket, fumbling for his handkerchief. Turning aside, he blew his nose with a loud honk into the colorless fabric before folding it back in his trousers. "It puts me in the crosshairs of a difficulty." His eyes cast out on the vacant room, as if trying to fix on something other than Kate and her lack of cash.

His brown eyes, uneasy now, disconcerted her. She had had no intention of letting her demoralizing money problem affect anyone else. She had to resolve the conversation and be on her way.

Turning to him she said, "Mr. Jones, it's Saturday. I'll have to wait until Monday to go to Western Union to check again." She noticed his shoulders straighten in relief and suspected he would be glad to be rid of her. "Where might I find you when I figure out my finances?" She moved her chair back and stood up.

"Not far from here," he jumped up to join her, "on Second, close to Mission Street. So far, two other ladies are coming with their husbands, and they would make good company for you," he said, with a slight bow. "There's not much time until we leave. Tell me as soon as possible . . . Thursday morning at the latest." His brow worried into a furrow. "Like I said, I'm awful sorry I can't save you a spot." He extended his hand, "until then, let me know what I can answer for you."

Kate put her hand resolutely against his palm. His face did not reveal whether he was grateful that the time before they left was too short to be feasible for her to find the money if her wire did not come, or whether he was favorably disposed to her joining the trip. The firmness of his jaw signaled the former, but his warm handshake the latter. She withdrew her hand, and with a swirl of her skirt, turned and departed.

Kate's feet almost tangled in her skirt, she was moving so fast going up the Occidental's stairway. Her heart beat rapidly by the time she got to her room. She had caused part of the problem by thinking it was prudent to count on the latest trust amount, instead of drawing from the savings account she was diligently trying to build. It was foolish to pin her hopes on finding a wire transfer Monday, but if there was not one, she needed a backup plan. She sat on her bed thinking of options, but was stymied.

EIGHT

Sunday, Kate had allocated all day to Woodward Botanical Gardens because it was one of the few sites open on that day. When she arrived, she discovered a hodgepodge of flowers, an amusement park, museum, outdoor theater, and a zoo, all occupying two city blocks in the Mission District. The owner, Robert Woodward, had made a fortune in the California gold rush. Since beginning the gardens in 1866, Woodward had continually added to them. For twenty-five cents, anyone could spend the day in four hundred acres of gardens and amusements. At the entryway, the man who greeted Kate and collected her money said, "You'll see that families flock here on the weekends."

As Kate explored the gardens, swollen gray clouds covered the sky with a flat light that made everything appear as if she were moving inside an Oriental painting. The wind sent leaves and dirt swirling, making her cling to her hat as she inspected the metal labels that identified plants. Many of the trees had been imported from Europe and even Asia. Kate spent the whole morning, head down against the wind, wandering the gravel paths past streams, small lakes, hillocks, even a manmade grotto and cavern. On the far side of the park, she found the zoo with over a hundred animals. Toward noon, mist joined the wind, and she escaped to the refreshment room in the arena for lunch. The wet weather kept her inside in the afternoon with most other visitors. She moved along with clusters of people to the ferneries, a conservatory filled with exotic plants and flowers. Then, returning to the entrance of the gardens, she went into Woodward's former residence just inside the park. He had turned it into a museum of natural wonders, with stuffed animals, birds, fish, fossils, and mineral specimens.

After so many hours of studying exhibits, Kate was chilled, tired, and ready to return to her hotel. Her mind was overflowing with information; she wished there were someone to *tell* about the amazing sights. Instead, back in her room she described everything in her journal and in letters to friends.

—·— ·— — ·

The telegraph office was unchanged when she entered it on Monday— the room filled with clacking machines and piles of orderly, stacked yellow paper. Hearing her enter, the thin telegrapher swiveled and greeted her. "Ah, Miss Sinclair, isn't it? You're back."

"Yes, I am, . . . Mr.—"

"Twindle."

"Mr. Twindle. Thank you for remembering me. You must get a great many telegrams, but I wonder if mine was among them?"

He twisted his narrow hands around each other in agitation. "I'm afraid we have no news."

Kate grimaced, even though it was not unexpected. Had the telegram arrived, she knew Mr. Twindle would have eagerly given it to her. In fact, she would not have been surprised if he or his assistant delivered it to her hotel.

"Did you check with the front desk?" He shook his head as if apologizing for asking. "Of course, you did. That would be the first place you checked."

"Oh well, Mr. Twindle," her voice caught. "I have a couple more days, but only that."

"We'll keep a sharp eye out for it. In the meantime," he hesitated. "Might you have another source?"

"No, everything is in Providence." Chagrined that she continually made her life an open book, Kate gathered her coat close for the weather outside. "Thank you for keeping a watch out for anything addressed to me, and I might come back too."

He bent at the waist in a half bow. "I'm sorry to disappoint you."

With a pull on the door, Kate left the fretting telegrapher behind and stepped out to the bustle of the street. Carriages jockeyed for right of way, and other pedestrians brushed against her as she walked along the congested sidewalk. Managing the traffic and curiosity about the store-fronts took her mind off thoughts of money. She spent twice as long getting back to the hotel as had her previous trip in the rain.

Seeing her approach, Peter remembered her and reached for her key before she asked. With it came a white vellum envelope. Her heart plummeted, seeing it was not from the Old Stone Bank. It was addressed simply to: Miss Katherine Sinclair, Occidental Hotel, and obviously hand-delivered. Too impatient to ask for a letter opener, she slid her finger under the flap and opened it.

910 York St.
San Francisco, Calif.
September 20, 1869

Miss Sinclair:

I was pleased to learn that you are still at the Occidental and haven't yet left for Yosemite. Would you do me the honor of dining with me tonight at the Lick House? I will fetch you at 7:00 if you are so disposed.

I would welcome your company. Please send a reply message.

Yours truly,
Frank Ellsworth.

Frank's writing slanted to the right across the page with square, masculine penmanship, absent flourishes as if constructed of straight pieces of string. She refolded the stationery and pushed it back in the envelope. *It's not an answer to my problem, but more complication.* Without even saying goodbye to Peter, she took the envelope and oversized brass key and left, barely noticing his baffled look about her reaction to the letter.

Back at her room, she tossed the envelope on the desk and hung up her coat. She unbuttoned her shoes and removed them before stretching out on the bed. *What to do, what to do?* Problems were mounting. There was no way to contact her trustee other than the telegram she had already sent. Ned Jones had explained his financial situation. She had to have the required cash to go. If she paid him with her cash, she would have little money when she returned to San Francisco from Yosemite—not enough to return home. Her parents disapproved of her trip to Yosemite, so turning to them was not an option.

Kate crossed her arms behind her head and lay back on the soft pillow. Her mother's reaction about her trip to California was not unexpected but still an enigma. Eugenia had always been interested in what was going on in the world. When her father finished reading the newspaper at breakfast and had gone to work, Kate's mother had her turn, commenting about news articles as she read them, inviting a response from her children, often challenging them with questions.

Eugenia devoted most of her early marriage to raising children and taking care of Will's needs. She had had little spare time, but when she did, she volunteered for causes she cared about. Will discounted what she did, when he paid attention at all, calling it "busy work for the fair sex."

As a young girl, Kate remembered trying to make sense of occasional afternoon conversations by her mother and her friends when they gathered around the dining room table. Eugenia had never shooed her daughter away if a meeting was still going on when she returned from school. Kate had poured herself a glass of milk and, with a fistful of Graham crackers, moved a chair close to the dining room door to listen from the edge of the kitchen. Sometimes she had to strain to hear the women's conspiratorially muted voices. Other times, they were in loud disagreement, like billy goats butting heads in a backyard. The passion of the speakers made an impression, even though it was a long time before Kate made sense of subjects like temperance, emancipation, suffrage. Once she was older, she began to understand not only the meanings, but that there were opposing strategies to accomplishing goals, and even sharp differences regarding the goals themselves. The right of women to vote was a frequent topic, but not all agreed that women should demand it.

In addition to the right of women to vote, Eugenia had been a proponent of the seminary movement—a counterpart of colleges for men. She encouraged Kate to attend for knowledge and confidence. Her father had been against it: "What's the point, she's a girl," Kate once heard him grump. Kate knew it must have taken out-of-sight persuasion by Eugenia to get Will to agree to pay Kate's tuition.

The opportunity had overjoyed her, thinking education would give her the freedom to make her own decisions. During her four years, she diligently completed assignments in subjects she knew would stay with her for a lifetime: grammar, logic, mathematics, music, astronomy . . . on and on. Her favorite had been debate. She could still conjure up the memory of Mr. Brown at the front of the lecture room, in a gray tweed jacket flecked with maroon and navy nubs. He stood vigilant beside the tall blackboard, chalk in hand, ready to pounce on sloppy thinking. Mr. Brown gave each student debate topics demanding her to make a persuasive case for whichever side of the argument she drew. As a freshman, Kate could utter no more than two sentences before she heard the stern rap, rap, rap of his chalk on the board. Mr. Brown admonished, "You must think before speaking." This had usually been followed by another disgusted rap of his chalk, "Start over and see if you can bring yourself to argue with wisdom and eloquence." How, she had wondered, could she argue with wisdom and eloquence when her voice trembled, and eyes stung with tears of indignation? But by graduation she had made a seamless defense of the most complicated topic, leaving Mr. Brown's hand motionless and a glint of approval in his rheumy eyes.

Kate had been a student at Mt. Holyoke Seminary and away from home when the War of Rebellion began, but she had read news accounts of the divisive debate of whether to continue the momentum for women's rights or to accede to the needs of Negro men for citizenship and their own right to vote. There was never unanimity among suffragists, but most believed to win anything, they had to choose one cause. Suffrage had to wait until the war was resolved. Elation filled their ranks when ratification of the Fourteenth Amendment gave citizenship to all men, including former slaves. Ratification of the Fifteenth Amendment, allowing all male citizens to vote, had not yet come, but anticipation that it would had mobilized women for their own effort to vote.

Mt. Holyoke had encouraged her to think logically and meet the world on her own terms, but when she returned home to Providence, her mother had an entirely different life plan for Kate. In her view, the time had come for Kate to fulfill her domestic obligation by finding a husband and then educating the children that would inevitably arrive. Educated sons were to go out in the world to seek a good occupation. Daughters, too, should be educated—to carry on women's supportive role.

Putting aside old memories, Kate propped herself up to a sitting position, reaching across the desk for the letter she had tossed there. Unfolding it, she reread Frank's words. They were as spare as his handwriting but she was ecstatic that he wanted to see her. She refolded the letter and slid it back into the envelope.

Life had become complicated with the wire transfer debacle. When planning, Kate had confidently scheduled an extra week in California for plenty of leeway before leaving for Yosemite, but the delay of money was giving her a dizzying sense of unease. She might never return to California if this trip failed. Realistically, she could do nothing more about her money, and even though being with Frank was a temporary happenstance, she was tired of spending all her time alone.

In her stocking feet she walked over to the desk and found hotel stationery with the distinctive "O" of Occidental on the top. She dipped her pen in the inkwell and wrote an appreciative note to accept Frank's invitation. Finished, she put back on her shoes, wool coat, and broadbrimmed hat. Until it was time for dinner, she would explore more of the city. On her way out, she dropped off the note at the front desk and asked that it be delivered to the address on Frank's letter.

NINE

By the time Kate returned to her hotel, not even her money problems could diminish her anticipation of dinner with Frank. She was desperate for company. The Lick House had been her second choice for lodging—both appeared equally comfortable from the descriptions, and either was a splurge. She had decided on the Occidental because the literary magazine, *The Golden Era,* was headquartered there, attracting well-known authors to stay while on a lecture circuit. The prospect of encountering a famous author was far-fetched, but appealing, nevertheless. With Frank's invitation, not only would she enjoy his company, she would get to see the Lick House.

As she started down the Occidental's grand staircase, she spotted Frank standing confidently on the red patterned carpet at the bottom, holding his hat as he waited. His neatly parted hair gleamed from brown to black under the blazing light of the chandelier. When she reached the bottom, he stepped forward to clasp her hand in a cordial handshake. "Miss Sinclair . . . Kate, good to see you again."

The strength of his palm pressed against hers. "Is San Francisco treating you well?"

She released his hand and found her voice, "Very well. I've seen so many interesting sights already, but not the Lick House. Thank you for asking me to dinner, Frank." Once again, his eyes captivated her. "I even made a trip to Western Union. How is your job suiting you?"

"We have a lot to share over dinner. You don't mind walking, do you?" He crooked his elbow, and she took his arm. "It's only a block up Montgomery and one with lamps lighting it."

"I like walking. I've passed by the Lick House several times but haven't been inside." Kate smiled. It was so good to share things.

"And I already know how much you like new opportunities."

She looked up, frowning, but catching his droll grin, nudged him with her elbow at his jesting. They both began to laugh, her soprano against his bass. He tucked in his arm gently, bringing her closer to him.

The four-story Lick House was constructed of stucco and stone, with cast iron pillars and pilasters on the first story, and pedimented windows on the second, third, and fourth. A tall doorman in a dark frock coat and a top hat greeted them as they entered the gilded interior.

"Oh my, I thought the Occidental was grand," Kate said, looking at the lavish interior.

"Wait until you see the dining room. I only stayed here for two nights before I moved into a modest apartment away from the center of town. Of course, anyone is welcome to eat dinner here, and they agreeably turned a blind eye to my inexpensive threads." He cocked his right eyebrow in humor, guiding her to a doorway at the side of the foyer.

"Frank Ellsworth, I have a reservation for two," he said to the *maître d'hôtel*, who led them through the throng of tables covered formally with starched white linen. Solicitously he helped Kate take off her coat and then pulled back a chair for her to sit. He took Frank's coat and returned to his station.

"All the light from the candles and lamps reflecting off mirrors and gold trim make it as light as day," Kate said, tipping her head back dizzily to look up. "It's like a palace."

"You're not far off," Frank said. "The architect wanted to mimic the interior of the Palace of Versailles in France. This dining room holds four hundred people . . . and, by the way," he whispered in mock confidentiality, "the waiter told me it's called a *salle-a-manger* in French."

"Impressive," Kate said, taking the tall leather-bound menu offered by the white-jacketed waiter.

"Or pretentious. The kings of France wanted to convince the world how powerful they were."

The waiter asked for their drink order.

"I'm going to have a whiskey; may I offer you something?"

"Sherry would be a treat, thanks." She had not had any alcohol since she left home, but tonight seemed the right occasion.

Kate took her time reading the list of offerings. The menu was not dissimilar from her own hotel's. The Occidental and Lick House vied to be the most elegant hotel on the Pacific . . . or maybe beyond. And, there was always the Cosmopolitan, the Grand, the Palace, and the Baldwin. San Francisco had no shortage of imposing hotels.

After the waiter took their orders, she asked, "Have you had time to settle into your job, Frank?"

"I have to confess, I didn't know how much there was to learn about the telegraph, or maybe how much I didn't know. I'm drowning in details, but I like that." He looked at her earnestly. "I like learning about anything that's new and changing," he laughed. "Some people accuse me of being too single-minded when I have a project. I had made inquiries before I took the job, but the Pacific Coast is really different than the East, where I was getting my information."

"I wouldn't have thought of that," Kate said, intrigued.

"I hadn't realized that, up until 1860, Congress had introduced several bills to develop a telegraph, but they never panned out. Finally, they got one passed. It didn't take long after that to set up a transcontinental system."

"Not nearly as long as the railroad," Kate said.

"No. It went fairly fast. It's a good thing. Can you imagine the war years without a telegraph?"

"I've read some people think it was the difference between winning and losing," she agreed.

"Western Union won the contract to build lines from the east coast all the way to Salt Lake City, no small feat," Frank was obviously warming to his subject. "Something else I discovered: a consolidation of companies called Overland finished the job, connecting a small network here in California to Salt Lake City and then Omaha, Nebraska."

They continued easy conversation as they ate their dinner—plates brimming with steaming cod baked in garlic butter, scalloped potatoes, and long fingers of green beans. Their meal finished with chocolate cake.

"The men in my office have a slew of stories about the first wires here. Some people thought letters on pieces of paper were somehow moving along the wires. They couldn't believe words could be transmitted with mechanical tapping—a code being sent by electricity still baffles people."

Kate chuckled, "I must admit, I understand the concept of Morse code but nothing about electrical transmission."

"That makes two of us," Frank said. "Have you ever considered just how isolated early California was before the telegraph? Back in 1841, when President Harrison died, they didn't get the news out here for four months. Now it's instantaneous." He leaned forward in his seat. "And that's just the beginning. Science is changing every niche of our lives."

Kate's mind spun with all Frank said. She needed time to think of the implications. As he lifted his cut-glass tumbler to savor the last of his whiskey, she asked, "Is science part of your job at Western Union?"

He set down the glass. "Not directly." For the first time, she saw a cloud darken his eyes. "Western Union told me I was being hired to help spread its network, but it is going to be more than sales. Since the telegraph came, no one wants to be without its possibilities. Those who have access are a step ahead, and those without are afraid they will be left behind."

"Do you think that's right?"

"It's not an empty fear," he nodded. "Communication boosts commerce and safety too. Railroads already depend on information across the wire to reduce accidents. It's no coincidence the telegraph developed alongside railroads."

Kate listened attentively to everything Frank said—it interested her. She appreciated that he was comfortable discussing the male world of commerce with a woman. Not many men were, in her experience.

"Western Union was early in the game of telegraphy, but now everyone wants to play because it's lucrative. I'm beginning to suspect my job is going to be fighting off competitors while selling as much as possible. I'm not sure what that entails yet, but I'm going to give it everything I've got."

"That doesn't sound so easy. Who are the competitors?"

"I don't know all of them, but one is Jay Gould." Frank's hand wrapped around his glass as if the gravity of what he was saying provoked another whiskey. "Perhaps you've read about him." He looked at her for a response. "He's been in the news quite recently."

Kate thought instantly of the widely printed Thomas Nast cartoons. "If Nast is right, Gould is a rapacious businessman—a bully if you ask me."

"You do know the rascal, although Nast does like to exaggerate."

"No wonder you're apprehensive," she said. "How do you compete with someone like that?"

"I'm not sure yet. But I know one thing: You're always looking over your shoulder to prevent a sharp blade from stabbing you in the back."

"That's dreadful! Are others in your office nervous?"

"I just recently met everyone, of course, but yes, they are on edge about tangling with the likes of Mr. Gould. The regional manager, Howard Zell, stays in the office most of the time. The rest of us are supposed to be out trying to spread the wires and keeping in touch with what's going on. We all realize that if Western Union is going to continue paying us, we can't let men like Gould flatten us."

"It doesn't sound like what you were counting on."

"Maybe I wasn't realistic about what I signed up for. I knew full well that there were other companies we would go against, but the appeal of California made me overlook the competition. Jay Gould is a smart and clever foe. Staying on top will be a challenge." A smile crossed Frank's face. "Kate, enough about business tonight; I've kept you here longer than I intended out of pure enjoyment of your company. Look," he made a sweeping gesture with his hand. "The dining room is no longer full because I've bent your ear for so long. Would you like anything else, or shall we be on our way?"

She looked down at the gold watch clipped at her waist. "You're right," she said with surprise. "It is getting late. The time disappeared."

The attentive waiter noticed their preparation to leave and hurried to bring the check and their coats. He held hers while she put her arms in and held Frank's as he paid.

"Frank, thank you for dinner. The evening has been such a pleasure— not just the food but the conversation."

"My pleasure." He crooked his elbow and she slipped in her hand with a comfortable belonging. They left the Lick House and walked unhurriedly down Montgomery Street, in and out of glimmering pools of gaslight. The lobby of the Occidental was filled with the see-and-be-seen crowd, enjoying their last drinks before returning to rooms or homes. At the front desk, she reluctantly released Frank's arm and took the room key offered by the night clerk. As she turned, Frank grasped her other hand in his. "When can I see you again?" His brow furrowed. "I forgot to ask what day you leave."

The question hung there, with its attendant complications. Kate greatly wanted to see him again. He captivated her with his wide range of interests. She admired his honesty in revealing the unanticipated problems at Western Union. It was unusual for a man to do so. He seemed without affectation.

She mused about a second invitation. Giving him a date might reveal the possibility that she may not go to Yosemite. Travel problems were hers to resolve and not something to bother him with. And Frank really should not have to buy her another dinner if they were soon going to part forever. Pleasurable as it would be, it would be taking advantage of him.

"What about tomorrow?" Frank asked insistently.

"Tomorrow?" she stammered, momentarily squeezing her eyes shut. *Too soon, but when?* Her eyes flashed open, catching sight of his intrepid face, "What a nice offer, Frank. Would you consider the day after tomorrow?"

"It's agreed," he said, releasing her hand. "I look forward to spending the evening hearing about *your* plans."

They parted at the grand staircase, where they had met just hours ago. The place was exactly the same, but Kate's emotions had gone through a sea of change, from the simple pleasure of having dinner, to a genuine connection with him. She hurriedly stepped up the carpeted stairway, her mind jumbled with thoughts.

Back in the familiar surroundings of her room, she began taking off her clothing, folding each item for the appropriate drawer in her trunk so she wouldn't have to search. The lightweight flannel nightgown freed her from all the restrictive underclothing. Sitting in front of the oval framed mirror, she pulled the hairpins from her chignon and let her hair fall to her shoulders, unconstrained. Her toiletries were lined up neatly next to the ceramic water pitcher. She picked up her hairbrush and began her bedtime ritual of one hundred strokes, her hair glinting blond in the gaslight. Anxiety about her finances beleaguered her. Done with her brush, she replaced it on the vanity and sighed. It maddened her to have things fall apart after her months of assiduous planning. She slipped into bed and turned off the lantern.

She thought of another dinner with Frank, enticed by his look . . . his voice . . . his language . . . his alert eyes. It was a scarce man, or woman for that matter, who did not resent Kate's inclination toward independence. However, at that moment her reliance on other people, especially the intractable Mr. Finney at the Old Stone Bank, made her self-sufficiency as firm as wispy clouds evaporating in the sunshine. The West might be reputed as the land of opportunity, but she was learning it was not without challenges. Both her money problems and Frank's allure were testing her.

TEN

On Tuesday morning, the fog burned away early, expanding the patches of fresh blue sky. The clatter of delivery wagons echoed in the streets as Kate made a third march to Western Union. When she opened the door, Mr. Twindle rose and shook his narrow head. She had steeled herself for the absence of news, but her heart sank to her stomach anyway. She did not enter the office; instead, she gave a dejected nod, pivoted, and silently left, closing the door behind her.

She had already decided that if Mr. Finney left her empty-handed, she would continue touring. There was no reason the possibility of forfeiting one part of her plans should ruin everything. She had decided to visit Nob Hill that morning, to see the mansions of San Francisco's nabobs. She continued north on Montgomery Street to Sacramento and Jones Streets, and turned on a walkway that began climbing a steep hill. Before long, the famous neighborhood came into view. The houses reminded her of pictures of English castles. Other tourists, some in fancy dress and others in simpler garb, were strolling along the streets gawking at the luxury. Kate found the architectural details both stunning and excessive. She sought out two mansions mentioned in her guidebook. They both belonged to railroad developers who had become rich building the transcontinental route that she and Frank had just taken. The four-story Stanford residence took up an entire city block, and up the hill was the three-story Crocker house, ornately fitted with Second Empire neoclassical finishes. Prominence exuded a gilded message of power and wealth. She tried to remember everything, to tell Frank when she saw him.

The morning was soft and still, blue sky shimmering, perfect for sightseeing. After she walked for blocks, examining the entire Nob Hill, she decided she wanted to see something different. Portsmouth Square wasn't too many blocks away. She stumbled along, reading her guidebook as she walked. Originally, the Yerba Buena Mexican community called it the Grand Plaza, until Captain Montgomery of the *USS Portsmouth* seized the town in July 1846, at the beginning the Mexican-American war. He raised the first American flag near the Mexican adobe customs house. The Americans renamed the town San Francisco, and the plaza became Portsmouth Square, in honor of his ship. Kate found the square a contrast to the opulence of Nob Hill and the area around her hotel. It was like an ordinary frontier town, ringed by mostly two-story commercial buildings such as drugstores, printing shops, and restaurants. Kate's fondness for the city was growing with familiarity. She glanced at her watch. One o'clock. It was time to return for lunch.

Once back in the Occidental dining room, she only picked at her food, knowing the next day was Wednesday, and the day after the deadline set by Ned Jones. Her neck was painfully rigid with tension. She put her refolded napkin next to her unfinished plate, acid filling her stomach. At least having dinner with Frank would rid her of solitude, if not worry.

ELEVEN

"Kate, you look splendid," Frank said as she descended the last wide steps of the carpeted Occidental stairway to their meeting place at the bottom. His newly-trimmed beard made him even more handsome than she remembered. He was such a welcome sight, she wanted to hug him.
"I have an idea," he told her. "What would you think of trying something other than hotel food tonight?"

"And I'll bet you already have a place in mind," she laughed happily.

"We can't walk. I'll have to hail a cab," he raised one eyebrow, questioning. "Still game?"

"Of course." At that moment she would have gone with him almost anywhere, walking, riding, or by any conveyance, just as long as she was with him.

The Old Clam House was a casual, one-story, white clapboard building next to the bay. Inside, they found a small table for two with an angular glimpse of the waterfront through a wide window.

"I'm going to have my usual whiskey; will you join me with a sherry?" Frank asked.

"That would be just right, thank you."

When her drink came, she held the first sip on her tongue before letting it glide down her throat. She had not realized how the burden of worrying alone was grinding at her. She looked across at Frank as he sat, relaxed and hatless, his hair blowing slightly every time the restaurant's front door opened. Fortunately, Kate had tossed her wool stole over her arm before she left her hotel room; she had now wrapped it snugly around her shoulders, her broad-brimmed hat firmly situated. They took their time opening steamed clams and mussels and peeling shrimp cooked bright pink on a brazier. For dessert, they ordered a plate of a local favorite, dark Ghirardelli chocolate.

Frank's ease and confidence drew her toward him. One topic of conversation segued into another as he exhibited his wide-ranging knowledge without conceit. He was interested in everything, but he didn't pontificate. He listened—really listened—to her thoughts on the subjects they discussed. She was lighter than air.

"I'm satiated," Frank said. "Not just by the food but also by your company. I confess I'm disappointed that you're leaving. I've rarely met anyone I enjoy talking with as much as I do you."

She felt her face flush at his compliment.

"When did you say you are going to Yosemite?"

"Friday." She straightened as the spell collapsed like a sandcastle in a wave. She gulped, "I hope."

"Hope? I thought you'd signed on with a guide."

She sketched it out for him, every frustrating trip to Western Union, Edwin Finney, and her need to pay Ned Jones the next day. "There's no leeway," she said, dismayed by the crassness of talking about money, "and there's no guarantee of a spot. The season for Yosemite is coming to an end. It's only mountain men and gold seekers who visit in the snow," she stammered.

With each of her exclamations, the furrows of Frank's frown deepened.

She tensed. Once again emotion had caused her to spill out information she never intended to reveal. Where was her promise to depend only on herself? Frustrated, she twisted her napkin and stayed silent, pulling into a shell where she often retreated to escape difficulties. Kate was sure he could sense her misery.

"Do you mind my asking how much you owe your guide?" He paused for an answer. "You don't have to tell me, but I might come at the problem from a different angle." His voice was kind, not judgmental.

Still, she hesitated, loath to talk about the actual amount with someone whom she had just met. In momentary escape, her gaze floated around the compact restaurant with its every table filled, chiming with tinkling china and lively voices. She blinked and retreated from the chatter of the crowd to the solitude of the two of them once more.

"It's not that I don't have the money. It should be here. That's the maddening part."

"Did you say how much you need?" His lips slit with a hint of a smile as narrow as the shell she was emerging from.

"It's a lot. Not that I'm always frivolous; I'm usually pinching pennies, even in travel. Except," she drew her hands together in her lap. "Except for this trip—San Francisco and Yosemite. I knew it would be expensive, but it will be my splurge. I *can't* go home without seeing Yosemite."

He listened attentively, occupying himself with a last drop of his whiskey.

Gloom permeated her. Across the table, Frank clearly wanted to be helpful. "It's two hundred fifty dollars," she blurted.

"That's quite a bit," he offered, "but not more than I expected. As I said before, I think you're right about seeing Yosemite, and visiting in the autumn may be a fine time. I've done a little reading about it myself. Most of the trees are conifers, but there are also maples, black oaks, dogwoods that will be showy with color, and probably others I've forgotten. I'm envious, as a matter of fact. If I didn't have to work, I would like nothing more than to join the group."

She drew a deep breath, imagining his accompanying her. What a relief that would be. "You would consider it?"

"I would, but since I just started my job, there's no time off, unfortunately. Have you thought of getting a short-term loan?"

Kate shook her head. "No—banks don't lend money to unmarried women." She did not add that she would not ask her father to sponsor her. "Loans also take time that I don't have."

"Would you like me to come with you? I'm new in town, but I do work for Western Union, and I can be persuasive about credibility and speed," he grinned.

"Why would you do that? We just met," Kate said with surprise.

Frank nodded. "We may have recently met, but don't forget we have a journey across the country in common, a connection of spirit if nothing else. And, may I remind you that we've spent some time conversing about our exploits and aspirations."

He needn't remind her of the conversations. She had never been so in synchrony with another person as she was when they talked together. Her strong opinions were met with sensible retorts; he stood his ground without being offended by what she said. Tonight, at the Clam House, as with their previous dinner at the Lick House, other diners had already begun to leave, having finished their meals while Frank and Kate lingered, not yet ready to part.

"Frank, I'm grateful for your offer. I want to think more about other options. I'll let you know if I wish you to go to the bank with me. Thank you." The old bugbear of not letting anyone too close—that fear of becoming dependent—reared up. In the past, she had given up anything that had demanded reliance on someone else. It was better to forego what was at stake than to be entangled in the end, but Yosemite stood athwart that premise. She had never wanted anything quite so badly.

She had been taught "neither a borrower nor a lender be." Her father had spoken harshly about those who stooped to borrowing as if, for any reason, running short of funds was unscrupulous—a blot on one's character. That was his judgment for men who borrowed, and she could only imagine the words he would use for a woman borrowing money—and even worse, for what he deemed a nonessential trip.

The next morning, she contained her emotions with Mr. Twindle's apologetic confirmation that nothing had come from the Stone Bank.

Overnight she had made her decision, encouraged by Frank's saying that a brief shortage of money should not stop her from going to Yosemite. She had decided to use the funds reserved for returning home to pay Ned Jones, and face any consequences of being penniless if the money had not arrived by the time she returned from her trip.

TWELVE

In the morning, Kate set out in search of Ahwahnee Adventures. Montgomery Street terminated at Market, a diagonal street extending out into a wharf. When she came to the intersection, she hesitated, not knowing which way to turn, but chose to walk left. It had been a good guess. At the second corner, she turned right and walked slowly, looking at storefronts on each side of the street. Salt and fish scented the damp air. In only two blocks, she found the office in a slim, redbrick and timbered building, with a window so narrow it barely contained the words "Ahwahnee Adventures," even when stacked on top of each other. At first, she thought the door was locked and the office closed. Her heart plunged. Then she realized that the doorknob turned and, with her shoulder against the moisture-swollen door, she gave it a hard shove and catapulted into the office.

"Good grief, what have we here," the startled Ned Jones said, leaping to his feet.

"Oh, I'm sorry," Kate said, repositioning her flat-brimmed hat that had fallen over her eyes.

"Ah, I recognize you from the hotel, Miss . . . Miss—"

"Sinclair," she said, after regaining her balance. "I've come to inquire if there is still an opening for the Yosemite trip." She was afraid of his answer.

"Now I remember, you had financial inconveniences. Did you fix them?"

"I'm hoping you still have room," she said, without divulging the cash in her purse.

He hesitated, taking a step toward his paper-stacked desk, but remaining closemouthed about a vacancy. They were doing a dance of position. Both had something to lose or gain.

After a few moments of silence, she could stand it no longer. "I do have the money to pay you, Mr. Jones," she said, straightening her shoulders, "if you still have room."

The skin around his eyes crinkled. "Then, Miss Sinclair, we have a deal. You recall that we leave tomorrow. Can you be ready that shortly?" He glanced at her with skepticism.

"My satchel is all packed and ready to go."

He pulled up a straight-back chair beside his desk. "Then please, take a seat. I'll get a copy of the contract and my inkstand is right here for you to use." He stretched his arm and leafed through a pile of papers before he found what he wanted. "Ah, here you go." He positioned it on his desk so it faced her. Sitting down at his desk chair next to her, he positioned it to give her space to read and sign the contract. "As it turns out, I still have vacancies. I don't suppose you know anyone who wants to come along?"

She thought of Frank and how wonderful it would be to have him on the trip, then looked across at Mr. Jones. "I'm sorry, I've just arrived in San Francisco." She saw a small, fleeting look of curiosity pass over Ned Jones' face, as if he had read her expression and suspected someone had occurred to her in response to his question. However, if he wondered who that someone might be, he kept to himself.

THIRTEEN

That night, thoughts about the strenuous days ahead would not leave Kate's mind. She tried to reassure herself that she had already endured a difficult journey in traveling to Colorado Territory. Yosemite would be a different kind of test, sometimes requiring saddled mounts and hiking on steep terrain. Giving up on sleep, she got out of bed, her mind in a sleep-deprived muddle. She pulled back the curtain to check the weather, but there was not much to see. The sun had not yet risen. Below, a street lamp shone in a barely discernible orb. It must be foggy but dry, she thought.

Before going to bed, she had taken every item of clothing and paraphernalia out of her big satchel, then slowly and carefully reassessed each piece before putting it back. When she finished, the satchel was bulging, but by kneeling on it, she forced the sides together, and managed to click the latches shut. Whatever might be missing, she would do without. Everything else was packed in her trunk, to be left behind in the hotel's storage.

The desk clerk was struggling to stay awake when she came down to the lobby just before six o'clock. The dining room was not yet serving breakfast. She put her satchel by her feet and waited, looking out the hotel door. No more than five minutes passed before a Concord stage, pulled by three pairs of matched horses, arrived. She was outside by the time Ned Jones got out of the coach.

"Good morning, Miss Sinclair," he said, taking her bag. He opened the stagecoach door and leaned down to jimmy her bag in a space beneath the back bench.

Kate stepped up into the coach and smoothed her skirt before squeezing in between two men, silently groaned about her position, but figured it was better than the short middle bench without full backs. She was the seventh person.

The guide seemed to read her mind. "This coach will get us to the wharf to catch the ferry for Alameda, and the one on the other side is the exact same. We'll all switch around and take a spell in the middle. Ten signed up, so I'll be riding inside." He closed the door and took his seat just as the coach began to roll. "We have more passengers to pick up." His half-smile did not reveal whether he would have preferred being on top with the driver and guard or with the tourists of whom he was in charge.

This stage had three benches—one facing forward and one back with the third in the middle. Each person had eighteen inches of space, and before long, the knees of strangers would be banging against hers while their thighs rubbed intimately. Each of the two doors had an Isinglass window and was flanked on each side by two larger openings. Dark, thick leather upholstered the walls and benches of the interior. The same dark cowhide hung across the large openings. Passengers could part these curtains to take in the view when the weather was not cold or rainy.

At the Lick House, where she and Frank had first dined, they took on a male passenger and at the Cosmopolitan Hotel, a second couple. Everyone was on board. Kate realized full well that traveling in a party of ten could either be an asset, if they were companionable, or an irritation, if they were disagreeable.

Ned Jones stood near one of doors as the horses trotted across San Francisco for the Alameda crossing. "I want to give you a welcome from Ahwahnee Adventures." He kept one arm raised, palm pressed against the roof of the swaying coach for balance. "We're all going to be living together for over two weeks so call me Ned, like everyone else in these here parts does. I'm going to show you land that is sure to startle your eyes. For most of three days, we'll be heading east, with only a few minutes to get out for changing horses every twelve to fifteen miles, more or less. There's no leeway at our stops, and we have the pleasure of three ladies so that delays things," he said, without apology. "Half an hour is allowed for a breakfast, lunch, and dinner. We've picked places that serve food—some heartier than others," he chuckled. "We'll keep on schedule so you can have time to see what you came for—Yosemite and Lake Tahoe—God's land. You'll see what I mean." His eyes half-closed in apparent reverence. "I'll tell you about some of the sights as we go along, and guides will take you other times, but right now I'll have a seat and let you explain something about yourselves to get to know one another."

Kate listened carefully, trying to get a sense of her travel companions. Uneasy excitement infused the coach as people described where they came from and why they wanted to see Yosemite and Lake Tahoe. Eagerness blended with apprehensive expectations. Some were voluble in their explanations and others hoarded their words and inner thoughts. They all had little else to do but talk since the only views were out the small windows; the big openings were still covered.

After crossing San Francisco Bay, everyone filed into the second stagecoach, taking the same position they'd had before. Although less foggy, the views were still only fast pictures of rushing scenery, glimpsed through the small Isinglass windows. It was not until the mid-morning exchange of horse teams that the driver pulled back the leather curtains to give a view of their journey. Seeing more at first unnerved Kate. The twists and turns in the roads made many stretches harrowing. Other conveyances traveled at varying speeds, going both directions along the route. Coaches and carriages proceeded at a fast clip, but fully loaded wagons, pulled by long teams of horses, moved laboriously. Often, they encroached on the middle of the road, passing with only inches to spare. Their coach rarely slowed, going down each hill at a full gallop and up the next at a trot. She held her breath, preparing for a crash each time their coach perilously careened around a blind corner, only to meet another vehicle barreling full speed from the opposite direction. The drivers skillfully avoided collisions, and she learned to relax and not watch so carefully.

The benches were hard, but the coach rested on leather braces, giving a sense of swaying instead of jarring. Nevertheless, Kate folded her stole and sat on it for padding. Ned was true to his word. Whenever the driver replaced the horses with a new team, Ned asked the passengers to shift seats, using some sort of prescribed rotation he kept in his head.

The first break was a rush of activity as passengers hurried off the stage, bumping against one another in their haste to use the outbuildings, drink a cup of water, and buy hardtack and jerked meat. It was what Kate had expected from her experience on her previous cross-country trip. Back on the stage in less than fifteen minutes, she took her new seat next to the door, where she at least had a firm surface to lean against. She was putting her purchases on top of her satchel when a lean man with ropy muscles moved next to her.

"I believe I have the seat next to you, Miss Sinclair."

"Of course, let me try to make more room." She pushed her satchel farther under the seat, while scootching left as close as she could get to the wall. "Do you have enough space?"

"Yes, that's fine," he said stiffly, edging himself into position and placing his heavy leather travel bag against his chest like a shield. He wore dark trousers, waistcoat, and a black wool frock coat.

Once he was settled, she asked, "Could you tell me your name again? I'm sorry, I tried to remember everyone but I—"

"It's George Johnson, Reverend George Johnson."

"I remember now; you've been visiting California for a month and decided to see Yosemite before the season is over."

"And I recall that you're traveling alone."

Ignoring the condescension in his tone, she responded cheerily, "I've come all the way from Providence, to see if Yosemite is as magical as the writers and artists portray it." She was not going to be cowed, but her initial relief at sitting next to the coach's side panel now was like being imprisoned in a corner. "Tell me again where you came from?"

"Michigan," he said, adding almost as an afterthought, "I was there for six years."

"Were you the minister of a church?"

He fidgeted beside her. "Part of my time there, I was a Methodist preacher. I had other jobs as well—like with the telegraph. I read about the Far West and decided to see if the church was adhering to its proper principles in California." He stopped and seemed to think of something else for a moment. "In each location, the elders think it's their right to vary the teaching to fit their own temperament, rather than strictly adhering to what is morally right. From what I've seen here, it's just the same." When the minister turned toward her, she tried to read his features, but his pupils were opaque and impenetrable. "That was the case in New York, Pennsylvania, and Michigan," he said, flatly.

"You've lived all those places?"

"And more, but so far I haven't found satisfaction in any of them."

Kate wanted to ask him how he defined satisfaction, but he continued talking.

"And now, I come here and discover a woman traveling on her own. What is this world coming to?"

She started to splutter a response, but he had turned with a shake of his head to stare through the window, lost in his own righteousness.

FOURTEEN

Kate held her neck rigidly upright against the hard, forward rocking of the stage as it traveled east. She no longer turned to look out the window because any movement caused a sharp crick in her neck. Coalescing drops of perspiration ran down her cheeks and even down the space between her breasts. The open windows provided no relief to the interior heat or reek of overheated bodies. Conversation had dwindled into impatient anticipation for the first overnight layover since leaving. Except for brief rest stops to exchange horses, they had been traveling day and night since leaving Alameda.

In the middle of the afternoon, they arrived at their lodging—the Oso House in Bear Valley, at the southern foothills of the Sierra Nevada mountains. Ned told them John C. Fremont—the American explorer, early California governor, and first Republican candidate for President—had built it. In addition to the expansive two-story hotel, with its airy, covered balcony wrapping the perimeter of the second floor above the main level porch, Fremont had established mines in Maricopa County. He had also built an elaborate residence that had burned to the ground three years earlier.

With rooms that had warm water in a pitcher, a basin for washing up, and a bed to sleep in, the travelers were convivial at dinner. Kate found an empty chair next to Stephen Graham, the banker from Philadelphia, and his wife, Diana. When Kate sat down, Diana leaned forward. "How are your accommodations? Ours are a bit cramped—not at all like our hotel in San Francisco." Diana wore a silky shirtwaist with gray, diagonal stripes and a dark tailored skirt—simple, yet her erect posture and the neatly parted ash-blond hair that puffed over her ears gave an elegant appearance.

"I barely spent any time in my room, just a quick wash up, so I could walk around the town in what was left of the afternoon," Kate explained.

"We were looking for the remnants of Fremont's mansion. I hear it was very grand before it burned. I doubt it rivaled our homes in Philadelphia," Diana sniffed, "but I'd like to see what is left." The woman's voice made Kate prickle. Something about it diminished the recipient. Her high-hat accent gave the impression of proving her superiority.

"The Main Line architecture would be out of place here," Stephen interjected affably.

"I don't know, Steve. A building is an indication of what kind of people live inside. It makes a statement anywhere."

"From what I've seen so far, nature does a fine job of architecture out here."

But Kate could see Stephen's words fell on Diana's deaf ears.

"Mr. Graham, my bank is the Old Stone Bank in Providence. Have you heard of it?"

"Please, call me Stephen, or even Steve. We're travel companions after all." A half smile lifted the corners of his wide mouth. His trousers were casual tweed, but a velvet collar trimmed his waistcoat, giving him an air of formality. A full head of auburn hair topped his square face, even though she guessed he was in his late forties, when some men's hair began to thin.

"And, please, call me Kate."

"Your bank is considered quite venerable in New England. I've heard of it, indeed."

"I've been trying to do business with it by telegraph in San Francisco. It has not been successful so far—maybe it's the distance?"

"No," he shook his head. "Distance shouldn't be a problem. I work for Jay Cooke & Company. Our bank was one of the first to use telegraphy. It's now possible to do business in any city, all from Philadelphia and, of course, other cities as well."

"Is it Western Union your company uses? I've become interested in the telegraph lately."

"Actually, it would be impossible not to do business with Western Union. It's bought up almost everything." He leaned back, taking a curious, closer look at her. "I dare say, Kate, I'm impressed by your interest. Most women—"

"If I may have your attention, folks," Ned said, rising to his considerable height. "You'll want to hit the hay early tonight, as we've got another busy day planned for tomorrow. I've arranged a brief tour of Bear Valley and the Fremont Mining property." He sniggered, telling them that Fremont's property produced more debt than minerals. "Then we'll return here for a quick lunch." He smiled, revealing stained teeth—from tobacco, Kate guessed. "And you'll want to eat up because we'll hop on the road immediately afterwards. If your traveling clothes need some washing, the laundry will pick them up tonight and have them ready for you tomorrow. Any questions?"

Kate had at least a dozen, but Ned's reminder about meals resonated. Best to eat now and leave the questions for the morning.

FIFTEEN

Mariposa had once had a mine with a forty-foot water-wheel for crushing gold ore. When placer mining dwindled, the town's business became logging. The hub of town was a white clapboard courthouse with black shutters and a tall rectangular clock tower, built before California had become a state in 1850. Kate and her companions spent the night in Mariposa, leaving before daybreak the next morning. Their stage traveled twelve miles south to Hussey's Steam Saw Mill at the end of the wagon road. The stage left them and turned around to reverse the route it had just taken.

The Husseys had cleared a large area for logging, fringed by hills abundant with pine trees. Logs of different lengths lay in neatly ordered stacks, ready for shipment. Kate's mood was somber and expectant. With luggage in hand, she and the other travelers quietly followed Ned. He directed them to the perimeter, where an open-sided, sloped roof structure stood for travelers waiting for mounts. Ned then walked down the road to four linked, wood-pole corrals adjoining a small metal-roofed stable.

Kate flinched and slapped at a stinging horsefly on her neck. She impatiently pulled at the veil she had wrapped over her hat to protect against insects, moving it so that it covered all her skin. The hat was made of heavy felt with a brim broad enough to provide a little shade but not enough to blow away in the wind. She was jittery, her nerves raw, no matter how she tried to calm herself. Her breathing came in short, shallow bursts as she imagined the steep, narrow trails that lay ahead. Beneath the wooden structure, they all stood or sat restlessly with little conversation, everyone betraying the same kind of apprehension that unnerved her. Even the most experienced equestrians appeared anxious about the rugged forty miles to Yosemite Falls.

Ned returned from the corrals followed by a muscular man, perhaps six feet tall, in leather vest and chaps, with worn boots that reached almost to his knees. "Listen up, folks," Ned said. "This here is our wrangler, Bob Young."

Bob removed his hat and nodded, revealing matted chestnut hair parted in the middle and a forehead that was alabaster from rarely being without cover from the sun.

"Bob will tend to the mules, making sure they're fed and watered. His position is at the back of the line, and he'll help with anything that needs fixin'. He's had a heap of experience in these here parts. Do you have any momentary questions?"

"I've never been on a mule. How do they differ from a horse?" asked Robert Davenport, a journalist in his mid-twenties who was documenting the trip for the *Gazette* in Annapolis. Kate had sat next to him on the stage for several hours and found him engagingly inquisitive, constantly jotting notes in his pursuit of an angle to give a story an interesting perspective.

"There's nothing more sure-footed than a mule, that's why we use 'em," Ned answered. "They're about as tough a beast as you'll find. All you have to do is keep a loose grip on the reins, and let your mule do the work. They're choosy about their position in line, but once they're in line, they do exactly what's expected of them. They know the route as well as me and Bob. You probably don't even need guides, except mules don't cook." He guffawed at his own joke.

Once mounted, they formed a line behind Ned, climbing steadily up a steep, narrow trail. Conifers mixed with scrub oak surrounding them in glorious profusion. Kate sat comfortably in the saddle, with her long canvas jacket extending partly over loose bloomers. Her well-worn boots were oiled to protect against moisture. Bob had tied her satchel behind her saddle, wrapped in a waterproof tarp that she could pull over her for cover in a rainstorm.

Since leaving San Francisco, the weather had been dry and sometimes suffocatingly warm. Breathing fresh air was refreshing after the closeness of the stage; nevertheless, riding was fatiguing. She had to squeeze her thighs to prevent slipping in the saddle. Her knees, continually bent at the same angle, hurt. Shifting positions at first relieved the pain of contact with the saddle, but by the time they took a rest for lunch, everything was sore. Her knees almost gave way as she slid off Jack, her mule. After steadying herself against the saddle to make sure she could still walk, she handed the reins to Bob and joined the others for cuts of pork on top of a thick, buttered slice of bread. Ned passed a tin of shortbread cookies. Horseflies swarmed, and it was an effort to get the food under her veil to her mouth without suffering stinging welts from the biting, buzzing pests. When she finished eating, Kate dipped her collapsible metal cup in the nearby creek and drank the cool water. Then she found a secluded spot to relieve herself. In half an hour, they were in the saddle again.

Four hours later, they arrived at Mariposa Pines, a grove of evergreens that opened to miles of valley formed by the South Fork of the Merced River to the north. In a large ring of stones, Ned and Bob quickly built a fire for cooking, but it was important, also, for smoking out the mosquitoes and horseflies that swarmed around them, relentless for exposed skin. After walking the mules to the stream to drink, tethering them, and giving them each a feedbag, the guides returned to the group with metal cups for everyone. Kate was sitting on the ground, legs to one side, on top of her folded waterproof tarp for padding.

"Hot apple cider, Miss Sinclair?" Ned dipped the cup in the large pail hanging over the fire. "Mind the cup; it's hot."

"I can't think of anything better right now." She pulled her sleeve over her hand before gripping the handle. "Thanks, and thank you for the trip. The trees are astonishing—as is the rest of the scenery, for that matter." She looked up at him. "Yosemite has already lived up to your description."

Ned nodded with a slim smile and filled a cup for the journalist, who had just arrived. "May I join you, Kate?" Robert Davenport asked.

"By all means."

He juggled his cup and gingerly sat down on a flat granite rock beside her. "Here, before you drink all your cider, may I offer you a little brandy? It's guaranteed to take away muscle aches."

She thought for a moment, then held out her cup so he could pour from the flask he had extracted from his pocket. "Thanks, I could gratefully dull some overused muscles." She took a sip of the warm liquid, content in the flickering firelight. "I don't suppose this will be a story you'll write about for your newspaper—getting a solitary woman tipsy?"

He laughed as he tilted his flask over his own cup. "I hope my readers are interested in something more consequential than a thimbleful of brandy, but tell me about your impressions so far. That might be worthy."

After only two sips of brandy-laced cider, relaxation overtook soreness. "Trees," she said. "I've never seen so many different types, and we haven't even gotten to the giant sequoias north of here. We are so remote, you would think nothing could ever harm the forests and waterfalls, but the gold fields were remote, too."

"Soon after gold, dirt and tunnels!"

"That's what I've read. I'm glad President Lincoln thought Yosemite was worth preserving."

Robert Davenport cocked his head. "Are you interested in politics?"

"My mother taught me to pay attention as a child, and I've never outgrown it. She was especially interested in women's issues. Do you report on those?" She knew she must look inquisitive.

"Ah, the reporter is being interviewed," he said, with a friendly light in his blue eyes.

Robert Davenport had a newspaperman's knack for remaining neutral while drawing her out, although she was sure he had opinions. Their conversation thrived while they hungrily ate generous portions of beef brisket and potatoes baked in the fire, all served on metal plates. Bob passed around a tray of cookies as Ned explained the sleeping arrangements.

"Me and Bob put up these frames a couple years ago. Some of you have already asked about them. As you can see, we put a horizontal beam between two trees. Then we cut down saplings and leaned them at an angle against the beams. While you were eating, we draped tarps we pack in with us. One hangs from the beam at the front, and the other over the sloping saplings. They don't quite reach the ground, except at the corners where they're staked. They give privacy and protection if it rains."

While Ned spoke, the others looked through the trees at the randomly clustered shapes in the shadows of the woods, like a ghostly tent town.

"Each lean-to will have two people, except one for Miss Sinclair. Kate, you'll be in one of your own and not too far from the one with me and Bob. We have a loaded rifle for bears, but we'll hang any food up high, a long way from the sleeping area, so we should be safe. That's about it. We'll come get you in pairs, show you where you'll be and answer any questions. After that, you can retire whenever you want.

By eight o'clock the sun had receded behind the mountains and, weary from traveling, most had left the fire.

Inside her lean-to, Kate took off her outer clothing, leaving only her chemise and drawers. She rolled up in the blanket and used her stole for a pillow. The night was warm but she knew the air would cool by morning. Sleep came immediately.

At first, she thought she dreamed that something moved beside her. She came awake quickly—it was real. She swatted the ground, thinking the movement was a rodent trying to get warm. Her hand hit only leaves, but she heard the sound of breathing close by. Her heartrate accelerated. Suddenly, a hand stroked her back and followed her curves around toward her breast before pulling away.

"Just checking to see if you're all right, or if you'd like some company, Little Missy, who's traveling all alone." The voice was guttural, barely more than a whisper.

"What do you want?" she hissed, trembling from her scalp to her toes.

The only answer was the rustle of someone moving through the leaves away from the lean-to. Scrambling up, she scoured her brain for clues to the identity of the disturbing visitor. Nothing came. Screaming was pointless—whoever it was had gone, but she was scared he might return. She searched in the dark to find her lantern. With the light, she put on her shirt, riding pantaloons, and boots. Pine needles clinging to the fabric pricked her skin. Sweeping back the hanging tarp, she looked around, and then used her lantern to locate the guides' tent.

"Ned, Bob," Kate kept her voice low so she would not rouse anyone else.

"Who's there?"

"It's Kate. Someone grabbed at me under the lean-to."

She heard movement, and then the front tarp opened. Ned and Bob stood there, disheveled, as if they had hastily pulled on their trousers.

"Someone was in your lean-to?" Ned asked.

"No. He touched me by reaching under the tarp." The lantern light wobbled in her shaking hand."

"Who?"

"I don't know, but he knew it was my tent."

"Might 'a been a wood rat—they've been scurrying to gather warmth for the winter. The durn things get into tents."

"No, no," anger overtook Kate's fear. "He said something."

"The wind is blowing—sounds like whispers. I heard them myself." Ned said.

"It was a man."

"He's gone now, I take it?" Ned asked.

Kate nodded, choking back a sob.

"Here's the best thing to do. I'll take my lantern and walk through the area looking for tracks or disturbances. Me or Bob will be awake listening the rest of the night." Bob nodded in assurance. "You've had a scare. Shout for anything . . . anything at all." Ned reached out to gently take her arm. "First off, I'll walk you back."

The light from their lanterns shone the way as they silently walked— Ned's arm guiding her. When they reached her lean-to, he pulled back the front flap. She hesitated, frightened to let him leave.

"Are you okay?" he asked.

"I think so."

"We're close if you need us. Call out."

Inside the lean-to, Kate stood at the flap to watch Ned trail off, lantern held high on his way to search. When his shadow melted into the night, she moved close to the center—away from the open edges. Without taking off her clothing, she wrapped up in the blanket and lay down on the leaves. Badly-needed sleep never returned.

— ·— ·— — ·

Before the sun worked its way up the edge of the mountains, the smell of burning twigs, bacon, and coffee roused her. Soon, she heard Ned and Bob walking through the campsite with wide metal bowls filled with warm, soapy water for each lean-to. Using a small cloth, Kate found washing somewhat restoring. She listened to the travelers straggle out, one by one, and pour a cup of coffee before gently lowering their sore bodies on to the ring of rocks at the periphery of the fire.

"Kate," Ned approached her as she emerged "Here's a cup of boiled water. I know you fancy tea. How do you feel?"

"Unsettled." She slipped her jacket sleeve over her hand and took the proffered hot metal cup handle, trying to keep her hand steady. "Thanks."

She sat down and opened the tin box she had put in her jacket pocket, spreading a pinch of tea in her cup. The aroma of oolong rose with the steam. She took small sips of the hot liquid as she furtively scanned the others for hints of who might have been depraved enough to reach his arm under the back of her lean-to. No one revealed himself, but she would be on her guard from now on.

After breakfast, they mounted their mules and fell in line, reaching the Merced River before mid-morning. Turning east, they followed a narrow path on the south bank, with splashing and cascading water at their left. Verdant pines of every height and diameter were unceasing. At last, they paused briefly at their highest point and began the precipitous descent. The saddles had no pommels, so Kate did as she was told and held on to the edge of the leather, giving Jack slack rein to manage on his own and take her with him, safe or not. Her boots were jammed in box-like stirrups that pinched her feet but gave her the balance needed to prevent her from catapulting headlong over Jack's withers. For three miles they zigzagged down, precariously descending four thousand feet. At the bottom, Ned waited for all the mules to arrive on level ground.

At last she could fully breathe. Kate leaned forward and gratefully stroked Jack's rough, brown hide, pulling her fingers through his tangled mane. The intrepid animal had taken her down safely, with little guidance.

Without a sound, like an artist revealing a canvas, Ned swept his arm across the panorama of granite crags rising on the other side of the valley.

She absorbed the beauty of the surroundings. One granite formation after another rose up to five thousand feet to touch the sky. This was why she had come—this melding of her humanity with nature. "It's even more than I expected," Kate said, to no one in particular.

"You can do more looking as we ride," Ned said to everyone. "Of course, the water isn't coming down near as much as early in the season, but you can still take in what nature has to offer in these here parts."

Kate heard Fritz Kroner on the mule next to her exclaim "Das ist Gottes werk."

She caught the German's eye and nodded agreement that it was God's work. Then she realized she could rule out enigmatic Fritz as the arm and voice in the night. His accent was certainly not a match. The knowledge that there was one fewer person to fear brought some measure of relief.

"Okay, folks. Gotta keep movin'. Only a couple more hours to get to Yosemite Valley, food, and a mattress."

SIXTEEN

When the procession of mules finally came to a halt, Kate gripped the hornless saddle to steady herself as she slowly slid off Jack, worried her feet would not hold her weight after so many hours of riding. Raising puffs of dust, she gave Jack's thick, dark coat grateful last pats. She took extra time, untying the leather thongs holding her poncho-wrapped belongings, determined to walk, not stagger, to the large, family-run inn where they would spend two nights. Ned had told them that owners George and Maryanne Davis had followed others with dreams of making a fortune during the gold rush. Like so many, they found little, so the Davises replaced their initial dream with a log guesthouse they built in 1864, surrounded by Yosemite's spectacular natural beauty.

The furnishings were spare; the Davises had not made a fortune from either gold or innkeeping, but Kate's room was clean, with a large, white ceramic wash bowl and pitcher of warm water on her nightstand. She peeled off her travel clothes and lathered herself with a square of soap that smelled like honey. Once she rinsed off and dried, she put on her change of clothing, leaned back, and collapsed on the straw mattress for a sublime hour nap.

At dinner, warm stew, rich with plump pieces of beef and chunks of vegetables, added to the celebration of being finished with the most difficult riding and halfway through their trip. As he often did, Ned knocked his knife against his glass and made a brief speech about the tour of the valley the next day and the trip to the Tuolumne Grove of Giant Sequoia the day after that. Warm apple cobbler was the last dish for dinner, but Kate's stomach was lurching and gurgling; something had not agreed with her. She decided to go to an outbuilding instead of her bedroom chamber pot. The temperature had cooled with the setting of the sun, and a fingernail moon hung directly above her. She walked urgently down the well-worn path to the outhouse and pulled open the door, grateful that the knobbed rope handle indicated it was unoccupied.

A minute or two later, feeling better but still a little queasy, she turned to pull the knobbed rope through the hole for the next occupant. As she bent, someone clamped her in a rough grip from behind. One hand covered her mouth, aborting her scream, and a strong arm encircled her, trapping both her arms.

"Come with me, Little Missy," the voice said, "you and I have a rendezvous." It was the voice from last night. Kate struggled and tried to focus on how to escape, but her captor pulled her along at an awkward angle. Her ankles twisted as she tried to walk without falling. She fought to keep up and to breathe under the steady pressure of his hand against her mouth. They kept going.

It got darker as they left the grounds of the inn. She must do something! With a burst of adrenaline, she kicked at his ankles. He lost his footing and crashed down on top of her, slamming her head into the ground.

When Kate was once again aware of her surroundings, he was gone. She had no idea how long she had been unconscious. Had he done more than fallen on top of her before he disappeared? Was he gone or just waiting? Her fingers flew over her undergarments, examining them for rips or tears. Nothing. There was no soreness anywhere except for her throbbing head. Her body and clothing seemed intact, thank God, but her heart pounded as if it might burst through her chest. *Where am I?* The slight moon above did little to illuminate the inky black. Her mind unraveled. *Would someone come looking for her? Where would they even start?*

She felt around for a stout, overhanging branch of the tree next to her, and pulled herself up, holding on until she got her bearings. Everything had happened so fast. They could not have gone that far. Without going too far from the tree she bent down and began exploring the ground with her hands—rocks and pine needles. Still squatting, she turned and searched the opposite way and, in a few yards, discerned a slight depression in the dirt. *If it's a path, which way? Was he just waiting for her?*

She had to do something. She stood up again, her instinct telling her to walk in the direction where her feet lay when she regained consciousness. It was just a guess, but she would try that way first. She scoured the ground for rocks and stacked up a pile into a cairn, to pinpoint her starting point if she had to. She might have to wait there until morning.

Surprisingly, the angle of her feet alerted her when she strayed from the narrow depression of the path. After tentative walking for a while, she saw a glow of light in the distance. *It must be the house. Oh please, let it be the house.* Progress was slow in the dark, but as she drew closer to the light from the house, walking became easier. The dark shapes of the outhouse and then the front porch came into view, and she wept in relief.

Entering the foyer of the lodge, she expected the other travelers to be there, worried about her disappearance. Instead, it was empty and quiet, with only distant sounds of conversation in the kitchen—the family doing dishes, she presumed. Why wasn't anyone looking for her? Kate stood alone in the light of a single lantern on the entryway table. *They must have assumed I went to bed.*

She had not been violated, but her perpetrator was getting bolder. This could not go on. Kate needed to tell Ned and Bob. Ned had announced their room number at dinner. She picked up one of the candlesticks from the table and lit it, then walked up the stairs, her boots making thudding sounds on the wood boards. Ned opened the door after she knocked, his eyes looking up and down. Leaves and dirt still clung to her clothing.

"What happened? Are you hurt?"

The room smelled stale—of tobacco and damp socks. Ned and Bob gave her the only chair and sat on the bed across from her, their brows furrowed with worry as they listened. Ned asked, "Did he take advantage?" He looked down. "You know . . . personal-wise?"

"No," she shook her sore head. "He just terrified me. He pulled me along, taking me somewhere—dragging me. We fell, and he must have left. I checked all over—he didn't harm me physically, well, except for my head." She balled her fists until her fingernails dug into her palms. "I'm scared. We have to find him before he does something more."

"Did you get a look at him?" Bob asked. "Something to go on?"

She shook her head. It was taking everything she had to choke back sobs. No matter how hard she'd tried otherwise, being a single woman had created a problem for the guides as well as her.

"If you come onto something, tell us," Ned said. "We'll be extra watchful—for anything that will help us get to the bottom of this."

Kate left for her own room, locked the door, and wedged a chair under the door handle. She took off her clothing and shook out the dirt, then fingered the bump on the back of her head. Miraculously, the skin was unbroken, but she had a nice goose egg, nonetheless. In her night dress, she washed up and brushed her hair, mindful of her wound. Several times during the night, gasping nightmares of shadowy men shook her from her sleep.

--- --- --- ·

The next morning started with a chill in the air as they began their seven-and-a-half-mile hike through the Yosemite Valley, a gorge lined with the breathtaking granite peaks they'd seen from a distance the day before. John Muir led them. Muir, a sinewy young man with a full scraggly beard, had been working in the nearby Tuolumne Meadow as a sheepherder since coming to Yosemite the previous year. With his rolling Scots accent and passionate reverence, Muir taught them about Yosemite's geology and biology.

Kate made sure she stayed close to people she trusted: The guides, Fritz Kroner, and Robert Davenport. "You're taking lots of notes," she commented to the young journalist, as they walked together along a deep section of the gorge.

"I was running out of ways to describe this place," Robert confessed. "Muir's details help."

Kate looked up at the granite formation against the cobalt-blue sky. "Muir's stories have put me in harmony with nature." She turned to face him. "Do you think reading words, or studying a painting, can do justice to Yosemite?"

"No," he did not hesitate with his answer, "nothing can take the place of being here, but not everyone is brave enough to come, so they should experience it in words and art, even if it's a far cry from seeing it in person."

"I'm lucky to be here." She had been convinced that the connection between humanity and the natural world was only understandable if experienced first-hand, in spite of any risk. After her terrifying experiences, she was having second thoughts about risk. There always seemed to be consequences for veering from the conventional, especially for women, who faced disapproval, or even punishment, by the rest of society for not following the norm.

SEVENTEEN

Rising early, and carrying a stout branch for protection, Kate walked through the smooth, still morning to see the crystal blue lake. She could not wait for the tour—she had to see it. Her group had arrived at the south end of Lake Tahoe late the previous afternoon, just as the sun vanished beneath the horizon. Navigating the rocky terrain, she breathed in every detail. *I must commit this to memory so I can pull it up in my mind over and over again.*

When she returned from her walk for breakfast, Kate came across one of their group, Suzanna Malcolm, in the main hall with its massive honey-colored logs used to construct the lodge where they stayed. Suzanna was a stout, matronly woman, who wore her gray-streaked hair in braids wound into a spiral at the back of her head. She and her husband, John, had spent their lives farming in Indiana, but now that the last of their six children had left home, they were looking for property in another place. They were typical of the "start over" crowd the West beckoned; looking for something better, even if they did not quite know what it was.

"Did you hear the news, Kate?" Suzanna asked.

"No, I'm afraid I haven't. I've been down taking in the view of the lake. I noticed there's a lot of activity here, at the telegraph office. I suppose it's because this is the first chance we've had to send a telegram since early in the trip."

"Uh huh, it's not just sending telegrams that has people excited." Suzanna shook her head. "No sirree, absolutely not."

"What then?" Kate frowned. Suzanna got excited about anything out of the ordinary; so far none of it had amounted to more than the minor inconveniences expected with travel.

"I happened to see the Grahams at the telegraph office, just after we got here," she said smugly. "Stephen turned pale when he read a telegram—looked real nervous. Ned told me he and Diana left this morning—by special arrangement. Remember, he's the bigwig banker."

"Do you have any idea what the telegram said?" Even though Suzanna's gossiping annoyed her, Kate was curious about Stephen Graham's reaction. Something serious must have happened if the couple had left the trip early.

"I'd be quicker with the answer if I understood it," Suzannah shuffled her feet nervously. "Something about the economy collapsing." She looked at Kate expectantly, as if waiting to see if Kate could solve this puzzle.

"What?" Kate said, incredulous. "What do you mean?"

The older woman shrugged. "At least you know more than you did before," Suzanna answered feebly.

"Well, so far, I don't know a thing. If it's true, it may affect us all," Kate said, starting to walk toward the front desk. "Maybe Robert Davenport has heard something from his newspaper. I better try to find him. Coming, Suzanna?"

"I might as well tag along, I guess. I'm always interested in a piece of news."

As long as it's gossip, Kate kept to herself.

Nearing the front desk, they saw a clutch of men, both from their party and other guests of the lodge, in a semicircle around the reporter.

Kate heard a man ask, "Are you withholding information from us to sell your newspaper?" His voice was sharp and hostile. She felt sorry for Robert, who looked stuck. He was backed up against a vertical log pillar, between the front desk and the small adjacent office that held a small telegraph operation.

"I know little more than you do," the tall, handsome newspaperman said, "But, I'll repeat it. Apparently, several men tried to corner the gold market. According to the wire, this was early in September. Jay Gould and Big Jim Fisk started buying up all the gold they could get. They planned to hoard it, speculating that the price would go up. They were gambling for a huge profit."

"So, what happened?" the angry stranger snapped.

"President Grant caught wind of the scheme and released some of the government's gold holdings," Robert said. "When gold was devalued, people started losing money. Apparently it caused a run on banks; some are even closing."

"Will it affect us regular people?" John Malcolm asked.

"I really don't know," Davenport shrugged helplessly. "I'm not sure anyone does." Obviously exasperated by the questioning, he stepped forward to break through the crowd. "I'm only the messenger. For those of us returning to San Francisco in the morning, there will be more news along the way. In the meantime, I'm going to pack up my things and take the tour of Lake Tahoe. We only have one day here." Kate watched him disappear up the stairs, leaving behind the murmuring crowd of companions and strangers.

Weak-kneed, Kate sagged into a chair in the lobby. Questions buzzed like swarming bees. The Stone Bank in Providence was old and stable. Could it withstand the collapse that Robert hinted at? If not, what would happen to her trust fund?

_ ._ ._ _ _ .

The stagecoach ride back to San Francisco was gloomy, full of speculation about the news and why the Grahams had returned early by private carriage. A few ventured his bank had failed, or even that he was part of the shenanigans.

Ned, a natural raconteur, diffused some of the concern by diverting their attention to the trip's highlights. At moments, the fulfillment of what they had accomplished rose to the forefront. However, the creepy sensation of being watched by her unknown accoster muted Kate's own elation about the trip, and the new concern about what bank failures might hold for her future added to her uneasiness.

By the time they reached Sacramento, new details amplified reason to worry. The two young schemers, Jay Gould and James Fisk, had almost succeeded after bribing dozens of government officials and buying over one hundred million in gold calls. On the Friday that she and the other travelers had left for Yosemite, gold prices had fallen from 160 dollars to 130 in ten minutes. The collapse was causing bankruptcies, stock market panic, and frozen credit. Kate feared more ruin was inevitable.

- .- .- - .

"Welcome back, Miss Sinclair. Glad to see you made it in one piece. Did you have any difficulty?"

The familiar aroma of jasmine blossoms made her feel almost at home and safe. "Thank you, Peter," Kate said to the desk clerk. "There were hardships; I wouldn't be honest if I said otherwise, but really, the beauty was even greater than I hoped. I'll remember it for as long as I live."

"Glad to hear it. We've managed to put you in the same room you had before, and already moved your trunk back in, so you won't have any delay."

"How considerate. I've been riding on a stagecoach night and day—it seems like forever since I slept in a bed." She turned to go upstairs.

"And, Miss Sinclair, a telegram arrived while you were gone." He gave a wide smile, knowing she would be grateful.

She grasped it quickly, relieved she did not have to go to the telegraph office for the information that had been an obsession before she left on her trip. Running her finger under the flap of the yellow envelope, she unfolded the terse message. FUNDS HAVE BEEN DEPOSITED IN THE WELLS FARGO BANK EDWIN FINNEY OLD STONE BANK. The telegram had come the day she left, which meant the date of this telegram was before the news broke about what was being called Black Friday—too early to reassure her about the stability of the bank.

"Peter, I'll be right back. I want to send a message."

"Of course, Miss Sinclair." He dipped his dark, curly head courteously, his cheeks always rosy. "We'll see that your note is taken whenever it's ready."

She desperately wanted to get out of her rumpled travel clothes and bathe, but she needed to arrange a meeting with Frank. In only a few minutes, she had penned a note telling him of her return and requesting a meeting the next day. She took the note to the front desk, along with a laundry bag of clothing worn on the trip for washing.

Fatigue from the long journey back to San Francisco mixed with the stress about bank failures. It was only late afternoon, but she decided to forego dinner, have a bath, and go directly to bed. When she closed the door, she locked it and once again wedged a chair under the doorknob for safety. It was more out of habit than necessity, because she was safe at the Occidental.

Falling asleep was blissful. She had gambled by spending almost all her money on the trip. The trust fund allocation allowed more than enough to remain in San Francisco a few more days and to buy a train ticket back to Providence.

Frank's note waited for her when she came down to the lobby in the morning. He would meet her at the Occidental at six that evening. Sleep in a safe environment and fresh clothing from her trunk had gone a long way to revive her. After breakfast she would go to the bank to get her trust money, and then to the railroad station to check schedules to return home.

— ·— ·— ·— — ·

The day's last rays of sunlight filtered through the tall, arched windows of the Occidental when Kate and Frank met at the bottom of the grand staircase. Her heart pulsed with affection when he took her hand. Their eyes locked.

"I've missed you, Kate."

And I've yearned for those entrancing eyes. Emotion overcame her. She hadn't realized, during her adventure to Yosemite, how much she had missed him, or longed to discuss the events of each day with him. On the way back, she had thought about how she would describe the trip. More than that, she had rehearsed how to thank him. He had encouraged her to find a way to go, even if her deposit had not arrived. However, at the sight of him, her well-thought-out words of thanks vanished.

"Frank, taking a chance and spending almost all my cash on the trip paid off. I'm not sure I would have done it without your encouragement," she blurted out.

"Old Stoney must have sent the funds."

"It's the Old Stone Bank," Kate laughed in spite of herself. "Yes, they came through, but what do you know about bank failures?"

"I'd be glad to tell you what I know, but only after hearing about Yosemite and Lake Tahoe. There's an interesting restaurant around the corner. We can walk to it." He crooked his elbow for her arm.

Linking arms made everything from her pelvis to her breastbone tingle, but she held him back. "Would you mind if we ate here—in the informal dining room? I've put our name on the reservation list. This is my treat."

"It's usually the gentleman who pays for dinner."

Her eyes shot up to gauge his expression. From the jocular look she read on his face, Kate knew he had not taken offense. "Without you, maybe there would not have been Yosemite to tell about," she said with relaxed happiness. "After all, you were the one who said I should go, even if I might not have any way to get back home."

"Ah, maybe that was part of the plan." He raised his eyebrows, the warm hazel of his eyes sending her a message she wasn't quite ready to acknowledge.

Laughing, he squeezed her arm. "Let's be on our way, *Mademoiselle*." They walked down the carpeted hallway to the nearby dining room.

It catered to those who wanted a small meal, rather than a multiple course, formal dinner. While still maintaining the Occidental's luxury, the room had a more relaxed, casual air. Even at the early hour of six, animated guests filled most of the tables. Uniformed waiters hurried back and forth to fill their requests.

When Frank and Kate took their seats, he asked, "Will you join me with a sherry while I drink my whiskey?"

For an instant, she hesitated, wondering if she dared add to the intoxication of just being with him. "Thank you. It's becoming a pleasurable habit." She caught his gaze and held it.

"Was the trip what you expected? I would give a lot to see what you did. Maybe someday!"

The waiter put down their drinks and took their dinner order, giving Kate a moment to sift out a few highlights so she would not ramble endlessly, determined to leave off the scare of her accoster. Instead, she recounted being squeezed for hours in a stagecoach, camping out, riding her sure-footed mule, and the glorious connection with nature that was reinforcement of her dreams of the exceptional, not the ordinary.

They ate broiled salmon, asparagus with hollandaise, and wedges of fried potatoes, as she continued describing the trip.

"But, Frank, tell me, what's been going on while I've been away. Jay Gould was somehow involved with Black Friday . . . and your Western Union as well?"

"Before I begin, should we consider Ghirardelli for dessert?"

Kate laughed. The tension of insolvent banks was momentarily dispelled, even the fear of her unknown attacker lessening under the spell of Frank's company. "Chocolate has become as pleasurable a habit as sherry, and I see the waiter coming our way, just in time to take our order."

While she listened to Frank, Kate let a square of dark Ghirardelli chocolate melt on her tongue, and then another.

"Jay Gould sticks his fingers in any pot that will make him money," Frank said. "He has a knack for figuring out what industries the economy is going to count on, and then, he and his ilk use any means to pursue them. He usually manages to keep it just above board, or officially legal." Frank took a bite of his chocolate. "He's a speculator and his thumb is always on the scale, wangling for a favor here, a favor there—government is complicit."

"He got his start with railroads, didn't he?"

"A leather tanning business in Pennsylvania first, and then, yes, the Erie Railroad. His critics, and there are many, say he manipulated the stock to beat out Cornelius Vanderbilt. Gould became Erie's president last year . . . with lots of help from New York's Boss Tweed."

"A banker who worked for Jay Cooke & Company left our trip a day early. We heard that many banks had collapsed because of Black Friday while we were traveling. There wasn't much information, but Gould was mentioned. Everyone was frantic about the news."

"I'm not sure anyone knows all the details, anyone beyond Gould and his cronies, but rumor has it that he wanted to increase the amount of shipping on the Erie. He thought if he and his pal James Fisk could control gold, it would increase the price of wheat and encourage western farmers to sell and ship on his railroad—and, of course, increase his freight business. Fortunately, President Grant and the government sold shares of gold and collapsed the scheme, but it caused panicky withdrawals of bank money."

"I'm concerned about the banks." The space between her eyes scrunched. "Since I gave up school teaching, I depend on my bank funds, slim as they are. Fortunately, my parents are happy to have me live at home—that helps reduce my costs."

"Your concern's valid," Frank's lips thinned. "Powerful men can drive the market up and down at will. If unscrupulous men have that kind of power, business . . . maybe even the entire economy . . . is all phony."

Kate paused, mulling over what he had said. "I never thought of it that way. Is Gould's interest in the telegraph about business or power?"

"Both," Frank said. "The Erie was the first railroad to dispatch trains using the telegraph. It owns its own telegraph, whereas Western Union leases to the railroads. You can bet Gould sees potential in the telegraph and probably Western Union. We just don't know what his plan is yet. No doubt he has one."

They continued their conversation until Kate looked around at the almost empty dining room. "We've done it again, Frank—talked until the waiters are stifling yawns, ready for us to leave. And, as usual, time flew."

He hurried around the table to pull out her chair. "Kate, I'd like to find out more about the banks and talk again. You haven't told me the rest of your plans. How soon do you leave?"

She hesitated. "I haven't made train reservations yet, but, I will soon. Let me have a day or two to get things in order and then I would like to meet again." Her breath caught at the thought of leaving and not seeing him again.

It was a slippery slope she was on, as steep as the ones Jack had navigated for her. If any man could make her forget her determination to pursue life's adventures on her own, it was Frank Ellsworth.

EIGHTEEN

Light from the chandelier reflected off the prisms of the glasses they clinked—his filled with whiskey, hers with sherry. Dinner appeared celebratory. Frank nodded a salute to her and took the menu the waiter offered him. Kate was not sure why or even what they were celebrating; logically, her mood should be somber, since it was the last time they would be together.

She had paid special attention to her appearance. Her white pleated blouse was starched and fresh beneath a rose-printed shawl that highlighted the pink of her cheeks. The chignon at the nape of her neck neatly captured every strand of her honey blond hair. Iridescent pearl earrings, unworn since she left home, were the final touch. If she was departing his edge of the world, her appearance should not matter, but her heavy heart told another story. If they were never going to see each other again, she wanted this evening to be a beautiful memory.

Sitting across from each other, they considered their menus carefully, as if the choice, too, mattered more this last time. When the waiter left with their orders, Frank turned to her. He looked impatient, as if he had been storing away something he had to say, waiting for the right time.

"Kate, something has come up at Western Union that might interest you."

She was alert at news of his work. "Is it something to do with Gould and his gold fiasco?"

"No," he shook his head. "Not that. No doubt he's conniving somewhere about another scheme, but this is a more everyday matter."

"Is it about your job?" Her lips puckered sympathetically. "Has something gone wrong?"

His eyes gleamed after her sympathetic reaction "Nothing of that sort, but it is about a job."

"Frank, don't keep me in suspense. I'm intrigued." She leaned forward, knowing she was acting petulant.

His face relaxed in a smile, as if charmed by her impatience. "Remember what you said about your bank?"

"Which time?" She compressed her lips, thinking of Mr. Finney and the delay of the money transfer.

"The time you mentioned your concern over being dependent on your trust fund."

"Oh, that! I remember all too well," Kate winced. "It doesn't give me a lot of leeway. Maybe I should go back to teaching."

From across the room, the waiter approached with a tray of food. Kate had requested steamed halibut with trimmings of acorn squash and a grated cabbage salad. Frank had ordered pork chops, applesauce, and mashed potatoes. She noticed a devilish look in his eye before taking her first bite.

"I may have a way to solve your problem and, at the same time, one of Western Union's."

"I can't imagine how."

"The company has a shortage of telegraphers."

"And?" she asked.

"And, the pay is good."

"What does that have to do with me?"

"You should consider applying."

"Me? I'm a woman." She narrowed her eyes in a what's-the-point gesture.

"Western Union has hired women telegraph operators before. Both men and women can almost choose their city, and we are in special need here."

"I don't know Morse code," she slumped back in her chair. She was annoyed by the useless line of conversation.

"You're smart enough to learn."

"I'd have to stay in San Francisco," she straightened up again.

"A job's waiting for you if you want it." He reached out for her hand. "I'd like you to stay."

The proposition, and his touch, sent her cockeyed. Thoughts and ramifications ricocheted in her mind like bullets without a target. Kate looked at him, her dinner barely touched, ready to spout out all the obstacles she could think of—as much for herself as for him.

"Where would I stay? I can't afford the Occidental."

"There are many women's boarding houses that are proper and inexpensive."

"What would I wear? All I have is travel clothes."

"San Francisco does have clothing stores," he teased.

"How will I support myself in the meantime? I don't know Morse code, remember?" Kate glared at him. But he would not take the bait.

"You'd have to go without pay until you're somewhat conversant with Morse, but after that Western Union will begin pay at a low level and increase it as you gain skills." Frank's answers were calm without obvious pressure.

She did not want to focus because a smidgeon of her mind knew the job was not the problem. She was avoiding the real issue—she had always been afraid of, and therefore resisted, developing a close relationship with a man.

"Frank, you're infuriating." But she hoped her face said otherwise.

"For now, tell me more about Yosemite. I like listening and pretending I'm there."

Kate looked down at the full plate before her and decided he was right. Letting the subject drop for a bit might be best, lest her emotions overwhelm her. He seemed to work more hours than would be expected, even at a new job. She admired his energy and dedication to work.

Her mood lightened as they talked and ate. When she shared added details of her trip with him it heightened her feeling of success. Once again, other diners departed while they continued their conversation. By tacit agreement, the evening ended with no mention of the job. It was clear the subject overwhelmed her. Her plan had always been to return to Providence, and more than that, independence dictated she should not get involved.

—·— ·— — ·

At the carpeted base of the Occidental's cascading stairway, Frank reached for her hand "Kate, I'd like to see you again. Could we set a date?" His eyes were determined.

"I'm not sure," she hesitated. "I'm not sure of the timing." Warmth and strength radiated through his hand. She did not want to let go. "May I send you a note?" She was too torn between leaving and staying to answer him right then.

"Of course." He gave her hand a squeeze before releasing it. "I'll look forward to receiving one. I won't say 'goodbye' until I know I must. Instead, I wish you 'goodnight.'" With that, he turned away and walked toward the Occidental's front doors.

Upstairs, Kate pressed the door shut, turning the key to lock it. She set down the candle in its brass candlestick, and lit the oil lamp, then blew out the candle. The light illuminated the flower-patterned wallpaper and sturdy mahogany furniture. She disrobed, but tugged a heavy wool sweater over her nightdress, knowing sleep right now was hopeless.

At her washstand, she unknotted her chignon and began the nighttime ritual of brushing her hair. Unnerving thoughts jangled her mind, one rapidly supplanting the other, without coherence. Gradually, the stroking motions of the hairbrush calmed her. Her breathing slowed as she began to make sense of what she wanted to do.

The easiest course of action was to make return train reservations according to her original plan. It would allow her to escape her feelings about Frank—feelings that intensified each time she saw him, and threatened her commitment to self-reliance. No feelings were worth the hurt they might bring. Furthermore, returning home would put an end to the preposterous notion of being a telegraph operator. Among other things, that would mean a tremendous fight with her parents. She was tired of battling with them and facing the disapproval of so many of their friends, and even a few of hers.

She knew she'd been fortunate. Her father had put down the idea of a college education for a woman, but Eugenia won Will over, and Kate had gone. After she graduated, teaching had been a profession both parents considered fitting for a woman; one they hoped would be temporary until she married. They had argued fiercely against her taking the Hills' children to Black Hawk. Only the escort of one of Nathaniel's business partners placated them. When she told them she wanted to travel from coast to coast on her own, they feared for her life and worried about her reputation. A job as a telegrapher would be another escalation of arguments. Eugenia and Will knew teachers, but not telegraph operators. Kate had had a passion for learning and travel; being a telegrapher had never occurred to her.

She put down her brush. Her life was getting increasingly complicated. Still, excitement tingled through her. Was a job as a telegrapher an impossibility or a challenge? She rolled her eyes. The job itself might not be impossible, but everything that went with it seemed to be. She massaged her temples with her fingertips while she thought, then released them. Slowly she stood up and moved the chair to the desk.

From her sloped leather writing box, she extracted paper and ink and began to make a list. First, she would have to move from the comfortable, well-situated Occidental to something less expensive. It would still cost money. Expanding her wardrobe would have to wait; her travel clothes would do for a while, so there was no need to go shopping. Enrolling in a telegraphy class was the sensible approach, rather than depending on an instruction book, even though it was surely more costly. Money, too, would be an issue. Opening her own account at Wells Fargo might be necessary—if they gave accounts to women. She would avoid turning to her savings that she had scrimped and saved to add to. There. That was enough planning for the moment. It seemed her mind was made up. Almost as an afterthought, she included it all in her daily journal.

Then, she pulled out a long sheet of paper, smoothed the surface on the blotter, and penned the words, "Dear Alice." Words flowed as she described everything . . . or close to it. She had not quite resolved *every-thing* herself. Writing to her closest friend often helped sort things out. It was as if their minds were synchronized, no matter how far apart they were physically. *Maybe we have a telegraph between us without wires,* she mused. She would wait until the next day to tell her parents about delaying her return, and send quick notes to Bill and Jim, too.

NINETEEN

At breakfast, Kate traded her usual newspaper for the lists she was making. She wanted to get started right away, to see what was possible. After finishing her eggs and toast, she went to the front desk.

"Peter, I'm doing some research, and wonder if you know of any rooming houses that take women."

"If you're thinking of making a change from the Occidental, I know of a few. In fact, my aunt lets rooms for ladies in her own home. It's too far to walk from here, Miss Sinclair, but it's respectable and, if you want, I can set up an introduction. It might just be suitable for both of you. My Aunt Mathilde is one of my favorite relatives," he said cheerfully.

"I haven't decided if I'll need one yet, but that's helpful, Peter," Kate brightened at the news. "I'd like to learn more about her house. It will be the first I look at."

With a note of introduction in hand, Kate found the tall narrow house, topped with a steep gabled roof. It had squared bay windows and decorative white wooden cladding that was badly in need of fresh paint but presentable, nonetheless. Kate took an instant liking to Peter's aunt, Mathilde Evans, and her British accent. The three-story house was usefully filled with small bedrooms and a shared lavatory on each floor. Residents helped prepare the meals and ate together at a big, round table in the dining room. Mathilde took Kate through all three stories, explaining the rules as they went along. She was a buxom woman, with a fleshy face framed by iron-gray hair. Weariness showed in her brown eyes, but, despite that, Kate could see she was a proud housekeeper with a fondness for the young women under her roof.

At the end of the tour, she opened the door to the vacant room. "You said you had a steamer trunk. It won't go up these stairs. The third floor is all I've got, but I'd be glad to store the trunk in the stable . . . for free."

"That would be such a help," Kate said. She looked around the room, finding it simple but somehow welcoming. "It's a nice room, and I like the house too, Mrs. Evans. I'm not quite sure how long I'll stay in San Francisco yet, but I'd like to pay for a month, if that's okay."

Mathilde frowned. "I'd like a longer time." She studied Kate, hesitating, apparently hoping for a change of mind. Finally, she said, "Oh well, I don't have anyone for the room right now, so a month is what we'll do. When can you move in?"

"What about tomorrow?"

Mathilde smiled in agreement and took Kate's cash for a month's rent with everything she had but two quarters.

There's no turning back now. Kate knew she had taken an impetuous step toward a new venture. She had no idea where her propensity for careful research had gone.

At the hotel, she thanked Peter for making the connection with Mathilde. "She is very nice. It's a bit of a sudden decision, but that's where I'm going to stay—at least, for a month."

Peter was radiant. "Glad to help, Miss Sinclair. My aunt is as upright as they come. You'll be safe there."

"Thank you, Peter."

Relieved that she had arranged for an economical place to live, she was ready to tackle the next item on her list—setting up an account at a local bank. Steeling herself for the inevitable resistance she was bound to receive, she exited the hotel for Montgomery Street.

A tall, uniformed doorman opened the ornate door to Wells Fargo Bank. She explained that, first, she wished to verify a transfer from the Old Stone Bank. He hesitated, as if he did not know quite what to do with her, and then directed her to a clerk who wrote down her information and disappeared. She could sense the surreptitious glances of the clerks as she stood waiting for a banker to come to the lobby. Since the transfer from her trust fund had been sent to this bank, Kate had decided to open an account here instead of keeping cash in the rooming house, where there was no security and lots of coming and going. The banker introduced himself as Mr. Millard. Kate reached out to shake his pudgy hand.

He was a flaccid older man with a plump body, encased in a typical banker's gray suit with subtle striping. "I have found the wire transfer from Providence you described. I can take you to a teller and have him give you cash."

"Thank you, but I'm here to inquire about opening an account in your bank to use for additional deposits and to withdraw funds for expenses."

Mr. Millard looked as if he had accidentally bitten the inside of his cheek. He didn't speak for a moment.

"It's a monthly payment from a trust fund." She wanted to kick herself for feeling she had to divulge the source of her money.

He looked down at the carpet instead of her. "Miss Sinclair, we usually don't open new accounts, unannounced."

For women. Kate had no trouble guessing what the banker had left unsaid.

"But," he continued, "given your association with the Old Stone Bank I think we might be able to be of some assistance." He led her to his desk, where they sat opposite each other, and Kate signed the necessary papers. She used the trust fund payment for her account and withdrew a small amount of cash for her living expenses. At the end, he handed her a slim, dark-blue account book that showed her balance and permitted her to deposit and withdraw funds.

"You may withdraw money as long as sufficient reserves exist," he stressed.

As if I didn't know! Ignoring the banker's condescending attitude, she breathed a deep sigh of relief. Money from the next trust fund allocation would build up her initial deposit, and she had a means of receiving money and paying bills however long she remained in San Francisco . . . assuming the banks continued to stay in business, of course.

— ·— ·— — ·

While staying at the Occidental, Kate's routine included reading the *San Francisco Chronicle* while she ate breakfast. Usually, her interest was in news reports, most of which came from the Associated Press via Western Union telegraph—the company that had inserted itself into every part of her life. Occasionally, columns of advertisements caught her eye. They told simple stories of commerce in San Francisco—what was being bought and sold, and who needed what. On this morning, the advertisements were what interested her most.

It was her last day at the hotel, and while her trunk was being taken by cart to Mrs. Evans' rooming house, she scanned the ads for telegraphy schools. As she did, her breathing grew shallow.

What am I doing?

But, after momentary panic, her trepidation about what she was getting herself into passed—she thrived on new adventures, and if she didn't act now, she would always wonder what might have been. After reading every relevant ad, she found at least three names to jot down as possibilities. Piqued by interest and growing enthusiasm about an interview, she pushed back her chair and went up to her hotel room for the last time.

97

Kate's third-floor room was under sloping eaves. On opposite, straight up-and-down sides were windows she could
open for cross ventilation. From one window she could
see the back of brick buildings, perhaps warehouses, and
from the other, a street lined with shade trees and modest
residences. Directly below was a stubble of grass surrounding the horse shed, where Mathilde had said she could
store her trunk. Kate had unpacked her belongings, and,
in several trips up the three flights of stairs, put them in
her bedroom. The battered chifforobe, with exposed scars
of dark wood protruding through the white paint, had
enough space to hang her clothing. Everything else went
into two large drawers at the bottom. If she were ever able
to afford anything new, there might be a space problem.

She arranged her hairbrush and mirror on the narrow
washstand; its tall, rickety legs warned her not to bump
it or the water pitcher might tip over, either onto the
desk or the adjacent bed. The mattress was thin, and the
blue-green patterned quilt, well-worn; however, looking
around, she was pleased with her sparse but adequate

new home. Even though temporary, it was her first residence, other than college, away from her parents. It gave her a base as she navigated learning something new. She was giddy with the prospect.

After getting everything put away, Kate took her map and set out to investigate three telegraphy schools. Visiting them, she found they all had similar setups, with a large open room filled with chairs and single tables holding Morse code straight key telegraphs. Training for men and women were in different rooms. All three schools wanted money right away, with no guarantee of employment at the end. Her head pounded from the pressure to sign up without assurance of something specific at the end. She left each school without a contract, although she knew she could not postpone the decision for too long. She had to have a job and income quickly. San Francisco was more expensive than Providence. Her deposit in the bank was a cushion, but would be used up quickly.

Back at her room, the aroma of dinner drifted up the stairs to her third-floor aerie, well before it was time to eat. Kate could not quite identify what it was. Beef stew? Pork? The scent did not do anything to alleviate her headache. She lay down until the dinner bell rang.

At the head of the table, Mathilde clapped her wide hands for attention. The six other boarders broke off chatting and took a long look at Kate, as she slipped into the last seat at the circular maple table for eight. Mathilde Evans assigned all boarders responsibilities at meals—setting the table, clearing, preparing food, washing dishes. Days and duties were listed on a small slate board in the kitchen. Since this was her first night, Kate was treated as a guest.

"Ladies, this is our new boarder," Mathilde said, sounding crisply British. A soft breeze fluttered through the lace curtains of the dining room windows. "Miss Katherine Sinclair." Mathilde turned to face her directly. "Kate, dear, tell us a little about yourself."

Kate had hoped to take stock of the others before she said anything about herself. There was no avoiding it now. "Thank you, Mrs. Evans. I'm happy to be here." She tried to assess reactions as she described, with little detail, crossing the continent by train and her excursion to Yosemite. She was well aware that the trip was an opportunity most of them would never have.

While Kate talked, Mathilde carefully ladled what Kate recognized as beef stew from a steaming tureen into individual bowls to pass around the table.

Kate concluded by saying, "I had planned to go back to Providence right after my trip, but changed my mind. I've decided to stay and train as a telegraph operator . . . first, I have to learn everything about it."

Kate saw only skeptical looks, until a slender girl sitting across from her said, "that's what I do. I'm Tess Shanahan." She had black hair, made full by its tight curls, and pinpoints of freckles dotted her light complexion. "It's not something you can do without learning. You'll have to work hard and learn to be fast. That's what gets you a job—speed and no mistakes." Her eyes were almost as dark as her hair and had an inflexibility about them.

"Tess, you're the first telegraph operator I've talked to," Kate said. "I honestly don't mind hard work. I just don't know where to begin. My mind is still swimming after visiting three telegraphy schools this afternoon. What's your advice for choosing?"

Tess was silent for a moment, thinking. While Kate waited for her response, she noticed gray, half-moon circles under the other girl's eyes. Whether it was fatigue from working, or something else in her life, Kate did not know.

"I suggest you learn on your own for two weeks." Tess paused.

Kate tried to read her expression, wondering if her hesitancy was about giving advice, or about the job.

"I still have my instruction books. I'll lend them to you, if you promise to return them. They cost me a pretty penny, mind you." Tess's eyes scrutinized Kate, probably to see if she looked honest. "After that," Tess continued, "choose a school where you can pass a test, instead of taking a long course before an exam. Learning something before starting school will save money and time."

The exchange obviously interested the other girls. They quietly spooned up their stew, occasionally soaking chunks of crusty bread in the broth as they listened.

"I promise to return the books. It sounds like good advice to study in advance. I wouldn't have thought of that, and I need to spare my costs." Some of her tension gratefully slipped away. "Will schools actually certify me after passing a test?"

"They all want your money," Tess nodded, "so you can present your conditions for taking the class. Of course, the directors are usually men," she rolled her eyes, "and most men frown at women making demands." Kate took in her hard eyes. "You just have to insist."

"That shouldn't be a problem," Kate tried to lighten the mood. "Some people already accuse me of being too pushy." Everyone joined in her laughter. "Thanks for your help, Tess; I really appreciate it." Kate picked up her soup spoon. The other girls were almost finished eating. "But you've listened to my story." She looked around the table, trying to catch each girl's eyes. "I'd like to hear what each of you are doing in San Francisco, if you're willing."

Tess had been forthright with her practical advice for a job as telegrapher. The others were more hesitant to speak up. Kate was caught off guard by their reticence. The conversations were sobering, and not what she expected. They were not tales of independence but, instead, hints of being trapped. The girls lingered after dinner, describing their work situations, and sometimes what led up to them. One was a scullery maid, cleaning pots and pans and polishing silver in a private home; a ghostly blonde was a cook's assistant; another girl, who appeared to be in her mid-twenties, worked making repairs in clothing for a seamstress. One worked in a laundry, ironing and folding shirts. Two sisters cleaned an office building at night. They all worked long hours for what Kate assumed was low pay. She found their language unpolished, some with remnants of a foreign accent. Most seemed to come from the city. Talk vacillated between unwillingness to openly admit that they were stuck, and an unexpected chance to express their plight.

When talk petered out, they got up from the table, some to do the dishes, others saying "goodnight" and retreating to their rooms. Kate started up the narrow stairway. Her tired legs were like lead weights with each step. At the top, she peeked down the hall to see if the other roomer on the third floor, Annie, the young girl with haunted eyes and stringy blond hair, was in the bathroom. Seeing the door open, Kate went in the small, white-tiled room, and then made short shrift of her nighttime rituals. Once in bed, her mind leapfrogged from her move to the new room, the visits to the telegraphy schools, and getting to know her fellow boarders. She had crammed as much as possible into one day, and it was just a start to her new life.

TWENTY-ONE

After breakfast the first morning, in her simple new home, Kate sat down to arrange her writing material. The desk was painted a much-worn gray with rose-colored trim and turned cabriole legs. The three-foot-wide desk had three small, square drawers above the writing surface and a wide one just below. First, she attended to her journal, jotting down descriptions of the past two days. After that, she reached for her stationery to write letters. The first was to her best friend.

> Dear Alice: You won't believe all I have to tell you. The first bit of news is that I have decided not to return to Providence quite yet. The second is that I am investigating a job. No, not teaching, but telegraphy.

Kate paused to grasp what she was writing, and almost giggled aloud, imagining Alice's reaction. Her pen dipped to refill rapidly, to keep up with the fast flow of her compact script, explaining about the money, her new lodgings, the potential job, and Frank. Putting it all on paper was joyfully cathartic.

Please keep up your correspondence at my new address, telling me all you and Nathaniel are doing in Black Hawk. Your descriptions always make me feel as if I am there with the two cherubs I escorted across the land. Kiss baby Gertrude, whom I look forward to meeting someday. Your affectionate friend, Kate.

Now it was her parents' turn. She had written several letters telling them all about San Francisco and describing the sights of Yosemite and Lake Tahoe. For all they knew, she had boarded a train across the bay from San Francisco and was on her way back to Providence. She had not given them a specific date, so they would not worry. Kate's pen hovered over the paper. Writing to them conjured up ghosts of other letters, even though those were tightly suppressed in her consciousness. Thinking about how much her life was changing brought painful memories of the past floating to the surface.

Her pen remained still as she remembered her thirteenth birthday. Dinner that night was a traditional family celebration. Her mother allowed the birthday girl, or boy in the case of her two older brothers, to choose the menu. Kate had asked for scallops, always abundant from one of the Narragansett Bay fisheries. For a cake, she wanted what her mother had made for birthdays since before Kate went to grade school—a spongy angel food cake, baked in a tube pan that left a hole in the center. Her mother placed a doll in the center of the baked cake, with a fabric dress bodice that extended to the cake's edge; she then decorated the cake with icing, making it look like a wide, fancy hoop skirt. Kate knew she was too old for princess cakes, but they brought such fond memories.

The princess with her cake skirt was the table's centerpiece. By Kate's place were two packages, wrapped in white, with curled pink ribbons on top. The family rule prevented her from opening them until plates were cleared and her mother had served the dessert. As she was savoring the plump white scallops, brown-edged from frying, Kate took sidelong glances at the packages, coaxing her to guess what they were. The rectangular one, from her father, was undoubtedly a pair of books. She could not guess what was in the longer package from her mother. Her brothers, Jim, sixteen, and Bill, eighteen, sat across from her, answering questions asked by their father, who always directed the dinner conversation. Every so often, when unobserved by their parents, one would jab the other's ribs with an elbow.

After the dishes were cleared, her mother returned from the kitchen with a serrated knife, a tub of vanilla ice cream, and a scoop. Kate blew out the slender candles as the others sang: "cheer her, cheer her, on this special day and many more to come," in a jovial, off-key tribute. Her mother cut the cake into tall triangles. The rectangular package from her father was the first Kate unwrapped. Carefully, she released the paper and uncovered two books. Both leatherbound volumes had gold-embossed titles. The first was Charles Dickens' *A Child's History of England*; the second, more green than brown leather, was *Flower Fables* by Louisa May Alcott.

"Thank you kindly, Daddy. You know how I love books." She left her chair to kiss him on the cheek, above his bushy, gray-flecked mustache. He parted his salt and pepper hair neatly in the middle, and in the last month, he had taken to using wire rim spectacles. He was still in his dark jacket and cravat from work.

"I know you're curious about other parts of the world, and Mr. Dickens is quite descriptive about life in London." Her father always spoke like a school master with a lesson. "The other reminded me so much of your independence." His eyes were partly teasing, partly disapproving. "It's a collection of fairy tales, written by a girl when she was not much older than you, and with an imagination just as fanciful." He patted her shoulder. Kate returned to her seat to open the second present. From the long package, she gently unfolded the tissue paper to find a doll with sea-blue glass eyes, staring at her from a wax-coated, papier-mâché face. Her long, creamy white dress had vertical pink stripes that her mother had replicated in the icing on the princess cake.

"Do you remember Nana?" Eugenia asked. "She died when you were six, but she made this doll for me when I was about that age, and sewed different clothes for her. This is the only dress that the moths haven't gotten to." Her mother's eyes shimmered with affection. "I know she'd want you to have her now. Maybe we can find the other clothes, too."

"She's beautiful, Mama. Thank you. I promise to take good care of her." Kate put her arms around her mother. "Nana used to read to me, but I don't remember much more."

A few days after the birthday celebration, Kate was in her room. The new books lay on her desk and the doll was protectively propped in the cane seat rocking chair. Kate looked over at the doll in the fragile, everyday dress, and was curious about the other clothes her mother mentioned. She stood up from her desk chair and decided to try to find them, even if they might be filled with moth holes.

A pull-down staircase leading to the attic was accessed by a door in the ceiling a short distance down the hallway from her room. On tiptoes, Kate reached for the chain and yanked hard, releasing the mechanism that unfolded the stairs. Occasionally, she had been up in the stuffy attic, when her mother was getting or putting away holiday decorations, or exchanging summer clothes for winter and vice versa, but rarely had she gone up by herself. At the top of the stairs, the room was orderly, but it was not clear how things were arranged. She walked softly over to the window, trying not to let her footsteps make the wood creak, and pulled apart the heavy, dark-green draperies to let in light. Surveying the boxes and bags, she determined that the oldest items were stored against the west wall, near the window, with newer things toward the middle, and out-of-season clothing hanging on rods along the far wall. Following along one wall, she discovered toys she and her brothers had outgrown. Behind them were even older items that may have belonged to her parents and were too sentimental to part with. Kate spied a small, doll-sized trunk. Crossing to pick it up, she unlatched the brass clasps. Inside she found what must have been the rest of the doll's clothing. Carrying the trunk to the window, she sat cross-legged on the floor and began examining the wardrobe that her grandmother had lovingly created. Her mother was right, much of the aging fabric was in dismal condition, but Kate could still tell it represented everything a young girl might need: school clothes, church and party dress, coat, shoes, hat, and a nightdress. She decided to take the trunk to her room and hold the clothes up against the doll, even if they were too delicate to put on her.

As she wrapped her arm around the miniature trunk, her elbow collided with something hard, shooting pain down her forearm. "Ouch," she said, rubbing her funny bone to take away the tingling pain. "What was that?" Behind the heavy drapery, was the edge of the pillar her elbow had hit. Looking down she saw a slightly different colored box squeezed into a cut-out portion of the pillar in a dark corner. It was flush, and looked almost as if it were part of the pillar. Curious, Kate pulled the box toward her. It took a while to extract it because it fit so perfectly in the space. She snapped open the latch at the back and looked inside. Letters were stacked in a neat horizontal row. She picked up an envelope to see to whom they belonged. Lacy handwriting addressed them to William Sinclair, with her father's office address beneath his name.

Why are they here if they're addressed to his office? Burning interest overrode her conscience and she opened the first envelope.

"My dearest Will, I will treasure our meeting forever . . ." The bottom of the third page was signed "With affection, Sally."

The next was similar, and the next—love letters to her father. She looked at the date of the first: October 12, 1849, four years ago. Hastily, she put the letters back in the box, with bitter regret that she had found them, but harsher judgment for reading something that did not belong to her. The box clanked as she shoved it against the wall and put the drapery back in place, covering it. She cautiously made her way down the ladder holding on to the trunk with one arm, clinging to the ladder with the other. Her trembling legs barely held her. Refolding the stairs against the ceiling, she returned to her room, still shaking. She set the trunk down in front of the doll and walked over to lie down on her bed.

She closed her eyes, trying to push out the dark, swirling questions. She was not sure how much time had passed before she heard her mother's voice:

"Kate, where did you find them?"

Kate leaped off the bed so fast, the blood drained from her head and she thought she might faint.

Eugenia stood at the door in her cotton day dress. She had put on a few pounds, but Kate thought she still looked pretty and knew so many things about the world. Kate could not fathom why her father might be attracted to someone else.

Eugenia entered the room, her gaze on the small trunk.

Kate's breath rushed out. Her mind had been on the letters, but her mother was referring to the doll clothes. "In the attic," she stammered. "I hope that's okay."

"Of course; I wasn't sure if I kept them or threw them away." Eugenia moved toward the trunk and unclasped it. "Let's look through these and see if any can be salvaged."

Kate sat down on the floor next to her mother, trying to steady her hands.

"We're both too old to play dolls, but just for a moment." Eugenia laughed, looking at her daughter. "Kate, are you alright? You look pale."

"I'm fine, Mama, really. Tell me about the clothes."

TWENTY-TWO

The aroma of coffee and cooking oatmeal brought Kate out of her tired sleep. Her stomach growled with hunger. Sleepily she looked around the pitch-walled room, taking a moment to recall where she was. *In my new life,* she remembered with a somnolent smile. Far from Providence and the secrets it held.

When she traipsed down the stairs to the dining room, she found the other boarders already up. She discovered some girls preferred to keep to themselves while others chatted happily, wide awake and ready for the day. Kate sat in the chair next to Tess, who silently waited for Mathilde to serve them a hot bowl of oatmeal. A vertical row of pearl buttons extended from the collar to below the waist of Tess's gray dress. It hung stiffly on her thin, angular frame, as if it were made for someone else and was there only accidentally.

"Here are the books I said I had. This one goes into the mechanics of the telegraph and the responsibilities of the operator; the second explains Morse code." Tess piled them on top of each other and pushed them toward

Kate. "You can have them for two or three weeks. I'm mostly through with them, but I want them back."

"I'll get right to work on them," Kate promised. "It's really all I have to do until I decide on a school." She turned toward Tess hesitantly. "Do you mind answering questions, if I don't understand something?"

"No, I guess not." Tess shrugged. "But I work long hours, so I'm not here very much."

"Thanks, hopefully I won't have many." Kate could not figure out how to get past the barrier that Tess put up. She thought another telegrapher would have liked talking to someone else about her job.

Kate turned to her breakfast, reaching for the dish in front to scoop a dollop of butter for her oatmeal. She added a spoonful of soft brown sugar and watched them coalesce and liquefy in the hot mixture. She missed the comfort of poached eggs and toast with a newspaper, in the elegant surroundings of the Occidental Hotel. It was going take time to get used to the house and other boarders. Curious about the telegraphy book, she flipped open the cover, carefully keeping it away from her bowl, and began to read as she ate and drank her tea. The first chapter told the history of communication, beginning with smoke signals and ending with the development of the telegraph. The history of communications was probably more than she needed to know, but it kept her interest. She could discuss it with Frank someday.

Finished with breakfast, she went up to her third-floor desk to continue studying. The second chapter explained mechanics. The machine itself was fairly simple. Kate looked at the diagram. There was a bar with a knob on top and a switch underneath. The operator pressed down against spring tension, completing the electric circuit of the battery, sending an electrical signal across a wire to a receiver on the other end. Telegraph companies had strung wire on poles between stations and receivers, often along railroad tracks, across the country. Even with the explanation and history, Kate found the idea of sending a message through a wire unfathomable. It was the magic of electricity, and maybe just a beginning, as Frank had said, with more inventions ahead.

After spending hours reading through the first book, Kate reached a standstill. The straight key machine might be as uncomplicated as the textbooks said, but she would never learn to operate it without practice on an actual machine, and that could only take place at a school.

She stood up to stretch. After a drink of water, she left the mechanics of telegraphy, and sat back down to tackle learning the dots and dashes of the Morse code alphabet. Commonly used letters had fewer dots and dashes: "e" was one dot, while "q" was dash, dash, dot, dash. She went over and over the twenty-six letters, until her mind was so jumbled, she could barely remember the order of the alphabet in English. *Enough.* It was time for a break.

She got up from her chair and jimmied open the window, testing the outside temperature. It was pleasant. She found her knitted wool shawl and wrapped it around her shoulders before going down the stairs for a walk, pledging to free her mind of dots and dashes.

Walking for over an hour, exercise and a breeze of humid air sweeping in from the Pacific Ocean, cleared her mind. Back in her room, she cut paper into twenty-six small squares with scissors borrowed from Mathilde. On each, she put a letter of the alphabet with the Morse code symbols on the back. Once done, she mixed up the scraps of paper, and began quizzing herself. If she missed one, she turned to a worksheet and wrote the letter's code five times.

By the end of the week, Kate was tapping out sentences using the tip of her pearl-handled nail file propped against her hairbrush. She was barely making five words a minute, far from the thirty words a minute she strived for. No, not strived for—it was mandatory, if she wanted to get a high-paying job. Her head bowed in fatigue. At this point, it seemed beyond possibility.

—·— ·— — ·

Tess had not been at dinner the last two nights. Mathilde did not allow girls to skip the evening meal without her permission. She could not afford to waste food. Tonight, Tess's seat was empty again. Just as Mathilde was serving soup, the dark-haired waif hurriedly took her chair at the other end of the table from Kate. There was no way to have a personal conversation. As she ate, Kate glanced up between forkfuls to make sure Tess did not disappear before they had a chance to talk. At the end of dinner, Mathilde served each boarder a piece of chocolate cake, iced with creamy, dark frosting. Tess ignored her dessert and excused herself from the table. Kate looked at Mathilde desperately. "I'll be right back." She bolted from the table.

"Tess, do you have a minute?" Kate still had her napkin in her hand.

"I dunno," Tess was startled. "I'm in a hurry." The girl's bony shoulders hunched forward.

"It won't take long," Kate said, in a bright voice, trying to sound appreciative. "I've been studying your books, and I think I'm ready to go to class. I need to practice on a real operator's key. You can't get very fast just using a nail file and hairbrush."

Tess met Kate's humor with a sarcastic look.

"Could you tell me the name of the school you attended? I visited three, but there's no way to tell if one is better than the other."

"Morris and Fenster," Tess shrugged. "I don't even know if they're still in business."

"Morris and Finnister?"

"Fenster, F E N S T E R," Tess spelled out with an impatient voice.

"Okay, thanks. Would you know of a second, in case the first is out of business?"

Tess turned, and Kate was afraid she was going to leave without answering, but she paused. "I've heard Smith and Woodward is okay, but I haven't been there."

"Thanks, I've already visited that one, but not the one you went to."

"You owe me my books back. Don't run off with them." Tess turned and walked up the stairs before Kate could answer.

Kate went back to the dining room to eat her cake. She was fuming, insulted by Tess's implication that she would steal her books. Kate didn't understand the other girl's hostility. If she had insulted Tess somehow, it was certainly unintentional. After dessert, Kate cleared the table—her duty for the day. When the last dish was in the sink, she used Mathilde's city directory to look up the addresses of the Morris and Fenster Telegraphy Institute.

TWENTY-THREE

Time passed as if it did not exist while Kate holed up at her desk on the third floor, memorizing Morse code and using her makeshift apparatus to practice it. She wanted to learn as much telegraphy as she could before registering for a class. Breaks from studying came for meals, to read and write occasional letters, and to write in her journal. There was so little to say she was tempted to do it in Morse code.

From Alice came: "I can only shake my head about your new 'scheme,' please respond with all the details!" In contrast, her mother wrote: "Kate, your father and I want you to stop this nonsense and come home. What will people think?" Kate sent occasional notes to Bill and Jim. She wished she knew them better, but they were not good about writing. Since they had gone out on their own while she was in college, and moved to Missouri, they were like distant remembrances rather than close family. She had no idea what they thought about her and had her doubts about their approval.

Her confidence grew, but Kate had reached the limit of what she could do on her own—there would be no fur-

ther progress without an actual telegraph key. She had visited the school
Tess mentioned, making four to choose from. All wanted her to apply.
In the end, she chose Morris and Fenster—not because Tess had gone
there, but because of the location. It was closest to the rooming house,
though it was still a streetcar trip with several blocks' walk on each end.
Class started the first Monday of November.

Before moving from the Occidental, she had written Frank. "Here is
my address at my new rooming house. Please forgive my absence while
I study and decide whether I want a job. I'll be in touch as soon as I
can." Retreat was typical for her; an idiosyncrasy at best, a dysfunction
at worst. She'd done the same thing in college during exams, or with big
written papers, escaping to the library, away from her friends both physically and emotionally. They were miffed, and told her so.

With the weight of so many life decisions, instead of writing Alice, she
turned to her journal, where she was always hard-edged honest with herself.

- Job as telegrapher—self-sufficiency but less freedom with long hours
- Telegraphy school in Providence—expectations—friends and family
  would not approve
- Telegraphy school in Providence—no costs for housing
- Telegraphy school in San Francisco—exploring a job easier but miss
  family and friends
- Rooming house—independence, but not much in common with the
  other girls
- San Francisco—companionship, wide-ranging conversations, Frank!
- San Francisco—keeping a relationship at arm's length difficult

She closed her journal, fearing the self-reliance she held so firmly was
slipping, under the subtle coaxing of an intriguing man, who asked nothing of her but that she be herself.

--- -- - ·

On Monday, Kate closed the front door of the rooming house tightly,
making sure the persnickety brass lock was secure before she left to

catch the streetcar. It was eight o'clock and most of the girls had already left for work. The two who remained were drinking coffee and chatting with Mathilde.

When she found the sign designating the trolley stop, she stood restlessly in the fog, surveying the surrounding storefronts while waiting. Ten minutes passed before she heard clopping hooves and a ringing trolley bell. Boarding, she tipped her gloved hand so the coins slid into the conductor's outstretched palm, and found a seat among the mostly dark-suited men in top hats. She watched nervously for her destination, but had no trouble exiting at the right place and walking to the Institute.

At eight thirty, half an hour before class started, Kate was the first student in the women's waiting room. The next scheduled trolley would have made her late. Gradually, other women began filling the single chairs lining the wood-paneled room. Some greeted others familiarly, since the class had been going on for two weeks. As the door opened and closed, she glimpsed men going down the hallway to their separate classroom. Just before nine o'clock, a middle-sized man in a long frock coat breezed through the waiting room, juggling his top hat while he fit the key into the lock of the interior classroom door. He beckoned students to enter.

Inside, there were three vertical rows of single desks, each with a telegraphy key on top. Wondering if some sort of order had been established, Kate hung back while others took their seats. One seat remained empty, near the left-side bank of windows. She took the seat and immediately fingered the wood and metal telegraph key. *Finally, the real thing.*

"Welcome to the two new students who have joined us, and to those who have been here before," the instructor said in a flat accent. "This will be your first day putting to use what you've learned about Morse code and practicing on a key. Let me explain the parts."

A prickling sensation spread over Kate's shoulders and down her back. *The voice, that gravelly voice, where have I heard it before?* She looked up with a start, examining the features of the instructor at the head of the class. He had gained a little weight, his cheekbones fleshed out, but without question, it was Reverend George Johnson, the insufferable minister from the Yosemite trip.

Head down for the next three hours, she concentrated on working the telegraphy key. At first, she struggled to quickly recall the code for each letter, but with each hour, it was easier. When the bell rang, ending the morning session, she was pleased with her results. Clicking out words in dots and dashes was becoming more natural.

She had put thoughts of introducing herself to Johnson out of her mind while she was working. The instructor had a list of class participants, so there was little chance of going unnoticed. Further delay would only make her appear weak. With her shoulders intentionally straight and confident, she walked up the aisle to the front desk where he stood. It was infuriating that she was meeting him again, especially in a position of authority. She disliked him and every other self-superior type like him. Johnson was putting his papers away in an oversized, worn briefcase. It appeared to be the same one he carried on the stagecoach.

"Reverend Johnson, I'm Kate Sinclair from the Yosemite trip," she said, offering her gloved hand.

He shook it limply. "I suspected it might be you when I read the list of students. Please call me Mr. Johnson here." He finished packing and closed his briefcase with a snap. "Continuing your independent ways, I see. What brings you to learn telegraphy?"

"There's a shortage," she said, refusing to be defensive. "And it gives me flexibility for income and location."

"Hmm," he said, clutching his briefcase handle. "There is need, but also competition for the best jobs. Most go to men, of course. Occasionally women—only those with special skills—are recommend for desirable positions."

Kate's heart lurched, but she maintained her composure. *He's just the type of man who dislikes all women because of his own demons. The ministry for him is superiority and control.* She restrained a smirk when she said: "I'm surprised to see you here as well. I thought you would get involved with the ministry."

"The ministry would be my first choice. So far I haven't found a church willing to let me preach the true word." He moved away from the desk edgily. "Like you, I discovered a shortage of telegraphers when I was in Michigan and found telegraphy an easy skill to learn as a backup." He looked down at her. "How did you fair today? Will we be seeing you tomorrow?"

"I progressed quite well," Kate said.

His expression did not change, but a shadow of doubt flicked across his eyes. "Until tomorrow then," he said, and strode out the door.

— · — · — · · — — · ·

Johnson had apparently taught many classes previously because he was knowledgeable, but his instruction was by rote, without humor or personal connection with his students. Kate gained as much from practice as instruction. Tuition in the course included optional practice on the telegraph key after class. For two weeks, she spent every afternoon working to increase her speed without losing accuracy.

Friday was the final exam. Students went directly to their seats after Johnson opened the classroom door. They barely greeted one another. Tenseness permeated the room—and Kate's own heart felt close to her throat. For two hours she focused on going as fast as she could without errors, shutting out the clicking of the other machines.

"Time is up. Stop where you are." Johnson abruptly announced, tapping his watch. "I'll post the results when I'm done."

Some women milled around in the waiting room, talking nervously about the test. Kate paced up and down the hallway—too anxious to sit down. Bile gnawed at her stomach. She thought she had done reasonably well, but feared that would not be enough. As a woman, excelling was the only way to get a job.

After what seemed like endless time, Reverend Johnson—now Mr. Johnson—opened the door and called them to the results he'd tacked to a corkboard. Most rushed forward to look at the list, but Kate approached apprehensively. She felt a pat on her back as she raised up on tiptoes to see over the cluster of students. On the top was her name. Thirty words per minute and only one error! Her held breath came out with a whooshing sense of relief.

"Congratulations, Kate! Well done," several girls said. "You have a job for sure," another added. Satisfaction seeped into her consciousness. She had done it—and without the cost of the first two weeks of instruction.

Reverend Johnson handed her a certification of completion. "Well done, Little Missy. Good luck on finding a job."

Kate had already turned to exit when she froze. She squinted and looked back, giving him a hostile, knowing look. His jaw clenched—he knew she knew. Holding on to the stiff paper certificate, Kate quickly left the classroom. Her emotions were flying like birds in a windstorm. She had to get away from Morris and Fenster Telegraphy Institute and Reverend Johnson. Opening the street door, she paused to unfurl her umbrella against icy drops of rain. She looked back to see if he was behind her. She had fortunately worn boots instead of ordinary shoes and began running in the direction of the trolley. Each step splashed up water, soaking the hem of her skirt and coat, but she didn't care.

Johnson had not said, "congratulations," but "well done, Little Missy." Her breath came in gulps. That same voice and horrid nickname haunted her dreams. There was no doubt. The holier-than-thou minister was the villain who had attacked her, and now the person who was going to recommend her for a job.

TWENTY-FOUR

The aroma of curry, chicken, and apples greeted her when she opened the front door. Mulligatawny soup, one of Mathilde's best cooking efforts, and Kate's favorite. Years before, Mathilde and her husband had lived in India, where he was stationed with the British Army. She had learned the recipe there. Kate hurried upstairs with her dripping coat. She unbuttoned her sodden boots and replaced them with dry shoes, without time to change her damp skirt, and made it back downstairs before Mathilde had ladled the first bowl of soup. Only half of the girls ate lunch at home. The others worked too far away and packed a lunch to eat, often while they continued to work.

The spicy soup was delicious and so was the bread—so hot that butter melted on it immediately. "I've passed my telegraphy course," Kate managed to say, after the first few spoonfuls.

"Oh, Kate, congratulations," the girls cooed almost in unison, with only a hint of envy. They did not begrudge her success, Kate knew, though it made their own jobs seem more meager.

"What will you do next?" asked Mathilde with a wide smile.

"I have to wait for the instructor." She swallowed hard, thinking of Reverend Johnson. "He'll send a reference to one of the companies—probably Western Union—suggesting that I be interviewed for a position." Now that Reverend Johnson knew she had figured out he had accosted her, she could not imagine what job recommendation he would give her. He had it in his power to do a different kind of damage than he had before.

"You shouldn't have a problem. Tess is always talking about a shortage of telegraphers," Mathilde said.

"Yes, if you're willing to go to any sort of office. I don't want to be in a far-off railroad station, so I've put down preferences for a spot in the middle of Providence," Kate hesitated, "and also one in San Francisco." She paused, thinking. Her plan had always been to return to Providence after Yosemite, but the temptation of learning telegraphy had lured her to stay. She had refused to think about what happened after the telegraphy school until she knew her test score.

"We hope you'll stay in San Francisco," Mathilde said.

"What a nice thing to say. I've grown fond of the city." Kate was hedging. She knew it was not just fondness for the city. Yet, everything was uncertain. She was not sure where she wanted to be or whether she really wanted a job. She *did* want the freedom to make her own decision. Doing well on the test had given her options all tangled with extenuating circumstances.

"Who decides?" Elizabeth interrupted her thoughts. Originally from Ireland, she cleaned offices at night with her sister.

"It's the company, but the instructor at the school chooses where to send the applications." Kate's breath caught and she put down her spoon. Her appetite disappeared at the thought of Reverend Johnson deciding her future. "I'm hoping my good score helps, but you can never tell."

"Kate, we're so proud of you. You've had your head bent over, working hard for weeks. All of it was worth it. Why so glum?" Mathilde asked.

"I won't know if I have a job for a while. All I can do is hope for the best." Kate's initial euphoria over her high score had evaporated like water drops on a hot stove. She sat quietly while the others finished, then excused herself to clear the table and do dishes.

Upstairs afterward, the rain drummed against her windows in hard liquid pellets. Kate was dispirited when she should have been elated. She had not only succeeded, she had come out on top. Disgruntled, she pondered if failing might have made life easier. She then could have returned to Providence and resumed life, without anyone being the wiser about her attempt to do something new.

She had resolved not to contact Frank until she had decided about a job and location, but recognizing Johnson changed her mind. She'd thought herself rid of the perpetrator. Her disgust about what he had done only increased with his ability to control her job recommendations.

Once she started the letter, her spasms of anxiety calmed. Writing to Frank lifted her spirits. It also confirmed how much she missed him. Studying for the telegraphy test had preoccupied her for so long she had thought of little else. As she wrote, descriptions of the boarding house and of school flowed, just as they might have over dinner together. She told him she had scored well on her test, but left the future ambiguous, because it was. Explaining Johnson would better be done in person. Finished, she sealed the envelope with hot red wax and walked downstairs to put the letter on the console where it would be picked up by the young boy who came after school to earn coins by delivering messages.

That night she lay in bed under the light quilt. There was no heat on the third floor, but warmth drifted up from below and, with it, any odor of cooking and noise. Her two windows were often propped open to generate a crosscurrent of air. Tonight, sleep would not come. Thoughts of George Johnson touching her made her shake with repulsion. She was becoming paranoid about the degenerate man. The application for the telegraphy institute had asked for her address. Johnson likely knew where she lived. Her third-floor aerie was safe but going out might not be.

She thrashed all night, and by morning had made a decision. Reverend Johnson should be punished, or at least banned from working with women. She needed an ally. Luckily, she and Tess were assigned to dish duty.

"Tess, was George Johnson your telegraphy instructor?" Kate asked, as she started scrubbing a stack of dishes submerged in warm soapy water.

"No, but I've heard about him."

"He used to be a minister; I met him on my trip."

"He sounds like a creep." Tess took a rinsed plate and began drying.

"I had a bad experience with him on my trip. He grabbed me."

"Really? The girls say he's a bully, but I'm shocked he was that bold."

"I'm afraid to think how far he'd go. Bullying isn't right either, you know." Kate started washing glasses, pausing the conversation as Mathilde walked through the kitchen, looking for something. Once she and Tess were alone again, she resumed. "He shouldn't be teaching women. We need to stop him."

"We? All I know is gossip. Is there a witness to what you said happened?"

"No," she admitted. Both Ned Jones and Bob Young had heard her complaints, but they hadn't actually seen anything.

"So?" Tess set her hands on her hips. "Whose word will carry more weight? A minister and teacher, or his female student?"

Kate shook her head. "I know, but we can't let him just get away with it. What he's been doing is wrong and he has to be stopped before he does something worse."

"Maybe so, but leave me out of it," Tess said over her shoulder, as she carried a tray of glasses to put in the pantry cupboards. "I need my job."

The dishes done and put away, Kate went upstairs feeling frustratingly powerless. Brooding over what to do, she decided Reverend Johnson was most likely not a threat during the day. Both incidents had happened in the cover of dark. Going out in the daytime surely was safe. She had to tell someone about Johnson. Kate had never seen him at the school in the afternoon, so, after lunch, she went to Morris and Fenster and asked to talk to the administrator.

When she knocked on his door, Kate's jaw was clenched so hard, she thought her teeth might crack.

"May I help you?"

"Mr. Armstrong, you may remember me. I'm Kate Sinclair. We spoke when I submitted my application. I just finished the class."

The small man with fair complexion pulled his reading spectacles up so they rested on his light brown hair. "Oh, Miss Sinclair. I do remember you, and congratulations. I saw from Mr. Johnson's list that you finished at the top. You'll give our school a good standing. What can I do for you?"

"It's about Mr. Johnson. I don't think he should be teaching female students."

Mr. Armstrong looked puzzled. "He's new, but he has good experience."

"He can exert too much control over women, perhaps he should teach men."

"Mr. Johnson said he was perfectly willing to teach women, in fact, it was what he preferred." Armstrong frowned. "A teacher who doesn't have control is not someone we want at Morris and Fenster. Do you have a specific complaint?" They were still standing in his doorway.

"No, not about here."

"Well, then, I wish you good luck. We like students who work hard and come out on top."

He reached out and shook her hand, concluding the meeting.

Kate could not move for a moment. She had been brushed off, not listened to. Disheartened, she walked slowly toward the exit.

—·— ·— — ·

A letter from Frank finally came. She slit open the envelope and absorbed the comfort of his words. He had been on one of his many business trips for Western Union, this one to Sacramento. He was delighted to find her note upon his return. "May I pick you up at six for dinner?" he wrote.

Kate ran back again to ask Mathilde to excuse her from dinner.

"Did you hear something about a job?" the kind landlady asked.

"No, not that." Kate shook her head. "But I am going to dinner with a friend," she smiled. "And I want to look my best."

The corners of Mathilde's dark eyes crinkled. "At least something made you smile. You've been so somber of late."

"This will definitely help, but now I have to run down the street to get my reply sent to Frank, quickly."

"Of course, it's a man," Mathilde said, as Kate rushed out the door.

Kate wished she had something different to wear. Frank had already seen everything in her meager travel wardrobe, but right now, she could not afford anything new. She took one of her silk scarves—the color of lapis—wound it around her neck, and tucked the ends in her crisp white shirtwaist, clean from the laundry. Then she pinched her cheeks for color. It was the best she could do. Glancing at the looking glass, she found the effect, with her light hair brushed shiny and restrained in a chignon, not at all displeasing.

A few minutes before six, she put on her dark wool coat and left her room. As quietly as she could manage, she stepped down the stairs to the corridor. Voices came from the dining room, where the girls had already gathered. They glanced curiously at her, but she passed by quickly to wait in the foyer. Patches of the last daylight came through the cut-glass sidelights flanking the front door. She stood restlessly by the console, empty except for a brass kerosene lamp. Mathilde kept it lit until ten o'clock—the time boarders had to be in their rooms. Soon a shadow passed the long, narrow window, and the knocker sounded. She forced herself to pause before reaching for the knob, not to appear too eager.

Frank stood on the front stoop, just as she remembered him. His cheeks were ruddy from his walk, and his brown-flecked green eyes danced. He gave her a wry smile and she fought the urge to press her lips against his. Despite her vow to remain free, she had trouble resisting him.

125

"Frank—"

"Kate," he interrupted, "my tardy response was not intended." Instead of continuing, he reached out his arms and pulled her toward him, encircling her in a warm embrace. She kicked the door shut with a backward thrust of her foot, so no one inside would see. Neither of them moved, fitting together like two interlocking pieces. Kate felt his heart beating against the pounding of her own and was suffused with all-encompassing serenity.

"I could stay this way forever," Frank said, after a while. "But then we'd starve, wouldn't we?" He gently let his arms slide away. "Someone at work told me about a small restaurant we should try—nothing fancy, but I suspect they have sherry." Even in the declining light, she could see his mischievous eyes as he crooked his elbow toward her.

Kate reluctantly gave up the intoxication of his embrace, slipped her arm through his, and they set off walking toward the trolley stop. Filmy clouds retreated, leaving them with the sun's last rays as they waited for their ride. Shoulder to shoulder during the trip, they enjoyed each other's company with little conversation, content to watch the setting sun growing fat and burnished like a golden portent, before disappearing behind the horizon.

TWENTY-FIVE

The blue-trimmed, white clapboard restaurant was redolent with the aroma of seafood. Gas sconces gaily lit the small space—there were only ten tables. The host led them to a table for two in a quiet corner, where they promptly received a menu and ordered drinks.

Frank leaned in close. "Kate, my travels relate to the conversation we had at our last dinner. I think you might be interested."

After spending so much time alone in her room, worrying about a future job, talking to him was like a release from prison. "I almost asked you on the trolley about your job, but I didn't want to pry." It seemed to her that he was always working . . . and always learning. She liked to think that was something they had in common. With a contented sigh, she took a sip of the sherry the waiter put in front of her, settling in for another round of Frank's encyclopedic storytelling.

"Pry?" he laughed. "I've been marking time 'til I had a chance to bend your ear . . . but I promise I won't go on for too long."

I'd like to hear it all—I'm interested." Although she had always enjoyed conversing with men, this was on a different level. To describe the other talks as superficial would be unfair, but this transcended to an exchange of mutual understanding. Frank did not realize that most men discounted women's opinions.

"I want to hear your plans, too." His eyes sought hers. "You didn't waste any time learning to be a telegrapher. I'm mightily impressed that you followed up on my suggestion, but not at all surprised that you did well."

Kate winced at his praise, dreading the inevitability of admitting that she did not have a job—and might never if it depended on a recommendation from the instructor and self-anointed minister.

Before Frank noticed her crestfallen expression, the waiter arrived with marinated green bean salad, a sourdough baguette, and plates mounded with iridescent shells of plump, broiled oysters, nestled under buttered breadcrumbs. With her first bite, sounds of nearby conversation and laughter receded to the background. A bubble of private conversation enveloped the two of them.

This would be why I would marry. This craving to share experiences and exchange ideas.

"My trip was to Sacramento, with many stops along the way," Frank said, chewing and savoring his first bite. "Hmmm, the restaurant recommendation wasn't off base," he said, scooping another oyster from its pearly shell. "It won't surprise you that the offices were mostly one-person operations." He fingered his whiskey glass while talking—a habit she had noticed before. "I debated whether to tell the telegraph operators I was coming, or surprise them by arriving unannounced." He pushed the glass aside.

"What was your hesitation?"

"One time, when I arrived in a small town without warning, I got off the train and found the telegraph office closed. I knocked on the door, but no one answered, so I wandered into town and asked at the first office for the whereabouts of John Horn, the telegrapher. The person I asked knew alright. He said he was sitting on a barstool, just like he was every afternoon."

Kate covered her mouth to stifle a giggle. "Oh, no."

"That was the end of him," Frank said. "I have occasionally discovered a telegrapher playing checkers with another operator—the other player can be close by or far away as India." He fiddled again with his whiskey glass. "I really don't have a problem with that. Business can be slow in small offices, and since telegraph messages can only go one way at a time, there is considerable waiting before the wires are cleared in the other direction.

"Someone told me some operators have devised Morse code symbols for positions on a checker or chessboard and are quite adept at long-distance games." Kate said. "I wasn't sure whether to believe it."

"It's true," Frank said. "There's actually a close fraternity of telegraphers all over the world."

"What did you decide to do about notifying telegraphers before your visits?"

"For this trip, I decided on a mixture of surprise for new ones and advance warning for those I'd already met. It's important to make sure customers are satisfied—if not, they are ripe to woo away from Western Union."

"That sounds fair—for the company and the operators," Kate said. Once again, she admired how dedicated he was to his job—how hard he worked.

"My job sometimes requires sleuthing," he continued. "I'm expected to learn about the competition." His expression turned more serious. "During my trip to Sacramento, I heard plenty of rumors about Jay Gould making moves to take over Western Union. It's my habit at each place to have an extended chat with the telegrapher, or more, if it isn't a single-person operation, as well as talk with other folks in town. I generally turn up all sorts of information . . . some even useful," he chuckled.

He was nonchalant, but Kate had an uneasy feeling. "Is there danger in trying to prevent powerful competition?"

Frank paused, spearing the remaining oyster on his plate. "I'm not making light of it. Stories waft through the air about those who try to stand up against powerful men. But there's probably bloat in all of them. Men tend to exaggerate to make themselves appear important." He shrugged, as if shaking off a threat. "The immediate danger, though, is having my job depend on figuring out how to thwart the opposition." He gave her an eager look. "Now, that's enough about me. It's your turn. It seems we are both going to be in the telegraph business. May I offer you Ghirardelli chocolate while you talk?"

The inevitability of telling Frank about her reference predicament had plagued her since she put two and two together about George Johnson. When she had sat curled up in her armchair, under the sloped ceiling of her third-floor bailiwick, she had agonized about whether to share all her concerns about Johnson, or whether to say nothing. She knew she tended to divulge small details to perfect strangers, but the real secrets of her life she kept locked tight. Frank's willingness to explain the burdens of his job disarmed her. Even more was his evident desire to listen.

At first she stalled, giving Frank an overlong description of incidentals; the more she talked, the more her defenses crumbled. Then she threw away caution. "You'll think it odd, but my telegraph training is related to Yosemite." She sensed him reading her face for emotions. It would be difficult to hide anything from Frank. Her eyes softened as she looked at his strong features so close to her. "Do you remember, I told you I found one of the men, Reverend Johnson, disturbing?"

Frank didn't answer, evidentially searching his mind to recall what she had told him. "More or less," he said, after a moment. "What about him?"

"He was also the instructor at the telegraphy school, but that's not all. When we were on the trip, he accosted me."

Frank lifted off his chair. "How? Did he hurt you?"

"No," she shook her head to dispel what he had not asked, "just scared me."

"I hope you reported him."

She shook her head. "When I told the guides about the incident, I didn't know who had done it—it happened at night. I only realized it was Johnson at the end of my class."

"That no-good so-and-so; I'm going to confront him."

"It wouldn't do any good." Kate shuddered, alarmed that Frank might get involved. She had had no success with her own attempts. "I have no proof. Right now, I have two worries. He may harm one of the women he teaches, and he controls what job I get."

Uncommon silence fell between them. Kate occupied herself with another dark brown piece of Ghirardelli, slipping it in her mouth before it melted on her fingers. She considered the futility of reporting Johnson—to whom and about what, exactly? She suspected Frank was mulling over similar questions.

TWENTY-SIX

Kate and Frank had agreed to meet for lunch two days after their dinner, on Sunday, a day he did not work, although she suspected he worked every day. The ferocious wind of the previous day had calmed, but rain was sending rivulets of liquid mud down the edges of the streets.

She was already in the restaurant's vestibule when she saw him step through the front door and rapidly shed his slicker. With a vigorous snap, he shook off the water. "Frank, I'm back here. There's a row of hooks for coats."

His eyes shone in the dimness of the entryway when he saw her, his lips bent in the crooked smile he wore whenever he had something he wanted to tell her. She laughed. Every time they were together, there was something new. Frank was her polymath, and she loved that about him.

They walked into the big open room, scattered with sturdy, golden oak tables and matching chairs; it was only half-filled with diners. The tall windows seemed designed to fill the room with sunshine, but today the light was as dim inside as out. She guessed lots of people were dodging the weather and staying in.

"You're brave to come out in this weather," Frank said, as if reading her mind. He pulled out the chair so she could sit. "But I'm glad, and I shouldn't be surprised."

"Maybe just foolish. Who knows if my clothes will ever dry." Her eyes followed him as he went around to the other side and scraped back his chair. "I'm happy I'm here."

They ordered bowls of clam chowder, which arrived thick and steaming, accompanied by crusty bread in slender twisted sticks.

"I have an idea," he said, his spoon hovering over the too-hot soup.

"That worries me, Frank," Kate frowned. "Not that I doubt for a minute that it isn't a good idea, but your job has enough challenges. You shouldn't concern yourself about something for me."

"Just hear me out. I don't have to do much to make a connection for you. I know some chaps at Western Union who are in dire need of telegraphers. The offices are small, somewhat out of the way, city offices—much like Mr. Tweedle's—not a big central location, but it would give you time to learn the ropes and gain experience for your next job."

"Twindle. It's Twindle," she said, a bit more crossly than she wished. She knew he was only trying to help, but the thought of relying on him so completely, chafed. She preferred to make her own way. More than that, his suggestion meant no longer postponing the decision about whether to return to Providence as planned or stay in San Francisco. Thinking intently about what he proposed, she forgot her food.

"It would be a way to bypass your instructor," Frank said. He submerged his spoon in his clam chowder and ate contentedly, giving her time to cogitate his proposal.

Kate broke a breadstick as if she was snapping a hen's neck for the stew pot.

Frank deliberately finished every drop of soup and two twisted, sourdough breadsticks. "Ah, those clams were deliciously plump. Or maybe . . ." he swiped the starched napkin across his russet mustache, "maybe food always tastes better when I'm with you."

"Frank, would you give me three days to think about it?" Kate hoped she had rinsed the acid from her voice when she said it because she was angry with herself, not at him. "You're so kind to try to help me. I'm struggling at the moment about what I want to do." She heard the pleading in her voice. "Even though I passed the exam, I don't know yet if I even want to be a telegrapher, or if I do, I'm not sure where."

It's the perfect solution—a job and the chance to put Reverend Johnson in his place at the same time. Why am I unsure? She knew the familiar impulse to retreat was raising its ugly head.

His frustration was palpable, and their lunch ended soon after. As they tugged on their raincoats in the dim vestibule, there was no magical parting, simply a move for the outside and a dash through the pelting drops in separate directions.

—·— ·— — ·

Thick, vaporous fog replaced the rain, reducing the movement of the city. Kate stayed inside the next day and did not go downstairs until dinner. Her third-floor room lately had begun closing in on her. Before taking her seat, she made a hurried trip to the foyer to take a perfunctory look through the mail. She shuffled through the few pieces of unretrieved envelopes, expecting nothing, but there in the disarray was a long, business-sized envelope with her name . . . and the return address of Western Union. Her heart thumped. She wanted to slit open the envelope that second, but she could not bear sharing the news, whatever it was, with others until she had absorbed it herself. Since she had skipped lunch, there was no foregoing dinner. Mathilde was flexible, but wasting food was inviolable. The letter would have to wait.

The girls were lost in supercilious chatter about dress lengths, bonnets, and waistlines. On other evenings, Kate joined in, but tonight, all her thoughts centered on her future—perhaps contained in the envelope hidden beneath the napkin on her lap. As soon as everyone had finished dessert, she escaped to the third floor, relieved that she had no chores that night. She turned on the gas lamp and fumbled in the drawer for her letter opener. In one long stroke, she opened the envelope.

The letter offered her a telegrapher's job in Providence. It detailed hours of work, pay, duties, rules, and a request to begin on December fifteenth. The letter still in her hand, she let herself fall straight backward on the bed. Someone had made her decision for her. She would take a telegrapher's job and the job would be in Providence. Her head rested on the pillow. Kate had always intended to return home after her trip to Yosemite, so it had made sense to list it as an option. Still, she was curious about the offer. If San Francisco needed telegraphers, why was Western Union asking her to go all the way to Providence? Despite her high scores, why had she only received one offer? And one a long way away, to boot. There could only be one reason. George Johnson gave the references for his students. Perhaps he'd eliminated the local jobs and promoted this one. Now that she had recognized him, getting *her* out of town got *him* out of a bind.

She sat up, clenching her fists. The Providence offer gave her little leeway to consider alternatives. In order to get there on time, she'd have to leave almost immediately. She moved to her corner reading chair and tried to press down the whirlwind twisting in her.

She'd convinced herself the appeal of telegraphy was extra income to grow her savings and a job where a woman could excel, even in competition with men. With the proposed assignment, she was unable to deny the truth any longer. The real allure of the job and of San Francisco was Frank. She'd never felt this way about anyone before. When they were together, the rest of the world slid away, so absorbed were they in their exchange of thoughts and ideas. Best of all his traits was his sense of humor. He made her laugh more than anyone had before.

Everything was moving frighteningly fast. The job, the relationship. She wanted to slow it down, to be able to think what was best. *Maybe there is no best.* She had made a pledge to live life on her own, and so far, had happily done so. A relationship was a commitment—a binding contract . . . or not.

With despair, she went over scenarios of how she'd tell Frank, imagining his response. Despite her inexperience, she knew he felt the same attraction she did. In his reasonable, measured fashion, he would make a case for staying. But she couldn't. A relationship . . . it was just too risky.

Kate rose from her chair and began taking everything out of the tall chifforobe and drawers of her desk to pack. She was making a logical decision. Providence was her home; her parents and friends were there. In many ways, this was the best solution. She could pursue her fledgling career in a comfortable, familiar setting. Yet, for the first time in her life, she found herself wishing she could embrace the illogical. She sent Frank a note by messenger, asking him to have a drink together the next evening.

His reply came quickly, agreeing to Kate's invitation. They met at the same restaurant where they had eaten clam chowder. With their drinks, a waiter had brought a basket of the same twisted sourdough breadsticks they had enjoyed before, but once again, Kate found she had little appetite. Across the table, Frank's expression was expectant and curious . . . maybe even hopeful.

Her own, she knew, was grim. "I got a letter from Western Union yesterday."

"And?"

"It was an offer for a job in Providence . . . it starts December fifteenth."

"You don't have to accept it. There are jobs here for the taking. I can see that you get one."

She erratically broke pieces of breadsticks, without eating them. "Frank, I'm overwhelmed. Being a telegrapher is a big step. It means financial freedom, but with it comes long hours of work. I'm honestly torn between staying here and working and going back to Providence, and maybe going back to teaching or tutoring." In her heart, she knew that would simply be one more way to avoid a relationship.

"You know what I'd like you to do."

Kate took a sip of sherry, looking into his serious eyes. "I think I do. You would be one of the reasons I would stay. But I've decided to take the job in Providence." Her heart wrenched; his face expressed so much hurt. "Let me explain. This may not be permanent. I want to see how restrictive I find the job closer to home. I may not like it and decide to travel. I may also enjoy my new occupation and decide to continue. Either way might bring me back to San Francisco. I now know from experience, it's easy to get here."

Frank gave a sad laugh. "Only you would describe over a week of train travel as 'easy.'" He sighed. "Is there anything I can say to persuade you to try telegraphy here?"

Kate shook her head. "There's no perfect answer right now." She knew getting away from Reverend Johnson also played into her decision, but she didn't mention it. She'd given him enough to process.

"This has come as a surprise—a disappointing surprise. I'm not sure what's gone wrong." It killed her to hear the bitterness in his voice. "You did nothing wrong; I can assure you. There are too many decisions right now. I'm so sorry."

"When will you leave?"

"In a day or two—I barely have time to get there by December fifteenth."

TWENTY-SEVEN

At dawn the next morning, scents of frying bacon and percolating coffee drifted up to the third floor. Kate had groused silently about odors from any part of the house migrating up the stairs to settle, in an invisible cloud, against the pitched ceiling of her room. Her solution was to bang open her two windows and stir up a breeze in the airless room. Today, however, the aroma made her take a nostalgic look around the room that had been home for over five weeks. It had not really mattered that the chifforobe was battered; it had been functional enough for her scarce belongings. The desk was modest, but she had spent hours and hours there, studying telegraphy and writing letters or in her journal. With the addition of a pillow, the worn easy chair became a cozy place to read or re-read the books she had tucked in her trunk, as well as others she borrowed from Mathilde. As much as things sometimes chafed at her, Kate would miss her room, and even miss the noisy mealtimes with the girls.

All of her clothing, books, writing material, and accessories now lay in organized piles on the cheerful quilt that covered her bed. She was already dressed in her tan gabardine travel skirt, shirt, and walking shoes when she went downstairs to get a key from Mathilde to find her trunk in the stable. On the way to the kitchen, she went to the foyer, and with fondness, ran her hand over the long, dark wood of the console. It dispatched news in and out of the rooming house and provided a lively gathering place for gossip as girls came and went with their mail or chatted with messenger boys.

The mist of fog had not yet burned away on this typically cool San Francisco morning. After breakfast, Kate went to the railroad office, purchased her ticket, and then returned. This was the last time she would walk these several blocks. Often, when she walked to her rooming house, her steps were weightless, as she recollected the details of her latest outing, whether it was exploring the city, being with Frank, or even learning telegraphy at the institute. Her mood was not as carefree this time.

The rooming house was quiet. Walking softly, she searched for Mathilde, and found her in the parlor, sitting in her overstuffed gray-green easy chair, her book askew on her lap, her heavy-lidded eyes closed. Kate sat down on the matching divan next to her, not wanting to startle her. Mathilde worked hard to make ends meet. The girls who boarded here came and went, with little attachment to the house or its owner. She gently stroked Mathilde's sturdy arm with her fingertips. Mathilde said something dreamily and then opened her eyes, shaking her head groggily.

"Kate, didn't you go out?" She reached down and closed her book, sitting up straighter. "Oh, I just wanted to do a little reading before it was time to start lunch. Did you want something?"

"Mathilde, I have something to tell you," Kate's shoulders slumped. "I've been offered a job in Providence. That's where I came from, remember?" she said, trying to sound cheerful.

"I guess that's good news, but I'm sorry." She took Kate's hand in her own. "You never gave me a bit of problem, and always did your jobs without reminding."

"I've enjoyed my stay here, thank you, Mathilde."

"When is it you go?"

"This afternoon. I have to be at the station by one, and I'll have to hurry. I've already arranged for the livery stable to pick me up, along with my trunk."

Mathilde looked at the gilded watch that hung from a chain around her neck, and jumped up." Oh, it's late, I have lunch to prepare. I'm sorry you're leaving so soon. Is there anything you need?"

"Thank you, Mathilde. I've folded everything, and it won't take long to bring things down to fill my trunk . . . and, Mathilde, I've paid to the end of the month. I don't expect anything back. I'm giving you dreadfully short notice and it may take you a while to get another boarder."

Nodding, Mathilde said, "So nice of you, Kate. Most girls don't know how hard it is to make a go of it here and take everything they can." She gave Kate a questioning look. "Maybe you'll think me nosy," Mathilde clasped her square hands. "What about your young man, Kate? I know there was fondness . . . I hope there isn't some difficulty?"

Kate pressed her eyes shut. She had hoped to avoid that question, not just from Mathilde, but also herself. "No," she shook her head, "there's no problem."

How could there be a problem with the smartest, most charming, handsomest man I've ever met? That he is perfect is the problem.

She gave Mathilde a frantic look. "I have to hurry—there's so much still to do. Thank you, Mathilde, I'll find you to return the stable key and say goodbye before I leave."

TWENTY-EIGHT

In the first month at the Providence telegraph office, Kate was overwhelmed. Discordant sounds of clacking telegraph keys and the constant staccato of incoming telegrams made it impossible for her to filter out what was extraneous. Her head ached from trying to concentrate. But, in retrospect, she realized she'd learned a great deal. The telegraphy school in San Francisco had used paper strips filled with dots and dashes for telegraphers to read and transcribe. In Providence, Kate learned, operators *listened* to clicks. An electrical current opened or closed, making the lever strike an anvil, producing a click. Telegraph operators distinguished a dot and a dash by the short or long interval between the two clicks of coded messages. Added to mechanical noise were the conversations of operators waiting to send or receive a telegram. Only two messages went at a time, and those, only in one direction. Bit by bit, she learned to hear what she was supposed to and shut out the rest.

When not in a queue to send or receive telegrams, telegraphers had other work to do. Kate proofread her longhand transcriptions before she typed them, checking carefully for accuracy. Often, she had to edit customers' messages. Senders paid for a certain number of characters, but sometimes did not count accurately, requiring telegraphers to take out words and abbreviate without changing the meaning. Then there were priorities to keep: Government messages were highest priority, followed by those marked urgent, then the full-price message, and last, the night message, which was less expensive because it might not go until the next day.

After scrutinizing stacks of messages to send, her eyes were red and sight blurred at the end of the day. She kept going because she needed to prove herself—errors, especially by women, were cause for termination.

Western Union's downtown office was at the side of the three-story, Italianate-designed Regal Hotel. The dark, wood-paneled room was long and narrow and contained eight small, square tables, each with a telegrapher key, typing device, and space for stacks of papers. At the side of the room stood a high desk, where head telegrapher, David McAnarney, usually stood by, rather than sat on, his tall stool. Kate guessed he was around forty years old; he had long, steely sideburns, a receding hairline, and thinning crown. His pinched lips usually held a cigarette, its burning tip shedding ashes on his desktop and clothes, filling the room with smoky fumes. Everything about him was gray, Kate thought grouchily.

He had just left the room for one of his breaks and some of the telegraphers were flapping papers to get rid of the smoke. As the newest employee, Kate had the last desk in the long row of five men and three women. Paula Young was nearest to her.

"Kate, do you ever wish you were in a far-off railroad station telegraph office where you managed everything yourself?" Paula was taking advantage of the head telegrapher's absence to chat. She was in her early twenties, with straw-colored hair twisted high on her head. Her muscular frame was squeezed into an obviously homemade, striped cotton dress, and scuffed leather boots stuck out under the hem.

"I don't know, Paula." Kate looked at the sturdy girl, wanting to be agreeable, but finding she was not in agreement. "That sounds pretty lonely, doesn't it?"

"I guess . . . maybe it's just because I was raised on a farm. That was lonely. At a telegraph office, you're always connected to someone, no matter how far away. And you get paid for it."

In the six weeks Kate had worked in Providence, she had sensed that, in addition to regular pay, the opportunity to rise to the middle class was a motivation the others in her office had in common.

"Is it the city for you, then?" Paula asked, sorting papers to prepare for typing while she continued talking.

"I'm not sure exactly where I want to be yet," Kate said. "Have you heard of the new traveling telegraphers?"

"You mean the ones who go from place to place to get offices shipshape?"

"That's it, exactly. There have been complaints about mistakes and indifference. That's bad for Western Union. Traveling telegraphers will go to an office and stay for weeks, or even a month in larger cities, to clear up the deficiencies. I don't think many telegraphers will be interested in going from one place to another, but I might. It would be a chance to travel."

"Ooh, that wouldn't be for me." Paula shook her head. "I want to find some place to do my job and earn my way, maybe put down roots." She faced Kate, "And, anyway, it's the men that would get those jobs. A woman traveling around, alone? I don't know." She shook her head again, before focusing on her work as Mr. McAnarney returned to his desk.

Kate resumed her own work, but a dark cloud settled over her. It had been a mistake to tell Paula about the traveling telegrapher job. Sabotage would surely not come from the young farm girl, but it might from someone else. All telegraphers heard stories about office competition, where one operator would send sloppy telegraphs under another operator's code to cause trouble, sometimes resulting in dismissal. Since getting her job in Providence, Kate had been diligent about fitting in. She intentionally never mentioned she had a degree beyond high school. She was the only one, even among the men. Her aspirations to travel had remained unspoken, too. She needed to keep her head down and work hard, although she knew it would take more than that to get a chance for the new position—she was short of experience, but limited interest in a high-travel position would be in her favor.

TWENTY-NINE

A soft glimmer of cloud-shrouded sunshine sketched soft light in Kate's bedroom. She remained, half-dozing, in her comfortable bed, a down comforter piled on top, with no desire to get up. Sunday was the only morning she did not have to be at Western Union at eight o'clock for ten hours of work. With the fuzziness of a dream, she remembered it was the day she would see Alice. Kate groaned. She wished the weather were better. The dull, overcast day was what Alice had grown up with, but by now, she must be accustomed to Colorado's crystalline, blue skies, with the intense rays of the sun insisting that you rise and greet the day. Kate pulled her pillow over her head and slept a few more minutes.

After breakfast, she walked three blocks up the hill, to the familiar, redbrick house, with its tall, slender columns framing the entrance. Kate took three quick steps up the stoop and grasped the cool, brass door knocker. She heard her knocks echoing inside the house. The door quickly flew open and, in the next second, Kate and Alice were a tangle of arms, kisses, and giggling. Alice's parents,

Harriet and Isaac Hale, joined the frivolity, making hushing sounds, warning against waking up one-year-old Gertrude, who was sleeping in a makeshift bed by the kitchen hearth. Alice explained that seven-year-old Crawford and five-year-old Isabel were on the third floor, in the playroom with a local nanny. She was keeping them occupied until noon dinner, giving Alice and Kate uninterrupted time together.

"Kate, let's sit in here, like we used to." Alice squeezed Kate's hand as they walked to the parlor. "We'll see how much catching up we can do before Crawford and Izzie come downstairs. They'll be over the moon to see you."

The horsehair sofa was a familiar place for conversation. "How are they doing at school in Black Hawk?" Kate asked Alice.

"Children are endlessly adaptable." Alice shrugged. "In no time, they acted as if they had never lived anywhere but a mining town. That's good and bad," the corners of Alice's sky-blue eyes crinkled. "Good they fit in so easily, and bad that they fit in with the other young ruffians of the town."

"Ruffians?"

"That's too strong, but several of the children there would much rather climb mountains than sit with a book or learn anything about culture." Her lighthearted tone belied her professed complaint.

"They do go to school, don't they?" Kate said, startled.

"Of course, and I'm realizing that nature has something to teach them as well as books. Don't worry," she touched Kate's arm lightly. "I value books as much as ever."

"What about you?" Kate shifted, looking Alice up and down, reading her expression as well as hearing her words.

"Honestly?"

"Yes, honestly. How do you really like living in a mining town?"

"Sometimes I shake my head in disbelief that I'm in a world that's rough and crude and so opposite from what I'm used to," Alice made a sweeping motion with her hand as her eyes took in the comfortable furnishings of her parents' parlor. "It's different, but it's fine. Best of all, our family is together, and our new little one is thriving in the high hills. I'm grateful that Nathaniel has had success after so much hard work."

Their attention was broken by Alice's mother, who came in carrying a gleaming tray loaded down with tea and iced sugar cookies.

"Here you are, girls," Harriet carefully balanced the tray and set it on the low table in front of them. "I'm keeping my eye on Gertrude—I'll let you know when she wakes." The half-bustle of her ruffled black skirt made a silky whisper as she hurried back to the kitchen.

Alice filled a teacup with steaming amber liquid from the pot, offered it to Kate, and then poured one for herself. "I do miss my friends . . . like you . . . desperately. There aren't many women or families in a mining town."

"Do you ask friends for dinner? You always entertained when you were in Providence."

"A few." Alice picked up a gold-rimmed plate and offered Kate a cookie. "It's not the same as the conversations we had with faculty members and their wives. They always had some new idea that challenged your thinking."

"You always complained that the men took the most interesting discussions to another room, while they smoked after dinner." Kate looked at her friend as she sat, relaxed, sipping her tea. Her face had grown rounder, but she still had a youthful appearance—full of the enjoyment of life.

"I remember," she laughed. "Nathaniel is better than most husbands about filling me in on what's going on in business and around the town. Did I tell you he's thinking of running for mayor of Black Hawk?"

"No." Kate's eyes widened. "You wrote he was being pulled into politics because of business. I shouldn't be surprised."

They sat only inches apart, looking much alike, in starched white blouses and dark textured skirts, while Alice explained Nathaniel's latest business challenges. Miners were almost doubling their gold production since he had built his now-famous smelter, and many objected to the rates he was charging. They were oblivious to how much money he had lost to his failures and the years it had taken to make it work, stretching his own finances thin.

"Others were eager for rewards," Alice complained, "but had neither the stomach nor the skill to risk everything. Nathaniel's always being tested." Her blue eyes clouded.

Kate silently agreed that Alice's husband often faced obstacles; however, she was not convinced that he had always minded doing so. In her mind, Nathaniel considered taking a risk as a challenge—a way to grow and learn, as long as the results were worth it. In that regard, she had much in common with him, but then, he was a man. While risk-taking was considered bold and courageous in men, women in the same situations were considered brash.

"Kate," Alice interrupted her thoughts. "Now it's your turn. I've read your letters many times over—thank you, but it's not the same as hearing your voice and having you beside me. Hurry, I want to know as much as possible. Oh, Kate, I miss you the most." She reached over and put her arms around Kate in a hug. Then, she leaned back against the smooth, black horsehair settee.

Kate took another cookie, with its glistening sugary topping.

Maybe, just maybe, if I say everything out loud, I'll believe it myself.

"So much has happened in four months, since I decided to be a telegrapher," she began with a smile, telling in words what she had already written. She described the comfort of the cross-country train trip, roughing it in Yosemite's spectacular surroundings, and visiting so many sites in San Francisco it seemed like a second home, as well as her course in telegraphy and Frank's role in everything.

"I'm spellbound. Honestly. I've never heard you describe a man like that before."

Kate smiled, her gaze unfocusing a little as she thought of Frank. The features of his face as he talked were as clear in her mind as if he were in front of her. "There has never been someone like him." The late-morning Providence sun had finally appeared, bringing streaks of light through the vertical, velvet-draped windows. "I've never met a man with such sharp intellect. He reads everything and remembers almost all of it, with the uncanny ability to recount it in a way that makes you interested in any topic. Dinner with him is like going to a personal lyceum . . . except he interjects the cleverest sense of humor. Sometimes he surprises you with a serious statement, and then you look, and one side of his lips turns down a little, while the other side lifts into a crooked smile, and you catch up with his wit."

"Kate, I'm flabbergasted. This is such a change. I hardly know what to say."

A half smile of acknowledgment flickered on Kate's lips.

"No, really," Alice looked straight at her. "Boys were always attracted to you—your blond hair, flawless complexion, dimples when you smiled. Even as your best friend, I was jealous, but whenever anything got serious, you quickly got immersed in something else—teaching, lyceums, volunteer work. You can't deny it."

Kate nodded, and then shrugged. "There were plenty of boys and then men who thought, and still do think, my freely expressed opinions are unladylike or even offensive."

Alice ignored her retort. "Tell me more about him. What's his job at Western Union?"

"Frank thought he was hired to make sure Western Union had lots of offices in California, to edge out competition. Everyone has an interest, now that so much news, business, finance—really all types of communication—come across the wires."

"You said, 'he thought'?"

"In a way, helping expand business is still what he does, but his real responsibility is outdoing the competition."

"Other telegraph companies, you mean? I thought Western Union was a monopoly; I've heard Nathaniel talk about that."

"Yes and No. Western Union sends most of the telegrams, but there are still smaller companies doing business. When there's financial success, others want some of the profit, especially powerful men and politicians. Have you heard of Jay Gould?"

Alice nodded. "The telegraph has even improved what news we get in Colorado. The railroad hasn't worked its way to Black Hawk yet, so we don't get as much news as San Francisco, or even Denver, but I read about Gould and Fisk trying to control the gold market last September. Banks and businesses are still in turmoil from that trick."

"So, you understand how powerful these men are. So far, there are just rumors Frank picks up from visiting telegraph offices, but danger is growing from competition by powerful men."

"What will Frank do?"

"He's gathering information now. His job takes him to all parts of California, so he listens to make sure he has all the facts and figures. He takes things seriously and lets work consume him."

"Does Western Union have a plan?"

"It's too early, and it's going to take courage even for Western Union to go head-to-head with the kingpins. Frank isn't daunted by that, but he's realistic. Men like Gould and Fisk can be ruthless if others get in their way."

Alice shifted closer so her knee gently touched Kate's. "Why did you take a job here and leave San Francisco . . . and Frank?"

Kate hesitated. "There were lots of different reasons . . . this is where I was offered a job, and I was always planning to come home." Kate knew Alice saw through the chimera. She could delude her friend less than herself. Kate did not tell Alice of Frank's letter that came after she left. It had been full of disappointment. He had said he would not give up hope that she would return to San Francisco. They still wrote every other week, but the hurt was there, even if he did not express it.

Alice's skeptical look was interrupted by the thumping footsteps of children running down the stairs, followed by jubilant cries of "Auntie, Auntie," ringing through the hall. Soon, Isabel and Crawford were clambering on the lap of their mother's favorite friend and their honorary aunt. Having been told Kate was coming for dinner, blond, curly-haired Isabel had prepared a picture for the occasion. She had drawn the three of them riding a train. From the kitchen, insistent wailing from Gertrude announced she had awakened and wanted to be fed. Their private tête-à-tête was over.

When Alice finished nursing Gertrude, they all retreated to the dining room, where Harriet had festively set the oblong table with a snowy-white tablecloth, red napkins that matched the tomato soup, and crustless ham sandwiches. Harriet was an older replica of her daughter, round of face and figure, with the same acute, blue eyes that missed nothing. Alice was on a path to look just like her in twenty-five years.

"Kate, tell us about your duties at Western Union," Alice's father gave her a paternal look. He was interested in what she did, but Kate suspected he would not have been happy if Alice decided to do something similar.

"Here you are, involved in the most modern science." Isaac Hale was a trim man, dressed precisely in a dark jacket and gray waistcoat, with deliberate hands, befitting his job as the owner of a watchmaking and clock business. Clean-shaven, his gray hair had thinned to balding above his inquisitive chestnut-brown eyes. "Who sends the most telegrams, government, or businesses?" He wanted to know.

"Government probably sends the most," Kate answered over the children's chatter. "There are all kinds. At railroad stations, operators receive orders from the dispatcher, for relay to the crew, to slow down or even halt a train."

"I send telegrams to order business supplies, but almost never personal ones. Do other people?"

"Sometimes," Kate replied, "but not too often. Even though rates have gone down, telegrams are expensive." She took a square piece of cake, iced in dark chocolate and nuts as the plate passed around. "In fact, telegrams can alarm people. We've heard some are afraid to open yellow envelopes, with good reason—telegrams often bring bad news. Unfortunately, we transmit plenty of that. Only something dire is important enough to spend the money."

Isaac nodded in agreement.

The conversation switched to old friends and families. Like Kate, Alice had two brothers, who had moved away from the area and visited only occasionally.

"Please send our regards to your parents," Harriet said. "We do enjoy seeing them at social occasions."

When Kate reluctantly bid goodbye, Alice said, "It was like old times to have you here."

"I'll stay in touch."

"Yes, you better . . . about everything," Alice said as Kate went down the steps.

THIRTY

Each step of the way home from the Hales' house was so familiar, Kate could have walked it with her eyes closed. Calculating exactly how many times she had taken the same path was impossible. Kate and Alice had always been in school together and became fast friends by the age of ten or eleven. They were as comfortable in one house as the other, sometimes having overnights on the weekends.

At the Hales' house, it was as if Kate were part of the family. At hers, it was more the two of them together. Kate paused on the footpath, trying to think why. There was something about the subtle detachment between Will and Eugenia that made time there feel different. *The letters.* They might have something to do with it, or nothing at all. She was not sure, but it made her think.

Pushing open the door, she called out, "Hello—I'm home." Pausing in the cool, unlit foyer to listen for an answer, Kate jumped when the grandfather clock next to her began sonorously chiming five. Walking down the hall to the kitchen, she smelled smoke.

Eugenia looked up, strands of hair falling over her eyes as she struggled with the damper. "I think I've finally got it," she said, half to herself and half to Kate. "If the flue isn't just right, it's been filling the room with smoke lately. It needs an adjustment, I think." She began flapping a flour sack towel to get rid of the fumes.

"The Hales send their regards," Kate said, walking over to open the back door to let in fresh air.

"That helps, Kate, thanks. I want to hear all about your visit and what everyone is doing when we're at dinner."

"Can I help with anything, Mama?"

"Thanks, Kate." Eugenia turned toward her, and Kate read the affection in her mother's azure eyes. "But no, why don't you rest? You must be tired after seeing Alice, and you have work early tomorrow." She hesitated.

Kate's body tensed. Her visit to the Hales's inevitably sparked Eugenia's regret that her own daughter was not living a life similar to Alice's, with a husband and young children. She braced herself for questions about why Kate didn't go back to teaching school, with more time and summers free. Kate knew her upcoming thirtieth birthday was like an alarm bell for her mother. No mother wanted her daughter to turn into an old maid. Their many quarrels on the subject never led to a change in opinions; they only intensified their individual opinions.

The breath Kate held released when, for once, Eugenia resisted. Instead, she said, "I want a full report about Alice and her family, and Daddy will want to hear about Nathaniel's business. So, let's talk at dinner . . . and that means I better get cooking."

"Thanks, Mama, I'll be back in a little while to help get things on the table."

Sunday was the only day Kate regularly ate with her parents. With work six days a week, there was little other time. During the week, her mother fixed dinner earlier most evenings for Kate's father and herself, and kept the food warm in the oven for Kate to eat when she got home at six-thirty. Those nights, Kate ate hastily, needing sleep from the day's work and rest for the one to come.

As they ate Sunday dinner, Kate told them everything she had learned about Alice's family and news that the Boston and Colorado Smelter had expanded beyond Black Hawk to Alma, Colorado, another high mountain town.

"If it's expanding, Nathaniel's smelting business must be prosperous," Will, said. "It took guts. Good for him."

"Black Hawk is prospering, but all is not necessarily happy, according to Alice. A year ago, miners were out of work and grateful for the smelter, but now they resent Nathaniel's profits."

Will took time to cut bites of pork roast before he answered. "Change always causes disruption. You can count on it." He took a forkful of meat and after he swallowed, said, "Without it, nothing moves forward. Change is ongoing, but I don't know if anyone's figured out how to make it easier."

Her father was right. Little in life ever stood still. "I heard all about Alice's brothers, in Ohio—so many people are moving westward. The frontier, the Hales call it, and we used to think of it that way too."

"Until Colorado and California," Eugenia added. "I still think of our boys in Missouri that way. Whenever Harriet and I see each other, we commiserate about all our grandchildren being so far away. She was ecstatic about Alice's visit."

Kate knew it was painful that her brothers and their growing families lived so far away. "Perhaps, with the railroad's expansion, Bill and Jim will bring the children for a visit."

"I hope so."

When conversation turned from business to grandchildren, her father appeared to slip into his private thoughts. Often gruff and unresponsive with his immediate family, he was charming when he was the center of attention. On occasion, he would ask business associates and their wives to dinner. Her brothers had been invited, and when they left home, Kate had sporadically been included when she was at home. At those dinners, Kate remembered the dancing candlelight, lively discussions, and being startled to find her father charmingly conversant. He exuded pleasure at being master of ceremonies, unlike the introvert he often was around his family.

A thought jolted her. *Maybe that was the side of his personality he showed to the woman who wrote the letters.* Kate glanced at her mother. When Will held court, Eugenia was silent, as expected; when he was reticent, she unquestioningly filled the silence with either small talk or, just as easily, matters of substance. She was a good foil for him, yet he took her for granted.

Kate's attention came back to the present and the familiar surroundings. Their dining room had two tall, multi-paned windows with green velvet draperies that Harriet drew at nightfall when she turned on the six-arm brass chandelier. She added candles on the table for special occasions. When the original seat covers had worn out, Eugenia needlepointed a colorful flower on a dark green background for each chair. Otherwise, Kate noticed little change in the room since her childhood, or the rest of the house, for that matter.

Everything was so familiar, and yet she felt out of place, being at home after time spent traveling to Colorado and California.

After dinner, Kate went up to her room. Shelves lined the east bedroom wall, some filled with books and others with memorabilia, such as the doll given to her mother by Kate's grandmother and passed on to her. She loved the familiarity, but there was a lack of ownership—it was her parents' home. Unsure of how long she would stay in Providence, she knew it would be foolish to rent a room somewhere else when there were three, unoccupied bedrooms.

That night, she lay under her rose-patterned comforter thinking again about the letters. They had not come to mind frequently, but they never really left either, particularly when she was in her father's company. The following week, the letters worked a wedge into her consciousness. She had only read a few. The fright so many years ago of thinking her mother had discovered her awareness of the letters made her shut them out of her mind—they had been too painful to accept. Now Kate wanted to know more.

"How was work, Kate?" Eugenia asked when Kate entered the kitchen at the end of the week. She had apparently heard her come in the front door and had begun putting dinner for her on the table. A plate with a swordfish cutlet, sliced apples, and a square of cornbread, next to a goblet of water, waited for her.

"There weren't many breaks today, Mama, but I can tell I'm getting faster all the time." Kate washed her hands and slid into her straight-back chair at the kitchen table. "It's more of a routine now, instead of having to learn so much that's new. The head telegrapher even asked me to teach a new girl—I guess that's a compliment," she smiled.

"Kate, Daddy and I are going to go to see Uncle Rob tomorrow morning and won't be back until late afternoon. We'll miss church and dinner. You don't mind being left on your own, do you?"

"Not at all. I'm not much company these days, and I use Sundays to get caught up." She looked up at her mother. "Thank you for cooking, Mama. The fish is delicious. I appreciate it so much, as well as Amber doing my laundry. I have so little time these days."

"Amber doesn't mind, and with everyone gone, the house gets too quiet. We're glad you're here." Eugenia turned toward the row of dark, wood cupboards. "What about a slice of gingerbread? I made it this afternoon."

"Oh, Mama, no, don't tempt me," Kate laughed. "I'm having trouble getting my buttons fastened with all your good cooking. Thank you, though."

THIRTY-ONE

The bedroom was cold in the morning. Kate put on her gray flannel robe and lit a fire in the fireplace. After the small strips of wood kindling caught fire, she added lumps of coal and crouched down, waiting for the flames catch. When sure the fire had taken hold, she replaced the screen. Walking across the room, she tossed her robe across the back of the chair and climbed back in bed. It was such a relief not to have to go to work, and it was inexplicably pleasurable to be on her own in the quiet house.

After a bit, the letters she'd long ago found in the attic above her began to nudge her consciousness. Were they still there? All she remembered of the letter writer was the name "Sally." She tried to think of the last name. So much time had passed, she wondered if the woman might still have contact with her father, or if she was still alive. The only way to know was to look at the letters again.

She got out of bed, and put on her robe again, tying the sash. She found her warmest slippers and brought the lantern with her. With rain outside there would be little light above. She walked along the hall to the pull-down attic stairs. Once the stairs were down and stable, she grasped the wire loop of the lantern again and climbed up. The big, open storage space had accumulated additional clothing and boxes since she had last been there. To even get to the western window with its dark green draperies, boxes and paraphernalia had to be shoved aside. She moved carefully, to be able to replace articles exactly as they had been. A stack of four large wooden boxes blocked the lower portion of the window. The boxes did not budge when Kate tried to shove them with her foot. She put the lantern on the floor and reached for the top box. It was too heavy to lift, so she slid it down, balancing it against her chest, and then carefully onto the floor. She did the same for the second. Panting from exertion, she sat down with a thud. When she regained her breath, she was able to stand up and slide the remaining two boxes a few feet across the floor to make space to reach behind the draperies, where they would stay.

Pulling aside the heavy fabric, she found the metal box near the windowsill, tucked in the cavity at the base of a column. Kate pulled the lantern over for light and sat on the floor to open it. She found the letters tightly packed in the metal box—there were more than she remembered. Her heart pulsed. She leaned back against the large boxes she had just pushed aside, wondering what to do next, knowing what she wanted to do . . . what she had to do . . . was wrong.

It was too cold to stay in the attic, so she put the letter box under her arm and carefully stepped down the ladder to the hallway, going up the six steps once again to collect the lantern. She decided to go downstairs to fix tea and toast and bring it up to the warmth of her room while she examined the contents of the box. Her stomach turned at the prospect.

Within half an hour, Kate was back upstairs carrying a tray. She arranged the tea pot, cup, and plate of toast on her desk on the opposite side from the lantern and metal box. She sat down, poured a cup of oolong, and began to read. Seventeen years ago, when she had accidentally looked at the letters, the shock of the contents had unnerved her too much to notice more than the first dates. Examining them carefully, she found the letters arranged chronologically, from the first on August

8, 1849, more than twenty years ago. She read a dozen letters—all reminisced about time spent together with words of endearment and signed, "Sally." Kate turned the envelope she had just read lengthwise to mark her place and then got up to scoop more coal onto the fire. *Who was Sally? Did I ever meet her? Does she still exist?* Curious, she looked at some of the letters at the back of the box. They were less ordered—almost crammed in. The latest date Kate found was June 2, 1869, seven months ago. There was never a return address.

An insatiable need to find out more about Sally had supplanted her guilt from looking at the letters. Kate began examining each envelope for clues. Midway through the stack of letters, one envelope had a pencil notation across the front in penmanship she did not recognize: "Andersen." There was no way for her to know if that related to Sally, but it was a start.

THIRTY-TWO

Reading the letters awakened all the confusion Kate had stuffed into the far reaches of her mind. They may have been out of sight and mind but one answer was clear. Her father's relationship with Sally had been more than a passing fancy. Over the years there were tense references about "need to make a decision between us" and others about "our bond."

Trying to put the mysterious pieces together, it appeared that some of her father's evening "business meetings" had been with Sally, rather than with clients or men who worked for him. Meetings in Boston, or occasionally New York, might have been trysts with Sally, as well as some of the Tuesdays and Thursdays her father routinely said he spent in his Providence office.

Her head ached from the pressure and the letters' revelations. Intense desire to understand the story, laced with resentment of her father's seemingly cavalier behavior had replaced the avoidance of seventeen years. She was no longer a young girl. Not knowing her mother's attitudes, or if she even knew of the affair, accelerated her curiosity—and frustration. Whether Bill or Jim knew or suspected added to the mystery. They had moved away from Providence and the liaison; if they knew about it, would they even consider it illicit? She wondered. A man's world differed from a woman's.

She had to work fast to find information contained in the letters. Any notes she took must remain undetected. Her journals lined one of her bookshelves. Looking through them, she found a travel journal with an empty section at the back. She would keep her notes there.

The letters from Sally appeared intentionally cryptic, with few names, dates, or places that might be clues. When Kate found any, she wrote them down. So far, there was not enough information in this one-sided correspondence to make sense of her father's relationship with the mysterious Sally. There were references to "H," but without context. Another question raised rather than answered.

Each quarter-hour chime from the grandfather clock in the foyer below reminded her of her race with time. Her parents would return by late afternoon. Even though they would have had a noon meal at her uncle's, Kate needed to offer them some small supper to welcome them home. At her mother's insistence, Eugenia had done all the cooking since Kate's return to Providence in December. Kate wanted to do something in return. Soup, bread, and fruit were all she needed to fix, but the soup had to be prepared soon to give it time to simmer. Beyond anything else, she had to return the metal letter box to its spot and stack the heavy wooden boxes just as they had been when she found them.

By two o'clock, she was famished and weary from searching for clues. In the kitchen, she loaded bread with thick slices of cheddar cheese, and made another pot of tea for lunch. Then she took inventory of the kitchen. She decided to make buttermilk biscuits to go with the soup. In the icebox, she found a meaty hambone, and there were plenty of jars of stewed tomatoes and other canned vegetables in her mother's neat pantry. Potatoes and onions were in the cellar. Soon, she had plenty of ingredients, but they required chopping. By the time she had everything prepared and the soup was on the back burner, it was after three o'clock.

She dashed up the stairs, amused to realize she was still in her night-clothes. She opened the metal box and made sure the letters were arranged exactly as she had found them. With the light in one hand, and the box in the other, she headed back up to the attic. Tucking the box in the invisible cavity was easy, but restacking the four heavy boxes was not. Piling them on top of each other required far more strength than it had taken to unstack them. She had left the bottom two in a stack, but the third required tilting and pushing to get on top. When she tackled the fourth, she was out of breath and her muscles quivered. Groaning, she tried but didn't quite succeed, and the box fell to the floor with a crash. She tried again. Straining, she managed to lift it onto the top of the pile and shoulder it into place. She bent over, hands on her knees, and gave herself a chance to recover. She'd done well; the attic looked just as it had when she'd entered it earlier in the day. Now, all that remained was to get dressed and wait for her parents to arrive.

With a sigh, she began to straighten, but a sudden, stabbing pain in her lower back stole her breath and brought tears to her eyes. She made a few more valiant attempts to stand, but each time the pain in her back returned with a vengeance.

In a woeful dance of slow, cautious steps and shallow breathing, she made it to the floor below. Only her stubborn determination to keep her attic visits a secret got her through the pain of folding the ladder back into position. Carefully, she ran hot water in the bathtub, sprinkled in a handful of Epsom salts, and soaked until the water cooled. Slowly, she stepped over the side of the curved, ceramic tub and gingerly dried off. The pain was manageable if she did not move too quickly, but it was obvious it would take days to completely heal. *Heaven help me. What will I tell my parents?*

--- --- --- -

"I still don't understand how you slipped on the carpeted stairs. Day-dreaming about some faraway place, I would guess." Kate's father shook his head, his lips pursed disapprovingly.

Kate had asked him to drive her to work Monday morning in the hope the ride would be better for her back than walking. However, the mystery of the letters and the fear she might accidentally give herself away made her as nervous as a trapped cat.

"I'm sorry, Father. I think the bumping of the carriage is making my back worse. Thank you for going out of your way, but I'll walk home." She gathered her coat and inched out of the carriage.

"Maybe you should take a few days off. You don't want to have chronic back pains at your age," Will said, grabbing the handle to shut the door after she exited.

Kate went into work disgruntled. Reference to her age rankled. Her father made it no secret that he considered an unmarried woman of thirty to be an "old maid." She wasn't sure what to do with the knowledge that he would rather see her unhappily married than happily single. In truth, that hurt more than the stubborn pain in her back.

———

The next week was agony at work—literally. All she could think about was avoiding any abrupt movement. Sitting on her hard, wood chair exacerbated the soreness; so much so that Kate kept to herself for the first few days, although she knew it puzzled her co-workers. Typically, she was outgoing and friendly. Fortunately, each day the pain lessened a bit more, and by the end of the week she moved more easily, albeit cautiously.

It had occurred to her that city directories might be helpful in her search for her father's paramour. Western Union offices kept them to verify addresses. Her office had a collection of city directories dating back almost twenty years. On her short lunch break Friday, she began looking through them. Using the only clue she had, one that might be wrong, she flipped to the first of the "Andersens" and paused. Sally might be short for "Sarah," and, if she were married, the listing would be under her husband's name. Most listings were, unless a woman ran her own business. As far as she could tell, Andersen was spelled with an "e" instead of an "o" at its end. It shortened the list a bit. But, even then, Kate had only managed to get through three directories when the press of work took her back to her desk.

THIRTY-THREE

The application process for traveling telegrapher turned out to be a snarl of bureaucracy. Kate sent four requests before a blank form finally arrived from New York. Most of the requested information was routine: name, address, age, experience. The latter would not be in her favor, since this was her first job, but she hoped her speed and efficiency would make up for her lack of experience. Still, she suspected men with lower scores still had an advantage.

Next, Kate needed a reference from someone at Western Union. The chain-smoking Mr. McAnarney was hard to gauge. He had asked Kate to train new employees, both men and women, because he did not want to spend the time. She thought he had been pleased with the outcome. Since she had arrived, the piles of waiting telegrams had diminished and work efficiency had improved.

There was more. McAnarney had not realized that in the two months she had worked in the Providence office, she had become the person to whom other telegraphers went with questions or problems. They came with hushed caution when McAnarney was on a break. No one dared threaten his authority. Kate realized she was most at risk if he thought she was trying to outdo him. Still, she hoped she had proved an asset to the company and worthy of a reference. It was a gamble, but she had no choice.

She waited for McAnarney to return from a break to approach him. Everyone had learned it was best to not interrupt him when he was bent over his work.

"Mr. McAnarney, excuse me for bothering you." Kate watched him take his seat on his high stool. "I want to submit an application for traveling telegrapher." She held up the application.

His gray eyes blinked in surprise—his brow squeezed with displeasure. He seemed momentarily at a loss for words.

"Miss Sinclair, that will be one of our most strenuous jobs. Why in the world would it interest you?"

Kate heard the unspoken "you're a woman," in his words. "I like to travel and also to teach." She stood ramrod straight, in the aisle in front of his high desk. Her shirtwaist, with tan stripes and puffed sleeves was tucked into a simple black skirt. She intentionally wore unassuming clothing to fit in with everyone else. Yet, she prided herself on exuding an air of confidence and knowledge. It seemed that most of her co-workers admired her attitude, although she was unsure about McAnarney. He might resent it.

He turned his head to exhale his cigarette smoke so that it would not blow directly in her face. "It requires all sorts of travel and sleeping in hotels."

"Mr. McAnarney, you do remember that I've already traveled quite a bit and am used to sleeping in unfamiliar places?"

Keeping his eyes lowered, he grunted. "Sleeping in hotels is not appropriate for a single woman."

"I took my training in San Francisco, where there are many respectable hotels and rooming houses," she shot back.

He nodded, but showed nothing, not even a flicker of remembering or caring. Kate was not surprised that he knew little about her, or the other employees for that matter. He kept to himself, consumed by his own responsibilities—whatever they were; Kate was not sure.

"It's not only the travel. You have to find ways to improve the offices you visit." He tapped off a half-inch of ash, barely hitting the ashtray, and added, "It's a big responsibility."

Instead of retorting, "And women aren't up to it?" Kate said, "I like to help people learn. You've seen me work with the others here." She stepped back from the exhalations of smoke, choking down a cough. She had made her point. It was she who had trained the most recent telegraphers and, in a way, retrained some of the old ones, while keeping up with her own work.

She paused when another thought occurred to her. *Being valuable might be a reason McAnarney would want me to stay, rather than recommending me for another job.* Either way, she had to take the chance. "All I need is your referral and I can mail this." With a slight smile to take the edge off her persistence, she handed him the completed form and an attached explanation of why she wanted the job.

"Would you like to talk about it after work?" He gave her a cynical look.

"I would be glad to answer any questions you have right now," Kate said, never taking her blue eyes off his gray ones, staring him down so she would not begin to shake. Since her experience with Reverend Johnson, she did not want to be alone with any authoritarian man.

McAnarney sputtered at her reaction. "Here, just put it here," he tapped the receiving-box on the corner of his high desk. "I'll take care of it."

Kate seethed at his reference to an after-work meeting—it insinuated interest in something other than business. Her destiny was in the hands of another officious man. She had no control over what he would say or whether he would send the application.

"Thank you, Mr. McAnarney," she said quietly, but he had already bowed his head over his deskwork. She was tempted to bump his desk and spill his overflowing ashtray, but she noticed the interested eyes of the other telegraphers, undoubtedly curious about her conversation with the head telegrapher. She turned and docilely walked to her desk at the back of the room.

On her walk home after work in the cool damp evening, Kate thought of Frank, as she often did, wanting to know what he had learned about potential Western Union takeover threats. More than that, she wanted his perspective on applying for a new position—if she worked up the courage to tell him. Her promise to herself was to wait to write about it until after she got a response to her application. If she was accepted, she would tell him; if she was rejected, she would not. Anything before that would appear to be asking for help. She was committed to a solitary life. In fairness, she should break off any relationship altogether, but Western Union bound them together—that, and the draw of his personality.

— ·— ·· — — ·

After finishing the dinner her mother had left warming on the stove, and washing the dishes, Kate went upstairs to her bedroom. Frustration over her meeting with McAnarney and his intimidation did not abate. Despite her previous commitment not to write Frank, she needed to communicate with someone, and had a change of heart. She dipped her pen in the ink, imagining what he might be doing three thousand miles away, and began to write. She described Alice's visit, living at home, and what was going on in Providence. Only in the last paragraph did she briefly note that she had applied for the traveling telegrapher position. She hesitated before writing any more. If she told Frank that McAnarney might block the application, Frank might try to do something about it, so she skipped any mention. Nor did she say anything about her overwhelming longing for his presence. With a swirl of hot wax, she sealed the envelope and glued on a stamp before putting it aside, to think about whether she should send it or wait until she heard about the job.

— ·— ·· — — ·

In front of her office in the morning, Kate retrieved the sealed envelope from her purse. Hesitating briefly, she opened the rectangular iron postbox with a clang and dropped the letter in.

THIRTY-FOUR

Kate had established a regular routine. Every morning, she got up early to walk to the Providence Western Union office. She spent ten hours sending, receiving, and typing telegrams in the busy downtown office. On Sunday, she played her role of Respectful Daughter in the same home in which she had grown up. Outwardly, her life was as ordered as a clock in Isaac Hale's watch shop. Inside, however, her mind tumbled with unresolved issues. At present, her life was one of half dependence, half independence. She was not sure the traveling telegraphy job would be hers; in fact, the head telegrapher just might fire her out of spite. Her relationship with Frank was a seesaw between the determination to end it and longing to go forward, all the way. And, since her foray to the attic, the letters from the past now haunted her consciousness. In short, her future hung in a state of uncertainty.

For two weeks, David McAnarney had said not a word about her application. He might have jettisoned it in the trash bin, for all she knew. However, at the beginning of the new work week, Kate passed his desk, saying a perfunctory "good morning." His head snapped up.

"Miss Sinclair, may I have a word with you?" His lips were pursed as he spoke, as if perennially poised to take a drag on his cigarette.

"Of course," Kate said, startled, nerves jumping, but McAnarney offered no more. "Shall I hang up my coat first?"

"Yes, do that." He took a puff of his cigarette. "This won't take long, but by all means, do hang up your coat."

Kate was not sure she had ever met anyone so exasperating. She hung her coat on the branched coat rack near her desk, put her purse in the desk drawer, and returned. The conversation would most likely be about the traveling telegrapher position, and if it was short, as McAnarney professed, she probably did not get it. Or perhaps she would be without a job at all. She sighed in frustration.

"Miss Sinclair, I have a copy of the letter that I assume you'll find in this envelope." He thrust forward an envelope from Western Union.

She took it from him, holding it but not opening it, wondering what was coming next.

"The company is willing to try you as a traveling telegrapher, if that's what you wish." He stubbed out the end his cigarette with a hard twist. "Have you really thought about this?" His eyes were steely gray embers.

Kate's heart pounded so furiously, she had to take a deep breath before she could speak. The job was hers!

"I have, Mr. McAnarney. Traveling interests me and, in addition, I think I can improve business for the company." She tried not to shrink from his gaze.

"Traveling is dangerous for a woman. Your lodging won't be fancy. Life will be lonely," he spat out.

Ignoring his fuming, she slit open the envelope with her index finger and shakily extracted the letter. There was too much detail to read while talking to McAnarney, but she was sure it was an offer. "I have to read it before I understand everything."

"Just so you know . . . I think you're making a mistake, but you can read the letter during your lunch break, not before. Then you can let me know what you decide."

Questions bubbled up. *When would the job start? Where? How much would it pay?* She stuck out her hand with impromptu eagerness. At first McAnarney did not even notice. He then gave her a limp, moist, hand-shake. Everyone else in the office had paused to observe their discussion, likely noticing that Kate looked nervous. They seemed even more curious when she walked to the back of the room and put the letter on top of her desk, a large smile on her face. McAnarney kept his eyes on her. There would be no reading it until noon, and no privacy unless she left the office.

"Is it good news?" whispered Paula, at the next desk, who Kate knew still wondered how "good" meant getting a job that required relocating every few weeks or so.

"I think so," Kate said under her breath. "I won't know anything 'til lunch, when I'm allowed to read it." She rolled her eyes. With a deep breath, she shifted her attention to sending the telegrams that had already piled up.

THIRTY-FIVE

Little translucent balls of ice blew sideways. Sleet—winter's indecision. It stung Kate's cheeks and obscured her vision. She stepped carefully through the slippery accumulation, worried any misstep might send her skidding and reinjure her back. The walk home took twice as long as usual.

Safely inside the front door, she shook her coat, sending drops everywhere, and hung it on a hook, putting her sodden hat and gloves on the shelf above. She then exchanged her wet boots for the dry shoes she had left next to the grandfather clock that morning.

"Kate, thank heavens, you're home." Her mother appeared like an apparition from the dark hallway. "It's dreadful out there. I was worried."

"Brrr, I'm chilled all the way through," Kate shivered. "I hope it's not like this again in the morning."

"Here, come back to the warm kitchen," Eugenia said, leading the way down the hallway. "Your dinner is ready." She paused. "Oh, and you received a letter. I put it on the table."

"Another one?"

"Another? Just one that I know of." Eugenia moved to the stove to ladle chicken noodle and vegetable soup in a bowl. Next to the place setting was an envelope.

Kate slid into her seat and breathed in the fragrant steam curling above the bowl her mother set down. She reached for a piece of warm bread from the basket. "Thank you, Mama." Even without touching the letter, she recognized the neat, forward-slanting handwriting, and her heart skipped a beat.

She took a spoonful. "I don't remember when soup and fresh bread were more welcome."

"I'm glad you like them. Daddy and I had some earlier. The bad weather called for it." Eugenia pulled out a chair and sat across from her. "Are you going to read your letter?"

"Hmm, not yet, I need to get warm first." Kate glanced over at her mother. "I might even save it for upstairs." Kate's mind jangled with the offer from Western Union and the frigid walk home. If she opened Frank's letter with Eugenia nearby, she would have to offer some explanation.

Two bowls of soup warmed and relaxed her, and after helping her mother with the dishes, she excused herself to go upstairs. Donning her nightclothes, she plumped her pillow so she could lie propped up, under her down comforter. Only then did she open Frank's letter.

San Francisco
February 4, 1870

Dear Kate,

It was welcome news that you've applied to be a traveling telegrapher. It suits your teaching ability and natural organization. Best of all, it might connect with the expansion of my own job. It appears Western Union considers the information from my visits around California valuable enough that they want me to expand the method into more states and territories. That will require working with others, possibly traveling telegraphers. They've asked me to come to New York at the end of February to discuss specifics.

I'm desolate from the lack of a dining companion who has an equal fondness for conversation, sherry, and Ghirardelli chocolate.

Let me know if I can help you secure a traveling position.

With affection,
Frank

Kate's heart pounded with joy. When both letters arrived at the same time, she feared they were somehow connected. Frank's was dated after the Western Union letter had been drafted. She had earned the position on her own, not from Frank's intervention.

She re-read the Western Union letter McAnarney had passed on to her in the morning. Both the job description and the pay were to her liking. The provisions of the offer required her to set a date to go to New York for a final interview. If approved, she would receive her first assignment.

Kate put both letters on her night table. There was so much yet to do and learn, but any more contemplation tonight was pointless. She turned off the lantern, and, for the first time in a long time, fell into satisfied sleep.

$$- \cdot - \quad \cdot - \quad - \quad \cdot$$

Two weeks was an impossibly short period of time in which to accomplish everything. Kate wanted to be in New York when Frank was there, and he had said he would be there the end of February. At work in the morning, she approached David McAnarney's desk before walking back to her own. His ashtray was not yet overflowing with ends and ashes.

"Mr. McAnarney, I've decided to accept Western Union's offer to travel."

McAnarney observed her with his gray eyes and gave a little shake of his head. He sighed under his breath but said nothing.

"Thank you for forwarding my application," Kate blurted, trying to get a response from the colorless man. "You probably read that I am to report to the New York office. If it's convenient, I'd like to leave here the last Friday of the month."

"Have you really considered the ramifications, Miss Sinclair?" McAnarney stood facing her at his tall desk, lips pressed together in an irritated, flat line. "If you leave, it's unlikely that I can take you back. By the way, have you finished all your work? Trained the three new ones?"

"Yes, sir. You'll be pleased that all three are doing quite well already. They'll speed up with experience." Kate forced her arms to hang, relaxed, at her side, while she stood on the opposite side of his desk. "I realize it would be unreasonable for you to keep my job open. I would never ask that." *Because I really don't want to ever come back.*

"If you say so," he said, sucking his cigarette into a red tip.

Kate guessed the gamut of what he was thinking: Women should be at home, not working; traveling was equivalent to being a harlot; perhaps, he even resented that she would now have a job equal to his, with more flexibility.

"Please let me know if there's anything in particular you would like me to do before I leave. I still have almost two weeks." Turning, Kate smiled as she walked back to her desk, feeling as if a gate had blown open, freeing her to explore the wider world.

─── ·─ ─ ·

Revealing her new venture to her parents was problematic. Traveling to distant places and staying alone in strange places would bewilder them, at the least. They might worry that it would call into question her reputation, especially among their friends. Kate needed to tell them soon, but it would have to wait for another day. It was Tuesday. Her father would be at his usual, late business meeting. She paused. *Business meeting?* The letters had raised questions about how exactly Will spent his Tuesdays. He might be working, or he might be with Sally. The relationship had lasted decades. There was even implication that Will had considered leaving Eugenia for Sally.

Kate wanted more than anything to understand what had happened between her parents. Did her father love Sally as much as he loved her mother, or more? Was it ignorance or determined acceptance on her mother's part? Kate's temples throbbed. Not knowing the whole truth tormented her. The secrets of the letters, long held in abeyance, had burned their way in her mind, like acid eating into her psyche.

Kate was determined to follow her one lead of Andersen with an "e" until it ran out. The opportunity to look through Providence's city directories would disappear once she was assigned to an office somewhere else in the country. She must use every brief lunch break to trace Sally.

By Wednesday, she could no longer delay. Her parents had to be told about her new job. She went straight to her father's study when she returned from work. Will and Eugenia had already eaten. "Father, I wonder if you would be so kind as to pour Mama and me a glass of sherry, and join me before I eat."

He looked up from his newspapers, probably financial reports. "Just give me a minute to finish and I'll be in." He adjusted his spectacles, his expression unchanged, and went back to his reading. Kate was not sure if he was curious or resentful about her interrupting his routine.

There was no doubt about Eugenia. She was curious. "Is this something about your letter?" She looked eager as she faced Kate. "You never said anything after it arrived."

"No, Mama; I want to tell you about some changes to my job," Kate said quickly, to dispel the notion of a possible beau. "Father said he'd be in shortly. He said he'd bring us each a glass of sherry. I'll go build a fire in the parlor and we can sit in there."

Flames made dancing reflections on the white porcelain tiles outlining the hearth. Eugenia and Kate sat on the horsehair settee, Will on a maple-framed leather chair. There wasn't tension between her parents, just distance, or, perhaps, indifference. Kate tried to remember if she had ever noticed passion between the two, but she could not. They rarely touched each other.

"I want to tell you about something new at work. I'm going to have a different job. It's called a traveling telegrapher. I'll be given short-term assignments at offices in other cities, to stay a week or more to make improvements." She ignored the sound of her father sucking in his breath. "It's much more responsibility—I earned it with my skills," she said, pausing to take a sip of sherry. "I go to New York the end of this month. After that, I'll receive my first assignment."

"Kate, I forbid it," Will erupted. "I can't have a daughter of mine galivanting around who knows where."

Kate kept her tone respectful but firm. "You know how I like to travel, and I've found a way for business to pay for it."

The lines around Eugenia's eyes deepened. "Kate, I agree with Daddy, it sounds daring—almost promiscuous."

You might ask your husband about promiscuous. Kate kept her thoughts to herself and her eyes steady. "Most of my days will be spent at work. Don't worry, Mama, Western Union will provide for my lodging at a reputable place."

"And then what?" Eugenia's voice trembled. "It sounds so lonely! You'll have no hope of meeting any nice, young gentlemen."

"In a way, my age is what makes this job appealing. I need to travel while I still can. This gives me an opportunity to see places and meet new people."

"But, Kate, you may not have a chance to . . . settle down." Dismay aged Eugenia.

Kate reined in her emotions. If she became defensive, the conversation would turn into the same old argument. Her mother wanted her to get married; and yet, Eugenia's own relationship was one of broken trust—whether she knew it or not. Her father believed all respectable women were married, but his respect for her mother—Sally, too—was questionable. Ever since she'd found those letters, long ago, Kate had viewed her parents' marriage as a case against making a marriage contract, not for it. The three of them were dancing a dance of caution to avoid the disharmony of a quarrel—each to a different tune, driven by the beat of his or her own music.

"I'm fortunate to have this offer. I need to try it. If it doesn't suit me, I'll go back to being a telegrapher . . . or even a teacher again." Kate let the remainder of her sherry slide down her throat. Peace would be maintained, even if nothing had been agreed on.

THIRTY-SIX

The morning Kate boarded a train in Providence for New York City, fat gray clouds hung in the sky, threatening to spit snow. She wore boots, wool socks, long underwear, scarf, overcoat, gloves, and a wool hat, in an attempt to allay the temperature, not expected to reach above freezing in either city. Through a series of free telegraphs—allowed by Western Union for company business—she and Frank had agreed to meet for lunch and spend the afternoon together. Despite herself, she could not wait to see him and discuss her new job before her appointment in the main office the next morning.

Carrying only a satchel for her two-night stay, she stepped off the train in the terminal near Madison Square and joined the throng of people milling about, looking for signs to the lobby and paid transportation. Two rail cars up from hers, she saw him, standing, square shouldered and alert, watching passengers exit the train. Spotting her, he walked down the platform in long, rapid steps. Kate did not even think of propriety. Her body reacted unhesitatingly, propelling her toward him to wrap her arms around his broad shoulders and inhale his clean scent. She leaned against him, astonished by her lack of restraint.

"What a nice surprise to see you, Frank! Did you think I couldn't find my own way?" She kidded.

"To say it's good to see *you* would be an understatement," he said, separating from her and resettling his hat. Kate ignored two nearby women, openly tut-tutting at her public display of affection. She would not let a couple of old biddies ruin her reunion with this wonderful man.

"Here, let me carry your bag," he said grasping it firmly.

"How nice not to have to worry about transportation. Thanks."

He crooked his elbow for her hand. "I have a hack waiting out front to take you to your hotel. I've been here for two days, so I know a little about the city. We'll pass by the office on the way to your hotel, so you'll know where to find it in the morning. My hotel is not far away. We both know Western Union's rule about separate lodging for men and women." He paused, the interior gaslights glinting off his brown-flecked green eyes. "I can't say there *are* other women travelers." He gave an amused, endearingly crooked smile.

—·— ·— — ·

Time passed quickly as Kate and Frank reacquainted themselves, and before Kate knew it, they were ordering bowls of fish stew and crusty bread for lunch in her hotel's dining room. The décor was spare: uncarpeted wood floors, thin white table coverings, and lightweight curtains framing the simple windows. It was frugal, but clean, and the waiters did not appear to object to their lingering in conversation for over an hour after their bowls were empty.

"Most of what I'm going to tell you won't be important for your meeting tomorrow," Frank said, "but some background might help."

"I'm a woman in a man's world. I need all the information I can get." Kate knew from experience that what Frank had to say would be detailed. All of it might not prove pertinent to her job, but it would be informative. She relaxed, now that her traveling was over, and simply enjoyed his presence.

He told her that Western Union's president, William Orton, had an office in the building she would visit, although he would not be part of her routine hiring and assignment meeting. Orton had come to the company after Western Union bought U. S. Telegraph Company and American Telegraph and Company with an exchange of stock in 1866. The company had since moved from Rochester to its current building at one-forty-five Broadway, in New York City.

"Was that the end of Western Union's competition?" Kate asked.

"The last major competitors—although there are still a few other, smaller independent ones. Orton's a smart man with a law degree, but his principal focus is business. He's innovative, too—he helped develop the ticker that runs on the stock exchange floor."

Kate had read of the specially developed machines that sent and received stock prices via telegraph lines and printed the information out on a long tape, using a series of alphabetic symbols and numbers. "They can send a company's name and stock price, can't they?" She blushed at Frank's admiring look.

"Exactly," he said. "Messengers are being replaced by the ticker tape, but sooner or later, that will disappear as well. Within a year, it should be possible to wire money electronically, rather than information alone."

"Mind boggling. All of that should help Western Union, I would think."

"It does," he nodded. "Even so, competition doesn't go away. It may come from a different source . . . another company . . . technology . . . or it might come from powerful men, wanting to control and manipulate the telegraph."

"Like Gould?" Kate asked.

"Men like Gould," Frank soberly agreed.

"Where does Gould stand now?"

"Quiet, but lurking. He hasn't taken any action lately, that we know of, but he hasn't gone away, of that, we can be sure. Gould is always interested in manipulating technology for a profit." Frank pulled the gold pocket watch from his vest. "Kate, I have a proposal. We're both busy all day tomorrow with our own appointments. What would you say to spending a couple hours this afternoon at the Museum of Natural History? It would keep us out of the frigid weather."

"I've never been," Kate said, happily surprised. "That's exactly what I'd like to do."

"And dinner afterward? We need to see if Ghirardelli has made it this far east," Frank said with a chuckle.

THIRTY-SEVEN

After her busy day at Western Union, Kate had bathed quickly and slid on a silky, heather-green dress with a slim bodice and box-pleated skirt, cinched in at the top to accentuate her small waist. Looking in her mirror, she was pleased with the results. It would be the first time Frank had seen her in anything other than travel clothing or winter woolens. And this would be their third meal together in less than three days.

She was rewarded for her pains. As she removed her heavy wool coat and scarf at the restaurant, Frank inhaled audibly and grinned.

"I now know why beauty is called breathtaking." He scooted her chair up to the table after she sat, then took his own across from her. "Truthfully, I like your company whether you're in wool or silk." He unfolded his napkin and placed it on his lap. "And I'm especially interested in your meeting today. Tell me about it as we eat."

After the waiter had taken their orders, and a stemmed glass of sherry and a tumbler of whiskey were in front of them, Kate began to explain. Much of her time had been spent waiting. It took a while for an employee to set up a test for her on the telegraph key. Kate had returned to the waiting room while her speed and accuracy were graded. She had passed. The next test asked her to explain in writing what she would do in special situations, such as non-payment or running out of supplies, or other problems that might arise. She waited again. After receiving praise about the results of both tests, she had to wait for someone to discuss her assignment. Of course, by then, that someone was taking his lunch break.

"While I was sitting with nothing to do," Kate flashed a look of annoyance, "I saw a medium-sized man, with a curly beard and receding hairline, dressed in a fine-looking cravat and waistcoat, go in and out of the office, twice. I heard someone say, 'Good day, Mr. Orton.' So, now I can say I've seen the president of Western Union."

"Well, you're one up on me. I'm surprised you didn't introduce yourself."

"Frank, you know I wouldn't . . ." She looked at his mischievous eyes and rolled hers in mock annoyance.

"What happened next?" he asked, chuckling. "What about the assignment?"

She told him the next meeting had been with Rodney Jackson, who she described as a weasel-faced man with darting eyes and narrow shoulders. His waxed mustache was as tasteless as his ill-fitting suit. He asked her to follow him to his office, which was little bigger than a broom closet with two chairs on either side of a scarred desk. He begrudgingly acknowledged that her successful scores qualified her as a traveling telegrapher.

"You know, Frank," she shifted in her seat, "he gave me a doubtful look, as if I somehow managed to have a man take the test in my place."

Frank shook his head in sympathy. "And then what?"

Rodney Jackson had told her Western Union would inform her, by telegram, of each assignment: location, work to be accomplished, and estimated length of stay. Offices could be those just opening, rapidly expanding, or those receiving complaints. Kate's visits would be anywhere from a few days, to up to a month, in the case of offices needing to be reorganized or cities with many offices. Western Union would secure her lodging, while Kate was responsible for arranging meals and transportation. Expenses would be reimbursed according to guidelines. Pay would arrive in the mail, although Rodney Jackson had said it wouldn't be long before funds could be wired directly to a bank.

"I had questions after his explanation," Kate said. "The fidgety little man answered most of them, although he was vague about how I would get offices to comply with what I recommend."

Their waiter had removed the empty dinner dishes, and was setting down small plates of ginger cake in pooled lemon sauce. They were not surprised that the restaurant had not known about Ghirardelli.

Frank shooed the waiter away, obviously keen to have his say. "Kate, I'm sorry about your treatment, but the job is what I imagined it might be." His words almost bounced with eagerness. "We might be able to benefit each other. Would you be willing to listen to an idea or two?" He started eating his dessert, giving her time to consider.

"Ideas about my job?"

Frank nodded.

"Even though the weasel resented that a woman got the job, it sounds all sewn up. What ideas are you talking about?"

"Did Mr. Weasel say where you would go first?"

Kate laughed, flicking her white cotton napkin toward him at his sense of humor. "Mr. Jackson thought it would be Boston, with a stay of two weeks. I'll know in a day or two."

Frank tipped forward slightly and looked at her steadily as he spoke. "You know that I visit telegraph offices to make sure they are running smoothly, to keep Western Union competitive. Reconnaissance is part of it," he frowned. "Travel connections and eating alone gets old, but I like meeting people and seeing new places."

She nodded with a smile, thinking of the similarities to her new job.

"In a way, people with my job identify the need for traveling telegraphers." His eyes sparked with a lively fire. "Why not work together? Pass along information as to which office needs help and which is an asset."

"Work together?" Her forehead scrunched. "I don't see—"

"If we were both in the same region, I would identify offices for you to travel to, and once there, you would gather information. I think I could also arrange for you to have breaks between assignments."

"Time to explore?" Thoughts cartwheeled through her mind.

"Of course, you wouldn't get paid for free time."

Kate was trying to absorb the possibilities. She had been told that there might be times without assignments . . . without pay. Frank's comments suggested that she might choose to take a block of time off. It would depend upon what offices needed attention.

"For the most part, I like being a telegrapher. The pay means independence and adding to my savings, but ten hours in the office leaves me no time to do anything else. Often shops and other places I want to visit are closed on Sundays." She pushed away her half-eaten ginger cake. "The dessert is good but doesn't compare to . . . Ghirardelli." She had almost said, "our chocolate."

Frank nodded. Kate knew he was trying to decipher her emotions before continuing. He had told her before that he considered her the most competent, self-sufficient woman he had ever met. He admired her genuine interest in business, politics, and understanding of the way things worked.

"Kate," he finally said, as if she questioned the veracity of the plan, "what I'm proposing is on the up-and-up. Adding free time would mean starting a new assignment a day or two after the previous one ended, instead of right away."

"Is it possible?" Kate asked. The thought of a job of substance with a few days between assignments to learn about a location tantalized her.

"I think it is, if I convince managers that you're adding information of value, in addition to doing your job. Days between assignments are just logistics."

Kate's cheeks warmed with color. "Frank, whenever we meet, you come up with a new idea. It's astounding." She pressed her eyes closed and slumped back in her chair. "And I don't mean to sound ungrateful. What you say has merit." She pulled up straight again. "No, no, not merit—it sounds too good to be true. When my friend, Alice, brought her children to visit her parents in Providence, I only got to see them for part of a day. Why? Because of work. Who knows when they will be back again, or if I will ever be in Colorado Territory? It was heartbreaking. And I haven't seen much of my closest friends in Providence since beginning work either."

"Long hours are a complaint I hear wherever I go. That, and loneliness at the single-employee offices, especially in rural areas." Frank noticed a crumb on his vest, and flicked it away. "Some of the more enterprising solo telegraphers have local residents visit the office, and it sometimes becomes a kind of community hub—imagine that." Frank beamed. "Clever! We can be clever, too."

"There is so much to consider. What should we do next?" Exhaustion from two eventful days made Kate lose focus.

"I'll be in New York until the end of the week, when I return to California. That gives me time to approach one of the executives I've met with before about the idea. Generally, it's the local manager who makes decisions."

Frank reached across the table and took Kate's hand, which she gave him willingly. "This arrangement may mean that we will get to see each other more frequently. It wouldn't be often . . . at least, not often enough for me, but it's better than you being in Providence and me in San Francisco."

Kate absorbed the warmth and strength of his hand, not ever wanting to let go. Yet, running through her mind was the advantage of being on opposite coasts—*no temptation*. The more time spent with the desirable Frank, the more likely she would be to let down her guard about not getting involved.

"Frank, it has been a lovely evening, with so many possibilities." She gently retracted her hand. "I am grateful for everything you've done." Kate looked across at his mesmerizing eyes. With all that had happened the last two days, she could barely hold hers open. "Will you forgive me if I ask you to take me to my hotel? My train back to Providence leaves early in the morning."

"Of course," Frank stood up to pull back her chair. As always, other diners had thinned to almost nothing, as one word added to another in Kate's and Frank's conversation. "I'll contact you about what we discussed?" he asked.

"Yes," Kate nodded. "I would like that very much. Thank you." She put her hand in the crook of his arm, her pulse accelerating.

THIRTY-EIGHT

The first of the pale-yellow envelopes that would soon become familiar bearers of future assignments arrived at her parents' home. It told Kate to report to Boston the following Wednesday, for approximately two weeks. Instructions were brief: make a thorough report of the main office with suggestions for improvements. She smiled at the last sentence. *Frank was right; there are similarities between our jobs.*

There was a knock at her bedroom door. "Kate, may I come in?"

"It's unlocked, Mama."

Seeing Kate reading a telegram, Eugenia gasped. "Is everything all right?"

"Don't worry, Mama. A telegram isn't just for bad news." Kate stood up and hugged her. "This is the way I'll be notified where my next post will be."

"But telegrams are so expensive."

"Not for Western Union," Kate laughed. "Let's go down to the kitchen and have tea while I tell you about it. They aren't sending me very far—Boston—they probably don't trust me yet, because I'm a woman."

"That's odd, Kate. I was at a suffrage meeting in Boston just before you came home in December." Kate and Eugenia started down the stairs as Eugenia continued. "Remember the first edition of the newspaper I was reading last week? It started in January." In the kitchen, Eugenia shoveled a chunk of coal to the fire to make the stove hot enough to boil water.

Kate knew the newspaper Eugenia referred to. Over dinner one evening, Kate had noticed a copy of the *Women's Journal* her mother had left behind on the kitchen table. Published by the leader of the American Woman Suffrage Association, Lucy Stone, and her husband, Henry Browne Blackwell, the purpose of the eight-page weekly was to persuade state governments to expand or grant women's right to vote. The author of that issue was a Negress, Frances Ellen Watkins Harper. She argued that *all* women should be able to vote. It was something Kate agreed with, but had been too busy to join the movement.

Kate's head shook involuntarily at her strong-minded mother's view that it was important for women to have a voice and a vote, while at the same time asserting that a woman's role was to be married and follow her husband's dictates. *Did Mama believe extramarital affairs were acceptable? Did Father think it was wrong for women to have a voice?* Kate shook her head again. Both were untenable.

"Here's your tea, Kate." Eugenia put down the steamy oolong. "What are you thinking about? You look like you're in another world."

"Thanks, Mama. Just thinking." Kate dropped a sugar cube in her cup and swirled it until rising heat from the tea made her spoon handle too hot to touch. She thought of Frank and wondered where he might go next.

"Kate, do you think this will harm your reputation, all this traveling? It may appear unseemly."

"Mama," Kate laughed gently. "Your suffragists travel frequently when they give speeches about women voting."

"I suppose so. Modern women are a different breed, aren't they? My generation always had chaperones."

Or better yet, a husband.

—·— ·— — ·

Before Kate left Providence for her Boston assignment, she and Eugenia hosted an afternoon party for friends she knew from school and volunteer work. It was Eugenia's idea, and Kate welcomed it. This would be a party of close friends rather than the "at homes" that included many women she did not know.

The sound of lively feminine voices reminiscing about growing up and going to school together filled the Sinclair home. Kate had always been admired for her high grades and seminary degree. Now, her job as telegrapher was a fascination. She talked and laughed until she had little voice left. Regret filled her as she hugged each of the women goodbye, not knowing when she would see them again. As she and Frank had discussed, free time was a rare commodity in the life she had chosen, and from here on, it would be even more scarce.

Kate and Eugenia were in the kitchen putting away the delicate good china when her mother said, "Kate, I think I had as much fun seeing your friends as you did. I'm glad we included their mothers. We had many good times when you were growing up."

"They remembered activities I hadn't thought about for years," Kate smiled. "And ribbed me about things I'd forgotten. I guess I was known as being pretty serious."

"And greatly respected."

Kate sighed. "It would be so easy to go to teas once a week and talk about bonnets and frocks, but that wouldn't make me happy for long."

"Most of them volunteer for worthwhile causes," Eugenia countered. "And, I do too. You're being unfair."

Kate met her mother's eyes, and for once backed down. She had not meant to disparage her friends. "You're right. I'm having trouble synchronizing my life with the people I've cared about for a long time. They all have obligations to their children and husbands, and still make time to volunteer. They have a schedule just like I do, but mine with Western Union is more rigid."

"None of us can have everything," Eugenia retorted, but after a brief hesitation changed the subject. "Are you all set for Boston?"

Kate suspected the original statement had deeper meaning than Eugenia wanted to pursue, and maybe she did not either.

"Almost. Even *I* should do a little shopping." She glanced at her mother, worried her remark sounded like criticism again. "I don't own much other than travel clothes. Oh well." She shrugged. "Maybe that's all I need. After all, I'm a *traveling* telegrapher."

Before leaving Western Union's Providence office for good, Kate finished examining twenty years of city directories. All told, in Providence, there were eleven Andersens—no Sally or Sarah—with three listings beginning with the single initial "S," and one with an "H," which she had included since there were two references to an "H" in Sally's letters. Kate carefully noted the applicable addresses in the back of her travel journal. Now that she had all four addresses, she wondered what she was going to do with them—and when.

THIRTY-NINE

Boston was monochromatic, the sun hidden in a typical New England winter sky. Kate was excited to get started with her new responsibilities. The Western Union office on the south side of Boston was large, employing eighteen telegraphers.

"Miss Sinclair, I'm Ross James, the head telegrapher here," the heavyset man said, holding open the Western Union office door at the Old Colony Terminus. "New York telegraphed the time you were expected. Here, I'll take your satchel for you and hang up your coat." His thick jowls appeared even wider thanks to curly, russet side whiskers. "I see you haven't been to your hotel yet. Do you need a break?"

"A break?" Kate puzzled.

"You know," he said, avoiding her eyes, "to clean up."

"Oh, you mean a toilet." She almost laughed at his embarrassment. "Not yet, thank you just the same."

"When . . . if you do," he stammered, "there's one down the back hall at the station. This one here is for men."

Kate glanced at the rows of telegraphers, who were giving her nervous, sidelong looks. Only three were women.

After hanging up her coat, James sat across from her at a small, round table. He looked at her with troubled eyes. "Miss Sinclair, exactly what is it that you want?" He fidgeted with his pencil. "I'll be honest. I don't need anyone telling me how to do my job, especially a woman."

Kate had thought ahead of how her visits might be perceived—she expected concern about losing a job and resentment over being judged by a woman. It was much easier for Frank to visit offices, followed by a trip to a nearby bar for drink and banter, all the while gaining trust and casually asking well-targeted questions.

"Mr. James." Kate looked directly at him with a smile she hoped looked friendly. "Western Union has asked me to visit various offices to see what we can learn. Then, when I go to other offices, I may take along the good ideas that I've gained."

"Oh," James' chunky shoulders relaxed a bit. "I didn't take it that way. Come to think of it, I'm not surprised they sent you here." He looked relieved and a little puffed up.

"I'm sure I'll learn quite a lot while I'm here," Kate said, trying to keep amusement out of her eyes at his changed demeanor.

"Has the number of telegrams increased in . . . let's say, a year?" Kate kept her question neutral.

"Hmmm," James muttered, scratching his wiry side whiskers. "I don't know offhand, but the ledger book would tell us." His eyes widened. "It would take a lot of doing to figure it out."

"Let's not worry about that now. I'm going to be here for two weeks, so we have time. Would you mind if I interviewed each of the operators?"

Suspicion clouded his eyes. "What for?"

"Good ideas," she told him.

Kate could tell he was not completely convinced, but he agreed.

_ ._ ._ _ _ .

Kate spent much of the next two weeks at the round table James had turned over to her for work. Interviewing the telegraphers was more difficult than she had imagined. Each had a different story about what brought him or her to the job. A few were forthcoming, relaying current and past work experiences in detail, obviously enjoying permission for conversation rather than work. Most were reticent. Kate was not sure if it was by nature or because they did not want to disclose anything that might harm their job, and most of the men were offended by questions from a woman. At lunch breaks, talk was freer—about their lives, or even gossip about past employees and the company, if Ross James was not there. Kate mostly listened, occasionally adding a comment, trying to gain their confidence; too often the men grouped together, away from the women.

During work time, she offered friendly suggestions from her growing experience to improve efficiency. Even the men had to listen because she represented Western Union and could be a factor in whether they kept their jobs or not. Women were more receptive to new ideas. Almost by accident, women became examples when they made the improvements Kate suggested. The men then followed, just to keep up.

Her biggest coup came when she asked, "Mr. James, you said information about the number of telegraphs was in the ledger. I need to make comparisons over time."

"I'm sorry Miss Sinclair," he muttered. "I'm much too busy to do that kind of thing."

"Don't trouble yourself with it. I'd be glad to do the calculations."

James looked her up and down, doubtfully. "I don't know, I don't think you'd understand much of it."

"All I need to do is spend time adding some of the numbers."

Ross James looked frustrated. "Alright, I guess there's no harm."

"Thank you. I'll work as fast as possible, I greatly appreciate it," Kate told him, restraining a cheer that she had access to the office ledgers.

FORTY

Upon her return to Providence, Kate had had the blessed luxury of free time—and unpaid break until her next assignment. She was peacefully cocooned in her comfortable bedroom, relieved not to have to jump out of bed, catch a train, or go to work. Until this pause, she had not realized how weary she was. The last two months had been hectic and stressful, with tests, interviews, travel, and working through the resistance to suggested changes at telegraph offices. During her Boston assignment, Western Union had sent her to three additional offices for short visits. Many of the men she'd met had been indignant about a woman interfering—she had no right—business was a man's world.

During the day, she had been surrounded by the cacophony of voices and clacking machines. After work, her life was silent and void of human connection. She had been at loose ends, in an unfamiliar setting, without the comfort of familiarity. Reading books or writing letters or in her journal helped fill time. She had known the sense of loneliness would only increase. In the future, distance would preclude respite at home.

After eating alone every night for two weeks, in and around Boston, Kate relished her parents' familiar company at dinner. Eugenia served sizzling, crumb-crusted cod, sweet potatoes, and cinnamon-laced applesauce. Her parents' reaction was guarded about her new job, but they made an effort to ask polite questions about her trip to Boston.

"How do you know if an office is 'up to snuff,' as you call it?" Will wanted to know.

"Through the numbers and talking to people. It took a while for me to be able to do either. At first the managers didn't want me to look at their ledgers, and people didn't trust I was there to help."

"Were you the only woman in the offices you visited, Kate?" Eugenia asked. "That must have been difficult if you were."

"There were a few in each office, and they were definitely easier to talk to, although even that took time." Kate gritted her teeth, remembering what an effort it was to get information.

"Do the women telegraphers believe women should vote?"

Kate laughed. "I didn't think to ask, but I will next time."

She had hungrily finished her food and asked for seconds. She had not eaten much in Boston.

"Are they paid as much as men?" Eugenia asked.

"I wish I could tell you." Kate shifted in her chair uncomfortably, regretting the unclear answer. "When I finally got the ledgers, the figures didn't really tell whether higher pay went to men because they had been with Western Union the longest or just because they were men. I confirmed that all the men made more than the women. What I was really after, and will be in the future, was how well each of the offices I visit operates. There are all sorts of ways to calculate the figures, I'm discovering, and it makes it hard to get to the truth." Kate looked from one parent to the other. Supposedly, she had been given the job because of her abilities; at that moment, describing figures that could disguise actualities did not make her appear competent.

"Kate," her father said impatiently. "I completely understand why these men don't want a woman snooping through their ledgers. They aren't your concern." His face flushed, the way it did when he was annoyed.

"But, that's the point, Father. Western Union wants to know this information and has given me the job of finding out. I can't assess a business, which is what I've been asked to do, unless I can see an accounting for it."

"We know you're trying hard, Kate," Eugenia interrupted, "but where is all this going to lead? It seems you've headed down an impossible path. With all these long hours and traveling, there's no time for you to be with other people."

Of course, by "other people," Eugenia meant *men*.

I have met a man. A man who shows me respect and gives me support. But is that enough?

"Maybe Daddy is right. This might not be a job for a woman."

Kate sighed. Eugenia, in her own way, was trying to calm any discord.

"Whether I'm working with men or women, nothing can be accomplished without information. Women have the right to learn just like men." She ground her teeth, longing to get up from the table, but that was against the rules. Civility was the watchword, especially if you were a woman.

—·— ·— — ·

The first full morning of what was supposed to be a hiatus from work, Kate spent at her desk outlining what she had learned about the Boston telegraph offices. She yearned to discuss her ideas with Frank. His experience would add the perspective she did not yet have. Her businessman father might have been helpful, but she could not ask him. He would see that only as weakness, proof Kate was in over her head.

No, she would have to do her best on her own. She experimented with a couple of ideas until she came up with a framework for the information she'd gathered in Boston. Ideally, she could use it in other cities, as she learned what was relevant to assessing and assisting an office. Her trial form had places for financial data from the ledger, as well as her observations on what made an office function well, or bogged it down. Since the position of traveling telegrapher was a new one, she really was not sure exactly what the managers of Western Union wanted. They might not know exactly either. Kate wanted to demonstrate that her visit had merit. Any reason she gave them to think otherwise would put her out of a job.

Finished with work, she caught up with her daily journal, wrote a letter to Alice, and then indulged in a long one to Frank. First, she explained the rationale for her approach to assessing Boston, asking him what he thought she had forgotten. Then, her words became more personal. She wrote candidly about the tension between the convenience of living at home and its constraints. Before she knew it, her crystal inkpot had run dry. There were four pages! She leaned back in her chair and stretched her arms, flexing and unflexing her hands, relaxing cramped muscles. Pressing a letter opener across the folds to flatten them, she coerced the lengthy missive into an envelope and sealed it with her insignia on hot red wax.

After that, she retrieved her travel journal from the shelf. She drew a circle around the four addresses she'd centered her search around, still uncertain what she would do with them. She smoothed a clean sheet of paper on the blotter and sketched a rudimentary city map, painstakingly entering major streets, then the streets of the address. She then marked each address. If she knocked at one of the doors, what exactly would she say? If there was no Sally, she could apologize and explain she had the wrong address. Finding Sally, however, created a different scenario. She was not ready to knock on any of the doors and introduce herself as Will's daughter.

FORTY-ONE

Two brief telegrams arrived the next day; both needed deciphering. One was from Frank: WU APPROVED COORDINATING INFORMATION LETTER FOLLOWS FRANK. She knew this referred to the conversation at dinner about Frank coordinating with traveling telegraphers—Kate in particular. More details were necessary before she fully understood how this would work. She wondered if he would be her supervisor. Would they work in the same city? Would she see him regularly? Her stomach fluttered at the thought. She looked down at his words, pasted on the buttery paper. Kate knew he had not yet received her latest letter. Her gaze drifted up to the painted enamel box where she kept all his letters. Her breath caught when she thought of the comparison. She saved letters just as her father had. Did he do it because of his deep affection for Sally, she wondered. The letters continued to tangle her mind.

The second telegram came from Western Union, instructing her to be in Philadelphia on the following Monday, for a two-week review of the main office. It included the name of her hotel and a final sentence: BOSTON REPORT RECEIVED. Kate re-read the perfunctory message. Telegraphs were notoriously brief, but some comment on her report would have been useful. It raised questions and answered little. Was what she sent what they wanted? Did the lack of guidance stem from their not knowing exactly what they wanted, or was it intended to thwart her efforts?

Kate did not worry over it too long. Soon, she would be traveling again. A shiver of anticipation rippled through her; Philadelphia was a city she had never visited.

—·— ·— — ·

Twelve days' work in Philadelphia went quickly, with the expected challenges to what Kate asked to look at and slow access to information. She had not accomplished all she wanted, but made some inroads with suggestions, which pleased her.

Saturday and Sunday had been free for her to explore Philadelphia. She had stayed in the same hotel room and paid for the extra days with her own funds. The desk clerk at the modest hotel had been eager to tout his city. As with touring in San Francisco, she made a list of what she wanted to see most and plotted a route to make efficient use of the distances. After sitting in an office for two weeks, being outside in mild spring weather felt like an escape. Everywhere forsythia and witch hazel burst with new leaves, and cherry trees burst with blossoms. Daffodils and tulips in front of Philadelphia's memorable, historic architecture added welcoming splotches of spring color. For two days she filled every minute exploring Philadelphia—walking to sites invigorated her. The extra free days were everything she hoped for.

The last evening, Kate sat in her cramped hotel room, working. At the back of a notebook, she kept track of her expenses, both those to be reimbursed and those not. Her report on Philadelphia took several hours. She put it in an envelope to mail at the railroad station before boarding her train to New Haven—her next destination.

The trip from Philadelphia to New Haven was a series of frustrating missed connections. She spent the morning breathlessly racing from one platform to another, only to find a train was canceled for repairs or other unspecified reasons. Each time meant a long walk back to the terminal to re-route her trip. When she finally arrived, late in the day in New Haven, she only had time to briefly introduce herself and say she would return in the morning before the Western Union office closed.

For the next weeks, Kate saw little but the inside of crowded telegraph offices, with their constant clacking, and her hotel room, with its fussy wallpaper and endless odor of stale food and cigarette smoke. She could have been in any city in the country. The frantic pace and lack of free time left her tired and discouraged.

—.— .— — .

Each office experience added to Kate's ability to spot inefficiencies. The offices in Boston, Philadelphia, and New Haven were short of staff and struggled to keep up. When Kate's suggestions made work easier, telegraphers became receptive, although, more often by women than men. As she had learned before, men grudgingly changed their practices only when they saw women getting ahead. And, when dealing with the head telegraphers, Kate framed her suggestions with hints that the results would bring a favorable report to the New York headquarters.

Kate had a second revelation after several assignments. The distance between an office and New York headquarters gave head telegraphers considerable freedom. They were accustomed to little oversight. Reports they sent to the corporate headquarters were filed without scrutiny unless customer complaints aroused attention. Even then, Western Union management was slow to react, believing the company was doing a public service and people should be grateful. Kate's visits upset the freedom head telegraphers were used to, aggravating their resentment of a "bossy woman."

Despite the struggle to obtain information and time-consuming travel with delays and missed connections, Kate found her new job satisfying. Meeting new people and seeing different places were worth the hassles. She liked the puzzle of solving problems and seeing the results of her work benefit the organization.

FORTY-TWO

Not until late May did Frank's plan for the two of them to work in the same location materialize. He had arranged for a month-long stint in the railroad and telegraph hub of Chicago. The iridescent blue of Lake Michigan dominated the landscape. Kate's hotel, the five-story Adam House was adjacent to Chicago's largest building, the intercity Great Central Railroad Station, with its offices above the passenger depot, including a telegraph office. The eight-track rail house sat just beyond. Frank stayed at a similar-sized lodging, the City Hotel, a short walk from Kate's hotel.

Her trusty guidebook stated Chicago's population was almost 300,000—nearly triple the number of a decade before. Immigrants accounted for half, and different languages filled the air wherever she went. It was even more crowded than New York, making getting from one place to another like walking a tightrope. Kate carefully stepped up on the wood-planked walkways, jockeying for position with masses of others. She had to concentrate on each step just to maintain her balance. One unexpected bump might propel her down into the street and, quite possibly, mire her in mud.

Every evening, after their day at separate offices, Kate delightedly met Frank for dinner. He sat across from her, strong, square, and earnest. He picked low-cost places to eat that would not raise the eyebrows of those in Western Union who reviewed their expenses. It surprised her how pleasurable she found it to see him every evening—to be able to discuss business, or anything else.

—·— ·— — — ·

"You were right about the offices being a hodgepodge. The one I saw today is well-organized but has little knowledge of what other offices are doing. Coordination would help," Kate said.

"Chicago has grown, helter-skelter, into the country's largest city. Businesses have a hard time keeping up."

"What caused such rapid growth—railroads?" Kate took off her hat, put it on the extra chair next to his, and smoothed her hair. Her hat was the latest fashion, without a crown, only a slight elevation in the center and a small brim that pushed forward to the hairline. Ribbons at the side tied under her chin to anchor it.

"Railroads are part of it," Frank said. "I'd say it's inventions in general—like the telegraph."

Kate took a bite of the roll she had buttered. It was stale, but that came as no surprise. Food in restaurants that fit their budgets was frequently unappetizing. Determinedly, she chewed and swallowed. "I'm only beginning to understand all the ways the telegraph has changed things. I'm lucky to be involved. You said inventions. What are others?"

"Surprisingly many. For example, it wasn't long ago that cattle had to be shipped alive to eastern cities. When it became more efficient to butcher them here, in Chicago, meat could be sent, but only in cold, winter weather. With the invention of refrigerated cars, butchers can now send meat off the carcasses year-round. And the market is booming.

People are consuming as much as can be shipped. Chicago is the beef capital of the nation."

Kate shook her head. "I would have never put two and two together about refrigeration and growth. Listening to you is always so . . . enlightening."

"And there is nothing better than having someone intelligent and responsive to talk to—beauty doesn't hurt either." He gave his endearing crooked grin, before she could react. "Do you have energy for a little work now that we've finished eating?"

"Certainly," she looked around the dining room. The waiters had already removed their plates, glasses, silverware, and even the napkins, and not many other tables were occupied. "We may be developing a country-wide reputation of being the last ones in a restaurant."

Kate showed him the notes she had taken during and after her visits, further explaining the standard framework for information she had created and had sent him.

Frank's admiration was obvious. "I knew it was a good decision to work in tandem, Kate. It's already useful. Establishing a format benefits all offices."

"But I need help in looking at the financials." Her brow wrinkled as she explained her recent experiences. "There's only so much you can learn without them."

Frank nodded. "It's not just you. I sometimes hit the same roadblock. I understand why head telegraphers don't want an outsider raking over their details, but our job requires figures."

"Do you see anything I should add?" Kate asked.

"I think we might want to know how many employees come and go, and there may be other small items." He closed her notebook and handed it back to her. "In general, it's worth adopting—very good work, Kate."

Warmth spread through her. As always, when she was with him, she was valued rather than discounted.

"Let's see if we can go even deeper. We want to know what we don't know."

Kate frowned, at a loss as to what he meant.

"At first, some piece of information might not seem important. We won't know until we consider everything from different directions . . . or when something else gives it new context. Basically, we'll be keeping track of what we hear even if we don't think it's important at the time."

"What exactly are we looking for?"

"That's the thing, we don't know. Earlier, we talked about how much change refrigerated cars made. Think of the telegraph. That technology has caused greater change, but other technology is bound to be developed that might either help or be detrimental to Western Union."

"You don't expect me to be a scientist?" Kate asked, nonplussed.

"Not at all. Would you consider being a detective?"

Kate moaned, too many thoughts spiraled in her mind to even laugh at his humor. Even a brief mention of playing detective shook her senses. She was already uncomfortably trying to find Sally Andersen. The need to uncover her father's separate existence and the mysterious "H" referred to in Sally's letters scrambled her consciousness. She finally managed a smile. "I think the long day has muddled my mind."

"My apologies, I got carried away. May we continue our conversation at dinner tomorrow?" He picked up his bowler and handed her own hat to her. "I see you've made a good choice in hats. From the wind I hear outside, the lake's breeze is trying to blow down the city. Tie it on tight."

After making a bow under her chin, Kate slipped her hand inside the warm angle of his elbow, shaking her head in wonder. *Not only does he know about inventions, he also knows about ladies' hats.*

It was evident to Kate that, like herself, Frank thrived on long hours of work. Separately, they visited a new office every few days, with an endless cycle of introductions and attempts to gain trust. Some information was slow in coming or withheld entirely. Afterward, during dinners together, they shared stories of the day's events. They finished the evening by filling in information on the standardized form Kate had created. It was only on Sundays that they put work aside for touring, although many of the city's buildings were closed. Kate still looked forward to the relief and enjoyment of free time together, even if only to view exterior architecture and landscapes.

During their time in Chicago, it had occurred to Kate that this was what it must be like to be married—having someone always there, to confide in and share experiences. At night, in the darkness of her hotel room, she admitted to herself that marriage to Frank was an appealing idea. She had no doubt she was falling in love with him. But was love enough?

Night after night, that question tormented her. Hadn't her parents been in love once, too? *I'm not going to fall into that trap.* As far as Kate was concerned, she and Frank did not need marriage—she would cherish his company as a friend; enjoy how he challenged her, without inflicting wounds.

FORTY-THREE

Discordant sounds of railroad stations had become a regular part of Kate's life—shrieking whistles, chuffing engines, the clanging of iron against iron. The grand technology of locomotion seldom went without a hitch, whether it was breakdown of equipment or faulty scheduling. The new rhythm of her life was syncopation rather than symphony.

Kate had now spent four seasons as a traveling telegrapher. The difficulties of travel had become something she managed rather than fretted about, but she still resented the time it took away from accomplishing work or sightseeing. Her travel log had grown; she'd visited fifteen different cities since she began in the spring of 1870. Most of her assignments had been close to the East Coast. The greatest distance she'd traveled had been her visit to Chicago with Frank. Since then, they had been unable to arrange a similar trip. They exchanged letters frequently—every other week, sometimes more—but they had not seen each other, and despite herself, Kate found she missed him terribly. His laughter and expressions, his knowledge and quick conversation and, most of all, the secure, relaxed pleasure she experienced in his presence, meant more to her with every passing day. He was the one person with whom she could truly be herself.

Outside her parents' house, a nor'easter was blowing sideways, banging shutters as it whistled by. Spring had not arrived in Providence. This was only her second time at home in over a year; the last was during the holidays in December. The kitchen, however, was as warm and welcoming as ever. She was enjoying the treat of toast and tea with her mother, especially grateful for freedom from schedules, assessing new situations, and being by herself.

"I hope you don't have to go out today, Kate." Eugenia had a heavy, cable-knit shawl wrapped around her shoulders and still looked chilled.

"Thank heavens, no. I have work that will keep me at my desk for days."

"Is your job what you expected?" Eugenia put aside the newspaper she had been reading. "You don't often speak of it in your letters."

"Some of it's better and some of it's worse." Kate smiled weakly. She was overtired from traveling, and sitting by the warm fire made her sleepy.

"Which is which?"

"Would you pass me the marmalade, please?" Kate took the jar of slivered orange rinds mixed in golden jelly. "I've learned a surprising amount about the business, how it works, and when it doesn't. I think sometimes I'm adding value—maybe even most of the time—but not always."

"I'm positive you're always valuable, Kate."

Kate sighed at her mother's discerning look. Was Eugenia noticing the dark circles under Kate's eyes and the lines of exhaustion on her face? Knowing her mother, she'd noticed all that and more. She spread a thick layer of marmalade on her toast. "I like the way you make this—not too tart, not too sweet."

"It's an old, old recipe," Eugenia said, smiling. "My grandmother's, I think." She poured more tea in both cups, obviously happy to have company.

"The travel can be a nuisance when it doesn't go right, and lodging is a mixture of comfortable and awful, but the time in new cities makes the rest acceptable. I like learning about different places—each has its own identity—I guess like people." She met her mother's eyes—the original copy of her own.

"I'm glad you're happy. Do you know your next assignment? Daddy and I savor the time you're here."

"Hmm. Not yet. I have to wait for a telegram, but I may have a little time here; thank you for having me." Kate took another piece of toast and spread it with butter and again layered on the golden marmalade. She had lost weight. Sometimes, while traveling, finding a place to eat was a nuisance—even requiring dodging men who thought a single woman was an invitation, so she did without.

"You might be interested in attending a meeting, if you're here long enough. The Fifteenth Amendment has given our fight new life. We've gotten past the sentiment of 'votes for all or votes for none.'"

Kate knew many women had put their own push for suffrage on hold until the Fifteenth Amendment had passed, giving all male citizens, regardless of race, the vote.

"We're trying to rally support for Victoria Woodhull. She's going to put our case in front of the House of Representatives."

"Mama, I admire what you're doing. We are all grateful. I'm so busy doing other things."

"But we're fighting for all of us—you, too." Eugenia cleared the table, clinking dishes into the sink.

"I'm doing my part in my own way. I'm proving women are capable of working." Kate pushed back her chair with a scraping sound.

"Without the vote, women can't be truly capable." Eugenia turned her back as she poured hot water from the tea kettle into the sink to wash the dishes.

Kate respected her mother's passion—they both were trying to effect change, and it was hopeless to argue. "If you leave the dishes, I'll do them." Kate waited for a response. "Otherwise, I have some work to do."

Eugenia bent over the sink without reply, looking upset, but whether the fact that her only daughter was not more interested in "the cause," or simply the differences between them, Kate could not tell.

The weather blustered for two days. Kate spent most of the time at her desk, staying warm by the fire in her bedroom's white-tiled fireplace. Her reports to Western Union started with a consistent method of facts and figures comparing one office to another. They then went on to use statistics to improve output. She found that harder. Personalities and even locations—urban versus rural, for example—played a part. Frank had commented favorably on her system, and particularly her effort to find even more information, to improve productivity and customer approval. Yet, the New York office remained mum. Her assignments were increasingly difficult—offices with obvious problems and/or recalcitrant managers. Kate was not sure whether it meant the men in New York had more confidence in her abilities or if they were hoping for failure by assigning her the impossible. Frustration made her lose sleep.

After completing her most recent reports, she pulled her travel journal off the bookshelf and turned to the back pages. Time remaining in Providence was uncertain, so she had to make use of the opportunity to do more tracking of Sally Andersen. During solitary moments, on train rides or in ill-appointed hotel rooms, she strategized. Nothing palatable came to mind no matter how long she considered the options. There was no other way than to visit the addresses she had on her list.

In the morning, the weather was cool, not rainy. At the stable, she rented a covered, two-wheel, single-horse buggy. If she was going to introduce herself, she might as well not look like she had just crossed a moor in the wind. The first address led her to a one-story, white clapboard house with a sloping, dark-shingle roof. Kate tied her horse and carriage to the hitching post and knocked on the door. A thin, elderly woman, with skin as wrinkled as crumpled tissue paper, opened the door.

"Excuse me," Kate said. "I'm looking for Sally Andersen. I wonder if she still lives here?"

The woman gave Kate a squint-eyed look. "I don't know who lived here before, but there's no one here by the name of Sally. Sorry, can't help you." She stepped back and closed the door.

Kate stood stunned. It had gone so fast. She thought for a moment about what had caused the woman's reaction. *Would introducing myself at the beginning have helped?* She shrugged. *Probably not.* She knew she looked respectable. Perhaps strangers at a door were always suspicious. Kate knew little more than she did before she knocked. The woman could have been a new resident, a housekeeper, or even Mrs. Andersen herself. She turned slowly and walked back to her buggy.

The other two visits were not as brief, but equally unsuccessful. One woman asked Kate to identify herself at the outset. She remembered the previous owners were named Andersen, but knew nothing else about them. At the last residence, a woman about Kate's age, opened the door. Her husband was Samuel Andersen, and she asked Kate more questions about what she was doing than Kate was able to ask about possible relatives. The trip had been a dead end.

FORTY-FOUR

Sending letters to places across the country had become a game between Kate and Frank—seeing how many times correspondence could reach the other at far-flung hotels. Both of them remained busy, traveling to different cities on opposite sides of the country, with little time for a social life. Now and then, curiosity and self-doubt made her wonder if Frank had established a new relationship. She never told him about the occasional man knocking at her hotel door, sure she was a traveling harlot rather than telegrapher. She wondered if women ever made a play for him, too. It would not surprise her. He was an attractive, successful man and, sometimes, he stayed in cities for weeks at a time. She wanted to believe he was so devoted to climbing the ranks of Western Union, he had no time to woo a lady. The truth was that she did not really want to know. It would hurt too much to be replaced.

His letters still brought comfort. They contained business exchanges as well as small talk but were mostly about staying in touch. Having Frank listen, even on paper, was surprisingly reassuring, and so was receiving his news. No one else understood what it was like to spend two weeks here, another two weeks there. They each complained about the not-too-clean, dingy hotels with indifferent employees, or occasionally exclaimed about rare, attractive lodging with competent staff, knowing the other, and only the other, would understand the significance of each.

Altoona was the first of several towns Western Union assigned Kate to visit for two weeks in central Pennsylvania. After Altoona, she would travel to Pittsburgh, and then the state capital, Harrisburg, the last of her six-week-long trip. On her last day in Altoona, after her assignment was finished, she used her free time for long walks, since there was little remarkable architecture or museums in the town. The parks and high mountain vistas were beautiful. As was her custom, at the end of each day, she wrote in her journal, describing distinctive features to remember the town. She tried hard to find something to recommend in each place along her journey, usually succeeding.

Frank's most recent letter explained that he was taking a trip to the East Coast, ending in New York City while Kate was in Pennsylvania. At Western Union headquarters, he intended to present the case for another joint project with Kate, similar to Chicago. New London, Connecticut, was one of the places he was thinking of. "Please respond by telegram if you agree with the proposition. I need to act quickly," he wrote.

The letter continued, with Frank's usual amusing stories about his travels and problems confronted at work. Instead of putting the letter back in the envelope, Kate re-read it, imagining Frank's voice. His words were naturally more economical on paper than when he spoke, but lyrical just the same. If the trip to New London were approved, she would not have to be content with words on paper; they would be together. She tried to convince herself that she would rather keep the relationship companiable instead of stirring up her emotions, but right away, she went to Western Union to send a telegram endorsing the work assignment.

In her journal, Kate described Altoona's hotel as clean but lumpy— not only the chair cushion, but also the bed pillow and the mattress. After her journal and letters, she tended to her business writing, sitting in the same chair in which she had read Frank's letter—straight-backed and uncomfortable. After finishing, she slipped on her night dress and moved to the bed with her book. She always used small, extra spaces in her luggage for books, to keep herself entertained in the evening. No matter how modest the hotel, there was usually a comfortable place to read. Propped upright against the headboard, she mused about the role of books throughout her life. In her younger years, they transported her to faraway places. Now that she traveled, books provided an anchor for her soul. Content, she recovered the satin ribbon marking her place, opened the book, and began to read.

—·— ·— — ·

Located in a stately, two-story Greek revival Railroad Station, the New London telegraph office was, indeed, Kate's assignment after leaving Pennsylvania. Introducing herself to the dozen telegraphers who worked there, she began getting a sense of the operations by asking wide-open questions to get people to talk. The first day of any assignment wore her out. Usually, she spent that evening thinking about what she learned, filling out her form, and sketching out a preliminary course for the rest of her stay. Tonight, however, was different. After more than a year, she was meeting Frank, not by letter, but in person. She looked in the mirror, seeing a tired reflection looking back. She knew Frank would understand. He seemed to work even harder than she did. He tended to get caught up in his work, devoting most waking hours to it. She picked up her light shawl and closed the door to go down to the lobby to wait for him. Frank had told her he would pick her up there after a stop at his own hotel.

She sat, relaxed, in the lobby, not minding the wait. When she saw him hurry through the double entry doors, she stood up to greet him. She breathed in his clean, soapy smell when he embraced her. A flood of emotions swamped her. Wrapped in his arms, she never wanted to be released.

"I've missed you, Kate."

"Hmm, me too. Thank you for your letters. They help."

"They're not enough. The constant hours of work are losing their appeal."

"I understand that." Her world was cut into two separate halves. When they were apart, friendship worked, but when they were together, she wanted more. Right now, Kate did not want to envision ever being separated from him. The closeness she was experiencing was beyond words, and she did not want it to end.

They stepped apart but stayed connected, her arm in his, as they walked three blocks to the restaurant. Even as night came, it was sultry and hot. Although she wore her coolest cotton clothing, drops of perspiration coalesced under her arms and between her breasts.

Frank had chosen a small, ordinary eatery with a simple menu. Its location, next to the coastline, with frothy waves fringing the blue expanse of Long Island Sound, redeemed the ordinary-looking restaurant. New London, at the mouth of the Thames River, was far different from San Francisco's Bay or Chicago's Lake Michigan. Once a whaling town, New London's economy had turned to manufacturing and transportation.

They both ordered perch sautéed in brown butter, boiled potatoes with parsley, and summer squash. When they ate at places like this, they nicknamed the food as "expense account meals"—sometimes it was barely edible and occasionally a surprise. Frank always paid for their whiskey and sherry personally, something Kate admired. Settled at the table with their drinks, their meal had turned out to be quite good.

"Tell me about your New York meeting. How was it?" Kate asked.

A cloud crossed his eyes. "Yes," he said, "I need to do that."

His tensed jaw puzzled Kate. She had begun eating, but Frank held back.

"Some of it had to do with the experiment of traveling telegraphers. Apparently, most don't make much difference, but a few do—"

"I'd like to know how they decide," Kate interrupted. "I've turned in reports and haven't heard a thing, other than 'received'. Knowing what's helpful and what isn't might benefit all of us."

"I couldn't tell either, until they showed me examples. The good ones were your reports. They were without attribution, but you had shown me your format; otherwise, I wouldn't have known."

Kate's was crestfallen that her hard work had not been acknowledged— and then annoyed, but she remained silent, listening to what came next.

"However, there's the rub. The weasel didn't exactly take credit for them, but the other two in the room might have inferred it."

"Rodney?" she asked, feeling numb. "Rodney was there?"

Frank nodded. "Rodney and two higher-ups." His cheeks reddened. It was one of the few times Kate remembered the even-tempered Frank angry.

"Calling him out in front of our bosses would have done no good." He took a full swig of his whiskey, emptying it, and thumping the glass on the table. "I needed time to think of the best way to let them know whose work is most productive."

"How dare Rodney take credit for my work—that skinny little caved-chested man." She was close to exploding, but it was not Frank who deserved her ire, it was Rodney. There was nothing to do but calm herself. "It's some consolation that my work is well regarded, but women never get credit." She sagged back against her chair in frustration. She saw a look of relief wash over Frank.

"At least you don't think it was my doing." He glanced around the room. He seemed satisfied that customers were still eating, and they were not holding things up. "I need to tell you the rest. Both Rodney and I were given a promotion to regional manager," he said flatly. "A promotion, of course, that should have gone to you."

Kate's jaw dropped again, stayed there for a moment. "It's not fair."

"No, it's not. I can turn down my promotion or even say I'll leave the company if a manager's position doesn't go to you," he told her.

Kate was touched by the offer but couldn't let him sabotage his own career. "What good would either do? Nothing would change, and if you stay, at least you have a little more control over what happens to both our jobs."

"I'm sorry it's the way it is. I wasn't making gestures by saying I'd resign. If it would give you satisfaction, I'd do it."

Kate shook her head, and shrugged in acquiescence, knowing his offer was not a solution. There was no solution. Her work was considered of value, but others would take credit for it. The disappointment made her sad . . . and unnerved.

They finished their dessert as they worked on their daily summary. Kate was exhausted. Her eyes caught his. "Frank, it's getting late, with a busy day for both of us tomorrow. We should let the poor waiters leave." She looked around to make sure she had everything she came with.

Frank hastily looked at his pocket watch. "It's later than I expected." He came around the table to pull out her chair. "Let's plan tomorrow as we walk back."

FORTY-FIVE

Two weeks disappeared like vapor. Their last day was a blissfully free Sunday, before they boarded separate trains the following day for different locations. Despite her unhappiness with the managers of Western Union, Kate allowed herself to spend her free time focusing on Frank. She'd have time enough to figure out what her next step was once they were separated again.

To escape the humidity-saturated heat, they bought ferry tickets early in the morning, crossing the Long Island Sound from industrialized New London to the farmland of Long Island. They found a grassy spot to picnic in the shade of a towering white lighthouse crowned in red. At night, the Fresnel lens on top shone for miles to warn ships away from the rocky coast. Kate reveled in the luxury of a free day together.

In the evening, Frank chose a restaurant near the beach. They ate shrimp the color of sunsets, nestled on beds of pearly white rice. Sherry and whiskey in their separate hands, talk drifted to what was next. Kate would be going sixty miles northeast to Providence, Frank in the opposite direction to Ohio.

"What are your plans at home?" Frank asked Kate. He was in shirtsleeves; she wore a white muslin dress embroidered with sprays of yellow daisies. Resting on the nearby chair was her yellow straw hat with white daisies banding the crown. A wisp of cool air came off the water, cooling the room only slightly. Outside, stars poked holes in the velveteen sky above the sound. She had not wanted to make their parting a reality by talking about it.

"I'll just slow down my life. I haven't been home since March. I'm looking forward to seeing friends. That's what I miss most with travel— companionship." She gave him a soft look. "Connecticut has been different because I've spent my evenings with you. Of course, I'm always exhausted from trying to keep up with you," she laughed. "No wonder I need to go home."

"Are you complaining?" Frank gave her a teasing smile—one corner up and the other down.

"Of course not."

"You know I keep a map and put marks on the places I've been—quite a few, as a matter of fact, but I've never been to Providence." His eyes locked with hers. "I'd like you to take me for a tour sometime."

Sights Kate wanted to show him stacked up in her mind. Just as quickly, alarm bells clanged. If Frank came to Providence, there would be no escape from introducing him to her parents, with all sorts of ramifications. Time momentarily stopped. She listened to the continuous lapping of the waves outside.

"Someday I hope you'll come," she said at last. Sighing, she laid her silverware across her plate, finished with eating, and changed subjects. "Frank, I don't want to spoil this lovely evening by talking about business, but I've forgotten to tell you about something. Do you remember I had assignments in south Boston?"

"That was last spring." He stroked his trim mustache with his napkin. His mood had dimmed.

"I went just after Easter and stayed over a month. In the local papers were reports of Alexander Graham Bell coming with his father to the Boston School for Deaf Mutes. The school was started two years ago." She could tell that his interest was piqued.

"He's not an American, is he?"

"No, he's a Scot, although his family has moved to Canada. I don't think I would have paid much attention, except for your interest in inventions." She looked at him intently, gauging his reaction. "Bell is an inventor of sorts, even though he is still in his early twenties. He's interested in words, and hearing, and people who can't hear. Bell is experimenting with the transmission of sound using tuning forks. Have you heard of it?"

Frank thought a moment, before saying, "not precisely, but something similar . . . from Germany. There is lots of interest in the sound of a voice sent by electricity. The device that inventors are trying to make work is being called a 'telephone.'"

"Telephone? Is it possible?" Her head buzzed at the thought.

"I don't think anyone's close yet. Remember, though, the telegraph was just an idea once, too. It took many years and more than one person to finally succeed."

"I wanted to tell you, even if I don't understand it." Kate smiled smugly, pleased that she had paid attention.

"Thanks, Kate. Western Union is lucky to have you." Frank reached across the table and put his strong, square hand on hers. "Unfortunately, not everyone will see it that way. We'll have to think carefully about how to talk about your work, and even what you're discovering. Men have egos. They don't like to be bested, *especially* by a woman." He gave her hand a squeeze before retracting his. "Competition can get ugly."

"What do you mean?"

"The managers may try to make you invisible—give you undesirable assignments and not credit you for successful changes."

Kate let her gaze wander, surveying the other diners as she tried to tally what Frank had said. Finally, she retorted. "It's still not fair."

"No, but you do have something in your favor. Some of the managers at Western Union not only value your work, they need it, to show results to those higher up than they are. Even the managers understand, maybe under the surface, that they can't afford to get rid of you." It was his turn to look smug. "All is not lost."

"I appreciate your honesty." Kate was disoriented from Frank's account of her situation. The travel, long hours, and lonely evenings in mediocre lodging were worth it, as long as she was doing something productive. Kate did not need a pat on the back for working hard, but someone else taking credit infuriated her. "Maybe Western Union isn't a place I want to work," she said, hotly.

"I wouldn't blame you if you left. I'm feeling guilty that I suggested working there."

"It's not your fault."

"Let me tell you of a possible solution I thought of, and then you can make up your mind."

Frank explained that when he first started working for Western Union in San Francisco, it was mere happenstance that allowed him to travel for his first assignment. The other employees in his office had families in San Francisco and did not want to travel. Frank had spent long hours on the road and had written reports about his findings.

"Like yours, they were useful to the men in New York," he said.

"Except they gave you credit."

Frank nodded. "And when I was in New York, the managers upgraded my responsibility."

"An upgrade? Will you still be in San Francisco?" Kate asked.

Frank fingered his empty whiskey glass. "Yes, I'll still be in San Francisco, but I'll coordinate those who travel to other telegraph offices in the western part of the country.

"You said the West, so you won't be my supervisor?"

"No." He shifted, looking uncomfortable. "Because you work mostly on the eastern half of the country, Rodney will still be your supervisor."

"The weasel." She grimaced.

"Here's the good news. With my new position I can help coordinate occasional assignments like the one in Chicago and here in New London.

"Oh," she brightened. I'd like that."

"I can also make sure your work is credited. I've already asked that traveling telegraphers in the east send reports to me as well as New York."

"Will it work?"

"It's not foolproof. New York is a long way from San Francisco, telegraph or not. However, it should make it difficult for the weasel to assume all the credit."

"Thank you; let me mull it over. It is so kind of you to always be thinking of me," Kate said, softly. She reached over and picked up her daisy-laced bonnet and pushed it firmly on her head, somber now that the day was ending. The activities had not been out of the ordinary, simply boating and picnicking, but she'd been with Frank. She looked across the table at him, with his trim russet beard beneath his brown-flecked green eyes and ruddy cheeks. His lips were drawn. She felt harmony between them; the simple joy of being together made a day out of the ordinary, but their time together was ending. When they would see each other again was uncertain.

Arm in arm, they strolled back to her lodging through the muggy night, fireflies winking yellow and white. They would have to wait to see how the future unfolded.

"I'll be in touch about arranging an assignment in common. It will be something to get my head out of work, something to look forward to."

"For me, too." She choked back her disappointment at parting.

A long embrace, so passionate it felt promiscuous, was their goodbye.

Frank slowly released her and turned toward the front door. "Remember, keep your ears open."

"Even if I don't understand." Kate gave an unseen wave and walked up to her room, alone.

FORTY-SIX

Providence weather was hot and steamy in July. Kate sat, propped against a pillow on her bed, lethargic from the heat. Her book lay unopened beside her. She heard Eugenia moving through the second floor, closing windows she had opened the night before to let in non-existent breezes.

Eugenia looked through Kate's door as she passed by. "Kate, are you ill?" She took a step through the open door; lines of concern etched her face.

"No, not ill, tired. My body won't move in this heat."

"Let me at least close the windows."

"Thanks, Mama, but I don't know if it's hotter inside or out." She reached over for her fan and gave a few waves in front of her face. "I can't even think."

"I hope the heat won't ruin your plans for the short time you're here. Have you arranged anything specific?"

Kate looked across at her mother, who wore a light muslin day dress. She thought Eugenia's graceful movements and erect posture made her look younger than her early fifties. "I've been on the go so much, I don't want to get too busy. I'm going to have tea and sandwiches with Agnes and Diane tomorrow. Friday, there is a lecture by A. G. Bell about communicating with deaf mutes. I'm tempted to go all the way to Boston for it—if I can muster the energy."

"A meeting in Boston?" Eugenia seemed to search her mind before settling on the information. "Susan Anthony is speaking in Boston Thursday. I hadn't decided whether to go. Daddy has a meeting that night, so he will be away. Maybe we should go together. "We could attend each other's meeting and spend the night in between." She watched for Kate's response.

Kate sat up. "It's a tempting invitation." She swung her feet onto the floor. "My only hesitation is getting on another train and staying in a hotel, because I do so much of that." She looked at her mother's eager face, knowing a trip together would be important to her. Like so many men, Will dismissed Eugenia's interests as either a waste of time or "harmless little fantasies." Kate had always admired her mother's causes.

"Of course, this would be different from work, and I'd love spending time with you. Thanks. Can I think about it until dinner?"

"Certainly. You can also tell me about your interest in the deaf." Eugenia shook her head, "You're always full of surprises. Now, it's time for me to get back to work, even in this heat." She shrugged with a sigh.

"I'd be glad to help."

"Don't you have work?"

"A little, but it won't take long. Why don't I dust the downstairs. We keep throwing open the windows and the dust comes in."

"Thanks, Kate. The heat has me moving slowly."

Kate pulled a simple blue cotton dress with eyelet collar and cuffs over the sleeveless chemise she wore to stay cool. Comfort was all she thought of. While she moved the feather duster across every surface, she thought about Eugenia's idea. Through her job, Kate had learned about people with all sorts of backgrounds—rural to urban. At lunch break, telegraphers talked about their families and what they did for a living. Many had ended up working in factories or doing manual labor, earning meager pay. Telegraphers had better pay and work conditions but few rights.

Others in the office often considered Kate a conduit to Western Union. If she gained their trust, she heard their complaints: the hours of work were long, even if not as repressive as a factory, and women suspected that men had higher pay and a chance for supervisory positions or desirable locations. Kate listened with a helpless sense of not being able to change anything. Society was as responsible for the restrictions as the company was.

The more Kate thought about Eugenia's suggestion to attend both meetings in Boston, the more appealing it became. She had read about Susan Anthony's assertions. They went beyond women's right to vote; she was also known to be adamant about better employment opportunities and higher pay for women. Kate decided the lecture would bring her up to date with the issues and, perhaps, help her with her job.

What to expect from Alexander Graham Bell's advertised talk on communicating with the deaf, Kate was uncertain. She was following Frank's advice to keep her ears open. She laughed at the irony; Frank would, too, when she told him.

- - - - - - - - - - - ·

Kate and Eugenia had decided to stay at Young's Hotel on Court Street in Boston's financial district because Susan Anthony was speaking there. The train from Providence arrived late on Thursday afternoon, giving them time to check in and have a quick supper.

Fifteen minutes early, Kate and her mother entered the large meeting room lined with tall windows topped by cut stained glass. At the far end, a podium sat in front of an ornate fireplace. The room was already full of women—Kate guessed seventy, in a space that might have held one hundred. Eugenia waded into the animated crowd, proudly introducing Kate to women Eugenia knew. Promptly at seven, a ringing handbell called them to their seats.

Susan Anthony stood confidently erect at the podium. She was tall, with dark hair, parted in the middle, pulled back over her ears and fastened in a twist behind her head. Kate thought her wire-rimmed spectacles made her look severe, but Anthony began with humor. "I don't know how you did it, but you managed to exclude the hecklers. Thank you." The audience clapped appreciatively. "It may take me a minute to adjust to not having to talk above shouting about the impropriety of women making speeches," she said with a smile.

Kate found Anthony an eloquent speaker, who roused the audience with her ideas—all the more convincing by examples to back them up. She kept her listeners engaged for the whole hour she spoke. When she finished, conversations erupted as attendees stayed and discussed her ideas. The topic of women joining unions to improve employment provoked the greatest reaction—on both sides of the issue. Unionizing had experienced a difficult beginning. Resistance came from businesses, government, and some citizens, both male and female. Even the unions saw no place for women among their ranks. Nevertheless, Kate knew support for the rights of women was slowly gaining ground.

Being there was like reverting to her childhood, when she was at the dining room door after coming home from school, quietly listening to the discussions of her mother and her friends. Since those years, Kate had something to contribute, learned from the women with whom she worked, as well as her own experience in the male-dominated workforce. She joined in the conversation, admiring the passion around her.

After they returned to their hotel room, Kate's mother unknotted her chignon and began to brush her gray-streaked blond hair as they talked.

"My friends loved you, Kate. They were so impressed with your job and what you had to say."

Kate could tell from Eugenia's expression she was ebullient about having her along. "I must have only told them the good parts," Kate laughed, letting her own hair fall to her shoulders, and picking up her hairbrush. Relaxing by rhythmic brushing was something Kate had learned from her mother.

Eugenia looked at her with surprise. "I thought your job was everything."

Kate ignored the implication. "I like different places and figuring out what's going right or wrong." She changed hands with her brush. "Train schedules and accommodations can be tedious, though."

"My friends would be grateful for your help."

"I appreciate what all of you are doing," Kate hedged. Crossing to the wash bowl, she mixed a paste of baking soda and salt to brush her teeth.

"Would you accomplish more working on the cause than your job?"

Kate shook her head. "It takes too long to get anything done, and I'm too impatient." Her eyes half closed as she thought of the hours spent to make so little progress. "No, my job suits me right now." Kate did not want the exchange to migrate into expectations. "I'll take the far side of the bed, Mama. Do you mind if I read a little before I go to sleep?"

"Not at all. I'll write in my journal and then get into bed."

"Goodnight, Mama."

"See you in the morning, sweetie."

‐‐ ‐ ‐

After breakfast, Kate and Eugenia walked from their hotel to Stephen's Church for the talk on hearing and speech. The building was constructed of red brick and embellished with stone pilasters. A white tower and cupola rose from the brick, topped with a weathervane in the shape of a cross. Inside, the meeting room was set up with chairs for fifty or so attendees. At the far end, two men sat by the podium, waiting for the meeting to come to order.

The elder of the two stood up to welcome everyone. Alexander Melville Bell was a medium-sized man with a full head of silver-white hair that flowed into a grizzled beard. He introduced himself as a professor of elocution, with an interest in phonetics and the way in which humans make and perceive sounds. After he described his work, he called on his son to give the presentation.

Alexander Graham Bell had a softspoken Scots brogue like his father. He was a slim man in his twenties. Dark hair, well-trimmed beard, and a mustache framed his angular face. His early interest in acoustics, he said, had been influenced by his father's and grandfather's occupations in elocution. When his mother's declining hearing resulted in deafness, he became preoccupied with sound.

When he described being a ventriloquist as a boy, the audience laughed at his story. He had convinced onlookers that his dog could speak and had become a source of entertainment in the neighborhood with his antics. More seriously, he described his work training instructors in visible speech. He had become proficient in understanding any language by watching lips. He was recently hired to train instructors at the Boston School of Deaf Mutes. In addition, he was experimenting with a harmonic telegraph, convinced that someday the sound of a voice could be transmitted by wire.

After the presentation, the audience gathered around, asking questions of the Scots father and son. Kate stood close, listening. Most queries were about visible speech. As she listened to their answers, she casually looked at the crowd to determine who had come to the Bells' meeting. She surmised many were family or friends of deaf people, who needed help in communicating. A few stood apart, not conversing. Perhaps they lacked hearing, she thought. Her glance came to rest on a woman who seemed familiar. What caught Kate's eye was the woman's tapestry purse. Its long, narrow cord went over her shoulder, leaving her hands free. Kate had noticed it the day before at the suffrage meeting, thinking how useful it would be to have free hands. The woman's purse was the same, but her dress different. At the second talk, she wore a cotton dress with wide, dark-blue stripes, four rows of ruffles down the front, and a bustle at the back. Her brimless hat sat forward on her light, braided hair. Still slender and attractive, she was in her early forties, Kate guessed.

The audience thinned as the Bells answered individual questions. Kate saw that Eugenia was talking to an acquaintance. Since the woman with the purse was nearby, Kate moved toward her to comment on the purse and both meetings.

"Excuse me, I noticed your purse. It's quite convenient to have one you can sling on your shoulder, freeing up your hands. It caught my eye yesterday. Am I right that I might have seen you at the Susan Anthony talk as well as this one today?"

"Were you there, too? Both were quite interesting in different ways." A smile lit her face as she stuck out her hand. "I'm Sally Andersen."

Kate's heart stuttered. "I'm Kate Sinclair," she uttered, before she could stop herself.

Unconsciously, their gloved hands stayed clasped, sending a message of recognition neither would admit. Kate watched Sally's vivacity collapse, unable to imagine what her own expression displayed.

"I wish I could stay and chat. A friend and I shared a carriage, and I don't want to keep her waiting." Sally turned hurriedly to head toward the door.

"There you are, Kate. Did you see someone you know?" Eugenia asked, coming toward her.

"Yes . . . no, no," she shook her head. "I don't know her."

"Is something wrong? You look pale. Should I get you some water?"

"I think I'm okay," she said shakily. "It must be the heat."

"Do you want me to hail a cab?" Eugenia took Kate's arm to steady her.

"Thanks," she stammered. "I think I can walk. I just got light-headed for a moment."

"Kate, I never knew most of what the Bells had to say. Thank you for inviting me." Kate listened to Eugenia's enthusiasm about the talk, all the while feeling as if someone had punched her in the stomach. The abrupt introduction made Kate realize that Sally might live in or near Boston, not Providence. Meeting the woman she had known for years only through letters was a shocking surprise. While Eugenia continued to praise the meeting, Kate's mind was frantic about what to do next. There was only an hour before they had to leave for the train station. *The library. The library will have city directories.*

As they entered Young's Hotel, Kate asked, "Mama, would you do me a favor and ask the dining room to pack some bread, cheese, and a piece of fruit? We won't have time for lunch here and it would be nice to have something to eat on the train."

"Certainly, are you going to lie down?"

"I have to do a quick errand."

"Errand? Where? You don't look as if you feel well."

"I'm fine now. I have to go to the library. I'll be back soon."

Kate left her mystified mother and ran down to the lobby. The desk clerk sketched a small map of streets to the Boston Public Library.

"Here you go, Ma'am," he said, handing her the slip of paper. "It's an easy ten-minute walk from the hotel, even in this heat."

Kate sprinted out the door and down the street, trying not to look too unladylike with her fast pace. She reached the library in record time. Inside the three-story, brick building, light streamed through the high, arched windows. The reading room was filled with patrons, sitting at oval tables, reading newspapers or books, some fanning themselves. When she asked, the librarian nodded in the location of the city directories. Kate walked to the shelf and pulled the most recent one off. Her shaking hands fumbled with the pages and she took a deep breath to calm herself. There it was. Under the alphabetical listings . . . one Andersen with the initial S. and a residential address. Kate needed to sit down to write. With two more volumes picked randomly from the 1860s and 1850s, she squeezed into an empty chair. Using the inkwell and square slip of paper from a neat stack, she wrote down the address. The residence had stayed the same in the earlier volumes. Kate checked to make sure her numbers were accurate, folded the paper, and tucked it in her purse.

No sense of relief washed over her—not finding Sally might have been better. Learning more meant confronting someone . . . Sally . . . her father . . . her mother? Kate was numb. She glanced at the watch at her waistband, knowing her mother would be waiting and worrying. After returning the three volumes to their proper places, she rushed through the oversized, arched doorway and back to the hotel.

FORTY-SEVEN

Managing the vicissitudes of train schedules, lodging, and telegraph offices shaped the pattern of Kate's life—there was more irregularity than routine. Travel clothes that did not show the dirt were her uniform. With experience, Kate had learned to take early morning trains to give herself leeway if there was a breakdown or schedule change, and for occasional touring. Navigating a town at night for a woman had to be avoided. A book . . . or two . . . helped transport her away from long hours in cramped, often dirty, railroad stations. After realizing that women were frequently given the least desirable room, she learned to insist on being shown available rooms at whatever lodging Western Union designated.

A few men she worked with assumed that women who traveled alone wanted company. Some asked her for dinner—some insistently. The more they pressed, the more she knew it was an invitation for more than an evening out. The memory of Reverend Johnson, far away though he was, still remained. At each of her hotels, she told the desk clerk that she did not want guests, and locked her door securely.

Kate spent many evening hours honing her financial skills, to be proficient with ledgers and bank statements. She became an expert in numbers, to dispel the notion of many head telegraphers that details of ledgers were something that went in and immediately floated out of any female's mind. She had learned to ask specific questions that were not easily evaded. It had helped when Western Union instructed that she be given access to all financial material.

Kate was amused to learn that she was becoming known over the wires. Telegraphers used snatches of spare time to send messages to each other . . . sometimes about her. When she arrived in Trenton, New Jersey in September, the head telegrapher, Bert Kline, greeted her, saying, "You look just like the wire said you would." He was a clean-shaven man with light brown hair parted on the left side. Kate guessed he was still in his thirties. He spent his time during her two-week visit trying to confuse her. She was pleasant but insistent. At the end, when she was ready to depart, he remarked, "They were right; we needed to be on our toes."

"Thank you, Mr. Kline. I consider that a compliment."

Her ability to spot inefficiencies improved. She questioned whether rates for telegrams written late in the day should receive a reduced fee because it would not be sent until the next day. The same amount of work and time were required—it saved the customer money but not the company, so Kate recommended against it. She also presented an argument against the different charges for a personal telegram, versus one sent by the government. Charged for each letter, personal telegrams were brief. The government's inexpensive rates led to lengthy messages. She received no response to that suggestion. More importantly, she found ways to make the work in an office flow more smoothly, reducing waste and frustration; when possible, she subtly used women to lead the effort. At the end of every assignment, she sent a detailed report—adding her name next to each page number.

— · — · — — · ·

It was spring of 1872 before Frank and Kate worked in the same city again—Richmond, Virginia. The city was built along a series of falls in the James River, that widened into a tidal estuary where it met the sea. The James provided easy transportation to seaports and water to power mills and factories. It had also been the capital of the Confederacy. By war's end, twenty-five percent of the city had been burned by departing Confederate soldiers determined to deny anything valuable to the victors.

Richmond began rebuilding as soon as the fire had been put out. Redbrick, iron-fronted buildings—both homes and business—began replacing the rubble. With the new construction, transportation changed from canals to railroads. Seven years after the war, Richmond was on its way to becoming a railroad and telegraph hub.

This trip was Kate's first to the South, and she had especially looked forward to sharing the experience instead of her usual solitary touring. She and Frank arrived from separate destinations on Saturday and spent Sunday exploring the city. Even a sprinkle of rain couldn't dim Kate's pleasure at being by Frank's side again. The cover of his wide, black umbrella created a special intimacy. Colorful chrysanthemums, pansies, and black-eyed Susans relieved the misty monochrome. In the industrial area, they came across a vacant lot filled with burned timbers and broken bricks. It sat across the street from a newly built factory that stretched the entire block.

"There are more charred remnants than I might have imagined," Kate said, looking at the ruins.

"The new hasn't quite covered up the old," Frank said somberly.

"There must be painful memories here."

"Ghosts of losing a cause and so many young men will haunt long into the future." Frank's eyes darkened. "Fire and war won't leave the minds of this generation . . . and maybe the next."

"And Chicago's fire, last fall." Kate added, remembering the good times they'd spent there together. "The reports gave me nightmares—flames, heat, falling buildings, and people desperately running for their lives. Can the city possibly recover?"

Frank stopped. "Yes, both Chicago and Richmond will. Over and over, we recover from loss and pain, even if the memories never disappear. Humans are resilient."

"You're probably right, but having been in Chicago two years ago made the fire more tragic to me—almost personal. Much of what we saw is gone."

"We need to go back to see how they've fared. Although, not for a while, I expect."

Kate didn't comment. As ever, she was impressed with Frank's philosophy—her time with him was too infrequent and too short.

—·— ·— — ·

They were again in the rain on their last Sunday together.

"I have to say I've learned as much about Richmond as I have about telegraph operations in the past four weeks," Kate said.

"The same with me—so much of the city is absorbed by rebuilding; they can think of little else."

They had come to the end of a boardwalk—the mud below it, nothing but liquid.

"We've been walking in the drizzle for a couple of hours," Frank said. "I'm ready to dry off and warm up."

"And have something to eat? Suddenly I'm hungry. Maybe we kept walking because we didn't want our last day to end." Kate smiled up at him. "It's been a glorious month."

Frank wrapped his arm around her shoulder, drawing her close under the canopy of his umbrella, disregarding the impropriety. "We passed a restaurant a block or so ago. Let's turn back and try it. Being with you made me forget about food—imagine that!" He squeezed her against him with a laugh. "Let's have a meal and talk about being together."

Kate nodded, but shuddered. Each day that brought the end of the assignment closer raised the dilemma of their relationship. Her resistance was rising, making her edgy.

Laughter and a merry bustle greeted them as they entered Crawford's Tavern.

"Look, how many people have come in from the rain to have lunch," Kate said to Frank.

Outside, the sky was dark and thick; inside, lanterns threw light on long tables, pockmarked with use. A hearth at the far end, near the kitchen, warmed the two-story, open room. Taverns in Richmond, Kate and Frank had discovered, were more than restaurants or bars. They were community gathering places where neighbors and visitors met to talk politics, celebrate, or commiserate.

The waiter who welcomed them found a table for two along the edge of the room. Frank and Kate ordered a dozen oysters on the half shell, accompanied by a glass of sherry and tumbler of whiskey.

"I really am famished." Kate tipped a craggy, gray shell to her lips and let the plump, pearly oyster slide down her throat. She took a sip of sherry. "I think they go especially well with sherry," she told him, taking another.

"You think everything goes especially well with sherry," Frank joked.

A man in the far corner picked up his violin and began to fiddle, adding to the gay din pulsating throughout the room.

After oysters, they ordered simmering chicken and dumpling soup, served in earthenware bowls. Frank took a spoonful of his soup, swallowing with a sigh. "I could spend every day like this . . . together."

"We both have to work. Remember? This is the one day everyone is free. That's what the merriment is about." Kate wondered when she had ever been so relaxed.

"Living in the same city would make afternoons like this a common occurrence." Frank looked at her, but she kept her head down, lifting up a piece of dumpling with her spoon.

His response was breezy. "I've never asked you if you cook."

Kate looked up. "Tomato soup," she smirked merrily. "More than that, really—my mother taught me—but she likes to cook, so I haven't had much practice."

She could read his unspoken thought. Time together had been an effortless compatibility of shared interests, admiration of the other's strengths, and breathless physical attraction. He wanted more and she pulled away, hating herself for doing so. His eyes looked sad. Kate sensed his struggle to switch gears from what he wanted to say. She picked up her fork to half-heartedly spear pieces of cinnamoned apples from her piece of pie and observed the boisterous crowd, leaving Frank to his thoughts.

After a few minutes, he turned to her with a half-smile. "I wanted to save the best about work for last."

Kate was interested but wary.

"Western Union has become interested in Colorado. Denver, as a matter of fact."

"Colorado?" Kate sat up straighter. She knew her eyes must be sparking question marks. "Really? Denver!"

"It's really not surprising." Frank shrugged. "The Denver Pacific Railroad now connects the town to Cheyenne."

"And the Union Pacific." Kate said.

"And the Kansas Pacific links Denver to Omaha."

"The bridge must be finished." Kate felt all the pieces fitting together, both for the railroads and in her mind.

"The bridge took three years, but when I board the train for San Francisco in the morning, it will be the first time I don't have to disembark in Council Bluffs and take a boat across the Missouri River to Omaha."

"We always said we took the transcontinental railroad in sixty-nine," Kate said, "but now it really is seamless. But tell me about Western Union's interest in Denver."

"Do you remember what Union Pacific's president, Thomas Durant, predicted when the UP bypassed Denver for Cheyenne?"

"No, I don't."

"Without railroads, Denver would be too dead to bury." His eyebrows arched. "Now, with its connection to Cheyenne and Omaha, Denver is far from dying—it's growing, and Western Union wants to be part of the boom. I have been asked to find out about the town's development." Frank grinned. "Instead, I recommended you for the job. It took a passel of letters back and forth from wherever I was to New York to convince them. I even threatened to resign, but they were finally persuaded because of your past trip to Colorado, and your connection with the Hills. No one else has that."

Kate was stunned. "I can't believe it! They agreed to send me? It's too good to be true, but if it is, thank you," she exclaimed.

She saw some of the sparkle return to his eyes. "When will it happen?" She was trying to tamp down her giddiness.

"I don't think the details are quite firm. In fact, you'll have to write me about them when they are." He gave her his crooked smile. "Will you promise?"

"Of course. I want to keep up our letter writing."

"I wish it were more, Kate. Work has kept me more than occupied since I joined Western Union, and it still will, but it won't be enough forever." Frank caught her eyes and held them with his for a moment. Kate wanted to respond, but she couldn't find the words she knew he wanted. She reluctantly dropped her gaze to finish her dessert.

FORTY-EIGHT

Providence in late summer was a spectacle of flowers in full bloom—it was one of Kate's favorite seasons. After more than a year, she was once again enjoying time at home. It came as a respite between two months in upper New York state and leaving for Colorado at the end of the month. Frank had been right about Western Union. Not long after they had met in Richmond, a letter with the official news about Colorado found her in Albany. Kate was ecstatic about going, and grateful to Frank for arranging it. From their conversations over the years, he had understood how much it would mean to her to visit to Alice and her family. They both knew Nathaniel's connections would help her gather information for Western Union.

As always, Kate made time to renew friendships at the ritual of daytime "at-homes," where women in silks and satins filled parlors echoing with lively camaraderie and gossip. Attending them reminded her of the forgotten competition of finery, and the dictates of *The Dictionary of Etiquette*—so different from telegraphers' lives. Friends she had known growing up told her about their husbands' businesses, how children were growing, and about their busy social calendars—who was invited, who was not. More and more names were unfamiliar.

The past spring, Kate had turned thirty-two, and each birthday brought growing distance from friendships formed half a lifetime ago. She sighed. It was like forcing two unmatched puzzle pieces together, and yet she knew that friends with shared experiences, even if long ago, helped give definition to her existence. She did not want her independence to always mean being alone, so she tried to fit in.

Kate had to shop before leaving for Colorado Territory. Knowing fall weather might be cold, especially in the mountains, she bought thick wool socks, heavy mittens, a new black felt coat, and substantial leather boots. She could not resist one shimmery, satin dress the color of violets, trimmed in frothy white lace at the collar, sleeves, and bottom of each flounce. It was the first fancy dress Kate had bought in years, influenced, she knew, from being with her friends.

Her large leather satchel would not be enough—this trip required a trunk. Normally, she would have asked the gardener, or even her father, to retrieve it from the attic. Neither had been around when she was ready to pack. She recalled, as a college student, occasionally bringing down the sturdy but lightweight trunk by herself. She hesitated, worried about re-injuring her back. She looked up. The opening to the attic was somewhat larger than the dimensions of the trunk. It would be possible to pull it to the opening and slide it down the slanted steps until it reached the ground.

Inside the attic, Kate grabbed the anchored leather strap on the vertical end, tipped it and pulled it a little way. She exhaled with relief; it was manageable. A finger of light shining through the parted dark green draperies beckoned her. Curious about whether there were more letters since she last looked, she reached behind the fabric and pulled out the box. Balancing the box on her hip; she opened the lid and extracted the last letter. There was no postmark. She would have to pull the letter out of envelope.

"What are you doing with that box?" a harsh voice came from behind her.

The box jettisoned out of her hand and clattered upside down to the floor. Disoriented, Kate gasped.

"How dare you touch those letters!"

Kate turned to see her father at the attic entry; his arms stiff, hands curled in knuckled balls.

"Father, you startled me." Her heart pounded in her ears.

"That's obvious. Now, what are you doing with those letters? Have you read them? They are private correspondence!"

"I . . . I . . . came up for my trunk." Kate looked helplessly over at the trunk lying sideways near the entrance. She reflexively bent down to pick up the letters spread out like autumn leaves at the base of a tree.

"I'll take care of those," he said, with quiet anger. "I'll deal with you later." Will stepped aside to let her pass.

Kate's legs shook as they met the first rung of the ladder. She thought about taking her lantern, but her father could not see to pick up the letters without it. She wanted to know why he had come home during the day on a weekday, but knew better than to ask. In her room, she closed the door. Leaving it open was an invitation for more of his spleen. He would have to knock. Sitting at her desk, she was too distracted to accomplish anything. After a while, she heard the scraping of his footsteps above in the storage space. There was a curious bumping sound and noise outside her bedroom. Kate realized he had brought down her trunk and put it outside the door. Heavy footsteps padded down the hallway.

It was the worst possible day for this to happen. She would have to face her father alone over dinner. Eugenia was in Boston, at a suffragist meeting. The morning after Kate had arrived from her most recent business trip, she and her mother had enjoyed tea and toast together, laughing over all of Kate's plans.

"Kate, would you be willing to cook for Daddy while I go to a meeting up north?"

"Of course." Kate poured another cup of tea from the flowered china teapot. The familiarity of the setting, and even the oolong, brought a sense of tranquility. "Which night will you be gone?"

"Wednesday. I thought Daddy would be gone, but his plans changed. If you're too busy, I can ask Amber to stay to cook for him after she cleans, but he would enjoy this so much more. You know how he hates to be out of his routine." Eugenia was polishing the chrome trim of the stove. She rarely sat still, finding small tasks to do while she talked.

"No, it will be fun to cook, since I rarely do it." In the back of her mind was Frank's teasing question. "Shall I get a chicken to roast?"

"I'll see that one is in the icebox. Are you sure you don't mind? I'll be here the rest of the time you're here."

"I don't mind at all. Are you making progress on the vote?"

"Some days I wonder—there is still so much resistance. Talking to a legislator personally, if one is willing, helps. That's what we're working on." Eugenia put away her polish and rag, leaving behind gleaming chrome against the black of the cast iron.

"Thanks, from all of us." Kate said.

The favor Eugenia had asked was innocuous when she'd asked it. Now, given her father's ire, Kate would do anything to escape the dinner or, at least, have Eugenia as a buffer. Throughout her life, she really had not spent much time with her father. Preoccupied with work, Will's main connection with his family was dinner-time conversation. Once his children were past primary grades, he asked questions about their schooling, demanding a high-caliber performance, especially of her brothers. His dogmatic views on everything, from behavior to politics, had been strictly expressed. No one questioned him.

If he was not at work, he was in his much-loved study, reading the newspaper or books. Occasionally he brought work home, spending hours squinting over ledger sheets. The small study was his, except when Amber cleaned it. There was no particular rule against entering—it was unstated. His three children had come to the door to ask a question and ventured to his desk if beckoned, but it was not a cozy place where the family gathered together to talk about the day. Even Eugenia limited her presence, merely sticking her head in the door to ask a question now and then. When Kate was young, her mother had spent the evenings with her children; now, she read alone while Will was in his study.

Sighing, Kate left the protection of her room for the kitchen. While the oven was heating, she rubbed the chicken with lard, added sage, salt, and pepper, and surrounded it with potatoes before popping it in the oven. She put cream in a bowl and took her frustration with her father out on it, whipping vehemently to top the apple crisp she had baked. She planned to pick green beans from the garden and steam them just before she served dinner. Wiping her hands on her apron, she surveyed her efforts.

Well, there's one meal I can cook.

The thought of trying to prove her prowess in the kitchen would usually have made her laugh. Tonight, it brought no humor. She walked up the stairs to her bedroom, planning to read, but knew her mind would be on the conversation with her father.

At five-thirty, she tapped on the doorjamb of his study. "Dinner's ready, Father."

He looked up from reading. He seemed groggy. Perhaps he'd had a nap. "Thank you, I'll be right in. I'm going to pour another drink. Would you like a sherry?"

"Not tonight, thank you for offering." Kate wanted to remain clear-headed. A second drink for her father was unusual. *He must be tense too.* She returned to the kitchen.

Kate put two dinner plates at his place, surrounded by the dishes she had prepared. Even though there were only two of them, he would serve.

"Do you feel well, Father?" Kate asked after taking her seat to his right.

"I have a little stomach upset. Nothing more."

"I'm sorry. I wondered why you came home early."

"I said I'm fine," he growled. He ate a few bites of chicken, chewing in silence, repeatedly wiping his abundant moustache with his napkin to keep it clear of food. Above his broad shoulders, his face was pale.

If the chicken tasted flavorful, she was unable to tell. All her senses were consumed thinking about what might come next. Finally, come it did.

"I want you to tell me what you were doing with that letter box." Her father's dark brown eyes were implacable.

Kate had decided not to lie. Will had drilled his family about truth-telling. Punishment had been swift and sure for her brothers and her when they'd been dishonest. She would not lie to her father, but revealing everything might not be necessary. "I found the box by accident and was curious."

"Did you read the letters?" His facial muscles clenched as he waited.

"Yes." She kept her eyes on his.

"All of them?"

Kate nodded. Her teeth clamped in dread. Loose pieces of her brain seemed to be tossing around, making coherent thought difficult. Will's controlled rage was typical, but more urgent than she had ever seen it. He did not yell or show anger physically. It was more subtle; disparaging comments—diminishing the ego. He was always in control and there was never any arguing.

"Isn't it wrong to read other people's mail?"

"It wasn't intentional," she tried to explain. "I—"

"If you read something that's not yours, it is intentional."

The coals in the small tiled hearth shifted, making a slumping sound. Kate cut into a piece of chicken. She was determined to eat whether she was hungry or not. Her father would not intimidate her. The skin of the chicken was crisp, the flesh juicy and fragrant with sage. Her potatoes had a newly-dug, sweet flavor, and the beans were perfectly cooked—not crisp or mushy. She'd cooked a good meal, despite her preoccupied thoughts.

Once her father's plate was empty, Kate crossed her silverware next to the food remaining on her plate.

She met her father's eyes head-on. "What does Mama know of Sally?"

She could tell Will had expected the question. His eyes darted away for a moment, the muscles along his sideburns tensing. Still, he maintained a purposeful calm.

"That is none of your business," he said, stiffly.

"Are you being honest if she doesn't know?" There was tacit understanding that no one stood up to Will. This was as close as Kate had ever come.

"Mother has chosen to have a life of her own. There are consequences. She knew it was my place to make the decisions in this house, but from the time you went to school, she badgered me to pay for you to go to college. Look what happened," he glared.

Kate felt his implication. Her mother had dared pressure him about Kate's education, and the result was an independent, unmarried daughter, who had discovered his separate life. She was not going to give him the satisfaction of cowering. "Would you like some dessert, Father?"

He recoiled in surprise. "No," he said sourly. "I told you. My stomach is upset. If you'll excuse me, I'm going to my study to read."

Kate remained frozen in her chair. She could count on her fingers the times anyone argued with Will—like that day, long ago, when she'd returned from the lake and overheard her parents. Most of the time, Eugenia did exactly as Will wished. When Eugenia went to the city, she planned her visits for times when her husband was also away from home. Did Will consider her mother's carefully conscripted behavior too free? Had he embarked on his affair with Sally to punish Eugenia for having outside interests? Or was that just an excuse for his oversized ego? Kate might not be close to her father, but the thought that he might be deliberately mean was profoundly disappointing.

After minutes—or maybe hours—she rose and went to the hearth to close the damper. Her mind kept somersaulting while she put away the leftover food and washed the dishes. Determining what to do was difficult . . . deciding what she owed her mother was even more problematic.

FORTY-NINE

The last ten miles of any trip were always Kate's favorite. She could finally put away worry about something going wrong and reflect on everything right—the interesting architecture, crops, animals, and glorious scenery she had seen along the way. As the train neared Denver, Kate inspected her clothing and laughed. It was the same tan travel suit she had worn to Colorado four years previously and, a year after, to San Francisco. The tan jacket topped a skirt of tan, black, and gray plaid that disguised any soil. Her clothing had not changed, but the ease of travel certainly had—for the first time, she rode in comfort all the way from the New York to Denver on the same train.

With a chuff, the train came to a halt at the Denver depot. She stepped onto the platform and squinted into the intense western sun. From a line of carters hawking business, she chose one to convey her small steamer trunk to the Larimer Street Hotel. It was only three blocks away, and she was eager to walk—the clear, oxygen-thin air invigorated her.

On her previous trip, Denver had been a brief hiatus before boarding the stage to Black Hawk, and she'd seen little of it. At the time, Denver's population was an emaciated thirty-five hundred, but, as Frank reported, the city had blossomed in the intervening years. Since the opening of the Denver Pacific Railroad in 1870 to the Union Pacific hub in Cheyenne, and likewise the Kansas Pacific east, a hundred people a day were moving to the reviving territorial capital. Locals relished the growth for a badly needed boost to the economy. Western Union forecast a spreading network of railroads to other towns . . . and with it, the telegraph. The railroad might be bringing more families, but Kate noticed the boardwalks of Denver fronted many more saloons than clothing shops. For all its growth, it still appeared to be a male-dominated, rough-hewn frontier town.

Her job was going to be different in Denver. Instead of making improvements at different offices, Kate would assess the potential of a community. It was what Frank did all the time. She thought about him, knowing he was in his element at reconnaissance. She pictured him in a saloon, casually slouched on a barstool, hand wrapped around a glass of whiskey. He'd make conversation with the locals and soak up information. Kate needed a different strategy. If her superiors in New York were waiting . . . perhaps even expecting . . . maybe even hoping for her to fail, she would prove them wrong. Not failing was more than a matter of pride. Kate found the prospect of her new job appealing—being untethered from an office all day might give her time to learn about a place and meet people as well as succeeding for Western Union. She looked forward to it.

After walking three blocks, she found her two-story, redbrick hotel. Each story had a row of three oversized oval windows, and above, an imposing false-front façade extending well beyond the roof. From her travels, Kate had become adept at casually sizing up a hotel. As she entered, she walked by a large, quasi-saloon/dining room on the left, and continued down the hall to the lobby and front desk. "Good afternoon, my name is Kate Sinclair. I have a reservation."

The clerk was a scrawny, older man with wrinkled skin and a skimpy beard. Peering through half glasses, he traced the list of reservations with his knobby forefinger. "Oh, of course, Miss Sinclair. Now I remember. You're going to be with us for a while. How do you do?"

"I'm glad to be here. Thank you," she smiled. "I wonder if you might have a room at the end," she pointed up and to the far corner, "since I'm staying a long time."

He hesitated. "I might manage that," he said, giving her a curious look. She was not sure his look came from the request or because she was an unescorted woman. He put back the key he had originally taken and picked another from a different cubby hole. "Your trunk's here already. I'll lug it up after I show you your room."

They walked up the narrow stairs to the back corner, away from the noise of the street and eating area below. She liked the room—small but not cramped, with a table for writing and another with a water pitcher and bowl, and the blue floral wallpaper was without stains or rips. A stout brass bolt on the door looked plenty safe.

—·— ·— — ·

The telegraph office Kate had noticed when she stepped off her train was her first stop after breakfast. The small, brick building next to the station served telegraphs along the railroads going both north and east. A bell tinkled as Kate pushed open the door. Inside, she saw a long table along the back of the room with cubbyholes above. Kate heard the familiar clattering of the telegraph where an operator concentrated on her work. "Just a minute," the woman said, without looking up. She wore a colorful ruffled skirt of blue, green, and burgundy stripes, topped by an iridescent tight-fitting green bodice. Strands of red hair escaped wildly from the coil she had wound casually above the nape of her neck. Finished with the telegram, she looked at Kate with amber eyes. She stood up and stepped to the counter.

"Do you have a telegram to send?"

"No," Kate moved forward and held out her hand. "I'm Kate Sinclair. I have a job similar to yours on the east coast."

"Aubrey O'Hare," the woman clasped Kate's with her strong, bare hand. "What company do you work for?"

"Western Union."

Aubrey retracted her hand; a cloud of wariness crossed her eyes. "You're not here to do us in, are you?"

"Not at all," Kate shook her head, unsure if what she said was true. "I look at different offices, trying to find ways to improve their efficiency. Would you have time to tell me about your work? I came when you might not be too busy."

"Are you trying to get my job, Dearie?"

"No, I already have a job," Kate said lightly.

"Oh, what's the harm." Aubrey opened the hinged gate for Kate to enter, and pulled a wooden chair to the table. "I'll only be able to talk in snatches, between telegrams, and if someone comes in, we'll make like I'm teaching you. No one would put up with women sitting around gabbing. Too many in this town don't like me having this job anyway, but I could use some company." Aubrey's wide, slightly rouged lips tipped up in a smile.

Sitting across from each other, their talk came in broken pieces. Whenever the telegraph clacked into life, Aubrey's wide fingers blurred with speed, tapping out messages. As the telegram strips piled up, she wordlessly pushed over a stack of buttery yellow paper and Kate took over pasting the word strips. As the morning lengthened, customers increased.

"Aubrey, I didn't know business was so good you had to get help," a customer chortled, giving Kate an interested look.

"Don't worry, Jock, I'm just showing her what I do. I can handle everything that comes my way just fine. Don't you worry none."

It was friendly chit-chat that didn't seem to disturb the flamboyant telegrapher. During short lulls between messages, any question Kate asked, Aubrey answered with a surprisingly detailed response. Her language was unpolished, but she understood her job and the telegraph business. Kate quickly learned that Aubrey also knew the town, probably in a different way than women with a more refined background. News flew over the wires to almost everywhere in the world. Local news was communicated across the counter. A telegraph office pulsed with the lifeblood of a town. Kate suspected their different lifestyles might form friendship—she was curious about what Aubrey's previous job was, but their shared interest in business connected them.

"Thank you for having me, Aubrey," Kate said at the end of the morning. "I learned a lot."

"You stay in touch with what you're up to, Dearie. We had a good talk." Aubrey gave a wave of her muscular hand as Kate went out the door.

FIFTY

Closing the door of the telegraph office, Kate tugged down the wide brim of her hat to shade her eyes— breathing in the clear, fresh air, absent humidity. Walking, instead of sitting in a dimly-lit office all day, was exhilarating. Denver was high but flat, with crenelated mountains stretching along the west. Larimer was Denver's main street. Kate decided to explore that first. Passing saloons, the assay office, and a bank, Kate came to a milliner and fancy goods store. She introduced herself to the proprietor, Eliza Babcock. The slender woman, probably in her late thirties, wore a plum-colored flounced dress trimmed with lace and frills. A small, crowned hat with rolled brim pushed toward her forehead over her light-brown ringlets. Kate thought her an appealing advertisement for her store.

Eliza was eager to impress a visitor about the growing town. She told Kate of the increasing number of school children and cultural activities. Traveling musicians, she said, had recently performed an Offenbach opera at

Apollo Hall across the street. Kate casually examined the selection of colorful grosgrain ribbon while she listened.

"Not all the growth is good, mind you," Eliza fretted. "The new dry goods store carries plain things, not nearly the quality of mine, but still, it's competition."

Kate bought a yard of navy ribbon and another of pale yellow before thanking Eliza, and saying she hoped to see her again.

Down the street, at the dry goods store, she examined a selection of linen handkerchiefs while making conversation, thinking a handkerchief would be a nice gift for Alice when she arrived in Black Hawk . . . and another for her mother. "Has the railroad made a difference for the town?" She asked the short, stocky male clerk.

"Two years ago, Denver was spiraling down to dead," he said, adjusting his wire-rimmed spectacles. "After the production of gold flamed out, a few of us hung on to see what'd happen with the promise—very uncertain—of a railroad." The clerk cleared his throat. "It was lean times, believe you me. There was a fierce battle between W.A.H. Loveland, with his Colorado Central in Golden, and John Evans and others, trying to make Denver dominant. Even with Jay Gould and the Union Pacific behind the Colorado Central, Evans and his group won out."

Kate became extra alert at the mention of Gould. She handed the clerk two handkerchiefs. "I'll take these."

"I'd say Denver has a chance now," the clerk said, tearing off a sheet of brown paper to wrap the purchase. "That will be six bits."

Kate counted out three quarters. "Thank you. I'm learning about your city. I can see it has promise." She turned and left the appreciative clerk.

After meandering the length of Larimer Street and back, Kate returned to her hotel for lunch. Afterward, she wrote letters, including mention of Jay Gould in one to Frank. She sent a note to Alice, thanking her again for her invitation and saying she would arrive in a week by stagecoach. Black Hawk was still without railroads and telegraphs.

The next morning after breakfast, Kate went to her hotel's front desk to inquire about Sunday church services. She expected they might be a place to speak to some of Denver's female residents.

The aged clerk said, "I'll start with the ones that have buildings. A lot have more hope than bricks," he told her. As he described the churches, pausing to think of the exact cross streets, Kate made a list with the paper and pencil she had brought from her room. There were more than she would be able to attend before her return east. She had to guess which were most promising. She started with the congregation led by Nathaniel Hill's friend, Reverend Tom Potter.

The chilly morning was a harbinger of changing seasons when Kate walked two blocks from her hotel to the Apollo Hall, where the Baptists held their Sunday service. Around forty congregants sat in rows of individual seats. She counted twelve women. At the end of the service, Kate introduced herself to Reverend Potter, who clasped her hand warmly. Tom was a medium-tall man with a lean frame and chiseled cheekbones. His eyes were intensely direct and completely focused on a person when he spoke.

"I hope you'll join us for coffee in the outer room. My wife, Claire, will want to meet you. In fact, she'll give me the dickens if she doesn't get to meet a friend of the Hills." His dark eyes laughed. "Most likely she'll be surrounded by children. She's a teacher."

The room smelled of percolating coffee and freshly baked goods when she entered. Tom was right. From his description, she guessed which one was Claire—a woman who held the hand of a young girl about three years old, while talking to two other children. Kate approached her, keeping a distance until Claire finished her conversation.

"Mrs. Potter? I'm Kate Sinclair, a friend of the Hills."

"From Providence, then," Claire smiled. "That's where I grew up. Please call me Claire; everyone does." Her dark brown hair, parted pencil-straight down the middle of her crown, was pulled back into a coil at the back of her head. She nodded toward the dark-haired girl with the same small nose and chocolate brown eyes. "This is our daughter, Agnes."

"Good morning, Agnes. I was a teacher, like your mama." She turned to Claire. "Do you teach all grades?"

Before she could answer, Claire was interrupted by a parishioner asking a question. Others stayed close, waiting to have a word with her before they left the meeting room for home. It was obvious the minister's wife was a popular member of the community.

"I'm sorry, Miss Sinclair. I don't mean to be rude. Sundays are busy."

"Please, call me Kate. Don't worry about the interruptions. I just like knowing about schools, since I was a teacher."

"We're growing." She lifted Agnes to her hip. "I teach all ages right now, counting on the older students to help the younger ones. We want to hire an additional teacher." She looked at Kate inquiringly.

Kate was caught off guard. "I don't think I'm interested in going back to teaching right now, but would you mind if I observed one day? I might even be able to help."

"That would be wonderful." Claire released the squirming Agnes, who was gleeful to be free. "The children would benefit from someone new."

Claire taught in a large, wooden building, with one open room. A side hall extending the length of the room held a supply cupboard and hooks to hang the children's outer clothing. The privy was outside. When Kate arrived on Wednesday to spend all day, Claire explained that next year the town planned to build a new brick school, with two stories. It would accommodate first two, and eventually four teachers. For now, thirty children, ages six to eighteen, filled the room with surprising quiet.

"Kate, how would you like to take the older children today? Tell them what you've been doing since you left teaching. Use the map on the wall if you wish."

"Talking about my adventures?" Kate smiled. "I might keep them until dinner time."

Claire quickly divided the room, asking twelve older students to move their chairs toward the blackboard where Kate could teach them. She had the youngest ones sit on the floor in a semicircle by the potbelly stove to listen to her read stories. The remaining ten moved their chairs toward the back to take a spelling test on their slate boards. Kate admired the way Claire managed the room with quiet intelligence.

"I've learned more than I taught," Kate told Claire at the end of the afternoon. "The children told me why their families came to Denver, and about their fathers' occupations." She knew she would learn more about Colorado politics and business when she visited the Hills. "Thanks." She embraced Claire, "It was delightful to teach again. Denver is lucky to have you."

"You held the children spellbound. I owe *you* the thanks. They learned from your being on your own and the way you've accomplished things. Let me know if you want to go back to school teaching." Claire winked.

FIFTY-ONE

Much of the thirty-five-mile stagecoach route from Denver to Black Hawk paralleled the Colorado Central Railroad tracks, newly built since Kate had taken this trip with the children four years ago. As she began the trip, the shimmering fall leaves of aspens and cottonwoods against the fresh blue sky reminded her of the gold that had lured miners to test their luck in Colorado's mountains thirteen years ago.

Eight miles from her destination, the scenery changed. Trees were scarce—used for building, she knew, and the route for the railroad was only graded, not yet built. Black Hawk was blanketed in smoke, making the lack of light like day's end instead of four in the afternoon. Kate suspected it came from the smokestacks known as "Professor Hill's Works"—the smelter that her friend Nathaniel had built to rescue Colorado Territory's mining economy.

Through the stage's Isinglass, Kate glimpsed Alice ahead, stretched up on tiptoes, waiting for the stage, just as she had four years ago when Kate had brought Crawford and Isabel to Black Hawk. This time, when she stepped down the iron stairs and exited the stagecoach, it was Alice who had the children. The usual greeting met her—voices talking one over another, hugs, kisses. Embracing ten-year-old Crawford, and Isabel, now eight, she was cognizant of their added inches and strong bodies. Blond-haired Gertrude squeezed into the throng, wanting to be part of the gaiety. No longer the chubby baby that Kate had met during Alice's visit to Providence, she was now a mobile toddler. Their changes were a reminder of the pace of passing time. It would not halt for her either.

They walked all together up the steep road toward the Hills' home. Crawford and Isabel showed their adopted aunt the school they attended, and Alice pointed to the brick and stone buildings, with ornate cornices and bracketed eaves that had been built since she had last visited.

"I'm glad to have you show them to me," Kate panted. "It gives me a chance to catch my breath." She laughed. "How could I have forgotten the altitude?"

"Because it only took you two days to acclimate, that's why," Alice grasped her hand. "I'm *so* glad you're here."

"Me too. I've missed your friendship."

As Kate unpacked her few things, she heard pots and pans clanging downstairs. Alice had just started to cook dinner when Kate stepped into the kitchen. Helping set the table, she asked Isabel about her favorite subjects at school. Crawford explained the rocks in his collection, and Gertrude showed her a handmade doll with a gingham skirt. The tender emotions flowing from one to another, the fondness, and the sense of family were what Alice had chosen for life. The appealing setting tugged at Kate, but she liked her own life, being on her own and her new assignment.

Nathaniel let in a gust of fall air when he returned from work, mixing the cool in with the warmth of frying chicken and potatoes. His whiskery kiss tickled her cheek when he wrapped his arms around Kate in a welcoming hug.

"How's our intrepid traveler?" He stepped back at arm's length to look at her. "Definitely no worse for wear," he said, taking her hands in each of his.

"It is so good to be here." She clasped his hands "Everything is growing: your children, the town, your smelter; I can't wait for you to tell me all about it."

Kate hoped to focus the visit on Nathaniel's work instead of her own. He would not be as favorable as Frank about her business world. Nathaniel was traditional about a women's role being at home. Like her father, he believed men were responsible for decisions, and women for the hearth, but his gregarious personality and a passion for what he did would dominate. She would learn by listening and with a few well-placed questions. Since she saw him last, Nathaniel had added a few pounds and his mustache was bushier, but the enthusiasm in his eyes was unchanged.

At the head of the dinner table, he served individual plates of fried chicken, mashed potatoes pooled with gravy, and warm apple slices. "This job of mayor takes time away from work," he complained, not too vehemently.

Nathaniel had been urged by some townspeople to run for mayor of Black Hawk because of his business experience; others fought against him because of what they considered his excessive smelting profits. Despite that, the election results had landed solidly in his favor. Since then, improvements to the town had increased his popularity.

"The railroad should reach Black Hawk next year," he said. "We've made progress, but there are still grumblers. What's important now is statehood—it's about time, after eleven years as a territory. I've joined the Territorial Council to fight for it."

With all the dinner plates served, the five Hills and Kate bowed their heads for grace. The children waited for their mother to start before hungrily beginning to eat.

"Why has becoming a state taken so long?" Kate asked.

"Politics," Nathaniel finally said after swallowing his first bite of chicken. "Voters turned down the effort in 1864, and during Reconstruction, President Johnson vetoed it. Since then, Congress has rejected an almost-yearly appeal, using the excuse of too few people in the territory."

He swirled a dollop of potato in the brown gravy and put it in his mouth, then swallowed. "With recent growth, Washington's excuses are running out."

Solving problems as usual, Kate thought admiringly. Nathaniel never sat back and complained; he got involved in a cause he believed in. His persistent leadership usually led to success.

FIFTY-TWO

During the day, Alice and Kate walked up and down the inclines of Black Hawk. Kate's labored breathing improved with each outing as she acclimated to the altitude. Sometimes they walked a mile to Central City, where an azure sky was more likely than one smudged by smelting. The spirit of a mining camp dominated by men still lingered, yet in both towns Kate saw touches of refinement emerging, with substantial commercial buildings and growing numbers of permanent homes. It surprised her that neither town was as rough as Denver. There were fewer saloons, and any brothels were out of sight.

Knowing Kate wanted to be able to understand the territory for her job, Alice introduced her to some of the local business owners—some more prosperous than others. All had different personalities and stories about what brought them to the mountains. Kate was especially heartened that women ran a few stores. She admired their savvy sense of business and their awareness of both local and national events. They were self-reliant, although not always by choice.

Kate kidded Alice about politics. "Did you notice that some were quite effusive about politics and the mayor? Others were dead silent."

"The latter don't think Nathaniel should be mayor." Alice rolled her eyes.

"They were outnumbered," Kate laughed, knocking Alice's bonnet askew with a hug.

The visit was rare free time for both of them, while Crawford and Isabel were in school and Gertrude stayed with a grandmotherly neighbor.

"Do you think you'll stay in Black Hawk forever?" Kate asked Alice, their arms linked in an outward expression of their unending bond.

"For the time being. Right now, moving isn't pressing, but it may be someday. Nathaniel's business is hemmed in by the mountains—there's not much room to grow, and even though I enjoy many of the people here, a wider circle of friends would be nice." She slowed her pace, and they unhooked arms. "What about you? Is your job what you expected?"

Kate sensed Alice reading her face for what she might not acknowledge with words.

"I'm not sure what I expected," Kate admitted with a shrug. "At first it was for income and to build my savings, but then it became more. I like the feeling of succeeding, even if it's often a battle."

"I'm not surprised." Alice laughed. "I'm surrounded. Both you and Nathaniel thrive on challenge."

"Except that he's a man." Kate frowned. "Success in business for men is applauded. For women, it's either discounted or resented." They stood at a street corner, in front of a grocery store's glass window, marked in oily chalk with the day's specials. In the distance, mountains gleamed with frosted peaks. "I might not have this job without Frank."

"Ahh."

Kate saw Alice's blue eyes flicker with curiosity. "He puts in a good word for me when my work is overlooked. That's given me opportunities—like this one in Colorado."

"How often do you get to see him?"

"Not often," Kate's initial scowl turned to a smile. "Fortunately, when it happens, we're usually in the same city for a month. It's like a seamless bond—not always agreeing, but always understanding."

"You must miss him."

Kate nodded. "It's a little like my affection for you. We have our separate lives and go our own way, although we write a couple times a month. No matter how long we're apart, we stay connected. It's not exactly the same, of course. You and I have had the same memories for so long, you are part of who I am. With Frank, it's newer, but he's part of who I'm becoming."

She paused and thought about Frank. One difference, left unsaid, was her indescribable passion for him. "Maybe I'm just nostalgic, being with you. I do like my job . . . traveling . . . meeting new people . . . challenge," she cocked an eyebrow at Alice. "Truthfully, it's people you care about that give life the most meaning. I miss that." Kate looked at her watch. "I know it's time to go. Crawford and Izzie will be back from school soon and I want to spend time with those cherubs. I'm running out of time."

FIFTY-THREE

Two inches of overnight snow did not keep Alice and Kate from their morning walk. After watching Crawford and Isabel disappear, crunching down the steep, snowy road, swinging their metal lunch pails. Under the smoky sky, the women discussed the merits of books they had read, debated politics, and laughingly remembered the past. Occasional, frosty breaths puffed out in disagreement, but, except for lifestyles, Kate was in complete accord with her friend.

It was their last night together before Kate was to return to Denver. Nathaniel appeared deep in thought as he mechanically put portions of fried beefsteaks, baked potatoes, and sliced peaches spiced with cloves on each plate. When everyone was served, Crawford took his turn at a blessing: "God is good, God is great. Thank Him for the food we take, Amen."

Nathaniel took only a few bites before turning to Kate. "We've talked about your job as telegrapher, but your intention still puzzles me." He quickly raised his hand, cutting off her explanation. "Before you leave, I want you to hear my concerns. It has more to do with the business than your job. Have you heard about the postal telegraph notion?"

Kate nodded, grateful Frank had told her about the concept that had been debated since 1866. "Yes. It's the idea that the government should run the telegraph just as it does the post office," she said, noticing a flicker of approval across Nathaniel's face.

"It makes sense for a number of reasons." Nathaniel paused for another bite, while Alice shushed Isabel and Gertrude's giggles with an upright finger pressed against her lips. "First, the telegraph, like the mail, is public business. I'm concerned about how much commerce is transacted by wire—if the post office isn't careful, it will be replaced. As a monopoly, Western Union has an undue influence over business and information. No one company should have that kind of power."

"What's the answer?" Alice asked what Kate was wondering.

Both she and Alice continued eating while Nathaniel described the four ideas being discussed. The first was for the government to charter a new company to contract with private companies for transmitting telegrams.

"A postal telegraph can be justified, under a provision of the Constitution, for public business," he said.

A second was to declare all telegraph lines as post roads and, as such, put under the control and regulation of the government. The third stipulated government build an entirely new system, while the last called for the government to purchase all lines from existing providers.

"Not only is Western Union a monopoly;" he said, his jaw firm in his vehemence, "the company manipulates the price of its stock, making it overvalued and artificial."

Kate was uncomfortable about Nathaniel's dismal view of her company. It made her feel culpable, even though it was ridiculous to feel she had influence. "Do you have a preference of the four proposals?" She asked.

"Not yet. Each has its pros and cons, advocates and skeptics. Monopolies are dangerous, especially one that influences information—we need some control."

When dinner was over, with the plates washed and stacked in the china cabinet, Kate called the children upstairs for a last bedtime story. Surrounding her on the bed, the three begged for more, and she relented until the clock chimed nine and their eyes drooped. She breathed in their innocence as she kissed each round, unblemished cheek, reluctant to leave.

A letter from Frank had found its way to the slopes of Black Hawk. *Dear Frank.* His words included lively descriptions of his travels, comments on current events, and newsy information. Every letter he wrote managed to make her laugh ... think ... and wish she were with him. She sat at the edge of the quilt-covered, narrow bed, using the side table for writing. After Nathaniel's discursive, she had plenty to relay to Frank, and things she wanted to know from him.

She was scheduled to go to Denver in the morning, and then on to many work locations before returning to the east coast. Leaving the friendship of the Hills made Kate sad, and also unsettled that Nathaniel considered Western Union a threat to the country's communication system.

FIFTY-FOUR

Flat-stemmed cottonwood leaves rustled in the fall breeze as Kate walked through Denver for the last time. The September sun, high in the sky, shone on the trees along the Platte River. Leaves had turned from pale green to yellow, like lanterns lighting Denver's otherwise colorless landscape. In the panorama to the west, the higher mountains had an early dusting of snow; and in the opposite direction, the flat grasslands stretched everywhere east.

Two men passed Kate with a nod and a tip of their hats. She recognized them as a banker and storeowner who, because they were Nathaniel's friends, had been willing to meet with her. Once they did, they became intrigued with her work and had introduced her to several other business leaders. She considered it a victory that she had gained their respect—if not, perhaps, their approval.

Down the street, a shop owner greeted her with a flutter of his hand as they crossed, going in different directions. By connecting with many different people, Kate had acquired a good sense of the town. She had become convinced that, with the railroad links, the dusty frontier town had potential for Western Union. Grating against her sense of accomplishment were Nathaniel's vocal opinions about monopolies, and men who desired to control telegraphs for their own benefit.

The following morning, she boarded the Denver Pacific north to Cheyenne and spent a week at its telegraph office. From there, she traveled on the Union Pacific east to Omaha, Des Moines, and Kansas City, each for a week. Finally, she returned to Providence.

- - - -

Another year had passed since Kate had been home . . . and since the confrontation with her father about Sally. She ached to resolve the issue of the affair—whatever resolution meant. Did she want her father to confess to Eugenia that he was seeing another woman? Or describe what the relationship was and who had Will's loyalty? And revealing the relationship would hurt Eugenia as deeply as it had hurt her, Kate knew.

The letters had been clattering around in her mind since youth. Not just clattering, but shaping the attitudes she had toward men—never trusting or getting too close. Frank was the one exception and, wonderful though he was, Kate was uncertain she could ever truly commit to him. Consequently, she had agonized about going home, yet her mother deserved her only daughter's company. Though Kate seldom returned, home was a touchstone—a permanence in her life.

Providence dripped with desultory midafternoon rain on her arrival. As she disembarked at the station, her tightly woven wool coat and hat kept the damp away. The uniformed stationmaster tried to ignore her, busying himself with other passengers, as if she must be expecting a man to escort her. However, a small coin from her gloved hand and polite request worked, as it almost always did, and he called a hack for her.

Inside the front door, Eugenia enfolded Kate into her arms. "Welcome home. We are so happy to see you. Let me take your coat—you're all wet."

Kate put down her big leather satchel—her trunk was coming later—and released her coat to her mother's hands. Along with the weight of her coat, the built-up tension about returning home was released.

"Rain is a nuisance, but it does rinse away the factory smoke for a while," Kate said.

"Come, let's go back to the kitchen. There is hot water in the teapot."

Sipping smoky oolong tea, Kate listened to her mother's news about her brothers and got caught up on local happenings. The warmth and familiarity of the kitchen was hypnotic.

"Are you going to see some of your friends?"

"I hope so. I've written notes saying that I'll be visiting. I do want to see them," Kate replied.

"It's good not to drift completely apart."

Kate nodded. "I don't want to give up friends altogether." Her attention shifted. "I might take a trip to Boston for a couple of days." She shuddered. "Ugh, the thought of more travel!"

"Is there another talk?"

"No." She looked into her mother's inquiring eyes. "Mama, thank you for the tea. You make me glad to be home. Can I do anything for you in the kitchen before I go upstairs and unpack? Some of my things may have gotten wet. I'll be back down to help get dinner on the table."

"You don't have to help, but I'd love your company."

— ·— ·— — ·

During her trip home, Kate had settled on what she knew was a cockamamie scheme. Knowing that her father would repel any questions, she decided to see what she could learn from Sally. Kate believed an unspoken connection had been made at the Alexander Bell lecture. There was no question that Sally had recognized her name, even if unacknowledged. That much, Kate believed. If, since then, Sally had learned that Kate was aware of the affair, the woman just might be forthcoming with an explanation. Of course, it was just as likely that Sally would refuse to meet with her or deny the relationship altogether. Kate did not know if anyone else was aware of the affair. She assumed keeping it secret must be a constant worry for both Sally and her father, whether the actual relationship was over or not.

Kate agonized about the best way to accomplish her outlandish idea. Sending a telegram was a possibility, although it might be read by someone else. Showing up at the address Kate had tucked into the back of her travel journal was another option, but it was the height of rudeness to arrive unannounced, as well as a gamble. Sally might easily be out for the day. In the end, Kate decided a note was best . . . to begin with. It took away the element of surprise, but surprise would not necessarily bring more information.

She sat at the mahogany desk with curved Queen Anne legs she had used since childhood. Everything, from simple arithmetic to increasingly sophisticated thinking, had all been done at this desk . . . and now, she embarked on this unexpected task.

In the right-hand drawer, she kept spoiled sheets of stationery to use for drafts. She tinkered with openings, endings, and what she actually wanted to say. For the most part, the words came quickly.

Providence
October 30, 1872

Dear Mrs. Andersen,

I hope you might remember meeting me briefly at the end of the Alexander Bell lecture in Boston, over a year ago. I remarked that we had both also been at the talk by Susan Anthony the day before. When we met, you were in a rush to meet a friend with whom you had shared a carriage, and we were unable speak further.

My travels take me away much of the time, and I have not been home since then. I am very interested in meeting with you. We have much in common.

It is possible for me to visit Boston on November 11 or 12. Kindly respond and indicate if either of those days might work and specify a place that is convenient. I will come to the place of your choosing.

Sincerely,
Katherine Sinclair

On the envelope, Kate included only her street address—no name.

The grandfather clock's five chimes reverberated up the stairs. Kate would let the thoughts in the letter steep, like brewing tea, until after dinner, and then put the words on a piece of good stationery. She slipped the draft under her blotter and went downstairs.

"Give me a job, Mama," Kate said, wrapping a white apron around her slender waist.

"What about cutting carrots?" Eugenia handed her three fat carrots, a knife, and a cutting board.

Kate rhythmically sliced carrots for steaming—they reminded her of gold coins. She popped the last piece in her mouth, savoring the sweet, crisp taste. Standing next to her mother in the cozy kitchen was pleasantly reminiscent of her childhood.

A little past five, Will came in the door, home from work. Kate smelled the damp air as he gave her a hug. It was not the fatherly bear hug of long ago, with his whiskery mustache tickling as he planted a kiss on her cheek. Instead, she absorbed his perfunctory arm wrap around her shoulders while his eyes refused to meet hers.

"May I pour you ladies a sherry?" He reached for his bottle of brandy, and with their assent poured sherry for them. "I'll be in my study; let me know when dinner is ready." He turned and left the kitchen.

At dinner with her parents, some of Kate's tenseness dissipated with the familiarity of being at home. The three of them occupied themselves with breaded pork chops, cabbage salad, and steamed carrots, while Kate talked mostly about Alice and Nathaniel, relieved to have so much news for conversation. She described the Boston and Colorado Smelter as going full throttle, and told her parents of Nathaniel's political activity.

"Nathaniel's interested in politics? It doesn't surprise me. He always liked to get things done." Will's erect posture made him appear interested, though he mostly kept his eyes lowered, concentrating on his food.

Kate would have liked to know if her father had the same concerns about monopolies and control of news as Nathaniel did, but she was afraid to bring up the topic of Western Union and her job. Instead, she said, "I knew you'd like to hear about what Nathaniel's doing."

She changed subjects, needing to talk about her stay. "Thank you both for having me. I'll be here for almost two weeks, if that's okay." She tried to sense Will's reaction without looking at him, suspecting she would receive a cold shoulder during the time she was at home. Without enough thought, she added, "I might go to Boson, but I haven't decided."

"Boston! For business?"

Eugenia and Kate both jumped, startled by her father's harsh voice.

Kate scoured her mind for a reasonable response. "Yes yes, business," she stammered.

"What kind of business?" Will's eyes narrowed.

"Just business I need to do." She caught her mother's perplexed look.

All three of them were still and silent. Eugenia looked at the three finished plates. "I have chocolate cake for dessert. Let me clear and bring it right out." She stood up, skirt rustling as she collected the plates, and hurried out, almost in escape.

While Eugenia was in the kitchen, Will muttered under his breath. "You better be going to Boston for your own business, young lady." His glower sent a shiver up Kate's spine and her mind emptied of anything to say. He pressed his lips firmly together. As always, he was on the offensive, yet Kate suspected somewhere inside he must feel trapped. He could not control what might happen to his long-held secret.

It seemed to take forever for Eugenia to return with the cake. Kate took a bite, drizzled with buttercream frosting, but her tastebuds were numb.

Do I dare send the letter?

FIFTY-FIVE

Providence weather remained in a funk—sometimes raining, but even when it wasn't, the air was so saturated it was like walking through fog. Kate refused to let the sodden environs keep her from going to her friends' "at homes." She moved through a room, looking for people she knew. When she found a long-time friend, laughter about times gone by came easily. However, once past the reminiscing, they haltingly searched for things to say—a once close-knit cohesion had unraveled. Kate was frustrated. Women new to the city were more in tune with what was going on than she was.

Sometimes, in larger homes, the hostesses included mothers. At those, Eugenia was elated to show off Kate. It amused Kate to listen to her mother brag about what she disapproved of. "Do you know Kate travels all over the country with her job at Western Union?"

In response, there was interest but also disconnect.

"I can't imagine," came one reply. "I still have my little ones at home all day. Then, there are so many social obligations—my husband is the vice president of First National Bank. And I probably overdo it with volunteer commitments."

Despite the pitfalls of some conversations, the advantages of retaining friendships outweighed them, Kate knew . . . at least for this stay in Providence.

—·— ·— — ·

Kate's heart reverberated with the metal clang of the postal box. The decision to mail the letter to Sally had not been an easy one. There was a chance word would get back to her father and cause even more damage . . . to everyone, but Kate had come this far. Some intrinsic part of her needed to fully understand when and how her parents' relationship had gone wrong—how her father could essentially live two separate lives. So, she sent the letter, worrying every day that she would get a response; worrying even more when she did not. By Friday, she still had not heard a thing. Since Kate had done most of what she wanted to do in Providence, she decided to go to Boston on Monday as planned, knowing the likelihood was more than even she would not see Sally. She had to try while she had the chance.

Life with her parents had reset to a new pattern, with both Kate and her father papering over the secrets they kept. After Saturday breakfast Eugenia had sewing projects, and Will said he would work on his new hobby of collecting stamps.

"Where do you get the stamps you save, Father?" Kate asked him.

"At first they were from—"

An insistent banging of the brass doorknocker echoed from the foyer to the dining room.

"What the devil?" Will shoved back his chair, tossing his napkin on the table in his hurry to answer it.

Kate strained to hear, but her father's words were inaudible. Soon he came back and dropped a thin yellow envelope at Kate's place. "It's from Boston," he said icily, looking over her shoulder instead of moving toward his chair.

Her head swam toward escape, but there was none. She placed the blade of her dinner knife under the flap, slicing open the envelope. Kate read the telegram out loud. CHELSEA 8:02 AM NOV 10 1872 BOSTON ON FIRE BUSINESS DISTRICT BURNING FIRE DEPARTMENT CAN'T CONTROL YOU SHOULD KNOW ETHYL BROCKHURST.

They all gasped. Kate was at a loss for words with the unexpected news. She had suspected the telegram might be from Sally, as had her father, judging from his expression when he handed it to her. The news of the fire whirled in her brain, so unexpected, she had trouble comprehending it. She shook her head, trying to identify Ethyl Brockhurst. The town of Chelsea was just south of Boston. Kate had spent a week at the telegraph office there a few months back. After a minute or two, her mind cleared. Ethyl was a tawny-haired girl from rural Massachusetts who worked in the Chelsea office. She was one of the many young women Kate had befriended when on a Western Union assignment. Ethyl had looked up to her as a teacher, doing everything to please, and had asked Kate for her home address. Ethyl had written her a note of thanks.

Kate guessed that, from the Chelsea office, smoke, and even flames sparking the Boston sky would have been visible. The poor, frightened girl had turned to Kate to tell the shocking news.

"Who is Ethyl?" Will demanded.

"I worked with her at the Chelsea telegraph office. She's probably terrified, being so close to the city." Kate forced her own words of terror back down her throat. She was sick, hearing about another fire, recalling the devastation in Chicago and charred, postwar remnants in Richmond.

"I need to find out more about this." Will shoved his hands in his pockets and took a few pacing strides. "I'm going downtown."

"It's Saturday," Eugenia said. "Offices will be closed."

"I need to try." He turned toward the dark of the foyer. "I'll be back with any news."

--- --- --- --- ---

News about the fire filled Providence. The fire had started in the basement of the Tibbets, Baldwin, and Davis dry goods warehouse, at the corner of Kingston and Summer Streets, early Friday night. Once the fire began, the flames were sucked up the wooden elevator shaft, rising to the roof. Steep-pitched, overhanging wooden mansard roofs were a common architectural feature of the district because they allowed for extra storage, and the city did not tax merchandise kept in warehouse attics. From this first building, flames leaped from rooftop to rooftop, quickly incinerating most of Boston's financial district. Thirteen people perished. So painful were the descriptions, Kate barely had the stomach to read the newspaper. She was relieved that the number was fewer than the hundreds who had died in Chicago, but her heart ached for those who lost loved ones. Many businesses were destroyed and, with them, people's livelihoods.

For days, multi-paged, special newspaper editions accusingly reported delays in extinguishing the fire. Boston had installed alarms throughout the city twenty years previously, but each one required an individual key, in order to prevent false alarms. The night of the fire, the fire department made frantic, time-consuming searches to find those who had each key. Firemen were further hampered by large crowds. Warehouse owners trying to salvage their merchandise filled the narrow Boston streets, joined by hundreds of residents who flocked to the site to learn what had happened. Old and leaky pipes were another problem. They had been a complaint of the fire chief for years, as were non-standardized hydrant couplings. And, once hoses got to the fire, water pressure was so weak that it could not reach the upper floors. Consequently, the fire spread, taking over twelve hours to contain. In the end, it destroyed 776 buildings. Kate was overwhelmed by the amount of damage to much of a city she had so often visited.

Too late, politicians stepped up to podiums to demand enforcement of codes and prohibiting wooden buildings crowded together along constricted streets. A black cloud of depression settled over Boston and far beyond.

Kate spent the next week in Providence, volunteering with her mother in efforts to help collect food and clothing for those who suffered losses. Throughout the week, her father remained stoic and tight-lipped. Kate couldn't help but wonder if he had heard from Sally. Irrational as it was to hope to meet with the woman, Kate chafed at once again being unable to resolve the issue of the letters.

FIFTY-SIX

Assignments in New England at the end of 1872 and into 1873 were grim endeavors. Life had tipped like cascading dominoes. The Great Fires in Chicago and Boston strained bank reserves to the point of insolvency. The economy spiraled down into a financial panic. To add to the crisis, a contagious strain of equine influenza had swept south from Canada, taking down large numbers of horses as it spread. The sad results had been evident in every town Kate visited. She watched horses wheezing on the streets, short of breath and too weak to work. One time, leaving work, she saw a skinny old nag, ears drooping, being led along. The wretched animal stumbled and fell right at Kate's feet, too sick to get up. She stood immobilized, watching the owner trying to get the pathetic beast to rise.

Thousands of animals died, littering the streets with carcasses because there were not enough horse-drawn carts to take them away. Bit by bit, construction slowed, coal was undelivered, and children did without milk. In desperation, men—some in work clothes, some in coats and top hats—voluntarily lined up to pull carts and carriages for people who needed hospital care. Without the essential labor of horses to build and operate cities, many cascaded down into economic disintegration.

The country was somber. News of failing businesses and economic distress coming across the wires took its toll on telegraphers. The former camaraderie and lively gossip during waiting times was absent. So many people were unemployed, even those with jobs became edgy with foreboding about what crisis might happen next. Kate moved through life mechanically, trying to avoid emotion because everything was so raw. Frank's letters were one of the bright spots during the misery. He wrote about his busy job, and also commented on the hardship around him in San Francisco.

———— ·—· —· — · ·

Warnings about the economy sounded before the Boston fire and the one in Chicago in 1871. As Kate understood it, railroads were at the heart of the issue. At the end of the war, government land grants and subsidies had caused a boom in railroad construction. As the tracks spread, so did wild speculation. The risks were great; the returns, slow to come. She was thankful her small inheritance was invested with the conservative Old Stone Bank, and not anything so risky. Yet, throughout her travels, she witnessed the way available cash fueled expansion of warehouses, docks, and other supporting businesses. The railroad industry employed more people than any other, except agriculture. As the speculation collapsed, newspapers began calling the times the Panic of Seventy-Three.

Postal deliveries slowed like everything else. Letters arrived intermittently during her travels, even with advance notice of locations and hotels. Her mail went into a forwarding spiral—rarely catching up with her. Nevertheless, she spent part of her empty evening hours writing long letters, never sure when they would reach friends in Providence, her parents, brothers, Alice, and especially Frank. When a letter did come, Kate read and re-read the lines. She found comfort in the words even if they were dated.

Alice's writing was a flow of ideas and impressions, one succeeding another just like her conversations. One moment she was recounting a small injury to one of her children; in the next, she was talking about the economy. In her most recent letter, Alice complained about economic pressure put on Western silver miners by the recent Coinage Act. U.S. currency had always been backed by both gold and silver; coins were minted from both metals. However, the Treasury Department was worried the rich, new Western silver mines would lower the price of silver, causing more silver coins to be minted and jeopardize the gold standard. Under the new law, the government no longer bought silver or minted it into coins. Alice feared that the price drop would no longer make silver mining profitable.

Since the Hills' personal finances were built on smelting gold and silver, Kate understood her friend's fears, and sympathized in a lengthy letter.

As much as Kate enjoyed Alice's newsy letters, the notes that sent her heart thrumming were from her loyal correspondent, Frank, though his every-other-week letters did not arrive with regularity. Delays meant long stretches without word, and then suddenly three or four letters came all together. When Kate arrived in Poughkeepsie in March, four neatly-stacked letters in his slanted handwriting slid out of the cubbyhole when the desk clerk reached for the room key. It took all her willpower to resist asking the clerk for a letter opener right then and there. With a deep breath, she tucked them in her coat pocket. Not until she was downstairs again, in the hotel's bustling dining room, did Kate unfold each letter—the earliest first. As she leisurely read and ate chunks of pork mixed with baked beans, the noise around her faded. Like his conversation, Frank's writing made seamless transitions from serious politics to light-hearted news.

> . . . San Francisco has not been spared economic distress. Like those in the East, banks are strained to stay solvent as customers withdraw funds to cover their illogical speculation.

You won't believe the latest Jay Gould story. He bribed the infamous Lord Gordon-Gordon, in an attempt to take control of the Erie Railroad. When Gould discovered that Gordon-Gordon was an impostor, he hired someone to kidnap him as he fled to Canada. The escapade almost caused an international incident between Canada and the United States and, as usual, Gould has escaped prosecution. Fortunately, his plot to control the Erie Railroad fizzled. Now he'll have to find something else to do. Mark my words: We'll hear more of Jay Gould. . . .

Always, in closing, he sketched scenarios with lively words of what they could be doing together and how impossibly boring dinners and touring were without her. *I miss you. With affection, Frank.* Kate tried not to dwell on those endings but, despite herself, returned to them over and over.

FIFTY-SEVEN

To Kate, New England's 1873 winter mimicked the hard-edged reality of the shrinking economy—dreary, gray, and bleak. There had been little cheer for months, and then, just as early shoots of jonquils and crocuses showed through the brown earth, Frank's letter came. Western Union had assigned them both to work in Boston for the month of May. Kate was ecstatic. Until she re-read the letter and let the idea sink in, she had not realized how often she went through her lonely life with a clenched jaw and gritted teeth.

The assignment to Boston was a puzzle. The city had not been mentioned by her supervisors. *Was it Frank's instigation?* City sites cascaded through her mind. The "Burnt District" had been widely described in newspapers, yet she could not quite picture the boundaries or damage. On the heels of this thought came one of her aborted trip and mission to find Sally. Should she resume that search?

The Great Boston Fire had caused dislocation of Western Union offices. Frank and Kate had instructions to make a plan to revamp Boston's telegraph system as the city rebuilt. After examining new needs, they were to recommend new offices. Some would be closed, others enlarged. Their proposals, rationales, and possible locations would be sent to New York for approval and further instruction.

Their separate hotels were only blocks apart, making an easy walk to work together. The lobby of the Parker House Hotel, where Frank stayed, had tall, leaded-glass windows with circular tables in front, providing guests a convenient place to meet. Even the most critical busybodies would consider it proper for Kate and Frank to be together there. Each morning, after breakfast, Frank took possession of one of the meeting tables and waited for Kate to arrive. She relished the way his eyes lit up when he saw her enter the lobby.

"Good morning, Kate, what do you have in store for us today?" He stood up in greeting.

She laughed as she hung her wet raincoat and hat on the nearby coat tree. "Are you following orders?" She wore a slim, light-brown suit with dark scrolling trim and a stand-up lace collar. She smoothed her skirt as she took her seat across from him. The suit was new; she had gone shopping when she'd heard she would be with him—a vain indulgence, she knew.

"You're the organized one. I just follow orders." His eyebrow arched with humor.

"And you're very persuasive when you disagree."

They truly did work together seamlessly. Kate laid out schedules and locations, listing what they wanted to accomplish along with a date for completion. Frank met with politicians and businessmen to negotiate what was possible. Separately, they visited different offices, assessing needs and efficiencies, just as they had on many previous assignments. Some days, they went together to look at property. Western Union had unknowingly instructed them to engage in their favorite pastime— exploring different parts of a city together. One such afternoon took them past some of the country's most important landmarks.

"Did you read why Old South Meeting House still stands?" Frank asked her. "It's where the Boston Tea Party was planned."

Kate stood still, looking over at the brick building, with its tall, imposing steeple. "No, but tears of relief come to my eyes to see so many old buildings saved. I can't imagine Boston without them."

Pointing up, Frank said, "Residents climbed up with wet blankets and rugs and covered the entire roof."

"How could anyone be so brave as to do that during a fire? Thank heavens they were—it's our history." She looped her arm through his as they continued on their way.

They spent every dinnertime together, occasionally choosing restaurants beyond their meager allowance. After dinner, they reluctantly returned to their individual hotels to write up what they had seen during the day for discussion in the morning, at their usual meeting place.

One morning, Frank said, "I know it's going to be grim, but I think we should see the site where the fire began. We need to know the scope of the ruins if we want an accurate planning map."

Kate had just arrived. "I think you're right." She put what she had written the previous evening on the table. "I've been focusing on the positive. It's astonishing, the big plans the city has come up with in only six months." Over every breakfast in her hotel, Kate had paid careful attention to local news reports because Frank always absorbed so many details of what was going on everywhere. She wanted to keep up with him. "They're going to make Boston bigger, of all things."

"Their plans are definitely impressive—I hope they all work." Frank looked up at the windows. "It's still raining, but shall we go out to take a look?"

"I don't mind the rain," Kate said, patting her raincoat that she had not yet removed.

"All right," Frank said, pushing back his chair. "Let's go now and do paperwork after lunch."

Kate found the site as overwhelming as Frank had predicted. They watched dozens of workmen digging up the rubble to take it away, raising a wet, acrid stench with each shovel scoop of ashes. Ghost buildings remained; sometimes granite and brick facades were propped up by long poles, in hopes of salvage.

"Take a look around," Frank told Kate as they walked down Summer Street, stepping out of the way of workers slogging rubble-filled carts through the mud. "This is the past, and the future will be different. Just like Chicago, recovery will take hard work and ingenuity, but it'll come."

"It's beyond ingenuity—they're actually moving hills?"

Frank nodded "The city is taking down five hills and adding the dregs from the fire to fill in some of the Bay, for more buildable land. Someday, people won't know Boston was a hilly place," he laughed.

"It's definitely an ingenious way to make the city grow."

"More land means more telegraph offices."

"But not in time for our project."

"Fortunately, not. We have enough to do." Frank gave her an up and down look. "Are you staying dry?"

"The rain isn't that bad, and it's not too cold."

"All right, then. Let's try to walk the perimeter of the 'Burnt District' before we go back for lunch and more work."

"You're a taskmaster," she quipped, "but a personable one."

FIFTY-EIGHT

Time passed by as quickly as a runaway train when Kate and Frank worked, ate, and laughed together. At night she fell into her bed with pleasurable exhaustion. Sleep was a continuation of the dream she was living. Not that she and Frank always agreed—for example, he thought government should keep hands off a private project; she believed some assistance was necessary. Kate was obstinate when it came to women's rights and petulant about losing an argument. Sometimes, Frank resorted to saying, "I guess we'll have to agree to disagree," and changed the subject. However, even their occasional differences of opinion made the time with him exciting. She would have hated him to retreat into a shell as her father did. Thinking of the comparison brought Sally to mind. For the present Kate was too busy to think about searching for her.

They generally concurred on work matters, although what they were trying to do did not always go smoothly. Politicians often stood in the way of an idea that would make their plan possible, with hints that under-the-table payment would be necessary in order to get a permit. At times, Frank found a way to circumvent a call for government interference, but other times not.

"I don't mind rules, if they're followed," he said, one day, pounding his fist hard on the table. "Projects should be approved on merit, not on the finagling of politicians and their cronies."

Kate sat back and listened, content to be his confidante when he needed to sound off. She found him open about personal and business matters, regretting that she was not entirely the same. He was as willing to listen to what was on her mind, even her strongest opinions, as Alice was. Nevertheless, as the days passed, she continued to hold back her deep secrets about her father's illicit relationship from both of them.

— ·— ·— — ·

The problem of Sally became an increasing irritation. The idea of leaving Boston without trying to find her was intolerable. Kate considered sending a telegram saying she was nearby, but too many telegraphers knew her name. Finally, she sent a note by messenger.

> I am in Boston and would appreciate meeting with you. I would be grateful if you would kindly respond to the Irving Hotel telling me a convenient time to meet.
>
> Yours in closing,
> Katherine Sinclair

After three days without a response, Kate decided to take action. Sitting at the small desk in her room, she labored to figure out what she would say when she saw Sally. The first scenario was an emotional rant, where she accused Sally of being disreputable, taking a married man away from his wife. That would satisfy her thirst for vengeance but nothing else. *What is it that I want?* Kate didn't consider herself a demanding person, and demands rarely had a positive outcome anyway.

Her temples throbbed as she forced herself to answer her question. First, she wanted to know how Sally met Will . . . and when? Next, was the affair still ongoing? Where was his loyalty? There was more, but those were the answers she desperately needed. She pressed her eyes closed, picturing Sally responding to her knock at the door in the same fashionable clothing she had worn at the meeting when Kate had met her. Kate would introduce herself . . . and then what? The next mental image was of the door closing in her face.

She pulled out the pins and shook her hair free. Reaching for the long handle of her brush, she began the nightly ritual of brushing her hair to relax—one . . . two . . . three . . . After she reached one hundred, she finished the rest of her ablutions, slid between the sheets, and pulled the rough, gray woolen blanket over her. Closing her eyes did not take away the images or bring any solutions—her thoughts were still spinning as she fell asleep.

Kate and Frank devoted the next week to office visits—more introductory than the usual week-long remedial work. Frank went to the south side and Kate, north, near Cambridge and the colleges. Arriving at eight, she found two telegraphers in the office. Esther looked to be in her twenties, and Norma was approaching middle age. Both were agreeable and easily able to answer Kate's questions. One filled in what the other did not know. It was obvious to Kate they had an amiable relationship. The office was one of the most satisfactory she had visited.

Toward the end of the morning, an idea began pricking at her, slowly turning into an insistent plan. Sally Andersen's address was nearby. Kate pictured a map. It would be too far to walk, but in this area, hacks were easy to find. She had already learned what she needed for Western Union and could spare time in the afternoon.

"Esther . . . Norma, it's noon. It must be your lunch time," Kate said, tipping the watch clipped to her waist. "I want to commend you both—your office is in perfect order. I'll give exemplary recommendations to Western Union. It's been a good visit, thank you. And now I'm going to take my leave."

"You don't have to leave, Miss Sinclair," Norma said. "I always pack too much in my pail and I'd be glad to share some of it."

"We like your company." Esther chimed in. "We like answering your questions." She looked over at Norma, who nodded in agreement.

"What a kind offer, thank you, but I have to tend to something now that I'm in this area. We . . . I am only in Boston for a short time with so much to do." Kate walked to the row of hooks and retrieved her coat. "I hope you'll forgive me. I wish all offices were this agreeable."

Kate shook their hands, put on her coat, and walked out the door. She almost ran down the street in her impatience. Small business offices filled each side, as opposed to shops or hotels that pedestrians would frequent, and in two blocks she had found a hack, waiting on a cross street.

"Take me to two thirty-two Hickory Street, please," she panted.

"My pleasure, Ma'am." The driver jumped down and opened the door for her. He wore a gray waistcoat and jacket above black trousers. A full moustache reached the edge of his frizzled gray muttonchops. "In a hurry, are you?" he asked quizzically.

"Not in a hurry, exactly," Kate answered, annoyed at herself for appearing harried. Now, more than usual, it was imperative she keep her calm.

"It'll take fifteen minutes, or so," he said, closing the door and clicking down the handle.

Only half noticing the passing buildings change from commercial to residential, Kate searched for words to say to Sally, but none came. What she was doing was brazen.

The hack came to a two-story, gray brick townhouse with house numbers above the façade. A long flight of wide, cement stairs led to a landing, with a door on the right and one on the left.

"Do you mind waiting?" she asked the driver as he opened the door and pulled down the step for her to exit.

"Not a bit; take what time you need."

At the top, she looked at the numbers on the two black mailboxes of the common stoop. The one on the right was number two-thirty-two.

Inhaling deeply, she grasped the door knocker. Her three knocks made a hollow sound. Saliva collected in her throat. From the side, she noticed the driver, his head craned to see what was happening. Nothing. She knocked again—this time harder. The brass sound reverberated but, still, no response.

"Mrs. Andersen, are you there?" Kate put her hands against the door, her head bowed. *I guess they're not—*

"Hey, what's going on here?" The voice came from behind her.

Kate gasped, "Who are you?"

"I live next door. Who are *you*?" He was a tall man, dressed in a shirt and waistcoat, but jacketless, as if he had been interrupted. Underneath his mustache, whiskers sprouted—it must have been days since he had shaved. He stood so close she smelled his sour breath.

"I asked what you're doing here," he said, balling his fists.

Kate leaned away from him. From the bottom of the stairs, the hack driver spoke up. "Do you need help, Miss?"

She shook her head uncertainly. Did this man mean her harm or was he just offended by her repeated loud knocking?

She straightened to her full height. "I'm looking for Mrs. Andersen. I thought this was her address." Trembling, she took a step back. "I guess she's not home."

"They haint here." The man un-balled his fists, his face relaxed a little. "They moved out, after the fire."

"Oh," Kate sagged with disappointment. The hack driver still stood at the sidewalk, ready to assist her. "I'm Katherine Sinclair. I met Mrs. Andersen at a meeting and wrote her a note to see if we could meet." The information was out before she knew it, proof of her discomfort. "Did she say where she was going?"

He shook his head, watching her carefully. "I haint heard hide or hair of her and her son since they left last November. Mail piled up; then the postman stopped delivering it."

Kate pressed her eyes shut over oozing tears.

"I'm sorry I can't be of help." The man's expression softened.

Kate looked up at him, knowing color had drained from her face. "Did she have light hair . . . and a slender build?"

He nodded. "And her son's fair, only a tad darker."

"You said she has a son." This was unexpected information. Kate thought back to the date of the first letter. It was twenty years or more.

"Herb's in high school—a nice kid. The two of them were neighborly. Sometimes, she put tins of food by my door—said they were extras that would spoil if somebody didn't eat them. My job," he stammered. "The downturn's been rough."

"What about the father?"

"He must've died or somethin'. She never said anything, but she and the boy had some means."

Kate grabbed for the railing to keep from toppling, overwhelmed by thoughts. Sally was gone, and "H" was not her husband, as Kate had imagined, but her son. Her thoughts crowded together. She needed to go somewhere where she could think more clearly. "I'm most apologetic to have bothered you. I'll be on my way now."

The man nodded and slipped back into his own apartment.

By the time she lurched down the first four steps, the hack driver had sprinted up to take her shaking elbow and guide her toward his carriage. "Where now, Miss?" he asked, his weather-lined face full of concern.

"The Irving Hotel, if you would be so kind. Thank you." She sat back and began crying in deep, gulping sobs.

———

She lay on her narrow bed. In four hours, she and Frank had planned to meet for dinner. Her mind was in torment about what to do next. Canceling dinner on the pretext of not feeling well would only concern him and lead to questions. However, her distress might cause a floodgate of explanation about a private family affair.

The room was cold, but she did not want to get up to light the fire, so she pulled the scratchy wool blanket over her. Resolution was impossible, now that Sally had left. Knowing she had a son made Kate nauseous. *Who was his father? Might she have another brother?* Kate cringed. The answers she wanted were unlikely, even if she had met Sally. God knew her father wouldn't enlighten her, even if she worked up the courage to ask.

Thoughts kept tossing through her mind along with the unpleasant realization that no explanation would have satisfied her. Her father led two lives—both of betrayal. He was disloyal to her mother. He might have a child by another woman. His deception was unconscionable. It left her too brittle to even open a book. She lay with her disconsolate thoughts until it was time to get ready for dinner.

FIFTY-NINE

A hazy sky transformed the setting sun into an orange orb as it descended ever closer to the horizon. Frank and Kate had agreed to meet in the Boston Common before sunset. They both wanted to explore America's first public park and to stroll the botanical garden's meandering pathways together before dinner. With the changing season, showy flowers burst through their winter earthen prison, lending color to the cool, overcast weather.

"You know they experiment with plants here, and study them," Frank said.

"Now that you say it, I recall reading about it somewhere. I just don't remember things the way you do." She smiled wanly, not quite able to shake the mood of the afternoon and Sally. *And Herb.*

"They use new ways to hybridize and propagate plants." He stepped over to read one of the labels. "Some people object to it—even to having these tags, but I like the information."

"Me too," was all Kate managed.

Eventually, they headed across the street, to a restaurant at the water's edge. So often, they found themselves near water. Twenty white-clothed tables gleamed under gaslight chandeliers. It was not a fancy place, but a cut above their usual cheap haunts. The economy had dispirited them from indulging in anything as fashionable as the hotels of San Francisco. Her edginess resisted the friendly surroundings, filled with low conversations and rushing waiters. From the corner of her eye, she caught Frank looking at her. He was undoubtedly trying to decipher her mood, sensing in that perceptive way of his, that she was out of sorts.

They ordered, and Frank sat back, comfortably. "My office visit wasn't anything out of the ordinary—two men and two women telegraphers. They do what is expected of them and don't look beyond. The economy has them worrying about their jobs and whether their money is safe in a bank. They know people who've lost their jobs—not just because of the fire. It seems like the whole world's cascading down. It was hard to reassure them. What is your news?"

His sharp eyes observed her and pleaded with her, in turn. She wanted to dump the whole sordid story of Sally and her son at his feet. More than ever, Kate wished to be free from the secret she had infuriatingly allowed to influence her existence. Frank would be willing to listen and would probably reassure her. It was she who kept herself trapped. And yet . . . it was difficult to rid herself of her father's shame.

"Mine was above the norm, frankly. Two women did the work quite well, but I know they must also have money concerns. I'm sorry for their worry. The world seems upside down," she said, simply.

Frank noticed the waiter coming with their steaming plates. "Another sherry?" he asked.

Kate nodded appreciatively.

The waiter delivered wide, shallow bowls of steaming seafood—mullet, hake, monkfish, and shellfish in a savory broth of tomatoes, leeks, and celery, with potatoes served separately. The warmth of the nourishing stew and sherry relaxed her a little.

"Kate, I've heard from Western Union. The mucky-mucks like our ideas. They want us to come back here in the fall to see about some of the changes."

Her spoon remained suspended midway to her mouth. "Really? You should be happy."

"*We* should," he said, smiling. He raised his glass for a toast. Setting down her spoon, she mechanically clinked hers against his.

"Before we get too satisfied, let me tell you that someone from New York plans to come to Boston in the fall to meet with us. You know what that means?"

"No."

"It means, most likely, that our ideas will become his."

"How can they be his?" Kate glared.

"He'll have seniority, and our ideas are good enough that he'll expect the credit."

"I thought that only happened to women."

Frank shook his head. "It's often the way a big company works."

Kate finished her stew and pulled out a sheaf of papers from her large purse. When the waiter had removed their bowls, she spread some of her neat outlines across the table. They talked about what was most important to get done before they left in a week—which offices to visit, land to see, and which city officials Frank should meet. It was a lot to accomplish in the time remaining, but putting the items in order made it more manageable.

"The New York office will have to deal with the politicians." He smirked. "Someone there can decide whether bribery is necessary to break up the permitting logjam."

Finally, New York might prove useful. "When I get back to the hotel, I'll make a list for both of us and give it to you tomorrow."

"Thanks, Kate. We make a good team." He paused, his eyes searching her face. "I think this is the longest time we've spent together."

"It was miraculous our stay was extended a little," she nodded.

"Still," Frank said, "it wasn't long enough. I don't want this to end."

When he reached across the table and covered her hand with his, Kate almost flinched with the intimacy.

"I'd like to broach something with you. We're not so far away from Providence and I'd like to do things honorably. I'd like to meet your parents and ask your father for permission to marry you."

Surprised, she jerked her hand away from his. The affection in his eyes turned to hurt. Kate hated herself for it. She was so inept sometimes. "Frank, you haven't even met my parents. My father—" she stumbled and shook her head.

"Every father is particular about his daughter. Will he think I'm good enough?"

"Not at all." *You're too good.* "This has come so suddenly. I don't know what to say."

"Surely, you knew my affection has been steadily growing, all these years. It really started when I first saw you."

Her heart wrenched at the pleading she read in his eyes. She found it hard to meet them.

"Thank you, Frank. My best times are with you. It's such a big step, I—"

"Just say 'yes' and we can spend the rest of our lives together, like we are now."

She shook her head. "I can't. It's too fast."

The suffering silence on both sides of the table immobilized her. After a few minutes, she gathered her wits and picked up the work papers and put them in her handbag. Finally, she met his eyes.

"Could you give me time? You said we're to come back here in the fall. Can we wait till then?"

Frank sucked in a deep breath. She read his eyes, asking an unspoken "why," with more disappointment than he had ever expressed to her. "I guess it's time to go," he said, flatly. He came around the table to help her put on her coat. "We both have work left to do." They stepped out of the restaurant into the cool night air and followed the pathway toward her hotel in silence, arms hanging loosely by their sides.

SIXTY

For the rest of the stay, Frank seemed distant, preoccupied. For the first time, their parting was awkward and brief. Their letters mirrored that for a time, but over the long summer, Kate was relieved when they grew more relaxed. Their tone had changed, however; the balance shifted from personal to business. Her own feelings were wrenchingly ambivalent. Some days, her temptation was to write him a letter that said "yes," over and over again. Other times, the thought of the risk made her light-headed with her ragged breathing.

In June, she found herself in New York. The reception was much like her first interview at Western Union. She was asked to sit in the waiting room, with no indication of how long she might have to wait.

"Mr. Shaffer will be with you shortly," the clerk assured her, and turned to his own work.

In less than five minutes, a tall, trim man dressed in a fashionably tailored jacket and waistcoat with striped trousers entered.

"Miss Sinclair," he reached for her hand and shook it firmly. "I'm Timothy Shaffer. Thank you for waiting. Would you mind coming to my office for a few questions? I'm going to be with you and Mr. Ellsworth in Boston."

"It's nice to meet you. Frank mentioned someone from New York would join us in the fall." The minute the word *us* came out of her mouth, it felt disingenuous. Because of her, there was not the *we* that Frank had offered. Her paranoia about trusting meant it was him and her, *not* us.

"Have a seat, Miss Sinclair." Shaffer cleared his throat, and Kate knew he had observed her hesitation. She took one of the two upholstered chairs across from him. His face was narrow, with high cheekbones framed with well-trimmed sideburns, and clean-shaven except for a thin mustache. His eyes were as dark and alert as a hawk's. Nothing, she suspected, escaped them.

"Why do you propose a telegraph office at Tully Street?" he asked, without preliminaries.

As they parried questions and answers, it became clear that Shaffer wanted to understand the logic behind each of their suggestions: closing or enlarging offices, how many telegraphers would be needed, locations of new offices. Kate sensed how minutely he weighed each recommendation, on the lookout for what was most likely to succeed and bring profits for the company. She found him a perceptive interrogator—his mind active, but his hands perfectly still as he questioned with complete concentration. He did not care where the information came from, even from a woman, as long as he got what he needed—for many reasons, and to enhance his own reputation, she suspected.

Back at her hotel, she filled sheets of stationery, detailing to Frank her conversation with Shaffer, and giving her assessment of the man with whom they would spend time in Boston. It took her longer to write than usual; her personal feelings getting in the way of work. In the past, when she wrote Frank, she frantically dipped her pen and scribbled across the pages, her hand competing to keep up with the freefall of her thoughts. This writing was more restrained. It seemed unfair to have postponed answering his proposal of marriage. She remained agonizingly unsure whether she was just *postponing* or turning him down. Yet, despite putting him off personally, she relied on him for counsel and consolation.

It was disgraceful, but she was too cowardly to commit to any other course.

SIXTY-ONE

Woes of the sinking economy filled newspapers all summer. By fall, everything Kate read decried the plight of the Northern Pacific Railroad. Begun in 1864, during the fervor for railroads, the company lay inactive for the first six years, unable to get adequate financing. Finally, in 1870, after an infusion of money, Northern Pacific began laying rails west from Duluth, Minnesota, tracing Lewis and Clark's route to the proposed terminus of Tacoma, Washington and the Pacific coast. Early progress slowed when construction crews confronted difficult terrain, battling bogs, swamps, and forests. Laying track was made more treacherous by frequent attacks by native tribes trying to halt encroachment into their homeland.

Kate asked for a desk copy of the *Boston Herald* when she checked into the Irving Hotel late on a Monday afternoon in mid-September. She had two hours to read until the scheduled dinner with Frank and Timothy Shaffer. Much of the news was about local projects, stalled because of dwindling funds. The national economic news was no better—the country remained mired in a devastating economic depression.

Frank and Tim Shaffer were staying at the nearby Parker House. Shaffer had sent Frank and Kate a schedule for the ten days they would be in Boston together. Interestingly, he had not included Kate in meetings with others, only on tours, when it was just the three of them. She decided to wait to see how he made decisions before she became miffed about being designated as a tagalong. The daily routine in the schedule he presented was much like the one she and Frank had established the past spring—investigative trips during the day, and review of business over dinner in the evening.

Shaffer stood with Frank in the entry of the restaurant when Kate opened the door.

"Good evening, Miss Sinclair," Shaffer took her fingertips and brought them up, as if he'd forgotten their business footing and might kiss her hand, but he caught himself just in time. "It's good to see you again." His topcoat was long and dark. Beneath it, a gold watch chain hung across his waistcoat. He looked debonair and confident.

"It's nice to see you again, Mr. Shaffer."

"Hello, Kate. It's very nice to be back in Boston."

Frank. How she wished *he* would try to kiss her. Their eyes locked as she shook his hand formally. Noticing Shaffer's astute eyes on them, she kept her greeting businesslike and turned to follow the waiter to their table.

Seated, they all ordered dinner, foregoing any alcohol by unspoken agreement. It was Shaffer's meeting, and Kate knew he would set the tone.

"Frank and I had a chance to do much of our business at the hotel." He looked at her, without any meaning Kate could read. "By the way, please call me Tim," he paused. "May I call you Katherine?"

"Kate," she said, trying to keep the coolness out of her voice. She looked across at Frank from across the table and interpreted his imploring expression as "trapped."

It looked as if it would be a long night.

"I want to see every site you included in your report," Shaffer told them a bit later, between bites of food. "Frank and I can meet with city officials—my position will give weight to Western Union's proceeding."

Kate wondered if "weight" meant greasing palms.

"I'm reconsidering where a new main station should be, but I'll decide that after I see—"

"The location of the telegraph office is premised on the route of the new railroad tracks, after the infill project," Frank interjected, his shoulders straight and voice hard. "The size is based on estimated population growth."

Frank's tone sent a message, Kate realized. He was not going to be Shaffer's errand boy. She hid a smile of approval behind her napkin.

Good for you, Frank.

Tuesday and Wednesday after breakfast, Frank and Shaffer brought a hack around to Kate's hotel so they could all go together to tour the "Burnt District." They went from one site to the next, so Shaffer could see firsthand what Frank and Kate had reported on during their previous visit. They both explained reasons for revamping Western Union locations in response to changes Boston was making after the fire.

"Mr. Shaffer . . . Tim, you wouldn't believe how much this has changed already." Kate gave Frank a quick look. "There's noticeable construction since last May."

Shaffer asked questions but was noncommittal. When he turned to Frank for an explanation of the supporting figures, Frank said, "Kate will know those. She put them together."

Kate explained them, while Shaffer listened impassively. As she finished, he even managed a grudging bit of praise.

"I've been a recipient of Kate's impressive command of details before. I think we have what we need for the day. We'll drop you off at your hotel," he said to her.

When Kate walked down the stairs on Thursday morning, she heard loud conversation from the dining room. She paused at the front desk for a morning paper, hoping to read it with her breakfast.

"Have you heard the news, Miss Sinclair?" The clerk pointed to the extra edition of the *Boston Herald*. "Jay Cooke & Company has gone bust. They say people are lined up at every bank, trying to withdraw money."

"What on earth?" Kate said, picking up the copy and taking it to a small table at the far end of the noisy dining room. She had planned on gulping down a quick breakfast before writing notes addressing the few specific comments Shaffer had made during their tour. Those thoughts fled, however, as she became absorbed in the news about the latest blow to the economy.

Northern Pacific Railroad had defaulted on over a million and a half dollars they'd borrowed from the large, Philadelphia-based Jay Cooke & Company bank. Making matters worse, similar financial crises were affecting Europe, and Cooke was unable to sell securities abroad. With his credit now worthless, the company declared bankruptcy. The newspaper predicted this was just the beginning of an even darker time for the economy.

Kate put down her fork, her stomach too unsettled to eat. She felt a tap on her shoulder. "Frank? What are you doing here? Aren't you going to a meeting?"

His face had a grim expression. "The meeting has been cancelled. I decided to walk over to let you know what's happening. Everyone in the city seems to be out." He nodded toward one of the dining room windows. "People are anxious. It's too much to fathom after enduring the Great Fire." He slipped into the chair across from her.

"Do you remember my telling you about the banker and his wife on the Yosemite trip—the Grahams? They were from Philadelphia, and he worked for Jay Cooke. They left Yosemite immediately after hearing about Black Friday."

He hesitated for a moment, thinking. "I'd forgotten, but now that you remind me, I do."

"He must be somehow involved in this."

Frank didn't disagree. "If he's still in banking, he'll be hurt—and he's not alone. Cooke & Company financed part of the North's effort in the war. When it ended, he had to find another investment. With the huge government land grants and desire to spread across the continent, railroads were a logical choice. They were expensive and slow to return any profit on money invested. Cooke got in over his head."

"The economy was already in trouble, and now this." A shiver of dread went down her spine. Kate wondered how her parents were coping. Would her father's business be in trouble?

"There's going to be a lot of pain." Frank's weariness and distress showed on his face. The surrounding noise made it hard for her to hear him.

"Kate," he leaned forward. "This isn't the time or the place to talk about our future. All summer, I was hoping it would be. Now, with the bank crisis and Tim Shaffer intruding into everything, nothing's right." His face was pale. "My feelings for you haven't changed. Tim thinks it's no use to stay in Boston; he says nothing can be accomplished here, and we should all leave. However, I'm hesitant to do so without some kind of understanding between us."

Frank's eyes were so dark and green and deep, Kate could have fallen into them. Suddenly she was seized by an apprehension that she might not see him again. "Frank, I'm so sorry this has all happened." Her soul was slipping down a precipice. "We *will* have our talk . . ." She glanced around at the near-frantic discussions going on around them. "But, not now . . . the mood is too bleak." She reached out to touch him, but he stood up, put on his hat, and walked away.

SIXTY-TWO

On Friday, Kate left Boston—the same day bank failures caused the New York Stock Exchange to close for the first time in its history. Tim Shaffer had sent a note to her hotel the day before, telling her Western Union had cancelled all assignments, "regretfully, without pay." With deep reservations, she headed to Providence. She had not been there for thirteen months, wasn't yet reconciled to what she'd learned about Sally and Herb Andersen.

Where else is there to go?

The Boston railroad station echoed with people clamoring to leave. Kate gratefully discovered that not many people were going to Providence. She waited at the counter for only a few minutes before she had a ticket for the Rhode Island train. It left in two hours. Glancing around, she happened to see a harried-looking Tim Shaffer, standing in front of a counter decorated with a conspicuous "New York City—Sold Out" sign. Kate quickly surveyed the rest of the cavernous room, searching for Frank, but if he was there, it was too crowded to find him. Pushing her way to the telegraph office, she went in to wire her parents of her imminent arrival.

—·— ·— — ·

Words of more failures came with each news report—affecting the populace like fingernails down a blackboard. Everything was screechingly discordant. A pall swept over both the national and international economies, and experts warned improvement might take years. The "at homes," where Kate would typically have seen her friends, were in abeyance, seeming too frivolous for the times.

"What was Boston like?" Eugenia asked as they lingered over breakfast and tea one morning. "I haven't been there since before the fire. It must be dismal."

"Yes and no. When I left, the city was in despair, but before then, it was already making plans for rebuilding. That's why we were there."

"We?"

"Another Western Union employee and I," Kate said, not looking up. She didn't want her mother reading her eyes until she'd had time to clear them. "Does Father still go to meetings in Boston?"

Eugenia shook her head. "He hasn't been since the fire either. Maybe the offices he usually visited burned down. I don't know."

Kate imagined other possibilities, marveling at her mother's innocence . . . or was it denial . . . or even acceptance? Questions spun like leaves in an autumn wind, skittering and lurching, never settling. Eugenia had made a life for herself in spite of Will's duplicity. Through a marriage contract, he ruled over his wife, yet was disloyal. Didn't that mean he'd forfeited the right to control her mother? Did Eugenia submit only because she didn't know of the affair? Did she still love her husband?

Was the answer never to let anyone control you? Kate had spent half her life believing so, but after so long on her own, she now knew the truth. Control was impossible to avoid—everyone answered to someone or something. Complete independence was unachievable.

So, where does that leave me? And Frank?

"Mama, do you want me to make the bread today? Maybe I should practice."

SIXTY-THREE

The houses surrounding Brown University were stately red brick, stone, or colonial clapboard in classic styles, individualized by their noted architects. Pushing out from the close-in neighborhoods called Campus Hill stood houses of more modest means, brick without embellishments or simple clapboard. Tree-lined parks and paths bound the neighborhoods together, with students, residents, and visitors frequently walking through.

Kate found an apartment on the campus outskirts. It was a rather odd configuration. It had its own bedroom, parlor, plumbing, and kitchen, but was still attached to a house. The couple who owned it had built the adjunct for her mother, who had recently died. Small as it was, Kate was happy that it had come up for rent just when she was looking. The furnishings were mundane and had lost their freshness, but Kate was sure that, with quality fabrics for bedding and curtains, and books on the shelves instead of knickknacks, the small apartment would suit her. It was also not expensive.

Since she had accepted a telegrapher job in Providence. She would be there until she decided what next. Her parents' house had been her birthplace . . . her coming of age . . . her refuge and anchor. It also summoned up ghosts of the past. It was time for a place of her own. At least for a while.

Eugenia was in the kitchen when Kate returned late in the afternoon. "What can I do to help, Mama?" she asked, adding hot water from the teakettle to the cool remains in the pitcher to wash her hands.

"Do you mind peeling and slicing the potatoes?" Eugenia handed her three large russets and a paring knife. "You were gone a long time."

Wrapping an apron around her, Kate began scraping the tan peel off the potatoes. She smelled an apple pie baking. She took a deep breath.

"I have news for you. I wanted to let you know before I tell Father at dinner."

"Is it about your job?"

"Partly. This Panic, as the newspapers call it, is affecting all business. Western Union notified me it had eliminated the position of traveling telegrapher. The executives in New York commended me and said they would help get me a job as a telegrapher at any location I choose."

"Oh, that's good news." Kate saw her mother's expression change, her brow creased. "Unless, you're disappointed?" Eugenia asked, uneasily.

"A little. I'll miss the freedom and higher pay, but even *I* have become weary of so many trains and dreary lodging." Kate tried to make it sound light and unimportant, but it had been a blow to get the news from Western Union. No more traveling telegraphers meant no more month-long assignments with Frank, and only duller, routine work.

"Do you know where you'll go?"

Kate picked up the wooden cutting board and began slicing the crisp, white flesh of the potato. "I'm staying in Providence. This is my home."

"Oh, that's wonderful." Eugenia turned from her cooking to face Kate. "It will be so good to have you."

"We *will* see a lot of each other," Kate hated herself for quashing her mother's joy. "But I've decided to move into an apartment."

"An apartment? What on earth for?"

"If I have my own place, I can come and go without disturbing anybody." Even to Kate, the excuse rang hollow.

"You've never disturbed us. We just rattle around here with all the space." Her mother quickly turned back to the pan, but Kate had noticed her eyes moistening. Even with her many activities, Eugenia's life must be somewhat lonely. Her father's indifference did not help.

"Don't worry, you'll see lots of me," she patted her mother's shoulder. "It's not far from the Hill—walking distance."

"When will you move?"

"In a couple days. My new job starts on Monday. I'm at a different Providence office this time, but still close." Kate had not wanted to go back to the office where David McAnarney was head. "It won't be as flexible as before, but I did get my first choice." Kate recoiled, thinking of the long days sending and receiving telegrams instead of examining budgets and devising efficient ways of doing things. No telling what the other fourteen people in the office would be like. There was already a head telegrapher, so she would not be in charge. Kate attempted to change her thoughts to the positive. "If I ever want to see friends, I hope you'll let me do it here. My new place is so small, it will only hold one guest . . . oh, maybe two, if they're thin," she said, laughing.

Eugenia turned, with a smile, shaking her head at the thought. Kate suspected she had just begun plotting entertainments to keep Kate close in her roomy parlor.

—·— ·— — ·

By letter, Frank informed her he had re-assumed his position as manager of the network of Western Union Telegraph offices in California. Like Kate, his wider travel had been halted. Even though their work in tandem had ceased, they maintained their common interest in Western

Union. Their letters became exchanges of events that might affect the company, with little about personal life. Kate gave him her new address, telling him she had moved to an apartment. Frank responded that he would be happy to look for a job and apartment for her in San Francisco. Kate imagined his earnest face and bright brown-flecked green eyes when he wrote it. It was his way of letting her know he was still interested, but also that he was not going to plead. She knew his sentiments; any next steps were hers.

— ·— ·— — ·

The new year came, with little fanfare. After three months in her new apartment, Kate had adjusted to the size. With permission from Elise and Mike Channing, her landlords, she replaced the curtains on the two windows with creamy alabaster linen that did not block the sun but provided privacy when drawn. Eugenia gave her a cast-off quilt with geometric flowers on a muslin background. She bought thick cushions for the rocking chair, where she read, and the desk chair, where she did her writing.

One icy March morning, when winter still kept Providence frigid, she and Elise Channing arrived at the trash bin at the same time.

"Are you tossing out the news?" Elise asked her.

"These are from last week. I was behind with reading my newspapers, but I finally caught up. Of course, there is another one waiting on my desk." Kate sighed. "I always seem to be behind on everything."

"Would you mind if I take them? We don't subscribe."

"I would like that. It's a shame for them to go to waste." Kate handed her the pile. She was glad to get rid of them. Long articles contained news of Jay Gould's success in gaining control of the Union Pacific. Accordingly, he had instructed the Atlantic and Pacific Telegraph Company to end its noncompete agreement with Western Union. Then, he convinced inventor Thomas Edison to sell his quadruplex telegraph system to Atlantic and Pacific. The quadruplex was capable of sending four messages simultaneously over one wire—two each way. Kate could just imagine Frank's reaction to the news. Even to her, it was obvious that Gould had made Western Union a target.

Elise was a short, compact woman, with gray mixing in her brown hair. Kate guessed she was in her middle fifties. She wore a heavy wool cape with a plaid scarf wrapped around her neck. They did not see each other often but exchanged pleasantries when Kate paid her monthly rent. Both she and her husband were interested in what Kate did, without being nosy. Kate felt secure, living at the back of their house, and appreciated their respect for her privacy.

"I have an idea, Elise. When I finish with the news, I'll come around and put it on your front stoop. Then, I won't be so wasteful."

"That'd be so generous. We'd both read it if it were here. Mike will be as glad about it as I am. Thank you again. We're so happy you rent from us."

"You can count on the paper. I'll try to keep up, so what I pass along is really news." Kate turned to go back around the house to her apartment.

"Cheerio," Elise responded, waving her gloved hand; the other wrapped around the stack of newspapers.

SIXTY-FOUR

Kate thought the Centennial International Exposition of 1876 was a fabulous place. Two hundred new buildings filled the exposition grounds of Philadelphia's Fairmount Park, stretching along the Schuylkill River. Streetcars running at short intervals whisked visitors from site to site, and the Pennsylvania Railroad ran special trains from outlying Philadelphia and from as far as New York City, Baltimore, and Pittsburgh. To accommodate out-of-state visitors, a committee sold tickets for available rooms in hotels, boarding houses, and even private homes.

Unfortunately, the humidity and the hot August air were suffocating. Kate had chosen late summer to go because Alice and Nathaniel would be there at the same time. Kate had managed a week off work only because she took it without pay. She'd been determined to make the trip. There had been distress that women's contributions would not be recognized at the exposition, and since her return to Providence, she had joined other women volunteers in soliciting support for the Women's

Pavilion. After the months of hard work, it was nice to see their efforts come to fruition.

She and the Hills had found rooms in a temporary hotel, built just for the exposition. The interior walls were sea green, and rose-colored velveteen draperies framed the windows—everything was fresh, clean, and modern.

Alice and Kate met for breakfast the first morning and made a schedule of sites they wanted to see. Nathaniel planned to attend a political meeting that day. He and others were hosting an exhibit on Colorado, celebrating statehood. After a fifteen-year effort, Colorado had become the Centennial State on August first.

"Have you looked at the list?" Kate asked.

Alice sat across the table from her, wearing a lightweight, cotton lace shirtwaist and a navy twill skirt with a wide, black band across her plump waist. "I have . . . a couple of times." She glanced again at the long sheet of paper the desk clerk had given them when they checked in. "There's more than we can possibly do in our five days here, but I suggest starting with the main exhibition hall, then the Women's Pavilion, and of course, the Colorado exhibit; perhaps Nathaniel will lead us through."

"I'd like that, if he can spare the time." Kate was eager to cheer about what he had worked so hard to bring about. She, too, was wearing the lightest weight fabric in her wardrobe. Her dress was gauzy and white, with a lace front, collar, and cuffs—all tied tightly with a deep-pink sash.

"Can you believe we're sitting here in Philadelphia together?" Alice asked.

Kate knew the twelve years since Nathaniel had gone west to explore mining propositions had not been easy for either of the Hills, especially at the beginning. Since then, her friends' lives and relationship had smoothed, while her own remained unresolved.

"What exhibits do *you* want to see most?" Alice asked, interrupting Kate's thoughts.

"Colorado, of course, and we have to visit the Women's Pavilion." Kate glanced across the table to read Alice's reaction to what she was going to say. "After that, would you consider the inventions in the Machinery Hall?"

"Put it on the list. I can always count on you to find something interesting."

Inventions fascinated Kate. She was envious of the men, and a handful of women, who devised life-changing inventions, many of which involved complicated science. Of course, she was most interested in Alexander Graham Bell's telephone demonstration—it was reported to send intelligible sound from one side of the Exposition to the other. Kate so clearly remembered the talk in Boston, when young Bell described experimenting with tuning forks to send sound. It had been some time now since she and Frank had discussed attempts to transmit sound electronically. The talking telegraph, or telephone, was then hypothetical; now, it had become a reality.

Walking along the paths of the exhibition, Kate and Alice sometimes had to jostle their way through the crowds, so many people had come. They fanned themselves as they chatted about what they were seeing; walking any distance brought rivulets of perspiration. Kate was damp all over, but deliriously happy to have someone to share the experience, especially her clever friend.

"America is doing herself proud, don't you think?" Kate asked. "The world can't think of us as a poor cousin any longer."

Alice nodded. "It's even more than I expected." They talked and walked until their feet ached and their voices were nearly hoarse. They occupied every minute until they met Nathaniel for dinner.

Almost all thirty-seven countries at the Exposition had food stalls, selling their native food. Aromas tempted passersby to take a break to stop and eat on their way to exhibits. The stalls were popular. They were small places, with high stools and half a dozen tall, round tables that sat four or six people. Alice and Kate had decided to try a different nation's food each night. With Nathaniel's agreement, they had selected the Café Leland the first night. The wait line snaked down the path, but some people carried away their French meal, and it did not take much time to find an empty table. Evening had done little to cool the temperature, especially in the small space.

"Thank you, ladies," Nathaniel said, looking around. "It's a good choice, and I'm famished." They had ordered coq au vin, scalloped potatoes, and Brussels sprouts, with a custard pastry for dessert.

"Have visitors come to the Colorado exhibit?" Kate asked Nathaniel.

"It's been a crush of people," he said, beaming. "The West has a fascination across the world. Everyone is congratulating us on statehood, and I've been standing all day. Happy as I was to talk to so many well-wishers, I'm glad to finally sit down. How was your day?" Nathaniel asked, slicing another piece of chicken.

"The Women's Pavilion was the highlight," Alice responded. "Did you know Kate helped raise money when they denied us a spot in the main hall?"

Nathaniel shook his head as he chewed.

"Nat, you wouldn't believe how many inventions came from women— they're all displayed at the Women's Pavilion." Alice's blue eyes lit up.

"I'll make sure to take a look," he said, using his fingers as a comb to brush a stray piece of food from his bushy moustache. "Well done, Kate. Was it your favorite, too?"

"I'm very pleased," she said, nodding. "Although my favorites are Bell's telephone and Edison's automatic telegraph system. Those two inventions were really the reason I knew I had to come to Philadelphia."

Nathaniel's eyes told her he was thinking about the inventions she had mentioned. "Bell's inventions might harm Western Union with competition. Edison's should help, by making it more efficient. Correct?"

Kate's eyebrows raised. Nathaniel was right; the two inventions would change the company. Since he'd always thought the telegraph company had too much control over information, she assumed Nathaniel would not object to competition by the telephone, if Bell could make it work. She'd already begun to see how Edison's device would automate telegraphy. Western Union had begun installing the machines that automatically transmitted messages at higher speeds than possible by telegraph operators. That helped the company because it did not need as many telegraphers. It had also reduced the pay for those who remained. Her stomach squeezed. The long hours were the same, but telegraphy was losing its prestige and meaningful pay. It was a blow to men, but hit women especially hard, as they attempted to gain a foothold to financial independence.

"You might have heard that Western Union faces competition from another company, not just the telephone," Kate said. She knew from Frank that Jay Gould had acquired enough shares of the Atlantic and Pacific Telegraph Company to control the company. His intention was to initiate rate wars with other telegraph companies, especially Western Union.

Nathaniel looked startled. "I was unaware Gould had made so many inroads with A and P."

Kate nodded. "Do you still think the Post Office Department should oversee the telegraph?"

Nathaniel scowled. "Your news makes me even surer." His eyes were firm, looking directly at her. "Mark my words, that wily Jay Gould intends to control Western Union as well as the Union Pacific. Many people can't grasp the connection between communication and transportation, but Gould can."

Kate understood Nathaniel's comments were not intended to be combative—it was not his style. Likewise, she hadn't introduced the subject to be argumentative. She respected his opinion and was not surprised he hadn't changed his mind. He remained convinced that it was detrimental to have any one company or individual in control of vital services. And he shared Frank's unease about Jay Gould.

Their conversation might have continued, but they had finished their meal, and the stares and harrumphing of those waiting for a table were growing insistent. The trio left the café, weary from their jam-packed day, and walked the mile to their hotel. Instead of talk about monopolies and Jay Gould, they laughingly reminded one another of what they had seen. Architects had designed the buildings to impress. The main exhibit hall was the largest building in the world, enclosing twenty-one acres. A wood-and-iron frame rested on 672 stone piers, complete with wrought-iron roof trusses jutting up from each one. Each side of the building had a portal for entry to different halls. Nations' flags flew everywhere. Exhibits from the United States were in the center of the building, with foreign exhibits arranged around the center, all determined by the nation's distance from the United States.

Countries had vied to outdo one another with a dizzying array of inventions, leaving Nathaniel, Alice, and Kate ebullient about the exhibits they had seen. They pledged to fit even more into the days ahead.

SIXTY-FIVE

After five days of inseparable time with Alice and Nathaniel, Kate could not bear to let them leave without saying goodbye at the station. Parting was wrenching, not knowing when they would see one another again. The last teary embraces lingered until the conductor's shrill whistle forced the Hills to board. Kate watched the locomotive snake down the winding track, the black smoke plume trailing and then dissolving in the atmosphere. With it went the memories of both long ago and just yesterday. When there was nothing left to see but empty tracks, she turned from the station with a heavy heart.

Kate's train did not leave until the afternoon, and in the meantime, she walked the paths of the exposition one more time, winding through the architecture and under the tree canopy of the Schuylkill River. The aromas had become landmarks for her. She knew which corner would smell of schnitzel, and farther on, in the middle of the block, spaghetti. It was Saturday, and crowds filled every space. The heat made her sticky. She dabbed away droplets at her temples with her handkerchief.

The exposition had thousands of devices, gadgets, and machines. Kate had picked only a few to study carefully, too overloaded with information to understand, or even look at, most of the others. The telephone, where she had already spent time with Alice, was different—she wanted to take one more look before she left. At the exhibit, she studied the telephone's dark cylindrical tube, bolted to a carved wooden plank, with wires spilling off the back. Morse code had once seemed unreal to her; a voice going over wires was even more magical. She stood still, listening along with the others hovering around. The sound of the voice was faint and hard to hear, but it was recognizable. Kate listened to the telephone transmission several times, trying to imagine how people would actually use it.

It was time for her to leave to catch her train. Kate looked around for an exit. The room was crowded with spectators, noisily sharing amazement at inventions. Her eyes lighted on a square-shouldered, medium-sized man with dark-brown hair and a trim, reddish beard at the far side of the room. He commented to someone with his slightly off-kilter smile.

Frank!

It must be her imagination, a phantom she had conjured because she'd wished him here with her so often. Her heart beat rapidly.

Could it truly be him? Of course, he would obviously find a way to visit the exposition. But right now?

She was lightheaded, but steadied her legs and started moving through the crowd with an intense need to see him, to be with him, to touch him. Visitors were clotted together, talking and observing in an unintentional blockade. Kate tried to keep her eye on him as she elbowed and bumped her way forward. She sensed curiosity at her frantic pushing but didn't stop. Far ahead, Frank walked unhurriedly toward a portal and exited the building. She kept her gaze trained on the back of his head, but then the crowd enveloped him.

It took long minutes for her to get to the place she'd seen him last. After walking through the door, she looked around, but there was no one familiar. She had to decide which way to go. Left, toward the internal railway station? She scoured the crowd—no luck. Taking a chance, she turned right and pushed through the crowds for the entire perimeter of the exhibit hall, searching for another glimpse of him.

Returning to the portal where they both had exited; she was breathing hard. Her hand shook, making it difficult to read her watch—four ten. She needed to leave her hotel no later than five o'clock to reach the railroad station and catch her train to Providence. She pressed her handkerchief to her moist face, then crumpled it in her fist. *I can't just give up when I am so close.* She searched the crowd again with tear-blurred vision.

It's no use. I've lost him.

SIXTY-SIX

Kate's joy during the Centennial Exposition—seeing Alice and Nathaniel, the success of the Women's Pavilion, being amazed by Edison and Bell—collapsed with her missed connection with Frank. It sent a distress signal ringing in her heart that she could not turn off. *What do I want from life?* The question had her in a stranglehold and would not release its grip.

However, her distress about the future could not halt the life she was living. Back in Providence, questions about the Centennial Exposition came from every-where—it was the first world's fair held in the United States, and everyone was curious about it. Recounting the details made her remember more of the exhibits than if she had slipped back into a routine of work without describing the exposition to anyone. With each telling, the unspoken ending haunted her.

Everyone wondered if a voice carried over a wire was just a plaything . . . the very idea seemed so impossible. Kate found her fellow telegraphers worried very little about the telephone. Automation, on the other hand, was a grave concern to them. Western Union had already placed three of Edison's devices in its Providence offices, replacing six telegraphers. In the past two years, the company had reduced salaries twice—all because of the worldwide economic depression, it had said. Now, it was replacing its workforce with machines.

"They make it cheaper for the company," Sophia, a dark-haired telegrapher, said. She was the youngest in the office. "I can barely survive now. I don't have parents or a husband to help fill in." The girl's brow furrowed above helpless-looking ebony eyes.

"I've heard a group is thinking of banding together to strike," the head telegrapher, Padraig O'Malley, said. "Machines or not, they couldn't get along without us. Would you strike, Kate?" Everyone turned toward her, waiting for an answer.

"I haven't thought about it, honestly." It was the truth. Since listening to Nathaniel's opinions about control, she had thought about the power of a monopoly, but not a strike to break it. She looked at the pile of telegrams ready to send by Morse code and another stack that had come in by machine. "Sophia's right, the new machines save the company money, but it still has to be fair to workers."

She looked at each of the other telegraphers, sympathizing with their dependence on their salaries. She was as perplexed as they. The fact that this affected so many people added weight to the problem. Still, she could not picture herself as part of a mob. Striking was so radical, but maybe radical was the only way.

"Let's tell one another as soon as we hear anything new," she said. "Then, we'll pool our information, and figure out what we should do."

They all agreed.

—·— ·— — ·

At night, comfortable in her apartment, Kate attended to correspondence. She wanted to share what she had seen at the Women's Pavilion with everyone who had contributed at her behest. She was pleased to explain that their donations had created a celebration of women. Female accomplishments were there for the world to see—or at least the ten million who attended the fair. Exhibits went beyond the important domestic work of women, with additional displays of women's achievements in philosophy, science, medicine, education, literature, and industrial fine arts, such as furniture and ceramics. One display featured eighty patented inventions, with each woman's name and, in some cases, her picture. Some inventors hoped science would free women from tedious work. There were even examples on display of women making a profitable living away from home—which did not always meet with approval. Much of society still considered women who worked outside the home to be troublemakers, not good, proper girls.

The tangible results of her fundraising efforts for the Women's Pavilion had changed Kate's mind about working on behalf of women's issues. Until then, most of it had seemed like endless frustration. With the success of the exhibits displaying women's accomplishments, she was encouraged to do more. She considered her stationary job in Providence routine, almost boring, compared to traveling from place to place examining offices. She needed something in her life outside of work—something to look forward to, where she could make new friends. Perhaps the women's movement could fill the gap.

Though exhausted from the workweek, Kate began going to suffragist meetings on Saturday evenings. Everyone was interested in the accomplishments of the exposition, and Kate was happy to tell them all about it, since none of them had been able to attend. At the same time, she was eager to learn about plans for what still needed to be achieved—equal pay, fair jobs, and of course, the women's right to vote. The cause drew every stripe of woman. Some women she found strident, with a hostile antipathy toward men. But there were plenty of others, like her, who simply believed in the potential of women. The meetings became Kate's social life.

Frank's letters came less frequently, but when they did come, slitting open the envelope made her heart warm, anticipating what he had to say. When she read the words, the sound of his voice filled her ears. She could close her eyes and imagine she was with him. It was still magic. She waited, but he never wrote about his trip to the Centennial Exhibition. Perhaps he thought it would appear like bragging. For her part, seeing him and not being able to catch him was too raw for her to mention. Instead, his letters were mostly about work:

> Our friend Jay Gould has come out of the shadows. You'll remember that he bought up stock of A&P until he finally gained control. Then, he upped the competition with WU. It's been a real problem for the company. Now, he's trying to sell A&P to WU. I'm sure this was all calculated. Gould stands to make a sizable profit, and WU has to gamble on the debt load. Purchasing A&P eliminates the competition, but I fear the high cost will take its toll. The company will become top-heavy with stock and low with profits. Then there's Bell. The telephone is not fully developed yet, and Bell is slowed with a patent suit. It's not a threat yet, but you can bet it will be.
>
> I had an occasion to go to The Old Clam House, the restaurant where we first had Ghirardelli chocolate. I can attest that it is still delicious. I can't speak to the sherry.
>
> All my best,
> Frank

The lack of constant challenges created a void Kate filled with deep thought. How she missed spending time with Frank! Regret began seeping into her soul. She put the letter on the side table and rolled over in the bed, where she had been reading. She was in a freefall, with nothing to catch her. Her heart was in anguish. She longed to ask him, face to face, what all this meant for her job. More than that, she wanted to be with him, to laugh along with him, and share the sights and sounds of different places.

SIXTY-SEVEN

Heavy paperweights anchored stacks of papers, keeping them from blowing in the breeze from the open office windows. The heat was oppressive and so had been the news waiting on each desk in the morning. Next to Kate, Edith Kennedy sat ashen-faced and grim.

"We barely can put food on the table, and now this." Edith was of average build with dark-brown hair fastened neatly in a roll at the back of her head, and eyes to match. Her clothes were simple, but always fresh and ironed. Her husband, Phil, was a mechanic for the New York, Providence, and Boston Railroad. They were both in their mid-thirties, with three children in early grades at school. Only because her mother helped with the children was Edith able to work.

"It's just not right. Our wages were low enough and now they've cut them again." George Morris stood up and slapped down the yellow telegraph that had brought the news. "We need to fight back." He was an overweight man in his forties, with a florid face that made him look to Kate as if he was one step away from a health crisis.

"Take it easy, George," Padraig O'Malley said. "This is all coming from what started with the Panic of Seventy-Three."

"Easy for you to say—you're the head. Our wages have been cut almost in half since the Panic."

"I got my cut, too." Padraig glanced dolefully at the open telegram on his desk.

"What do the rest of you think?" Morris looked down the aisle at the other telegraphers. All were men, except Kate, Edith, and Sophia. "I say we do something about this." His flushed cheeks quivered, daring them to disagree.

Some nodded, while others were grim, but noncommittal.

"This started when B&O Railroad cut workers' salaries three times in six months. Workers there are calling a strike—workers in other places too." George remained standing, as if in challenge.

"All they'll do is call in the troops—federal or National Guard. It's hopeless to strike," an older telegrapher said. "I hear unemployment is up to fourteen percent. I need my job."

"Soon you'll be working for nothing," said another telegrapher. "Talking about the National Guard, I'm thinking of joining. At least that way, I'll get paid."

"They're all just tools of the companies—that's probably you too, Padraig," George snarled.

"That's enough from you, George," Padraig O'Malley rose from his tall stool. "Sit down and shut up or you'll be jobless. That'll give you plenty of time to strike." He looked down the line. "Get to work, the rest of you. We have to deal with this the best we can." He sat back down and began examining the ledger.

The only sound was mechanical clicking, as the telegraphers attended to accumulating messages. The mood and the heat festered. It was not until O'Malley had left his desk and gone out of the room for a break that Edith leaned forward and asked, "What do you think we should do? Would you strike?"

Kate shook her head, unsure. "I've thought about it before, and still don't know what's right." Her brow scrunched in a frown. "I understand that businesses are in a hard spot, too, but that doesn't mean workers should do all the suffering. Without us, they won't have a company. I just don't know—"

"I want to join the strike," Edith interrupted. "I hear thousands all over the country are gathering." Her eyes looked troubled. "But I can't. My Phil's wages have been cut three times. I don't know how we'll feed the children. I have to keep my job. Maybe that's business's hold on us— being desperate for pay traps us."

Kate could only shake her head in sympathy.

The suffragist meeting that week was less restrained than the telegraphy office had been. Fiery sentiments inflamed the rhetoric.

"We're making little progress in the vote, and not much more in decent jobs. They pay us less, and then cut us when they want—there's no loyalty. We have to fight back."

"Hear, hear," the others chimed.

"They'll just put us in jail," a doubter replied.

"Let them—the more the merrier."

Cynical laughter rang out. Kate stood with three women who had become her friends since she joined the organization. Francie, Nadine, and Judith did not seem like firebrands, but resolute in their determination to improve opportunities for themselves . . . and all women.

"We won't get ahead unless we stand up for ourselves, and that means striking," Francie said. "Are you willing?"

"I just don't know." Kate held back a delirious laugh, imagining her parents' reaction to finding her in jail. Eugenia would not think the cause worth incarceration. "I can't demand more without the will to take a stand, but so far, striking is too big a step."

"Don't decide before you listen to the plans," Francie prodded her.

--- --- --- ·

The Great Railroad Strike, or as the newspapers later called it, the Great Upheaval, began a week after their conversation. Kate and her friends did not strike—railroads were the focus. They did, however, go together to a protest after work, where they stood, hesitating, at the fringe of a growing crowd.

"We're the only women I can see." Nadine shouted to be heard.

They were propelled along in an emotional wave of unruly demonstrators, some carrying flaming torches, many yelling anti-business epithets. They inched ahead, shoulder to shoulder, until the jostling melee bumped Kate and she was separated from her friends. She struggled to find the others. Spotting the bright blue scarf Francie wore in a sea of black and gray, Kate pushed, shoved, and slapped at the hands intentionally grabbing her until she reached her friends.

"I thought we'd never find you," Nadine wailed. The four linked arms so they would not get separated again. Along the fringe of the crowd, policemen helplessly swung billy clubs against the intensity of the crowd.

"This isn't what I expected," Kate shouted. "I want to leave."

"The coppers are just beginning to understand that we're stronger than they are," Francie said. "This will give 'em a lesson."

"Let's go, Kate," Nadine said, turning. They left Francie and Judith and fought to stay upright as they plunged against the crowd's momentum. It took half an hour of pushing and shoving to be free.

"I didn't think we'd survive," Nadine said, snuffling. "Where do you live?"

"Near the Hill," Kate said, still hearing the pulsating crowd behind her.

"I live the opposite direction. I better get going."

"Will you be all right?"

"I'll have to be."

"I'll see you, then," Kate said, and ran for her apartment.

--- --- --- ·

Back safe, Kate rhythmically brushed her hair in front the mirror, reliving the protest's tumultuous events. Her shoulders shook, knowing how close it was to anarchy. Protests were becoming more frequent—not just on her side of the country or even the United States; financial problems were undoing most of the world's economies. She looked at the mirror, questioning her reflection. *Pay . . . fairness . . . equality. All are crucial.*

Is insurrection the only way to get them?

She sincerely hoped not.

SIXTY-EIGHT

Economic gloom had afflicted all work at Western Union. Kate suspected it was the same in banks and stores and other enterprises—everyone was wedged in a vice being screwed tighter and tighter. In the past, office camaraderie, especially during slow times, had showed itself in lively talk, improvised games, and chatting with distant operators. Now, those times were dispiritedly silent.

"How low do you think Jay Gould can cut the Atlantic and Pacific's rates without going out of business?" Edith asked Kate.

"He always manages to have reserves, no matter what kind of rate war he inflicts. Western Union can't keep lowering rates to match him, but buying A and P to make the competition go away might break the bank."

Kate and Edith kept working while they talked, quietly looking down or straight ahead, so O'Malley would not be aware of their conversation.

"The other day, I overheard two men say that Western's stock is watered. Whatever that means."

"It means the company's value isn't worth the price of the stock." Kate gave Edith a sidelong glance. "It's only one of Western Union's problems."

— ·— ·— — ·

Before long, the inventors who had held Kate spellbound at the Centennial Exhibition had become factors at Western Union. Months before the exhibition, Frank had told her that Alexander Graham Bell and his backers had offered to sell his telephone patent to Western Union. At the time, president William Orton had been preoccupied with improving his telegraph system, and had also protested the asking price of one hundred thousand dollars as outrageous for a technology that had not yet proved useful.

In only two years, Orton had realized that the telephone, however imperfect, was gaining popularity; it was also providing substantial income for Bell. Orton tried to jump ahead with something even better by hiring Thomas Edison to improve Bell's original concept. Edison's tinkering with the telephone infuriated Bell, and he sued Western Union for patent infringement. Kate was able to follow the contentious litigation in copious newspaper articles.

These days, she found little joy in going to the office, mechanically doing her job. Her reduced salary provided little incentive to stay. Everything about the direction of her life was wrong—her job, her relationship with her parents, and most of all, Frank. She yearned for someone to confide in. Her mother's opinions about her job were already known. Alice was far away; and Frank's letters had become all business, except that he was working with a new woman, "who has great promise."

New rumors riffled the office every day, particularly at lunch. Kate bit into a gold-red apple while she unwrapped her chicken and buttered bread.

"I heard that Western is going to give up the telephone," one of the male telegraphers said through a mouthful of food.

"We're in the business of telegrams; let them do it," another retorted.

"Bell is making money hand over fist. I don't have use for a telephone, but a lot of folks do," someone else added.

Even the head telegrapher, O'Malley, could not hold his tongue. "Signing a contract to give up the telephone would be shortsighted, and a high price to pay to settle a dispute."

O'Malley's words rang in Kate's ears when she read in the newspaper that Western Union had done just that. In the contract to settle the patent suit, Western Union agreed that its business would be the telegraph and money transfers; Bell's business would be the telephone. Kate was not sure the telephone would ever supplant the telegraph, but it was one more blow to a company that had lost its appeal to her.

She decided to resign.

The kitchen was warm from the robust fire in the kitchen hearth. Outside, a November frost clung to the bare tree branches—crystalline against the gray sky. Kate and her parents had returned from church, and Eugenia was putting final touches on midday Sunday dinner. Kate placed the cherry pie she had made before leaving on the top shelf of the oven, above the roasting turkey. The coalescing aromas were reminders of past Sundays and holidays.

"Kate, is what you're telling me about quitting your job good news or bad?" Eugenia asked.

"Probably some of each." Kate pulled open the silverware drawer to set the dinner table. "I've been thinking about it for a while. The job's become repetitious, with machines taking over part of our work. You've read about the economy. Father says it has affected his business, too. Western Union is not the only company to cut wages. I need a change."

Eugenia paused her napkin folding, eyes alert. "What kind of change?"

"I've been writing Alice. She's invited me to Washington."

Eugenia paused to put the three folded napkins by the silverware. "Oh, that's right. With Nathaniel in the Senate, they would be there, instead of Colorado."

"I've been dying to go see them ever since they moved east while the Senate is in session. Now, I'll have the time to do it."

"I remember you were in a swivet when you couldn't go," Eugenia smiled.

"If I tour around with Alice, I can see parts of Washington, D.C. most visitors can't."

"When will you go?" Eugenia asked, vigorously whisking the gravy to dissolve the lumps.

"Western Union said I could stay as long as I want, but now that I've decided to leave, I'm ready to go." Kate did not add that quitting was only one step toward fixing her convoluted life.

"Does that mean you'll go to Washington soon?" Eugenia looked over at Kate, who was getting three glasses from the cupboard to set the table.

Kate shrugged. "It depends on a lot of things. Alice wants company, but she also has responsibilities as a senator's wife. We'll see."

SIXTY-NINE

Humid cold filled the flat, gray sky in Washington—not much different than Providence had looked when Kate left it that morning. She was relieved the predicted snow had not yet started. She watched through the window as the train pulled next to the long platform, filled with people hurrying to a train, or impatiently waiting for an arrival. After scanning the crowd, she picked out Alice, standing close to the station doors with a black-capped porter next to her. Alice had instructed her to bring more than her usual travel clothes in case there were "necessary social occasions." Even from a distance, Kate saw Alice's clothing was more formal than it had been in Black Hawk.

After the train lurched to a final, hissing stop, Kate stepped down the iron stairs and waved to catch Alice's attention. Soon they were in a familiar embrace.

"Welcome, Kate. I've already made lots of plans. I'm glad you could come so soon."

"I've never been here, and now I have a personal guide." Kate turned and gave a tip to the train's porter, who had lugged her large leather suitcase down the steps, handing it off to the porter waiting with Alice. He pushed ahead of them to a line of hacks in front of the station. Once the suitcase was loaded in the back of the carriage, they set off for the Hills' rental house.

The entire first floor was designed for entertaining, with an expansive parlor and attached library so guests could spread out during a large party. The dining room extended into a separate wing that could be closed off after dinner for men to smoke, drink, and continue their conversation, uninhibited by the presence of ladies. Upstairs, three extra bedrooms provided space for overnight guests.

"Quite a bit grander than Black Hawk, isn't it?" Alice said, after showing Kate through.

"It's beautiful, but I liked the simplicity and your handwork in the other," Kate said, taking another look at the stylish décor, and marveling at Alice's adaptability. "It's so good to see you again."

"I didn't plan anything for tonight, since you just arrived. Go freshen up. I have a cook now, so I don't have to worry about dinner, and Nathaniel won't be home for another couple of hours. We have a little time to catch up. Come back down when you're ready. Fifteen minutes later, Alice directed Kate to the small alcove between the kitchen and the formal parlor. The small room, painted cherry red, accommodated Alice's desk, comfortable rocking chair for reading, and an easy chair.

"It's taken me a while to get caught up with my wardrobe. I guess it's an understatement to say the capital is definitely different from Black Hawk." Alice laughed and poured tea for them from a pot that the cook, Gisela, wearing a black dress, white ruffled apron, and cap to match, had brought on a silver tray. "Afternoon tea always restores me. Unfortunately, I'm tempted to have something to eat with my tea. Even some of my new clothes have had to be let out, with all the dinners we go to." Alice's lips turned up in an amusing smile. "I should muster some restraint."

Kate sat on the easy chair, next to Alice's rocking chair, with her feet propped up on a needlepointed stool, a knitted wool shawl around her shoulders. The heat from the next-door kitchen did not entirely warm the small space. A gas lamp cast cheerful light through the room. "I honestly could stay here forever. There is so much to see and do, and so many important decisions being made."

Alice shifted, reaching for a gingersnap from the plate next to the tea service on her desk. "People are constantly coming and going without much permanence. In some ways it's easy to make friends—there are so many people—but, you must be on guard and learn who are friends, and who merely use you for what they want. It's a political city."

"It's much like what Nathaniel and . . ." Kate faltered. "It's like what he's always saying about men who use their power to get their way." She knew Alice filled in the name she did not say.

For once, Alice did not press her. "Now that you've quit your job, I would love your company here, but I worry about what you'd do the rest of the time."

Kate thought for a moment, "You're right. Life would be different for me, because I don't have the connections you do." She groaned. "I guess I could be a telegrapher."

"I hope you're joking."

Kate dropped her feet off the stool and sat upright. "Yes. Ugh. I've had enough of that job, and anyway, machines have changed the work. The company isn't the same as it was when I began." She reached for the teapot to refill her cup but hesitated. "Alice, is it too early for a glass of sherry?"

"Not at all." Alice extended her arm and rang a bell on her desk. In a few minutes, Gisela hurried in. Alice made her request, and in a few minutes the cook returned with a cutglass decanter of sherry and two crystal glasses.

"I'll join you," Alice said, much to Kate's surprise. "It's a while until dinner, and Nathaniel doesn't drink spirits, but Washington has induced me to enjoy a glass of wine now and again." She filled both glasses and then reached over to clink her glass against Kate's in a toast.

"Kate, what *is* next for you? You always have a plan, but I haven't heard you mention one."

"Hmm," Kate exhaled. "Perhaps, for the first time, I don't have one."

"Does that trouble you?"

"Maybe . . . no, not maybe, it does," Kate admitted to Alice, as well as herself. She reached toward the gleaming tray and took a gingersnap. "The telegraph gave me a dose of experience and reality. There's lots out there to do, but there's a price for each decision a person makes. Who knows what I should do next?"

"What about Frank? When I listened to you talking about him, you were in a different orbit."

"I used to drink sherry like this with Frank." Kate raised her glass, watching it reflect a spark of lantern light through the cut crystal. "He made everything electric, with his conversation. We were always the last ones out of a restaurant." Kate's laugh was thin, remembering those evenings.

"What happened?"

"Me," Kate said, nearly revealing the role her father's letters had played, as well. Alice knew her father; their parents were friends. It wasn't possible to unveil the letters, even to her closest friend. Frank was the only one she might have, or could have, trusted with her secret.

"What would you like to do? Really like to do?" Alice pressed her.

Kate almost slid into her usual arguments about depending only on herself, but something held her back. "Frank gave me every opportunity for what I wanted." Kate's voice quavered. "More than wanted—needed—but I couldn't accept. I'd like to spend time with Frank."

There, she had finally said it. She had peeled back the layers of her life and faced the stark, naked truth.

"You didn't have to give up yourself to have a relationship—it's more sharing than succumbing."

Kate knew Alice was trying to soothe her.

"I can see, from your wonderful family, that mutual affection can be worth what you have to give up for it," Kate said around a sob. "I've made a terrible mistake, because I'm so stubborn and illogical. I was trying to avoid being hurt," she admitted, tears streaming down her cheeks.

"Is it too late?"

Kate nodded, unable to say anything.

"Are you sure? Oh, Kate, be fair to yourself."

"In several letters, he's told me about a new work companion, but I think she might go beyond work." Another wave of sadness washed over her.

Alice did not speak for a moment. "I've never known you not to go after what you want. You just told me what you want. You need to contact Frank."

Kate sniffled. "Too much time has passed."

"You don't know that for sure."

She sighed. "Maybe you're right, Alice. I should write him—I owe him a letter, but I don't know exactly what I'd say."

Alice looked at her watch and stood up so fast, Kate was startled. "Not a letter, a telegram. We just have time before the office closes. Let's go." She grabbed Kate's hand.

"What will I say?" Kate repeated, feeling somewhat dazed.

"What you told me—and you might beg for his forgiveness."

SEVENTY

Kate had sent the telegram, and while she waited for a response, Alice showed her the city. Normally Kate would have soaked in everything, but she could not concentrate on anything but Frank. Anxiety consumed her while she waited. She knew Alice was trying to keep her busy every second to distract her. Alice explained that the nation's capital city had fallen on hard times during the Civil War, and it still showed more than a decade later. Many officials had complained that it was a national embarrassment, with its dirt roads, wooden walkways, and open sewers. Some began an effort to move the capital to another city, even proposing St. Louis. After much persuasion, President Grant gained Congressional support to hire an architect to modernize Washington. With lavish plans to fit his ego, Alexander Robey Shepherd oversaw design and construction. His budget escalated to three times its initial estimate, bankrupting the city after the Panic of 1873. Fortunately, enough improvements had been made to lure a few millionaires, who built mansions in the city, and others followed. By current count, Alice told Kate, the District of Columbia had grown to 377,000 people, and attracted visitors from all over the world.

Kate and Alice walked to different sites, only returning home when the last light drained from the gray sky. For two nights, Kate accompanied the Hills to political dinners.

Three days after sending the telegram, Kate thought she might faint when the houseboy handed her a buttery yellow envelope. It took Kate a moment to calm her shaking hands to get it open. Even then she closed her eyes while she unfolded the paper, fearing the response. Finally, she mustered courage to crack open her eye and slowly peek at the words. ARE YOU SURE FRANK.

Kate handed the yellow missive across the table. They had come home from sightseeing to have lunch. Alice had a meeting afterward. "Well?" Alice asked after reading it.

"I've never been more sure of anything."

Alice smiled. "Hallelujah! Do you want to stop by the telegraph office on our way to Mount Vernon?"

"Yes, I have to let him know right away—thank you. But would you forgive me if I stayed home this afternoon? I need to follow my telegraph with a long letter—there's so much to explain, if I can. You can never go back in life with more thought and deliberation. Frank didn't say what he wants to do, so I don't know. All I can do is hope."

— ·— ·— — ·

His last telegraph came to the Hills'. LET'S TALK IN PROVIDENCE FRANK.

Kate left Washington the following week.

Alice had been overjoyed with the news that Frank was on his way. "Remember, Washington is not far from Providence."

But Kate smothered any excitement. She did not know where she stood, or what her future held.

It was the beginning of December by the time he arrived. Providence was gray—low hanging storm clouds melding with factory smoke. Frank checked into his hotel before coming to her apartment to take her to dinner. He was guarded as they sat down at the table. Kate knew he must be carrying the hurt of rejection—the hurt she had inflicted—with him. As they talked . . . and drank. . . and ate, he relaxed and, consequently, so did she. Unwilling to harbor any more secrets, she told him about the letters, of possibly having a half-brother, and that, to the best of her knowledge, her mother did not know.

For a while, he did not speak. "What you've told me will take time to digest. I'm sure, together, we can figure out some way of finding out your father's relationship to the other woman—if you still want to know, but right now, I want to think about us," he said. "I want to meet your mother and father." He reached over and took her hand. "And I intend to ask his permission to marry you."

Kate's heart was a sea swell of emotions: ebullience, incredulous, nervous, but sure. "I don't know what he'll say, but I know what I will." She looked into Frank's brown-flecked green eyes. "Yes. My answer is yes. I should have known, from the start, it was a mistake to let the past, one I wasn't even responsible for, rule my life. But now, with you, there's a future."

ACKNOWLEDGMENTS

When I'm writing, I feel as if I'm all alone on an empty stage, with only a single chair, table, and computer for props. The lights are dim. It's a solitary occupation to dream up ideas, research history, and bring a story to life out of nothing. One after another, actors join me, playing essential roles with wisdom and guidance. Without a supporting cast, there would be no final performance of words in a book, no filling the theater with an audience of readers.

I am indebted to the supportive cast of many. Once again, Cotheal Linnell brought her sharp pen and edited the initial draft—that first attempt to make sense of the complexities of plot and characters, put on paper like pieces of a puzzle caught in the wind. Thanks, too, to John Kingman, Hadley Fisher, and Sheila Bender, for reading other early versions and questioning assumptions. As the manuscript took final form, Eva Fox Mate, with a magician's wand, critiqued and edited it. Dan Pratt designed the cover and interior with his creativity and sharp eye for detail. Jay Kenney, former lawyer, now apple cider maker, created a map to give the story visual context. My gratitude to all of you, and to those who cheered me on, for making possible a finished book.

ELLEN FISHER, 2022